Volume Two in the

ghosts
of the past

mark mitten

MILFORD
HOUSE
an imprint of Sunbury Press, Inc.
Mechanicsburg, PA USA

MILFORD HOUSE

an imprint of Sunbury Press, Inc.
Mechanicsburg, PA USA

For information about special discounts for bulk purchases, please contact Sunbury Press Orders Dept. at (855) 338-8359 or orders@sunburypress.com.

To request one of our authors for speaking engagements or book signings, please contact Sunbury Press Publicity Dept. at publicity@sunburypress.com.

FIRST MILFORD HOUSE PRESS EDITION: March 2021

Set in Adobe Garamond | Interior design by Crystal Devine | Cover by Mark Mitten | Edited by Abigail Hensen.

Publisher's Cataloging-in-Publication Data
Names: Mitten, Mark, author.
Title: Ghosts of the past / mark mitten.
Description: First trade paperback edition. | Mechanicsburg, PA : Milford House Press, 2021.
Summary: When a body is discovered in a mine shaft, high in the mountains above Quandary, Sheriff Breckenridge "Breck" Dyer and Deputy Jenny O'Hara follow the evidence to a cryptocurrency conference at the ski resort.
Identifiers: ISBN : 978-1-620064-59-7 (softcover).
Subjects: FICTION / Crime | FICTION / Westerns | FICTION / Mystery & Detective / Police Procedural.

Product of the United States of America
0 1 1 2 3 5 8 13 21 34 55

Continue the Enlightenment!

CHAPTER 1

Wallet Guy

The air was so cold that she could see her breath. It was coming out in hazy puffs. Deputy Jenny O'Hara had a small headlamp strapped to the brim of her helmet, and everywhere she turned, a cone of light cut through the darkness, illuminating a narrow tunnel of rock the color of charcoal. The roof and walls were uneven, and she kept banging her head, which was why Cash had given her the helmet in the first place. It certainly wasn't a fashion statement.

They were in an old mine from the 1800s. Tunnels, tram rails, rickety old boards, dripping water, flapping bats, and enough old beer cans, it could be mistaken for a recycling center.

"You sure this isn't going to collapse?" Jenny asked.

"This part is pretty stable."

"And you know that . . . how?"

"I've been down here already. Explored half this mine, and it hasn't collapsed on me yet."

"Well, that's halfway comforting."

Cash was the young punk who managed the Quandary Ski Resort year-round. Shoulder-length straight blonde hair. Couple big fat earrings. And he reeked like weed. Probably half those beer cans were his. A few winters back, he spent a snowy weekend on the slopes and liked it so much he never left town. He took a job teaching kids how to snow plow on the bunny slope, then worked his way up to manager.

Regardless of his character faults, Jenny was glad Cash was there. No way she was going to crawl through these tunnels without someone who knew the layout. There were a lot of twists and turns, and she was completely lost. How many old, manky ladders had they climbed down? He kept calling it the three hundred level, whatever that meant. All Jenny knew was that the further they went inside the mountain, the more nervous she got.

"What about dead air pockets in places like this? People blackout and don't even know what happened."

But Cash didn't hear her. He was totally at ease and had strolled on ahead, shining his headlamp at all the interesting objects he came across.

Take control. Relax. Count to ten. Jenny never thought of herself as claustrophobic before, although the only caving experience she had was a guided tour in the Cave of the Winds. But that place was a walk in the park compared to this. They had background music, rock candy, and T-shirts. Wheelchair ramps!

"If this is going to be my forever home, I'm going to haunt the crap out of you, Breck."

But Breck didn't hear her. He wasn't there. He had the day off and had turned his phone off, too, naturally. Claimed he was going fishing at the tiny lake near his cabin, even though he'd never caught a single trout in his entire life. What was he doing fishing in October anyhow? *One last time before the lake freezes,* he said. Whatever. Jenny left a mean little note on his desk, so he would know where to dig for her body.

The breathing exercises worked. Kind of. She started to feel a little calmer.

"Hey, check this out." Her voice echoed. She ran her fingers across a vein of glittery white rock in the wall. "This has got to be worth something."

Cash came back to see what she was looking at.

"Quartz. Ain't worth a dime." He smiled, just like she had seen him smile at toddlers on the bunny slope. "But you know what? Gold and quartz are sometimes found together. A hundred years ago, the miners must have followed this quartz vein, hoping to hit the pay dirt."

He was patronizing her. Jenny hated being patronized.

"I didn't know they taught mining at Dope Smoke College."

"They don't. I'm taking business administration classes."

It was a joke to lighten the mood, but it flew over his head. Cash started talking about the courses he was taking at the community college in town, but Jenny tuned him out. It hit her. The three hundred level. Did that mean they were three hundred feet underground? Before she could ask, Cash stopped to study a wooden chute sticking out of the ceiling. It was made of thick planks of rough-cut lumber.

"We aren't going to crawl into that shaft, are we?" Jenny asked.

"No, this is an ore chute. I don't remember seeing this before."

She felt her stomach sink.

"Are we lost?"

Even though he was wearing a headlamp, Cash was also packing a big flashlight in a belt holster. The sound of Velcro was loud as he got it out.

"This little bad boy is called the ThruNite TN12," he said. "I'm going to put it on turbo mode. Don't look directly in the beam."

He clicked on the flashlight and shined it into the ore chute. It was so bright that Jenny had to squint.

"There's a pretty big cavity above us. Where they dug out the goods. What they would do, is slide chunks of ore down this chute, where it landed in a tram cart. Then they wheeled it outside for processing."

"Everyone knows that." She didn't. "Now, where did you find the wallet?"

"It can't be too much further."

He turned off the fancy flashlight, put it back in its holster, and led the way further down the tunnel until they came to an intersection. A wooden box was lying in the dirt, stenciled with black lettering: *Fuse Rate, forty-six seconds per foot.*

"Okay, here we go. I remember this old dynamite crate." Cash pointed at the right fork. It was a side tunnel. "I found the wallet in there."

Jenny didn't like what she was seeing. The passageway was smaller than the other tunnels they had been in so far. Even the rock itself looked different. Soft and crumbly. Thick timber beams framed the ceiling and walls—probably to keep it from caving in. Her pulse started pounding at the thought of crawling back there, but she did it anyway. This was an investigation.

About halfway down the tunnel, Cash knelt by a pile of gritty mud.

"It was laying right here."

She knelt beside him. The dirt floor was damp, and her feet sank in. She saw other footprints in the muck, but they could have been Cash's from the last time he was there when he found the wallet.

"This place stinks. Like something died, bloated and burst in here." Jenny covered her nose. "Smells like my fridge."

"Well, this is the exact spot. I remember because it was next to that old shoe."

She angled her headlamp to see what he was talking about. Sure enough, a black shoe was stuck in the mud. She picked it up and frowned.

"This isn't *old.*"

It was an Oxford-style dress shoe. She showed him the label. Calvin Klein.

"I thought it was some miner's kicks from back in the day," he said.

"No. This is what you'd wear with a tuxedo."

Cash had swung by the Sheriff's Office earlier that morning. Said he found a wallet in the old Keystone Mine over the weekend. No cash, no credit cards, or even a driver's license to make an ID. But it did have a key card to a hotel room in Quandary—The Hyatt Residence Club. That was a red flag in Jenny's mind. It cost three hundred bucks a night to stay at the Hyatt. And that was in the offseason.

Besides, the thrill-seekers in town, whether climbers, cavers, paragliders, or wingsuit fliers, all wore hiking boots and slept in tents. They didn't wear Calvin Klein dress shoes, and they certainly didn't pay three hundred bucks a night for a fancy hotel room.

"Where does this tunnel lead?"

"I don't know. I didn't go any further. Feels freaky in here."

Jenny didn't believe in ghosts, and she wasn't superstitious. But there was something about this narrow, crumbly little side tunnel, somewhere deep inside the earth, that was giving her the shakes.

"Perfect place for a mountain lion den," she muttered.

Taking off her backpack, she pulled out a plastic evidence bag and put the shoe in it. When she shined her headlamp further down the tunnel, she saw more footprints in the muck.

"If you didn't go down there, who did?"

"Wallet guy?"

Jenny had to crouch so she wouldn't hit her head on the timber beams. There were shallow puddles of water everywhere, but it was impossible to avoid stepping in them. The further back she went, the smell got worse. Then the passageway ended abruptly.

There was a hole in the floor. Three feet in diameter. A black void.

Jenny felt the hair on her neck stand up again. The miners, a hundred years ago, had built a lumber collar around the opening and suspended a winch over the shaft. She laid down flat on her stomach, in the mud, and crawled over to the edge. But the pit was deep, and her headlamp didn't shine very far down. She couldn't see anything in the gloom. Except for . . . what *is* that?

"Cash, let me borrow your fancy flashlight."

He handed it to her. Jenny clicked it on turbo mode, and she saw straight to the bottom.

"What's down there?" Cash asked.

"Wallet guy."

CHAPTER 2

Little White Lie

The General Merchandise and More was sitting at the halfway point on the mountain highway between Quandary and Alma. It was just a few miles from the turnoff to Breck's cabin, and he stopped there all the time for gas and snacks. They sold earthworms in the summer, but it was October, and the worm bin was long gone. But Breck wasn't there for fishing bait. He was on his way to Frisco to speak with a lawyer.

Breck grabbed a Gatorade from the cooler and took out his wallet. There was a middle-aged man with long stringy hair working the register. Breck didn't recognize him. Every time he went inside the store, there was someone new behind the counter.

"Did you get fuel?"

"Yep."

Breck pointed out the window at his Jeep parked at the pumps. The gas pumps were so old, they didn't have a digital display or a credit card reader, but they were newer than his Jeep. It was a 1977 CJ7, and it still had the original soft top, even though it was shredded in a few spots, and the snaps holding it in place had long since rusted tight. The only thing that wasn't original was the engine. It was a Corvette transplant, which was good for car chases but bad on gas mileage.

"Gas and Gatorade. Anything else?"

"How about a pack of American Spirits. The green ones."

The man fished out a package of cigarettes from a shelf behind the counter. Breck heard a voice behind him.

"I thought you quit."

He turned around. Seneca Matthews, the mayor of Quandary, was stand-ing by the candy bar rack with a Hershey bar in his hand.

Breck looked outside again. The large plate-glass windows were dirty, but sure enough, the mayor's high-end BMW was out there, parked at the other pump. Where did that guy come from? He was like a bad penny.

"Some people smoke because it calms the nerves," Matthews said. "Rumor has it, the DA is going to press charges against you."

Breck tossed some money on the counter, pocketed the cigarettes, and head-ed out the door without waiting for his change or saying a word to Matthews.

The day before, Breck got a letter from the District Attorney's office. It was a notification that they were opening a criminal investigation to determine whether or not they would press formal charges against him. Someone had filed a complaint and accused him of working with a Mexican drug cartel to set up an illegal cannabis operation in Quandary County. Breck knew the "someone" was Matthews. This was payback because Matthews was the one who actu-ally *did* work with the cartel, but it all fell apart when Breck busted the cartel operation and put a stop to it. He just didn't have enough evidence to prove Matthews was involved.

But the truth was an easy thing to twist, wasn't it?

The General Merchandise door flung open, and Matthews was on his heels.

"This sure is bad timing, isn't it? Only two weeks until Election Day. Do you really think people are going to vote for someone who is under investigation?"

Walking around to the driver's side of his Jeep, Breck opened the door and tossed the Gatorade on the passenger seat. He needed to get a drink holder one of these days. How many times did he shift gears with a cup of coffee sloshing around in his hand?

Breck had told Jenny he was going fishing, but it was a little white lie. He wanted to figure out a plan before he told her what was going on. After all, the DA hadn't charged him with anything official. Not yet. It was just scare tactics and intimidation so far, and maybe that's all it was meant to be. But Matthews was right about its impact on the election.

And wasn't that convenient?

Breck knew Matthews had talked Chief Maxwell Waters, the police chief in Alma, into running against him for sheriff, because Waters did whatever Matthews told him to, and that's what Matthews wanted.

A rubber stamp sheriff.

So what could Breck do to defend himself? The first step was finding an attorney who would represent him on a shoestring budget since he was broke.

That was another point of contention. Matthews, in his capacity as mayor, had slashed the city's budget for law enforcement services. Breck's paycheck got slashed in the process.

He pulled out a cigarette.

"Are you going to light that right here? By the gas pumps?" Matthews took a couple of steps back. "At least wait until I've pumped my gas before you blow this whole place to hell. And if you want to take the easy way out, go ahead. But wait until I drive away. That BMW is brand new."

"Everyone will know this is a witch hunt." Breck took out his keys. "Even if it goes to trial."

Matthews smiled. He tore open his Hershey bar and took a bite.

"Maybe," he said. "But all that matters in the voting booth is the court of public opinion."

Breck slammed the door, pulled onto the highway, and gunned it. Talking with Matthews was a waste of breath and a waste of time, and now he was running late.

He pulled a piece of scrap paper from his pocket—the Law Offices of Hoyt, Hoyt, and Frederick. The address was in Frisco. How was he going to explain the situation? Hello, my name is Sheriff Breckenridge Dyer, and I've been accused of corruption by the mayor of Quandary. The District Attorney just launched an investigation, but I'm up for re-election in two weeks, so if you could get me exonerated before then, that would be very helpful. One more thing. I'm broke. Do you accept Monopoly money?

CHAPTER 3

Crazy Day

It wasn't much of a day off.

The Law Offices of Hoyt, Hoyt, and Frederick were located in a tiny office suite in a crappy strip mall in Frisco. Breck never saw the Hoyts, and Jamey Frederick was a girl in her mid-twenties who wilted when he told her what was happening with the DA and Matthews, the cartel accusations, the election optics, and his non-existent bank account. It took hours to explain everything adequately and not come off sounding like a conspiracy theory nut.

But she must have been desperate for a new client because she agreed to represent him.

The sun was going down by the time Breck finally made it home. He parked the Jeep next to the cabin, but instead of flipping on the TV, he decided to watch the stars come out. Damp yellow aspen leaves covered everything on the deck—the floorboards and handrails, the ratty old lawn chair, and the barbecue grill. It must have rained a little while he was gone. Breck got a towel from the kitchen, wiped the leaves off the chair, and sat down with a heavy sigh.

He took out a cigarette and lit it. Matthews was right about one thing. Smoking calmed his nerves, and he did have a lot of reasons to be nervous.

Someone began honking their car horn.

Breck stood up again, and looked down the dirt road. A pair of headlights was racing his way. It was a 1980's Jeep Cherokee with walnut siding. He recognized it instantly. It was Cash's vehicle. As it pulled up to the cabin, Jenny jumped out of the passenger seat. She was covered in mud.

"Turn on your phone, Breck, for the love of God!" She ran across the deck, waving her cell phone for emphasis. "I've been trying to call you. Don't you check your landline, either? I left a dozen messages."

"Sorry, I just got home. It's been a crazy day."

"Well, I had a crazier day. I found a dead body."

"What? Where?"

"In the Keystone Mine." Jenny frowned. "And you would know that if you'd check your messages."

"What's up, sheriff." Cash rolled down his window and gave Breck a surfer pinkie-thumb wave. Then he looked at Jenny apologetically. "Hate to ditch you, sister, but I gotta roll. I got the night shift at the resort, and boss-lady don't like it when I'm late."

"Wait! We need you to guide us back inside the mine. There's no way I can find the way on my own. That place is a maze. Can you skip work? Please? Tell Tya it's police business, a recovery operation. She'll understand."

"I guess. You want me to call her?" Cash asked. "Right now?"

"Right now."

Cash took out his phone and dialed, but didn't get through, so he got out of the Cherokee and wandered around looking for a cell signal. Breck stubbed out his cigarette in a flowerpot. Jenny watched him with a look of severe disapproval on her face.

"What's this crap?" she asked. "When did you start smoking again?"

"Today."

"Why? Oh, who cares. Just don't do it around me." She picked at her muddy clothes. "I guess I don't need to change if we're going back in that mine."

When the sun went down, the temperature went down, too. It was getting chilly. Breck put his hands in his pockets. He leaned against the wood railing, and it creaked under his weight.

"So, the District Attorney has opened an investigation. He thinks I was conspiring with a Mexican drug cartel to profit from the sale of illegal marijuana. Sound familiar?"

"Gee, I wonder who told him that?" Jenny shook her head. "Matthews. That guy would throw his own grandmother under a bus. He probably already did."

Commandeering Breck's lawn chair, she eased down and groaned.

He could tell she was tired. While he spent the day lounging in a lawyer's office in Frisco, she spent the day risking her safety, following a lead into the depths of the Keystone Mine. It was one of those forbidden attractions that everyone in Quandary knew about. The "No Trespassing" signs didn't do any good. At one point, years ago, the mine entrance had been sealed off with a locked steel mesh door, but people had long since pried it open.

"So you found a body. Do we have a name?"

"No. We did find a wallet, but there was no ID. Just a hotel key card."

"What did the victim look like?"

"It's a male, that's all I can tell you. Facedown in the bottom of a mine shaft. We'll need to rappel just to reach the body."

"I've got everything we need, down in my basement," he told her. "Harnesses, ropes, webbing, carabiners. We'll need to set up a z-pulley to retrieve the body."

"You have all that stuff?"

"Yep."

They had been watching Cash. He walked up the road, down along the lakeshore, then back to the cabin, staring at his phone the whole time. But he never found a cell signal.

"Come on inside," Breck told him. "You can use the landline."

He went into the cabin and flipped on some lights. It had been a long day, and it was going to be a long night. There was a body inside the Keystone Mine, and they couldn't just leave it there. It could have been an accidental death, or it could have been intentional, and if so, it was a crime scene. Either way, time was of the essence.

CHAPTER 4

What's Your Name, Fella?

When Breck rolled the body over, a coil of intestine squirmed out of the dead man's belly like an eel out of water. As soon as it happened, Jenny, who was shining Cash's fancy ThruNite flashlight from above, vanished, and the mine pit went dark.

"Oh, Good God," was all Breck heard. That, and some dry retching.

"I can't see. Jenny! Shine the light down here."

A while back, Breck had purchased a nice new Petzl headlamp, but like a fool, he had bought generic AAA's. By the time they descended to the three hundred level, he could barely see his hand in front of his face.

"Jenny, come on."

Setting up a solid anchor for the rappel line had been tricky. In a recovery situation, Breck would normally place rock climbing gear in cracks and crevices in the surrounding rock. He brought a backpack full of spring-loaded cams, pitons, wired nuts, and old-school hexes, but nothing in the dank tunnel was reliable. Everything was too soft and crumbly. The old winch suspended over the shaft was his only real option for a rappel anchor, so Breck threaded a piece of webbing around the metal spool. It creaked but held.

"Sorry," Jenny called. She appeared again at the top of the shaft and trained the light down, so he could see.

The pit was about fifty feet deep. A century ago, the miners had used it as a trash dump. It was full of old junk and rubble. There was also a rusty cable and a metal bucket laying at the bottom, which was probably attached to the winch at some point. Beside Breck's boot was the leathery hide of a small animal that fell in a long time ago, just like Wallet Guy. Maybe a fox or a marmot?

He examined the dead man's face.

"What's your name, fella?"

It was bruised and bloody. Lips split, black eyes. Some of the bone structure in his face was broken. But was it from the fall? Or did someone beat him senseless first?

"Pronged on a sharp piece of lumber." Jenny's voice echoed. "Hell of a way to go."

"Safe to say it was the technical cause of death. He definitely bled out. I don't see any gunshot or tool-mark wounds."

The mystery man was wearing an expensive-looking business suit and one Calvin Klein dress shoe. Breck checked the label on the man's collar. The logo was written in Italian, or French, or something European. There was nothing in his pockets except a white silk pocket square in the front of his jacket, monogrammed with the initials JA, and a bear emblem embroidered with golden thread.

Spotting a glass bottle lying nearby, Breck picked it up and unscrewed the cap. It was cheap Smirnoff vodka, and it was still half full. The label looked new. Breck leaned close to the dead man's face and sniffed. It smelled like decomp, but not liquor.

"Does he have a cell phone?" Jenny called.

Breck checked his pockets.

"Nothing. Not even spare change or chapstick."

"You think this was an accident?"

"Nope."

The county didn't have an official coroner, and the closest thing to a morgue was a spare gurney at the Quandary County Medical Center.

"Send down the rescue basket," Breck shouted. "Let's get him out of here."

"Will do. Hang on."

The ThruNite beam disappeared, and Breck was in the dark again.

Who was this guy? Breck had never seen him before. But if he had a Hyatt key card, then he wasn't a local.

The best guess, based on its condition, was that the body had been down in the mine pit for 48 hours, give or take. No one had filed a missing person's report yet, which was odd. Dressed like he was, with the fancy suit and monogrammed handkerchief, it was hard to imagine no one cared or noticed he was gone. There was a wedding ring on his left hand, too. Platinum. This man was somebody's husband, business associate, colleague, competitor, and friend. And one of those people killed him.

CHAPTER 5

Creepy Currency

It was a good thing Cash had come along. The rescue basket never would have fit in Breck's Jeep, but it fit perfectly in the back of the Cherokee. Breck could have called an ambulance to transport the body, but even if he had, the road was too rough for any vehicle without four-wheel drive.

Leaning inside the back of his Jeep, Breck dug around in the shadows, trying to find a box of granola bars.

"You want a Clif Bar?"

He tossed one at Jenny. He was going to give one to Cash, but the guy was busy exploring one of the mine shacks. They could see his flashlight beam through the slats in the wall.

The moon was out, and the stars were bright, and they had a good view of the entire Ten Mile Range. Breck had hiked a lot of the peaks, and recognized most of them by name, even in the darkness. The Keystone Mine was sitting at 11,000 feet of elevation on the ridge below Red Mountain. True to its name, the dirt capping the summit was a deep auburn color. The mine entrance looked like a dark doorway cut into the mountain slope, right above a big cone of crumbled gravel, with an abandoned ore cart parked on the rails.

"What time is it?" Jenny asked.

"It's almost midnight."

Breck got out a thermos, and using the hood as a table, poured a little coffee into paper cups. Caffeine would help, and it would warm them up, too. It had taken a ton of effort to get the body out of the pit.

"Check it out," Jenny said. "You can see Quandary from here."

Breck brought her one of the cups. Sure enough, the city was twinkling in the valley down below—the streetlights on Main, the Safeway parking lot, county fairgrounds, and the hospital. There was a blinking red light on the cell tower, and the landing strip at the airfield was easy to spot.

Cash came out of the mine shack.

"Do I smell coffee?"

Jenny pointed at the ski resort in the distance. Even though there wasn't any snow yet, the ski slopes were lit up like a freeway.

"Hey, Cash. Whoever took your shift must be a complete rookie," she said. "They forgot to shut off the chair lifts."

He came over to see what she was talking about.

"No, we keep it running until midnight now. Ever since the Tordenskjolds put in a café on the top of Peak One, people want to ride the lifts just to hang out and do what we're doing now."

"Recover bodies?"

"Look at the city lights."

Sven and Tya Tordenskjold were the owners of the ski resort. Sven was always out of town, and Tya ran the place. She was also on the city council, and that's how Breck knew her. He usually attended the meetings to give them a monthly Sheriff's Report, listing all the crime data for the month.

"So, what was a guy in a fancy suit doing in that mine?" Jenny asked. "We know he was staying at the Hyatt. We can start there, see who the room is registered to. What else can we do?"

Cash pointed at the ski resort. "Dude was at the conference."

Breck and Jenny both turned in surprise.

"What conference? How do you know that?" Jenny looked betrayed. "And why didn't you say something earlier?"

"Sorry. That guy's face was jacked up." Cash shuddered. "Threw me for a loop. But now that we're out here, I can breathe again."

"What conference?"

"We're hosting an international finance shindig. The theme is cryptocurrency. They got a whole lineup of speakers, vendor booths, that sort of thing. The dead guy was there. I know I saw him."

Over on Peak One, the ski runs and the chair lift suddenly went dark. Breck checked his watch. Midnight. Almost on cue, a cold wind began to blow along the ridge. It was mid-October, and it was surprising not to see any snow on the mountain tops yet. But it was coming. It was just a matter of time.

As soon as the wind hit her, Jenny held out her hand.

"It's freezing. Give me your keys."

Breck reached in his pocket but realized she was talking to Cash.

"What? You don't want to ride back with me?"

"Your heater sucks."

Cash handed over the keys to his Cherokee. Jenny got in the driver's seat and started the engine. Then she rolled down the window so she could still be part of the conversation. "So, what is creepy currency?"

"Digital money," Cash said. "It's all online. Kind of like the stock market. People buy in, hoping the price goes up."

"That sounds stupid."

Cash shrugged. "I guess. But people get rich off it."

Breck got the thermos and poured everyone a second round.

At least they had a good idea of where to start now. It should be easy to figure out the victim's name from the Hyatt registry and then ask around at the cryptocurrency conference. And that wedding ring had to mean something.

The more challenging question was going to be, who killed Wallet Guy, and why? Whoever did it took his ID and credit cards. Somehow they missed the hotel key card or didn't think it was important. Were they trying to make it hard to identify the body? Or was it just a robbery gone wrong? If so, they sure went to a lot of trouble. They had to drive Wallet Guy to the Keystone Mine, miles from town, and force him to climb down ladders and walk through dark tunnels. Then they shoved him into a fifty-foot deep pit and left him to die. That was pretty sadistic.

"Is that conference still going?"

"Yeah," Cash said. "It runs through the rest of the week, ends Saturday."

Jenny fiddled with the knobs on the Cherokee dashboard until she found the heater fan and cranked it on high. Then she leaned out the window again.

"Hey. You say this currency conference is an international thing? What if the person who killed Wallet Guy flew here from Guatemala or something? We've got a week to figure it out, or they're gonna fly the coop."

Cash walked around his Cherokee and got in the passenger seat. He didn't even complain that Jenny had taken the wheel. Breck went around to the back of the vehicle to double-check the rescue litter was secure. It was going to be a bumpy ride back down the mountain. And a chilly ride in the Jeep—Jenny was right about the heater.

CHAPTER 6

Silver Label Club

Even though she had a multi-million dollar mansion built into a forested slope above Quandary, with a private access road, an exclusive view, and every high-end appliance and furnishing available, Tya Tordenskjold had a fully furnished 800 square foot apartment installed inside the ski resort. It was supposed to be for those occasional late nights or long weekends hosting events when it wasn't worth the effort to drive all the way home, late at night, and then drive all the way back in the morning. But Tya had been staying at the apartment for six months straight.

During those same six months, her husband, Sven, had laid claim to the house and stayed there when he wasn't jetting off to Norway. Sven had a mistress in Norway. And a mistress in Vail, according to the credit card receipts and the photos a private investigator had shown her.

Tya didn't sleep well when she knew Sven was in town. She slept better when he was out of town, or better yet, out of the country, even though she knew he was finking around. The moment he got in his Hummer and revved off to Denver International Airport, a dark cloud lifted, and she could breathe a little easier. Laugh a little lighter. And, of course, white wine helped take the edge off, as well.

Tya loved white wine.

For a birthday present to herself, she installed a floor-to-ceiling wine refrigerator in the apartment, right where the portrait wall had been. It used to be covered with black and white photos, a series of them, all very professional. Tya and Sven in black turtleneck sweaters, heads tilted. White aspens, white clouds, white teeth. His arm coiled around her, Rolex facing the camera. And that smarmy

Sven smile. Every photo was staged for the camera, like everything about him was staged, and now all those photos were gone, dumped down the trash chute, one by one, in a glorious free fall of tinkling glass and shattered dreams.

Who needs memories when you have wine?

The refrigerator was immense. Tya was a Silver Label Club member at every vineyard in Paso Robles, and a new box of wine was waiting for her every time she went to the post office. Chardonnay, Sauvignon Blanc, Pinot Grigio, Moscato. At this rate, she might need to build another wine fridge. The apartment had a guest room. Why not convert it into a walk-in cooler?

The sun was starting to rise. Tya stood at the window looking for deer in the dawn's early light while the espresso machine steamed and gurgled. It wasn't even six o'clock yet, but the intercom in the kitchen beeped. She went over to the wall and pushed the talk button.

"What is it?"

"Mrs. Tordenskjold, pardon the early intrusion." It was the girl working the front desk, Cash's fill-in for the night shift. She was a weird one and always tried too hard to sound professional. "But there is a woman at the front desk asking for you by name. She looks . . . disheveled. I think something unusual is going on here. Perhaps, the police may need to be summoned."

Tya didn't want to be called *Mrs.* anything anymore, but no one knew she and Sven were having marital problems. She hadn't broadcast the information, certainly not to the staff, and she wouldn't tell her employees until the divorce details got finalized. Maybe they would have to sell the resort if it came down to it. If so, all these people would be out of a job.

"And you say she is asking for me? By name?"

"Yes, ma'am."

"Well, what is *her* name?"

"I do not know. The woman is pretty frazzled right now and keeps speaking in a foreign language. She is currently hiding behind the reception desk, by my feet. I think she is scared of something."

The cryptocurrency conference was in full swing. There were a couple of movie stars in attendance, including several foreign actors. Maybe some stalker was causing trouble—things like that had happened before.

"Okay. I'll be right down."

The espresso was going to get cold. Tya took a quick, final sip, then checked a mirror to make sure she looked presentable, went out into the hall, and pushed the elevator button. The resort was a three-story building, and the apartment was on the top floor, but it would only take a minute to get down there.

Tya loved the ski resort. What if she lost it in the divorce? That would be a tragedy. Dark lumber and corrugated metal on the exterior gave the building a historic-modern mine-camp vibe. And inside, it was like a little slice of paradise. Besides the conference hall, there was a tourist shop, spa, sauna, a food court for a quick meal, plus a nice sit-down restaurant for a proper dining experience.

The restaurant chef was from Paris, and he had some serious culinary skills. As soon as he learned Tya had moved into the upstairs apartment, he began sending up special plates for her supper every night. His name was Jean-Baptiste, but he insisted she call him JB. Maybe he was kissing up or hitting on her, it was hard to tell, but either way, she got good food out of it. Just thinking about it made her hungry. When the elevator door opened in the lobby, Tya caught a whiff of the breakfast buffet, but she forgot all about it when she saw who was crouching behind the reception desk.

"Hedda?"

It was Hedda Asbjorn, in her pajamas and socks, and she looked terrified. She was so scared that she didn't seem to recognize Tya, even though they were friends.

"Are you okay?"

Hedda and her husband, Jansen, were from Oslo, and they were in Quandary for the conference. Jansen owned and operated a Scandinavian cryptocurrency exchange. He was one of the main speakers at the conference. Sven and Tya were Norwegian, too, and both couples had vacationed together, gone on cruises, and of course, skied the slopes together.

"Shall we alert the police?" the desk girl whispered.

But Tya wasn't listening. She couldn't believe Hedda Asbjorn was huddling behind the reception counter in her pajamas. The bottoms of her socks were filthy, too. Finally, Hedda's eyes came into focus, and she gripped Tya's forearms.

"Help me!"

"What's going on? What happened?"

"I got loose and ran, and I didn't know who to trust or where to go, so I came here."

Her words were tumbling out, almost too fast to understand. She was speaking Norwegian, but Tya understood.

"What are you talking about?"

"They broke into our room. Tied us up with duct tape. They threatened Jansen, struck him, and took him away. I haven't seen him for a couple days. I finally got the tape loose, and. . . ."

Suddenly she went pale, eyes wide, frozen.

"Who? Who did this, Hedda?"

Then Tya followed her gaze.

A man had just walked into the lobby from the parking lot. Dark hair, clean-shaven. He was tall and cut like a bodybuilder. He locked eyes with Hedda for a long moment. But then he noticed Tya was standing there, staring back at him, and other people were stopping to stare, too. He turned and left, and Hedda collapsed on the lobby floor.

CHAPTER 7

In The Icebox

Jenny put the Cherokee in park but left it idling while they unloaded the rescue litter from the back.

The Quandary County Medical Center was barely bigger than the 7-Eleven across the street. It had an examination room, an operating room, patient rooms, a lounge, a lobby in the front with a Coke machine, and a laboratory in the back that doubled as a morgue.

The doors stayed open around the clock in case there were overnight patients or emergencies, but most of the staff went home at the end of the day unless a call came in.

Because it was such a small show, Jenny knew everyone who worked there. There used to be four nurses on staff, but now they were down to three, and they all shuffled the duties around—surgery assistant, reception desk, ambulance crew, and janitor. Jenny liked all but one. Melinda. She was sour on life and never got any of Jenny's jokes. Doctor Heller was the only doctor. He was a recluse who lived in Frisco and commuted the ten-minute drive to Quandary every day. Red sports car. Mid-life crisis.

Jenny ran inside to get a gurney with wheels, so they wouldn't have to carry Wallet Guy another inch by hand. After dragging the rescue litter through the mine, her arms and shoulders were sore. Plus, she was dead tired. It had been a slow, bumpy drive down the mountain, and it was way past her bedtime. She checked her watch. It was almost her wake up time—if this were a normal day, her alarm would be going off.

When she saw who was working the graveyard shift, Jenny swore under her breath. Melinda.

"Got extra room in the freezer?" Jenny asked.

"Barely."

She spotted an empty gurney in the hallway and grabbed it.

"We just pulled a dead body from the Keystone Mine. It was pretty nasty. Guts everywhere."

Melinda didn't respond, but that was no surprise. As a rule, Melinda was unresponsive.

"I'll be right back."

Jenny wheeled the gurney past the reception desk, through the empty lobby, and out the automatic doors. Breck was waiting in the parking lot beside the Cherokee, and together, they transferred the body from the rescue litter onto the gurney as the sun began to rise. While they were working, Cash crawled across the console and got behind the wheel and began channel surfing on the radio.

Breck took out a twenty-dollar bill, went to his window, and handed it to him.

"What's this for?"

"Gas money. Thanks for guiding us through that maze. I wish I could offer more."

Cash turned down the radio. His clothes were just as muddy as theirs.

"Happy to serve, bro."

"Don't use it to buy weed," Jenny said, slamming the back door closed. "And no trespassing means no trespassing. Stay out of the mine from now on, got it? If you fall down a shaft, who's going in after you? Not me."

Cash leaned out the window and grinned at her.

"You're pretty hardcore, deputy. Do you want to go paragliding next weekend? You like pizza?" He waved the twenty in the air. "It's on me."

"No, and no. But thanks anyway."

She slapped the side of his truck with the palm of her hand to indicate the conversation was over, and he should drive away. Cash got the hint, did a u-turn, zipped through the parking lot, and they watched his taillights disappear.

"You love pizza," Breck said, smiling.

"He's going to spend that twenty on weed."

"Probably."

"Let's get this guy in the icebox before he gets any more ripe."

They pushed the gurney back inside the hospital. Melinda saw them coming and silently led the way, propping the lab door open for them. A walk-in cooler was built into the back wall, with another corpse parked on a second gurney, covered in a plastic shroud.

"What happened to that one?" Jenny asked.

"Rollover on I-70. State Patrol brought him in."

Jenny started to peek under the plastic but stopped. "You know what? I think I've seen enough entrails for one day."

Unfolding another plastic sheet, Melinda began spreading it over Wallet Guy. His intestines were inside a Safeway sack, taped to his waist like a colostomy bag. Jenny wanted to explain and tell her they had no choice. Yeah, it wasn't very dignified or professional, but recovering a body deep inside a crumbling mine shaft was tricky business, and they had to improvise. But Melinda didn't even blink and draped it over him and shut the cooler door, and that was that.

Breck gave her a side glance like he was going to ask a question.

Melinda noticed. "What?"

"So . . . how is Michelle doing these days?"

Michelle was the nurse who quit. Jenny knew Breck was worried about her. He had taken Michelle out on a single, solitary date, once upon a time. But the previous year, a baddie from a Mexican drug cartel shot up the hospital, and she took a bullet in the spleen. After that unfortunate incident, Michelle decided Quandary wasn't as safe a place to work as downtown Denver.

"I heard she got a job at Saint Joseph's, maybe?" He shrugged.

Poor Breck, he was prodding for information. Jenny felt bad for him, and apparently, so did Melinda. She finally ginned up a pity-smile.

"Michelle's working at Craig Hospital now. She posts a lot of pictures of her cat on Instagram. And she went to Country Jam in Grand Junction this summer. That's about all I know."

Jenny buried her hands in her muddy jacket pockets. She was ready to go home, take a hot shower, and go to sleep.

"Hey. We should get out of here."

"Yeah." Breck nodded and ran his fingers through his hair. He turned to Melinda again. "We'll swing by later with a camera to take evidence shots."

Melinda shrugged.

"Fine with me."

They walked out to the parking lot and got in the Jeep. Breck put on his seat belt with a dull click. He dug out his keys but just leaned back and closed his eyes for a couple of seconds.

"Danny just bought a fancy DSLR," he said. "I guess he's getting into photography now. He won't loan it to me, but if you ask, he might."

"Okay. I can do that—later. First, I need sleep."

"Me, too."

Danny was Breck's younger brother. He owned the brewery on Main Street. Jenny knew there were times when they got along and times when they didn't. Maybe this was one of those bad times.

They drove back to the Sheriff's Office, and Jenny jumped out with a wave. She lived in a rental cottage a couple of blocks down Main Street, but her purse was sitting on her desk.

"When I get home, I'm going straight to bed, and I'm going to sleep till noon," she said. "You should do the same."

But Breck shut off the engine and got out, too.

"I'm too tired to drive home."

Jenny flipped on the office lights and went to her desk. Mine mud soaked her socks, and every step she took squished. Her boots used to be waterproof when she first bought them. How many years ago was that?

Breck took off his muddy jacket and hung it on the coat rack, then walked straight into the jail cell and laid down on the cot.

"Pull the blinds when you leave, okay?" he said.

The little red light on the landline telephone was blinking. Jenny pushed the playback button to hear the message.

"This is Tya, at the ski resort. . . ."

CHAPTER 8

Charm And Disarm

Every spring, Mayor Seneca Matthews paid a landscape company to plant a big garden right out front. It was a colorful sea of columbine, alpine lilies, and Indian paintbrush. The smell of wildflowers made City Hall seem feminine and friendly. Who could be mad when they breathed in such whimsical vapors?

Matthews hated the smell, but it was strategic. Emasculate his enemies before they even set foot inside the building. Charm and disarm.

Unfortunately, by October, the flowers were dead. But even if they had been alive, the scent wouldn't have any effect on his ex-wife when she was in a rage.

Valerie Matthews blew past his secretary, Brittany, and right into his office. She wielded a crumpled manila envelope in her hand like a baseball bat, swatting things off his desk. Pens, papers, and his can of Diet Coke all went flying.

"They're evicting me!"

"Easy, Val! Easy does it."

He jumped out of his chair, keeping the desk between them.

"Easy does what, Seneca? Nothing about what you've done is easy!"

She glared around at the larger objects on his desk and ruthlessly tipped over his computer monitor. Brittany was watching through the doorway, snapping her gum. Matthews glared at her. If that girl tried filming this on her iPhone, he would fire her on the spot.

"Why don't you take your lunch break now?" He waved her away like a wasp, but she didn't move.

"I just clocked in a little while ago. It's barely eight in the morning."

"Just leave! Go to Starbucks or something."

Brittany put on her sunglasses, tucked her iPhone in her back pocket, and shot out the front door.

"We're talking about my *home*, Seneca." Valerie's face was dark with rage. "You had an obligation. A court-ordered obligation. Now, where am I supposed to live? And where is our daughter supposed to live?"

"To be fair, Aspen doesn't live at your house anymore, does she? I know she's renting that little apartment by the college."

"Where did you hear that? Did she tell you that herself?" Valerie smirked. "Oh, that's right. Aspen doesn't talk to you anymore."

Matthews winced.

"Listen. It's not as bad as it seems," he said. "The bank must have sent that out by mistake because I've already paid the—"

"Shut your lying mouth, Seneca. I was just *at* the bank."

It had been over three years since the divorce. The first thing Valerie did was move out of their home in Quandary and buy a new home for herself, in Frisco, with a view of the reservoir. As part of the settlement, he was supposed to pay the mortgage, HOA, and utilities. That meant he was paying for two houses. Then, Aspen got accepted to the university in Boulder, and her freshman year was insanely expensive. Matthews couldn't afford to send her back there for her sophomore year, but he could afford to enroll her in Quandary Community College. Even so, life was expensive. Especially during a campaign year, and his number one priority was getting re-elected. If he lost his job, what would he do? Go back to real estate? His realtor license had long since expired.

Valerie wagged the envelope in his face.

"I have to pack up all my worldly belongings and go check into a hotel. Although how I'm going to pay for that, I have no idea. No clue! Did you know I had to sell my SUV? But I made enough to cover groceries for a month or two, so it wasn't a total loss. But once that little nest egg is gone, I'll be eating out of a garbage can."

Matthews blew out air, a defeated exhale, or at least that was what he wanted her to think. He even slumped his shoulders.

"I am so sorry, Val. This wasn't what I wanted to happen. Believe me. I love you, and of course, I love Aspen, and I never wanted anything like this to happen."

She knocked over his desk lamp.

"I'm going to rent a storage unit in Frisco, book a room in the Hyatt, and send you all the bills. Then I'm going to sit down with my lawyer, and you better not do anything stupid. Not one stupid little thing."

Valerie spun around and left, her heels clicking on the floor like firecrackers.

A room in the Hyatt? Was she kidding? Renting a suite there was more pricey than a house payment.

Matthews looked out the window. He had a good view of the parking lot from his desk, and he watched as his ex-wife got into a Ford Focus. It was a cheap little rental. Valerie paused with one foot in the door and cast a glance at his BMW, which was sitting in the special "Mayor of Quandary" parking space by the curb. Was she going to key his new car?

"Don't you dare . . ." he muttered.

But Valerie must have read his mind and simply drove away.

Matthews immediately picked up the phone and dialed the Hyatt Residence Club. The manager, a young man named Zachary, answered after a couple of rings.

"Quandary Hyatt."

"This is Mayor Matthews."

"Good morning, mayor. How may I help you?"

"How is business this week, Zachary? I understand a lot of those people attending the cryptocurrency conference have been staying at the Residence Club this week."

"Yes, sir. We are booked solid."

Matthews sank into his leather desk chair and tried not to sound too happy.

"Booked solid? That is fantastic. As mayor, I just want to see our city's businesses thrive. If the Hyatt is doing well, then I'm doing well."

"Is there anything else, Mr. Mayor?"

"Nope, that's it. Take care, my friend."

After he hung up the phone, Matthews looked around. His desk was a disaster. Broken lamp, scattered papers, and his computer monitor was face down in a pool of Diet Coke. He started to yell at Brittany to come to clean up his office, but then he realized the girl was gone.

CHAPTER 9

Or Something

Everything in Tya's third-floor apartment at the ski resort was either white, or powder green glass, or lacquered wood. An oil painting of a winter mountain scene, an Edvard Munch reproduction, hung above the desk. A row of novels by Per Petterson and Karl Ove Knausgård lined the mantle above a natural gas fireplace. A massive bronze eagle hovered over a walnut podium. It was all so sterile, so high end, Breck felt out of place in his mine-muddy jeans. He kept checking the rug, hoping he wasn't leaving any boot prints behind.

Tya had her arm around Hedda, whose eyes were vacant. They were seated on a white leather sofa. The woman was in shock, and even though she was safe, she had lapsed into silence and wouldn't answer any of Breck's questions.

"What about the security footage from the lobby?" he asked Tya. "Can you show that to me?"

"Sure. I can pull it up on my laptop."

Gently extracting her arm, Tya got up and went to her desk and turned on her computer.

Jenny was standing near the windows, looking outside. The apartment had a perfect view of the ski slopes on Peak One.

"Look at these clowns."

She pointed at the chairlift. A couple of mountain bikers took a seat and got whisked away, clutching their bicycles in a death grip.

While Tya clicked on the keyboard, Breck joined her at the desk, leaning close enough so they could whisper.

"Are you sure Hedda speaks English?"

"It's her second language. She's very fluent. This whole ordeal has really rattled her, though."

"Aren't you from Norway, too?"

"Yes. I was born in Lillehammer and went to university in Oslo. That's where I first met Hedda. We were both business majors. Of course, that was fifteen years ago. I've been living here for the last decade, so we only see each other once a year. Vacations mainly."

"What's her husband's name?" Breck asked.

"Jansen. You know what? I have a photo of him." Tya clicked the mouse a few times, and a promotional poster appeared on the screen. She pointed at a row of headshots. It was a list of all the speakers for the week. "That's him, right here. Jansen Asbjorn. He owns Bear Coin Capital."

Breck remembered the dead man's pocket square was stitched with the initials JA and a bear emblem.

Jenny came over to see.

"That's Wallet Guy," she said.

Tya glanced up, confused. "Why do you call him that?"

"Has anyone reported him missing?" Breck asked, trying to avoid saying too much, too soon. "Or noticed his absence?"

Tya shook her head.

"No one has said anything to me. But Jansen isn't scheduled to speak until Friday night." She frowned. "I wonder what the kidnappers want with him. I mean, he's rich, so they must want money. Maybe they drove him to a bank or something?"

Or something was the correct answer. But Hedda wasn't in any condition to hear that her husband was dead.

"Let's go ahead and take a look at that security footage," Breck said. "If we can identify the kidnapper, we can get some answers."

"That guy this morning. He was pretty scary looking." Tya clicked the mouse, brought up a series of video files, and began sorting through them by date and time stamp. "I feel so bad when I think about it. Can you imagine someone breaking into your home and duct-taping you to a chair? It must have been terrifying."

Over on the sofa, Hedda put her face in her hands. Did she overhear what they were saying?

Jenny noticed, too. She went over and sat down and started to put her arm around her shoulders as Tya had done earlier, but Hedda scooted away to the far side of the sofa, trembling.

"Hey, it's okay." Jenny smiled. "We're here to help."

But Hedda wrapped her arms around a couch pillow and closed her eyes tight. Tya spoke to her in Norwegian, something reassuring, but it didn't seem to make a difference. The woman seemed completely shut down.

"She doesn't know who to trust. That's why she ran here." Tya pointed at her laptop. "I've got the right time code cued up. You want to see this, too, deputy?"

Jenny eased off the sofa, trying her best to act non-threatening, and went over to the desk. Tya hit the play button. The security camera in the lobby had a wide-angle lens, and they could see the entire area including the front desk and the sliding glass doors that led to the parking lot. They watched as several individuals walked in and out. A silver-haired man in a suit stood outside, taking an early morning smoke break. Then he stubbed out his cigarette and came back inside, heading for the elevators.

"This is 5:48 A.M.," Tya said. "Okay, here she comes."

Hedda ran into the frame from the parking lot, wearing pajamas and socks. She began slapping the automatic glass doors until they slid open, then dashed inside the lobby. As soon as she spotted the girl at the reception counter, Hedda ran straight at her, arms waving, face creased with fear. Then, she dodged around behind the desk and crouched down.

"You'll see me come down to see what's going on. Just as I get there, the guy chasing Hedda steps inside the lobby. Now, watch closely." Tya fast-forwarded to the right spot and hit the play button. "Hedda freaks when she sees him."

Sure enough, a large athletic man stepped through the sliding doors and looked around. He spotted Hedda peering over the reception counter. When he noticed Tya and the desk girl standing there, he spun around and left, striding across the parking lot until he was out of sight.

"So, who was that?" Jenny asked.

"I don't know, but he looks familiar." Tya shrugged. "Before you got here, Hedda told me a little bit about what happened. She said two men held them hostage. I think it's pretty obvious that the guy on the security footage is one of them."

Breck pointed at the screen.

"Have all your staff take a look, see if anyone recognizes him. Can you print me a screenshot? I want to head over to the Hyatt Residence Club and see if this guy is on camera over there."

Tya hit the print screen button, and a printer softly hummed out a copy. Breck folded it and put it in his back pocket.

"Let's roll," Jenny said. "We can get the manager to let us in the Asbjorn's room. See what we can find there."

But Breck didn't think that was a good idea. Their main suspect had trailed Hedda into the ski resort lobby. He knew she was in the building. What if he was stalking her, waiting for them to leave?

"Until we have a little clearer idea of what's going on, one of us should stay with her at all times."

He thought for sure Jenny was going to argue, but she just patted her hip holster.

"No problem. I can take that sucker. But give me a call if you need a backup for any reason. It's just a short jog across the highway, and I can be there in a heartbeat."

CHAPTER 10

It Only Took One To Get The Job Done

The Hyatt Residence Club wasn't a typical short-stay hotel. They didn't rent rooms—they rented condo-style "residences." The Asbjorns were staying on the third floor, in a two-bedroom suite overlooking Quandary. Southwest decor, lodge lamps. It had a full-scale kitchen with stainless steel appliances and granite countertops. A massive stone fireplace on the far wall dominated the living room.

Quite a place.

Breck walked around. The fridge contained take-out boxes from restaurants, bottles of Perrier and Stella Artois, artisan bread, and a package of raw salmon. Fresh produce filled the crisper—avocados, tomatoes, and green leaf lettuce. Honey-dijon mustard in the door. Almond butter. How long had they been staying here? Just a week for the conference? Because that was a ton of food for one week. Several wadded up plastic bags from Safeway were lying next to the toaster. Breck felt sick for a moment. He had used a Safeway bag to transport Jansen's intestines out of the mine. He rubbed his eyes and took a deep breath to clear his mind. The man had suffered. There was no question about that.

Walking into the master bedroom, Breck counted half a dozen suitcases stacked in the closet, but they were all empty. The Asbjorns had settled in. All their clothes were hung up on hangers or folded neatly in dresser drawers. Hedda's jewelry was arranged on the dresser according to earrings, necklaces, and bracelets. It all looked expensive.

Heading back out into the great room, Breck spotted a laptop on the dining table and some paperwork, but it was written in Norwegian. A couple of pages had dark, bloody smears and smudges, and a ballpoint pen was caked with dried blood, too. Had Jansen signed something under duress?

Then Breck walked over to the fireplace. Two chairs were out of place, with duct tape stuck to the arms. Spare rolls of tape were lying on a coffee table.

This is where it happened.

Poor Jansen. No wonder his face looked so messed up. A candlestick was lying on the floor, with blood on it, and the carpet was blood-spattered, too. There was a row of matching candlesticks on the mantle, but they all looked untouched. Breck frowned. It only took one to get the job done.

The Asbjorns had been duct-taped to these chairs. Hedda must have witnessed everything, watching while they interrogated her husband and beat him bloody. That was cruel. Why not lock her in the bedroom? What was the sense in that?

Breck went over to the windows. From the third floor of the Hyatt, the city of Quandary looked peaceful and silent. It was a sea of treetops, cars driving back and forth, and people walking and talking and shopping, going about their merry way.

"Sheriff?" It was the guy from the front desk, Zachary. He was the manager of the Hyatt. He leaned in the doorway, nervous about coming in any further. "I looked at the registry like you asked. The Asbjorns checked in a little over a week ago and had booked this suite for the entire month of October."

"This room is a crime scene." Zachary had given him a plastic keycard to access the Asbjorn's front door. Breck held it up. "I need to hang onto this for now. And no one is allowed in here except me or Deputy O'Hara."

"Okay."

Breck pulled the printout from his pocket, the screenshot from the ski resort, which showed the kidnapper in the lobby.

"Do you recognize this guy?"

Zachary studied it closely and nodded. "Oh, yes. He is a guest here. Kind of."

Breck gave him a look.

"What does that mean?"

"I don't know what his name is, but he works for a foreign businessman who is staying in our presidential suite, a man named Mr. Khodorovsky. He is Khodorovsky's bodyguard."

They stepped out into the hallway. Breck ran yellow caution tape across the doorway. As they walked towards the elevator, Breck pointed at a security camera.

"Are your cameras working?"

"Yes."

"Show me the footage?"

"Sure. The monitors are down in my office."

They rode the elevator down to the main floor, and Zachary led the way to his office—a small room behind the welcome desk. As they walked, Breck noticed more security cameras. They were everywhere—the hallways, the elevator, the lobby. Whoever invested in the Hyatt Residence Club had spent a lot of money on décor and furnishings, and they hadn't skimped on the surveillance system, either. That was good. Since the bodyguard was staying at the Hyatt, there should be plenty of video evidence to track his movements. There were only so many ways to get in and out of the building.

"I want to see all the footage you've got from a couple days ago, starting with that camera near the Asbjorn's room."

"No problem," Zachary said. He led the way into his office, which had a row of flat-screen monitors mounted on the wall. He sat behind a small desk and began tapping on a keyboard.

Seeing a comfortable wicker chair with thick cushions in the corner, Breck eased into it. He hadn't slept all night and was suddenly feeling lethargic. He had to fight to keep his eyes open. They had stopped by the General Merchandise on the way back from the Keystone Mine. Breck bought a can of Coke, and Jenny purchased a can of Red Bull. She swore by them, but Breck hated those kinds of energy drinks. They tasted like tin-flavored acid.

"You got a coffee maker here?"

"Out in the lobby, you'll see a big painting of an owl. Right beneath that is a Keurig."

"Be right back."

Heaving himself up, Breck headed into the lobby.

The owl painting was easy to find, but trying to figure out the coffee maker was another story. *How do you work this thing?* He pushed the silver button on the machine, but nothing happened. He examined a tray of little plastic pods filled with coffee grounds. It was some brand he had never heard of. Breck chose one and looked around for help, but the lobby was empty.

"Whoever designed this should be in jail," he muttered.

He nestled the pod back into the tray. So much for that idea.

"Sheriff?" Zachary called from the office doorway. He looked spooked. "Somebody erased all the security footage. The whole thing. It's wiped clean front to back."

CHAPTER II

Time To Schmooze

Matthews circled the ski resort parking lot to find a spot that wasn't any-where near an aspen tree. He hated coming out to his nice new BMW, only to find little yellow leaves pasted to the windshield and hood. The car had less than 10,000 miles on it. He didn't want leaf goo any more than he wanted a door ding. That was why he parked crossways, taking up two spaces.

After he cinched his overcoat, Matthews hustled across the asphalt, fumbling in his pocket to push the key-fob lock button. Behind him, the taillights flashed. *Bwoop-bwoop.*

It was shaping up to be a miserable autumn day. Dark clouds had just started to creep over the mountain tops, and the forecast said rain. The creek running past the parking lot had fresh ice all along its gravel banks. He even smelled wood smoke. Someone had their fireplace going. It better not be winter yet. Matthews hated winter.

When he entered the ski resort lobby, he gave his overcoat to the girl at the reception desk and paused to read a promotional poster board perched on a metal tripod. Cryptocurrency. What the hell was that? Matthews didn't know, and he didn't care to learn, but there were important people in town for the conference. People to mingle with. People not to be ignored. Like Colorado State Senator Dana Stayne. She had the worst last name for politics, and the critics loved to riff on it. Her opponents in Congress called her a stain on the United States Constitution. A stain on democracy. A stain on America itself. The internet trolls weren't quite so elegant.

But those in her orbit knew her as the Ice Queen. When crossed, Senator Stayne could be one brutally cold lady, and Matthews wanted to stay on her good side. She was a master at dredging up dark secrets and dirty laundry and leaking it to the press at the worst possible time. More than one politician went down in campaign flames, and more than one mayor lost a re-election bid. Even a fatal car accident on Wolf Creek Pass a couple of years back was rumored to be her handiwork, but of course, that was a pure conspiracy theory. Or was it?

The elevator door slid open, and Deputy Jenny O'Hara stepped out and nearly walked right into him. Matthews glared at her.

"What are you doing here, O'Hara? Moonlighting as conference security? I thought I paid you to patrol these streets."

"Mayor McCheese. I thought your jurisdiction ended at the golden arches."

Matthews was about to launch into her, but people were stopping to look. Besides, she wasn't alone. Tya Tordenskjold popped out of the elevator, too. There was a time and a place, but this wasn't it.

He gave Tya his best smile.

"I was hoping to bump into you. Guess what? I was having dinner the other night in that wine bar up in Basalt—with Kevin Costner. Kev ordered a thousand-dollar bottle of Pinot Blanc that tasted like pears and black licorice. I thought you might like to try it, so I bought you a bottle. It's back in my office, but maybe I can swing by later?"

More than once, with Sven out of town, she had complained about his infidelities over a glass of white wine.

"I don't have time to talk right now," she said.

"Not a problem. We can save it for a special occasion."

Another woman was standing there with them, dressed in a bathrobe with the Quandary Ski Resort logo. Matthews recognized her. That was Jansen Asbjorn's wife. He was one of the super-rich crypto CEOs at the conference. But what was her name? Heather? Olga? Something like that. Matthews almost greeted her, almost apologized for the redheaded deputy's rude behavior, but there was something wrong here. Tya had an intense look on her face, the deputy was covered in mud—and why was Asbjorn's wife in a bathrobe? Before he could ask, all three of them marched outside to the parking lot. A valet drove up in Tya's sporty Land Rover. It was solid white. The same color as the wine she drank.

Where were those three going? Matthews watched them drive off, but he had more important things on his mind. He brushed the lint off his sleeves.

Time to schmooze.

The conference hall was buzzing with voices. It was a large room with a vaulted ceiling and wrought-iron chandeliers hanging from giant wood beams.

There was a spotlit stage with two chairs, ferns, banners, and a giant projection screen, but no one was up there at the moment. People were standing and chatting and networking. Matthews had timed it perfectly. The last thing he wanted was to sit through some nerd lecture.

As Matthews shook some hands, and joked about the weather, he worked his way around the room until he spotted the senator. She was tall, razor-thin, in her late 50s. Gray pantsuit. Pearls. Several younger women flocked around her, holding iPads and cell phones. That was another thing. She despised men, and her entire staff was female, and not one of them was Caucasian.

"Senator Stayne, it is a pleasure to see you here. Glad you could make the conference." Matthews went in for a handshake. Her grip was soft and limp. Her fingers felt like frozen little cucumbers. "I hope you are enjoying your time in Quandary."

"Seneca Matthews. The charming mayor of this charming little town." She smiled, though her smile and her eyes seemed detached. It was a little unsettling. "November sixth is coming up quickly. You worried?"

Matthews chuckled, a warm self-deprecating three-yuk beat.

"Oh, Dana. My campaign momentum is rock solid, and the polls are there to prove it. The Quandary Herald publishes a new one every week on their website. I believe the good citizens of this *charming* little town know I'm the right choice. Zero worries. Besides, my opponent is just a local-yocal wannabe."

Stayne raised her eyebrows.

"Is that so? I wouldn't underestimate Johnny Tibbs. From what I hear, he has a great deal of rapport with this community."

One of the senator's pencil-skirted lackeys leaned in, cradling her iPad. Whisper, whisper.

"You may want to double-check those polls," Stayne said.

Matthews worked up that chuckle again. Johnny Tibbs. The guy ran a dude ranch on the outskirts of Quandary, and his term on the city council was up. Now he was gunning for Matthews' seat as mayor. That little cowboy prick.

"Have you had a chance to consider my request?" he asked.

"You want my endorsement?" Stayne pressed a cucumber finger to his chest. "My name on your campaign? That doesn't come cheap."

Quandary wasn't a big city. If it weren't for the ski resort, it wouldn't even be on the map, but Matthews was slowly grubbing his way up the food chain.

"You know, I was talking to Kevin Costner the other night over a thousand dollar bottle of Pinot Blanc. We were at that wine bar up in Basalt. He thinks Quandary would make a great location for his next feature film. Spy flick, big budget. But he's concerned the film incentives in Colorado aren't quite competitive enough. He's thinking about filming in New Mexico instead."

Stayne looked impressed.

"You get Costner to film here, and I'll endorse you for mayor of Quandary. Hell, I'll endorse you for governor."

"No problem. Easy as baking a pie."

As soon as he said that, Stayne's face fell. Her lady gaggle looked dizzy with horror.

"Not that it is a woman's role to bake pies." Matthews stuttered. "It's a little known fact that I like to spend a lazy weekend baking pie, myself. Never let my ex-wife in the kitchen, back when we were, uh. Flour, apples. Mix it up, pop it in the oven. I do it all the time. Easy. And I'll get you Costner, just as easy. Easier, in fact."

Matthews let his eyes drift across the room, and he waved at a fern.

"Why, hello there, Joe, I see you," he called to no one. "What's that? Sure, I'll be right over. Pardon me, Senator. Enjoy the conference."

Plucking a champagne glass from a passing tray, Matthews got lost in the crowd as quickly as he could and gulped it down. Politics was ninety percent smack talk—everyone knew that. Connections were currency, but embellishments were part of the game. Right? How many times had he used that movie star line?

Ducking into the restroom, Matthews got out his cell phone and Googled Kevin Costner.

CHAPTER 12

Sensitive Subject

Tya drove with both hands on the wheel, used her turn signals, and braked when the stoplight turned yellow. Riding in the passenger seat was a strangely peaceful experience. Jenny was used to riding shotgun with Breck in his old clunky Jeep, gripping on for dear life. Its engine was loud, the wind whistled through the soft top, and the heater didn't work. But the Land Rover was sophisticated, with a digital touch-screen in the console, rear camera monitors, Bluetooth, GPS, and lo and behold, drink holders. There wasn't even a CD player, but somehow soothing classical orchestra music was floating around her. It was magical.

Jenny glanced back at Hedda. The woman still refused to speak or even look her in the eye. Whatever she went through, it must have been very traumatic. But at the same time, they needed her to make an official statement, saying that the man in the ski resort lobby video was her kidnapper so that they could arrest him.

The next stop was the Sheriff's Office. Maybe Hedda could relax there, far away from what happened, safe inside a law enforcement structure. But as soon as Tya pulled into the small parking lot and Hedda saw the sheriff star logo on the front door, she started hyperventilating and chattering in Norwegian.

"What's she saying?" Jenny asked.

"I don't know." Tya turned around and put her hand on Hedda's knee. "Let me talk to her."

Jenny wished she knew Norwegian. Having the ability to speak in a foreign language would be fun, like German or French, or Spanish, for that matter. She could successfully navigate the menu at Casa Bonita, but that was about it. Back when she worked for the Denver Police Department, she spent many hours patrolling the airport terminal's curbside. The language barrier used to drive her crazy because Denver International Airport was just like it sounded, international, and trying to explain why people couldn't park in the loading area and wait for their cousins from Egypt could get awkward.

"I don't know why, but she doesn't want to go inside with you." Tya looked apologetic. "She doesn't trust you. Or Breck."

"That's weird. Tell her we're the good guys."

"I did."

Hedda was firmly holding onto the seat belt as if she expected Jenny to force her out of the vehicle.

"Hey, I am not going to hurt you, okay?"

She tried friendly gestures—a thumbs up and okay sign. But Hedda shook her head firmly.

"What are we going to do?" Tya asked. "If she doesn't want to go inside the Sheriff's Office, I don't think we should drag her in there."

"No. But we can't take her back to the Hyatt, that's for sure."

They sat in the Land Rover, idling. A few small raindrops hit the windshield. The sky was overcast now. Jenny pulled a plastic juice bottle out of the drink holder. It was from Tya's fridge. All organic. The label said *Minty Winter Fell*. Dragon fruit, carrot, ginger, and mint. Bizarre, but tasty.

Maybe Breck had some answers by now or at least some new theories. After she took a glug of juice, Jenny took out her cell phone and dialed, but it went to voicemail, so she tried the Hyatt Residence Club, but the call dropped before anyone answered. The cell service in this town sucked. There was only one tower in Quandary, and whenever the clouds rolled in, the signal went to crap.

"You know what? Let's just take her back to my apartment," Tya said. "She can stay in the guest room until you figure out what happened. All she needs is a safe place and some time to recover. Once she's had a chance to process what happened, I bet she'll be willing to talk about it."

"I don't know. The kidnapper followed her into the lobby, remember? Until we arrest him, it's too dangerous for her to stay there."

"Okay, not the resort. But what about my house? There's an eight-foot security gate at the base of the driveway. No one gets in there without the right code."

Jenny thought it over. More raindrops pattered on the glass. Tya's mansion on the mountain? That would work.

"Okay. But let's head to the hospital first and get her checked out by a doctor."

"What about Jansen?" Tya whispered. "Are you sure we shouldn't go back to Hedda's room? What if the kidnappers try to call her at the Hyatt and demand a ransom? Or is Breck waiting by the phone?"

Jenny took a deep breath and tried to play it cool. There would be no ransom call. The worst part was, Hedda would need to confirm the identity of the body, and it wasn't a pretty sight to behold. But one thing at a time. The woman was still in shock over being kidnapped.

"Breck's got that part under control. All we need to do is keep Hedda safe until she's ready to talk."

Tya looked suspicious. "You know something, don't you?"

Jenny glanced over her shoulder. Hedda looked like a feral cat. Time to change the subject.

"So what's up with Matthews hitting on you?"

Tya shrugged. "Is that what he was doing?"

"If Sven were standing there, he would have body-slammed him into the floor." Jenny smiled. "I'd love to see that."

But Tya's voice went cold. "Sven is out of town."

Jenny was surprised at her curt answer. Sensitive subject?

"Too bad."

As they drove, Jenny lapsed into silence. Maybe she was too jacked on Red Bull and pushed the conversation a little too far. For some reason, joking about the mayor was off-limits. As a member of the city council, Tya might feel uncomfortable razzing Matthews behind his back. Unless the problem was Sven? Who knew? Maybe it was just bad timing. After all, Hedda was in the backseat, trembling like a leaf.

One time, Tya dropped by the Sheriff's Office. She told Jenny a bear had broken into their mountaintop mansion when Sven was in Norway on a business trip. It shook her up. After that, Tya was so nervous about bears that she couldn't even step out on the back deck to barbecue chicken. So she bought a .45 Magnum handgun and wanted to learn how to use it safely. On the weekends, Jenny began taking her to the gun range on Boreal Pass Road to shoot Diet Coke cans in a cut-bank. That qualified as fun in Jenny's mind and Tya enjoyed it, too. Even though they were from two different worlds, they became friends. They even went to the Quandary Brewery for burgers and beer to celebrate the day Tya got her concealed carry permit.

Friendship was hard to come by, and Jenny didn't want to ruin this one. She had been working in Quandary County as a deputy for almost four years. When she first hired on, there had been several other deputies and a dispatcher. Two of them were female, and Jenny became good friends with both of them right off the bat. Those were fun times—movies, dancing, and dining out. But that was around the same time Matthews got elected mayor. In his infinite wisdom, he slashed the funds the city spent on patrol services, which was a big blow to the Sheriff's Office budget. Breck had no choice but to whittle down expenses—and staff. All the other deputies, and the dispatcher, lost their jobs in the process.

They drove past a billboard that read *Re-Elect Matthews For Mayor.*

"We should head up to the shooting range again before the snow flies," Jenny said. "We can use that thing for target practice."

The corner of Tya's mouth creased into a smile.

CHAPTER 13

Mud Knots

"They sell horses?" Brittany was confused. "At the fairgrounds?"

"As soon as I punch my time card, I'm heading straight over there."

"Can I come?"

"Definitely."

The day had dragged by, but Aspen's shift at High Country Pizza was almost over, and she could barely hold it together. She missed horses.

When Aspen turned twelve, she took horseback riding lessons. It started simple. Introductory level stuff. Ground lessons, wheelbarrows, and poop rakes. How to groom. Then she learned to sit in a saddle and work the reins, and it didn't take long before Aspen was memorizing dressage patterns and begging her mother to buy her show clothes. But somewhere along the line, she got into skiing, and her dad made her choose. One hobby. Just one. So, she sold her English saddle and bought a pair of K2 Shreditor alpine skis.

"How can you afford a horse?" Brittany asked.

She was sitting at one of the round dining tables by the storefront window, sipping on a fountain drink while she waited. The lunch rush had finally tapered off, and the place was empty. There were crumbs and crumpled napkins all over the tabletops.

"At the auction, they always go cheap, and I've been saving my tips all summer." Aspen ducked into the janitor's closet and came out with a spray bottle and a rag. She began cleaning off the tables. "They've got the catalog preview online, and I saw a seven-year-old dun gelding that will show Training Level dressage, with no reserve."

"What does no reserve mean?"

"It means they start the bidding at zero dollars."

"They have a catalog? At an auction?"

"Yep. That way, people can know what's coming and figure out what they want to bid on beforehand. There's a lot of horses, so hopefully, no one else will want him. If I have enough leftover, I'm going to buy some new barn boots. There's a pair of purple Ariat lace-ups on Amazon I've got my eye on."

She was trying to stay positive. Keep her chin up. It had been a challenging year, filled with disappointments. First, her dad made her withdraw from the University of Colorado in Boulder and forced her to transfer to Quandary Community College. Then he made her sell her Volkswagen Beetle. She had cried and begged and then demanded an explanation. But her father wouldn't say much, except to say that life could be tough, so toughen up. Matthews were fighters.

Well, Aspen was a fighter, and she argued his ear off until he finally gave her some real answers.

The family bank account had bottomed out. The Matthews went from rich to poor overnight. Her dad was still fuzzy with the details and would only say that a significant business deal fell through. But one thing was crystal clear: while Aspen was renting a one-room studio apartment and drove a crappy secondhand car, her father lived in a 5,000 square foot home up on Eyrie Road, the street where all the rich people lived, and he cruised around town in a sparkling, factory floor BMW. *I'm the mayor, and this is an election year. Who would vote for me if I lived in a duplex?* So he got to keep his lifestyle, and everyone else had to sacrifice. Her mom lost the house in Frisco, and Aspen had to quit CU Boulder. C-frickin'-U? Fatherly love, people. That's what it looked like.

"I have a straw cowboy hat at home," Brittany said. "I really miss line dancing. There's a country music club in downtown Denver called the Grizzly Rose. People say it's awesome."

Going back to the janitor's closet, Aspen got a broom and started sweeping the floor. People were messy eaters.

"If we go, you'll have to drive," she said. "I don't trust my car. Not all the way down I-70 and back. I feel like it's going to break down at any moment, and of course, it'll happen at the worst possible time."

"I still can't believe your dad made you sell the Beetle. I loved that car."

"Yeah. Me, too."

Aspen's parents had gotten a divorce on her 16th birthday, a little surprise present that made the day feel *really* special. As an obvious ploy to buy her affection, her father purchased a Volkswagen Beetle, brand new, and gave it to her the day she got her driver's license. It was a "sorry we got divorced and ruined your Sweet Sixteen" makeup gift. After the divorce, Aspen moved in with her mom until she graduated high school, and then moved in with her dad to spend the winter in those Shreditor skis. The slopes were practically in his backyard. Her mother only lived ten miles away, in Frisco. But ten miles might as well have been ten million miles when the roads got icy.

But it didn't matter now. The Beetle was gone forever. Just like her mom's house, CU Boulder, and all the trust she'd ever put in her father, Seneca Matthews, mayor of Quandary. It was all gone.

Gone. Boom. Adios.

Aspen took off her flour-speckled apron and tossed it in a bin behind a metal rack full of cardboard pizza boxes.

"We've got time to stop by the feed store. I need to buy a lead line and a halter."

"Where are you gonna keep a horse?" Brittany looked extremely skeptical. "You don't even have a pickup or trailer."

"I can stable him at the Tibbs ranch for free and borrow a saddle for free, too. All I have to do is clean stalls on the weekends and tie mud knots on the trail horses. Elk season is about to start. I'll have to wake up at five in the morning to get everything done before the hunters ride out, but it's totally worth it."

"Sounds sadistic. If it were me, I'd spend all that tip money at the outlet shops in Dillon, get a whole new wardrobe, and get buzzed on Mocha Frappuccinos."

"Hilarious."

"Dead serious."

"I know you are."

The time cards were hanging on the wall next to the time clock. Aspen punched out and took a pizza box from under the heat lamps. Someone had called in a lunch order for a large pepperoni and mushroom but never showed. When that happened, she got to take it home.

"Free food! You want a slice?"

"Yes, I do."

"Let's eat in the car on the way to the tack shop."

They went outside and got into Aspen's car. It was a 1986 Toyota Corolla, or the Crapolla, as she liked to call it. It was a flaming piece of junk, a far cry from the Beetle, but at least it had wheels. Brittany balanced the box on her lap and picked out a slice. Aspen reached in and took one, too.

"I love it when the pepperonis are really crispy like this," Brittany said.

"I used to . . . but I think I'm getting sick of pepperoni. Hazard of the job."

"How long has it been since the last time you rode?"

"Too long."

Picking off the mushrooms, Brittany flicked them out the window onto the sidewalk, one by one.

"I used to date a cowboy who wanted to be an equine veterinarian. Remember Laramie?"

"Maybe," Aspen said.

"Kind of a mama's boy. But he knew horses."

Aspen barely remembered Laramie. He was one of Johnny Tibbs' wranglers, the previous summer, but only for about a month before he quit. Brittany dated all kinds of guys. Football players, UPS drivers, forest rangers, and school teachers. There was no method to her madness.

"What happened to that hipster guitarist? The one we saw playing at Starbucks last weekend?"

"He bought me a latte, and we talked." Brittany cringed. "But his beard smelled like garlic, and I swear I saw chia seeds."

Putting the key in the ignition, Aspen started the car and turned on the radio. She found a country station to get into the right mood. Six months of tips added up to five hundred dollars. The Ariat boots cost seventy-five, with free shipping. That left four hundred and twenty-five as her maximum bid. She knew there were going to be thousand-dollar horses in that sale ring, but there were also going to be some that nobody wanted.

Hopefully, no one would want that dun gelding—except her.

CHAPTER 14

The Bachelor

"Seventy-five, seventy-five, seventy-five, eighty." The auctioneer was an old-timer with white hair, and Aspen could barely understand what he was saying. "Eighty, eighty, lookin' at eighty-five, eighty-five . . . yep! Sold at eighty-five dollars to Number 103."

A high school kid in a cowboy hat led each horse into the sale ring, hand-walked them back and forth a few times in front of the auctioneer box, and then took them back into the barn after the bidding ended. The sale ring was in a bright, warm indoor arena at the Quandary County fairgrounds, which was good since the sun was going down, and the temperature right along with it.

"See? What did I tell you?" Aspen said. "You're missing all the action."

Brittany brushed the dirt off the bench and sat down next to her on the bleachers. She had gone to the concession stand to buy cotton candy.

"That auctioneer talks a mile a minute."

"While you were gone, three horses went for a hundred bucks each. That's cheap."

"Why didn't you buy one?" Brittany asked and pinched off a bite of cotton candy.

"Because I'm waiting for the dun gelding I told you about. Besides, half of these are strays, or they've been abandoned, and who knows what their story is. Maybe they're broke, maybe not."

Aspen held up her auction catalog and pointed at a photo of a tan-colored horse with a black mane and tail, and a black stripe down its back.

"See? That's him."

Brittany took the booklet in her free hand.

"Be careful, you're going to get it all sticky," Aspen said. Then she pinched off some of the cotton candy and ate it herself. It was pink and tasted just like bubblegum.

"It's like reading the classified ads. Here, listen to this one—*Sorrel for sale. Good cutting horse. Very cowy.*" Brittany chuckled like it was the funniest thing ever. "What does that even mean?"

The next horse for sale was a thin quarter horse mare. She was uneasy with all the new sights and sounds. The handler kept snapping the lead line to get her to stand still, but it only made the situation worse. The mare whinnied and reared while the auctioneer talked.

"Another stray. Look at those ribs." Aspen frowned at the handler. "That stupid kid!"

"So, who would want to buy a stray?"

"Number 103, apparently. He's already bought a whole bunch."

Seated in the next section, a man waved a white piece of paper with bid number 103 printed on it. He wore a dark brown Stetson and a dirty, canvas, western-style button-up vest. When he wasn't bidding, he took sips from a Coors can balanced on his beer belly—or scratched his crotch.

"I don't see a ring on his finger." Brittany giggled. "I bet he's going to be on the next season of *The Bachelor.*"

A couple of old cowboys raised their hands, and the bidding continued a little longer, but it was obvious no one was interested in paying too much money for a skinny stray mare. The auctioneer banged his gavel.

"Sold. Hundred dollars to Number 103."

The guy spotted Aspen and Brittany staring at him, and he held up his beer can. "Girls want one?"

"Marry me!" Brittany shouted, rolling her eyes.

Aspen put her face in her hands.

Once again, the young handler brought out another horse into the sale ring. It was a well-groomed sorrel and looked healthy, young, and strong. The auctioneer got on the microphone again.

"Easy going, no buck, no bite, gonna start the bidding at ninety-five, ninety-five, how about a hundred?"

The bleachers were full of men and boys wearing cowboy hats, pearl snap shirts, and Wrangler jeans. Hands shot up, and the bid price quickly climbed to a thousand dollars and kept climbing.

Aspen flipped through the catalog until she found the description.

"*Five-year-old cutting horse. Heading, heeling, dragging calves to the fire.* No wonder this crowd wants him so bad."

"Why don't you bid on him?"

"Are you kidding? He's already way over my budget. Besides, I ride English, not western."

Brittany nudged her.

"Hey. Check out the Bachelor."

Aspen looked over at Number 103. Now, he had a paper tray of nachos balanced on his stomach. He reached in and extracted a tortilla chip. Yellow cheese dripped onto his canvas vest, but he didn't seem to notice.

"This is going to sound sick and twisted, but now I'm in the mood for nachos." Brittany stood up and brushed the dirt off her pants. "I'll be right back. Save my seat!"

Seeing her get up, the Bachelor whistled at her. Brittany gave him the middle finger and then headed down the stairs. A few minutes later, she came back empty-handed.

"Sold out," she muttered. "How can a concession stand run out of nacho cheese? That's like the Red Cross running out of blood."

Aspen sighed. She was enjoying the auction and couldn't wait to bid on the gelding, but at the same time, it was hard to concentrate, given all the chaos in her life.

"I hope my mom is going to be okay."

"You should have seen her at City Hall this morning. She was livid. I got out of there as quickly as I could, but it was brutal." Brittany put her hand on Aspen's shoulder. "I don't care if he is your dad. Mayor Matthews is a full-blown crap bag."

"Welcome to my world."

With Brittany working the front desk at City Hall, it was like having a spy in her father's office. More than once, Aspen got a play by play of an argument between her parents. All the dirt, all the details. But this one was worse than ever. What was her mom going to do now? She didn't have a career or even a part-time job. She had been living on the money she got from the divorce, and the house in Frisco was supposed to be part of the settlement. But it turned out, the mortgage was in her father's name all along. Aspen used to love her poppa. Moon over him. Defend him. But all these dark little secrets were flying like fireworks on the Fourth of July.

"There he is!" Aspen felt her heart skip a beat. The dun gelding was in the sale ring. She waved, and the horse trained his coal-black eyes right on her. "Did you see that? He sees me!"

"This little fella don't rope, don't dally, but he'll prance around all day long if you wear a top hat." The auctioneer's voice rang over the loudspeakers. "No reserve. Do we have an opening bid? How about ten dollars? Anybody want a ten-dollar horse?"

Raising her arm, Aspen held her bid card high. The auctioneer started asking for fifty bucks, but none of the cowboys showed any interest. She felt relieved. Which one of them would be interested in a dressage horse? They wanted ranch horses, rope horses, and trail horses.

But then the Bachelor waved his card.

"Fifty!" he called.

"Number 103 bids fifty dollars. Do I hear seventy-five, little girl?"

Aspen raised her number to bid again.

Watching her, the Bachelor grinned and tipped his hat.

"What the heck?" Brittany asked. "Can't he tell you want this horse?"

"It's okay," Aspen whispered. "I've been watching that guy. He hasn't paid over a hundred bucks for any of the horses he bought."

She caught the auctioneer's eye.

"Little girl's putting up seventy-five for the prancing pony. What about you, 103? How about a hundred?"

Sure enough, the Bachelor bid a hundred dollars.

When the auctioneer asked for a hundred and twenty-five, Aspen waved her bid card. This was it. She winked at Brittany and mouthed the word, *boom.*

"I imagine we got a sale at a hundred an' twenty-five dollars," the auction-eer announced. "But it's my job to ask. How about a hundred and fifty?"

Carefully setting his nacho tray on the bleachers, the Bachelor raised his number over his head. Aspen was stunned, and so was the auctioneer.

"One-fifty from 103! Hell hath frozen over. Now, we've got a bidding war, folks. Am I gonna get one-seventy-five from the girl with the long brown hair?"

Aspen was determined to win this war, but the Bachelor kept bidding against her, and the price kept going up. Two hundred. Three hundred. Four hundred. A woman with glasses and hand-cut bangs was sitting in the row right in front of them. She turned around and gave Aspen an odd look.

"Better outbid that man if you want that horse to live," she said.

"What do you mean?"

"Don't you know? He's a kill buyer."

Aspen went pale.

"What does that mean?" Brittany asked.

The lady shrugged apathetically. "Sells 'em for meat."

The auctioneer's eyes darted back and forth between Aspen and the Bachelor. He spoke a mile a minute, with the mic pressed against his mouth like he was gnawing on it. He was hard to understand, and it was stressful trying to follow the quick talk.

"Four-twenty-five to Number 103."

"Four-fifty!" Aspen waved her bid card furiously.

She felt a sickness in the pit of her stomach.

"Meat?" Brittany was shocked. "As in, to consume? Are we talking about dog food or Canadian bacon? What are we talking about here?"

"He buys all the cheap horses and trailers them to a slaughterhouse," the lady with the glasses said. "Sells 'em for a quick buck."

"Is that even legal?" Aspen asked.

"Not here. But it is in Mexico."

The loudspeakers crackled as the auctioneer's voice rose.

"Number 103 bids four hundred and seventy-five dollars. What's it gonna be, what's it gonna be?"

"Oh, my God." Aspen stood up and held her number high, one last time. She had hit five hundred and couldn't go any higher, not even a penny. She wouldn't be able to afford those nice purple boots, but it was worth it if she could save the dun's life.

But the Bachelor called her bluff. He raised his bid card one last time.

"Sold for five hundred and twenty-five bucks." The auctioneer looked genuinely surprised and pointed at the kill buyer. "That is one high dollar hamburger."

The Bachelor looked over at Brittany and Aspen. He smiled and raised his Coors can in the air. "Marry me!"

CHAPTER 15

Save All The Pretty Horses

After the auction ended, Brittany and Aspen skirted around the building to find the holding pens. What they found was a maze of scratched-up metal panels wired together into stalls. Horses paced and pawed the ground as the girls walked by.

The Bachelor was loading all the horses he bought into a rusty stock trailer. Aspen did a quick headcount. There had to be a dozen crammed in there already.

"What's your problem?" Brittany cracked her knuckles like she was going to start a fistfight. "You are one sick puppy."

The kill buyer scowled.

"Get out of here. This area is off-limits, except to legitimate buyers."

"Why did you outbid me?" Aspen asked.

"To teach you two a lesson." He smiled, but it wasn't a playful smile this time. "You can't always get what you want. Now, scat!"

Using a whip, he forced the last horse inside, then slammed the gate shut. The entire trailer rocked and shook. It was obvious there were too many horses in there. Aspen stepped on the wheel well and peered through the window slats. Sorrels, blacks, bays, a palomino. Then she saw the dun gelding—his eyes wide with fear.

"Get off my trailer."

Aspen jumped down, butterflies in her stomach. "Let me buy him off you, please. I've got five hundred dollars right here. I can get more."

"I said, scat." The Bachelor had a clipboard with all the bills of sale and transfers of ownership. He flipped through the paperwork, searching for something he couldn't find, then flipped through it a second time. "What the hell?"

"Come on, pal," Brittany said. "Be reasonable."

"That damn Palamino ain't got no Coggins." He slammed the clipboard against the side of the trailer. It made a loud clang and spooked the horses. "Settle down!"

Aspen wanted to push past him and open the trailer. Set the horses free. Yell and scream and chase them until they ran far away, deep into the forest, where they could become wild horses and live new lives in the high country, free and clear, grazing mountain grass and drinking fresh water from the creeks and streams whenever they got thirsty. Never again would they worry about being crammed into a metal tin can and taken away to be shot and skinned and processed so some beer belly in a filthy brown Stetson could turn a profit.

Aspen felt powerless.

How could there be people in the world with such a low view of life? How could this guy wake up every day and look himself in the mirror?

"Come on, let me buy him, please." She showed the Bachelor a bank envelope filled with cash. "It's all right here."

But he didn't touch it.

"Just take the money," Brittany said. "You can use it to buy a new vest that isn't covered in nacho cheese."

The Bachelor smiled again, a little playful this time.

"Tell you what. You girls can buy any of these horses that your little hearts desire. But you have to go through my website."

Aspen immediately took out her cell phone, opened a web browser, and got ready to type.

"Really? Okay, okay. What is it?"

"Double-ya, double-ya, double-ya." He spoke way too slow, dragging it out. "Save All The Pretty Horses, dot com. Every one of these beasts will be posted on there by noon tomorrow. All prices final, so don't even think about haggling me down. That ain't how I work."

Aspen stared at her cell phone in disbelief. It was real. The Bachelor had a website with horses for sale. There were a bunch of photos. He had labeled each one with a made-up name, like Rodeo and Blackie and Sorrel #5, and each horse cost one thousand dollars. Every single one.

"What is this?"

"It's called a horse rescue."

"A thousand bucks?" Aspen's mind was reeling. "Can I make payments?"

He laughed. "Nope."

"It took me all summer to save up five hundred. It'll take a couple more months, but I can do it."

"Gonna be too late by then. If them horses don't sell in two weeks, they're going to Mexico."

After flipping through the paperwork one last time, he climbed inside his pickup truck and slammed the door. There was a hokey magnetic sign stuck to the door that said Blue River Horse Rescue.

"Come on, Aspen. This is a scam. We're out of here." Brittany took her by the arm. "This guy murders horses for a buck, and we're calling the cops on his ass."

But the Bachelor just laughed at them.

"Go right ahead. I am a straight-up businessman, and it all checks out. For instance, I don't cross no state borders without a Coggins on each horse. Now I gotta call out the damn vet to write one up. He takes so long. It might buy you an extra week if you're lucky. I won't get out of town before Halloween at this rate."

Aspen looked at the stock trailer again. The horses inside were still shuffling around, banging into each other. She could smell manure and urine, strong in the air.

"What's wrong with you?" Brittany muttered. "This is inhumane."

"Hey, I'm doing this community a service." He got serious. "Think about it. All these horses show up, and nobody wants to deal with them. What? You wanna see 'em starve out in a field somewhere? Eaten by ki-yotes? *That's* inhumane."

"It's against the law," Aspen said.

"That's why I truck 'em to Mexico, and yes, they get chopped up for meat. That's just the way it is. But they ain't suffering, they ain't starving. And neither are whoever winds up eating 'em. It's a win-win. And yes, I pay my bills in the process, so what's the harm? It's called the food chain, gals. That's just the facts of life."

The horses scuffled inside the trailer again. The *gong* of hoofs striking the sidewall was loud. Aspen spotted the dun again, his black eyes peering out at her as if he knew what was happening. He even whinnied at her, and it broke her heart.

"You don't care about rescuing these horses. You prey on people's consciences. That is the most evil thing I have ever heard."

"You suck," added Brittany.

The Bachelor reached into his vest pocket and pulled out a key ring. He found the right one and put it in the ignition. The engine began to rumble, and black diesel fumes pumped out of the exhaust pipe.

Aspen couldn't help it. She started to cry. There was nothing else she could say to make him change his mind. She had tried reason, logic, money, and guilt, but none of it was enough. She had five hundred dollars, but she needed five hundred more. Where was she going to find that kind of cash? Delivery tips wouldn't begin to cut it, her mom didn't have anything to spare, and her father was a selfish miser.

"Hey, blondie." The Bachelor leaned out the window and winked at Brittany. "Marry me!"

CHAPTER 16

Stake Out

"Why don't *I* stake out the lobby, and *you* go get Danny's camera?" Jenny asked.

"Danny likes you better."

"He's *your* brother."

"Exactly."

Breck handed her the keys to his Jeep. They were standing in front of the Hyatt Residence Club curbside entrance. Now that Zachary, the manager, had identified the man in the ski resort photo as the bodyguard of a foreign businessman staying in the Presidential Suite, all they had to do was wait in the lobby until he made an appearance.

"When you get back, we can snap some photos of the crime scene while we're here," Breck said. "Two birds with one stone."

Jenny weighed the keys in her palm.

"I hate driving stick shift after dark."

He took out a five-dollar bill and handed it to her.

"Hey. Can you buy me a coffee somewhere? We may be here all night. There's a Keurig in the lobby, but it doesn't work."

"I'm not transporting any hot liquids until you get a drink holder. They sell them for ninety-nine cents at Flying J's all across the nation. But I'll keep this for my trouble." She tucked the cash in her back pocket. "Am I going to run out of gas?"

"The brewery is five minutes there and five minutes back. You'll be fine. Trust me."

Of course, Jenny was smart to ask. The gas gauge didn't work. Every time he filled the tank, Breck wrote down the mileage in a notebook and did the math so they didn't wind up puttering to a stop in the middle of the road. It was one of many things about the Jeep that Jenny didn't like—and she wasn't shy about voicing her complaints. Another one was the fact that the suspension sat too high off the ground. She had to squirrel her way into the driver's seat.

"If I'm not back in a half-hour, call a tow truck."

Jenny opened the door, grabbed the frame, bounced a couple of times, and somehow crawled her way inside. The valet was sitting in his booth nearby, watching with a smile. Breck wanted to smile, too, but didn't.

"You need to install a handrail or something," she said. "I don't think this vehicle is ADA compliant."

"I don't think being short qualifies as a disability."

Jenny popped the clutch, and the whole thing lurched forward, but she managed to power through first gear and disappeared down the street.

Breck could have let her stake out the hotel alone, but the man they were looking for was nothing but sinew and vicious enough to kidnap, beat, and shove someone down a mine shaft. Confronting someone like that was far more dangerous than slapping the cuffs on a shoplifter at the 7-Eleven. Of course, Jenny could handle herself in a serious situation. She had proved that more than once, but there were other reasons Breck sent her to the brewery. Well, maybe just one reason—he didn't want to be the one to ask Danny for his expensive camera.

The natural gas fireplace in the lobby was radiating heat. Breck went inside and started walking straight towards it, but the moment Zachary spotted him, he urgently waved him over to the reception desk, knocking over a can of Sprite in the process.

"Sheriff! I've got our CEO on the phone, and he would like to speak with you."

Breck went over and took the receiver.

"Sheriff Dyer speaking."

"Good evening, sheriff. This is Bradford T. Williams, Jr., chief executive officer of the Hyatt Residence Club, national office. I heard about the unfortunate crime that occurred in the suite on the third floor, there at our Quandary branch. As I understand it, Mr. and Mrs. Asbjorn were held against their will. While other hotel brands have been the location of burglaries like this, it is shocking to hear the Hyatt Residence Club can now say the same."

"Okay."

Breck watched Zachary sink into his chair behind the reception counter. The guy looked physically ill. He was clearly terrified of the CEO and probably thought he was going to lose his job.

"While I know this is a sensitive police matter, our board is deeply concerned about the emotional status of our other guests once word gets around. Is there any way to keep this unfortunate event from the press? Keep it under the radar? I hate to think any of our guests staying there might feel unsafe, based on such a statistically rare event."

Breck frowned. A statistically rare event? The emotional status of his other guests?

"Mr. Williams, this is an ongoing investigation," he said. "I can't comment on it any more than that, and I'm afraid brand optics aren't my priority."

"I understand, sheriff—very noble approach. If I can be so bold, perhaps I can speculate that if word gets out and damages the good name of the Hyatt Residence Club, our board may find it necessary to investigate the competency of the local Sheriff's Office by petitioning the state governor's office for a gainful resolution. Litigate for damages, should it be warranted. This is a difficult situation for both of us, and it's nothing personal. Please, take no offense."

"Okey-dokey."

Breck hung up the phone and pointed at Zachary.

"Tell me again. What was the name of that foreign businessman? The one staying in the Presidential Suite."

"Khodorovsky."

People started flooding into the lobby. The conference must have let out across the street. Breck turned around and watched. It was an odd mix of young millennials carrying vape pens, women with top-knots and bohemian skirts, and middle-aged men in power ties. They chatted as they walked by, and Breck had no clue what they were talking about.

"Did you sign up for the cryptomining session?" someone asked.

"No, Matt McCall will be talking about the Halvening during the same time slot. Gonna be epic."

A small group of college-age young men sat down in wicker chairs near the fireplace, bantering in hushed tones, but Breck heard every word.

"Dude. I just bought a new GPU for my hard drive. I'm gonna mine Bitcoin."

"Don't waste your time, bro. Bitcoin is dead. Charlie Lee said that at the 4 o'clock sesh."

"Of course, he would say that. He invented Litecoin. Don't listen to that BS."

Then the bodyguard entered the lobby. He was shadowing another well-dressed man, clearly his boss, Khodorovsky. They went straight to the Keurig beneath the gigantic owl painting. Stretching out a sinewy arm, the bodyguard seized a dark roast coffee pod, placed it in the machine, and pressed the start button. To Breck's surprise, the Keurig began to squirt hot coffee into a paper cup.

CHAPTER 17

Shattered

The moment Jenny saw Johnny Tibbs straddling a bar stool in the Quandary Brewery, she knew her chances of getting out of there in a timely fashion were zero to none. The man was an unfettered extrovert, especially when he had a little alcohol pumping through his veins.

"Hey Danny," Tibbs said. "Where do cowboys cook their meals?"

But Danny was busy operating the beer tap behind the bar, pouring a pint of ale. He didn't even pretend to engage, so Jenny stepped in to deliver the punchline. It was a joke Johnny had run by her at least a dozen times on as many different occasions.

"On the range, *ba da boom*."

"Why, Jennifer. I couldn't have told you that one before. I just made it up." When Danny set the pint glass in front of him, he immediately took a foamy sip. "Got another one. Hey Danny. What do cowboys put on their salads?"

Again, Danny chose to ignore the question. He placed a cardboard coaster on the bar in front of Jenny. "You want anything to drink?"

"No, I'm still on the clock." Then she snapped her fingers. "Ranch dressing."

"Hell, no. Cowboys don't eat no salad." Johnny smiled his classic easygoing smile. "But if I buy you a beer, can we call this a date?"

"Nope."

She grabbed one of the flat plastic menus lying on the bar. It was tempting to order a hamburger since it was supper time, and she hadn't eaten anything since breakfast, but she needed to get back. Breck was waiting for her, and the bodyguard could show up at the Hyatt at any moment. Who knew, he might walk into the hotel lobby and see Breck's sheriff star and do something desperate.

Or, he might act like an innocent bystander, but either way, he was dangerous, and she didn't want Breck to confront him alone. The first step was to ask those basic questions they would ask any suspect and see how good the man was at lying. Once they got Hedda to start talking and a formal accusation, they could swoop in and arrest him. Plus, time was not on their side. The bodyguard was only in town for the conference, and that meant he would hop a plane at the end of the week and jet off if they couldn't make a case against him first.

"It's five o'clock somewhere," Johnny said. "Let me buy you a beer, Jennifer."

"It's five o'clock here," Danny said.

There was a clock on the wall near the silver brewing vats. Jenny glanced at it. She remembered seeing the conference schedule printed on a poster board at the ski resort. The last session for the day was supposed to end at five. She was cutting it close. She needed to get Danny's camera and get out of there.

Johnny pointed at the colorfully labeled tap handles.

"There's a new one you're gonna like. Danny calls it Pine Beetle Pale Ale. He makes it with actual ponderosa pine nuts, handpicked along the creek out back. Ain't that right, Danny? And local hops. Tell her how they grow them Chinook hops in Paonia."

Jenny sat down on an empty barstool.

"Can I borrow your new camera? We've got a crime scene to document."

Danny was always so taciturn that it was hard to gauge what was going on in his brain. His big bushy beard concealed half his face, making it even harder to judge his reactions, but at the mention of his camera, an eyebrow went up. Jenny held her breath. Was she treading on thin ice here? Did Breck and Danny have a fight or something? Or was this just typical brother crap?

"Did Brecky make you come here?" he asked. "He borrowed it last spring to take a picture of a tire track in the mud, and I didn't get it back for two weeks. Why doesn't the Sheriff's Office have their own camera?"

Jenny gave him a heart-warming smile.

"Cuz we're broke."

Tibbs reached over and patted her hand. The smell of beer on his breath was strong, and he got a little too close when he spoke.

"You know I like Breck and everything. But, Jennifer. You should transfer to Park County. They have actual police cars you get to drive around in, and a full CSI team over there, just like the TV show."

Danny glanced past her through the brewery windows. The Jeep was parked right out front, but it was just a silhouette.

"Is my brother coming in?"

"Nope. He's waiting for me back at the Hyatt. That's our crime scene." Jenny shrugged. "That's why we need the camera."

There was a bowl of pretzels sitting on the bar. Tibbs ate one and then began to chuckle to himself.

"Hey, Danny. Knock, knock."

But Danny walked around the bar and headed towards his office. He waved at Jenny so she wouldn't leave. "Hang on. I'll be right back."

Tibbs leaned a little too close again.

"Hey, Jennifer. Knock, knock."

"Who cares?"

"You're supposed to say, *who's there?*"

"No, I think that's right."

It would be nice to have a real patrol car. And suitable equipment. They used to have all that and more, but Breck had to sell a lot of essentials to generate some kind of income, just to make ends meet after Matthews decimated their budget. They tried applying for federal grants, but nothing ever seemed to come of it. Jenny knew the boys in Park County. They drove Chevy Tahoes and got decent paychecks and three weeks of vacation.

Danny came back and set a black nylon camera bag on the bar.

"This is a Canon 7D DSLR. Use the lens cap when you're not shooting photos, and don't let Breck touch it. This thing cost a chunk of change."

Before Jenny could say thank you, the door opened, and a woman walked into the brewery. She was a pretty brunette in her 30s, with weepy red eyes, and she was carrying a plastic helmet. Jenny didn't recognize her, but Danny did. His expression got weird. Jenny looked at the woman and then back at Danny. Who was she? What was happening?

"Hi, Nickie. I haven't seen you since the . . . memorial." Danny spoke in a gentle tone. "How have you been?"

"Is Breck here?"

Nickie carefully placed the helmet on the bar and stared at it, waiting for an answer. Her voice was raw and cracked.

"No."

"Good. I don't want to see him ever again."

Since she was sitting right there, Jenny got a close look at the helmet, and it was in bad shape. The top had caved in. The sides were shattered. Grit was embedded all over the surface like sugar on a donut.

"They found him, Danny," Nickie said. "It took ten years for the glacier to finally release his body. Ten *years*. But they finally found him."

What was going on? Whose helmet was this? Jenny studied Danny, but he was in a different world now—the same world as Nickie.

To his credit, Johnny Tibbs sat very still. No jokes, no sidebars, and no loud mouth commentary. The air had changed, and everyone could feel it.

"Okay," Danny said.

"This was Kyle's. I want you to give it to Breck, so he'll never forget what happened. He can look at it every day and remember what he did. Tell him I'll never forgive him. Tell him that for me, Danny. Okay?"

"Sure, Nickie," Danny said.

CHAPTER 18

Drunk Cowboy Sponge

After Nickie left, Jenny watched Danny's expression slowly return to normal. He reached for the damaged helmet sitting on the bar but hesitated, flexing his fingers as if he wasn't sure he should touch it.

"Where did you say Breck was?" he asked. "Can you get him over here?"

"He's staking out the Hyatt. We're waiting for a suspect to show. It'll be awhile. You want me to take this to him?"

Danny took a step back.

"Yeah. Okay."

But Jenny didn't get off her bar stool. On the one hand, she felt a sense of urgency to get back to the hotel and help Breck. But on the other hand, something heavy had just gone down at the brewery, and she wanted answers.

"Who was that Nickie chick?"

"It's a long story."

"Give me the Cliff Notes version."

Danny cringed a little.

"It happened on a cliff, all right."

"What did?" she asked.

He opened his mouth but closed it again, glancing uncomfortably at Johnny Tibbs.

Johnny was sitting on his stool in absolute silence, eating pretzels, and absorbing everything they said like a sponge. A drunk cowboy sponge. It was obvious Danny was hesitant to open up in front of an audience, but Tibbs either didn't get the signal or didn't care. He ate another pretzel.

"Enjoying the show, Johnny?" Jenny asked.

"Yep."

There were several framed photos hanging by the bar. They were mainly Quandary locals, smiling or making silly faces, hoisting their beer for the camera. Jenny was even in one or two.

Danny picked a certain one off the wall and brought it back to the bar. It was an old picture of Breck and another guy dressed in technical mountain climbing gear. They were wearing down coats and insulated bibs, carried ice axes, and wore heavy boots with crampons.

"See this guy? That's Kyle Oberland. He was Breck's best friend and climbing partner back in the day. Nickie and Kyle were married."

Jenny studied the picture. They were posing in front of a small yellow tent, balanced on a narrow, snow-covered ridge, with drop-offs on both sides. The tent barely fit. One step in the wrong direction, and it was a vertical free fall. Jenny couldn't believe what she was looking at. It was hardcore.

"This doesn't look like Colorado," she said.

Danny nodded.

"This is Nepal. They flew out there ten years ago to do some big mountain called Annapurna. It's got this huge south face that is nothing but cliffs and steep slabs of ice and monster avalanches. Twenty-six thousand feet high. You can hardly tell from this photo, but it is sick."

Jenny wanted to ask all kinds of questions. She knew Breck had all that rock climbing gear in his basement from when they went to recover Jansen Asbjorn's body in the Keystone Mine, but she had no idea he had been to the Himalayan Mountains. Wasn't that where Everest was? She glanced at the helmet and then at the photo again. It was the same one Kyle was wearing.

"This was their last bivvy," Danny said. "Later that day, a storm rolled in before they could make the summit."

"What's a bivvy?" Tibbs asked.

"Bivouac." Danny tapped his finger on the snow and ice stretching above them. "You can barely see it here, but they climbed right up the middle of this bad boy. They got most of the way up before the weather turned. It was so far off the deck they had to rappel a couple of dozen times and burned through all their gear on the retreat."

It was clear this story didn't have a happy ending, but Jenny had to ask.

"So, what happened?"

"Kyle wasn't as experienced as Breck was. About halfway down, he set up a bad rappel anchor. As soon as he leaned onto the rope, it popped."

Over the past four years, Jenny had known Breck as a boss, a mentor, and even a friend, given how much time it was just the two of them. They talked about many things, but most of their conversations revolved around paperwork, speeding tickets, double-parked tourists, and whether they should stop at Subway or 7-Eleven for lunch.

"Wait a minute." She was confused about something. "If Breck was stranded up there, how did he get down?"

Danny shrugged.

"When he fell, Kyle took the rope with him. Breck had no choice. He had to down-climb with only his axes and crampons. Vertical ice in gale-force winds. Digging snow caves at night. Somehow, five days later, he made it down alive. He spent a week looking, but he couldn't find Kyle's body. When Breck finally got back to Kathmandu, they had to amputate half his toes due to frostbite."

Tibbs gulped down the last of his beer. "I met Garth Brooks once."

Taking the photo, Danny carefully hung it back on the wall. Jenny checked the time and then picked up the camera bag. Stopping by the brewery was only supposed to take ten minutes. Breck would be wondering where she was. He probably called a tow truck by now.

"I gotta go."

"What about the helmet?" Danny asked. "You want to take that, too?"

Jenny hesitated.

What would happen if she showed up at the Hyatt with Breck's dead climbing partner's helmet? What would she say? Was it her place to even try? That was a lot of psychological baggage to drop on him, out of nowhere, in the middle of a murder investigation. And after hearing the details, Jenny didn't want to touch it any more than Danny did. That would be wrong.

"Just leave it right there, okay? Don't let anyone mess with it. I'll tell him to swing over as soon as we're done."

CHAPTER 19

Happy To Provide Translate

Where was Jenny? Breck wished she was there, but he was going to have to do this solo.

The bodyguard was even bigger in person than he appeared on video. He was wearing a tight black sports coat with a silver shirt, open collar, and his neck was all cords and veins and tendons. The seams on his jacket looked like they were going to rip apart if the guy flexed a muscle. His boss was in his fifties, with thinning black hair, too black to be natural at his age, and he was thin as a rail—the foreign businessman.

Time to say howdy.

"Mr. Khodorovsky?"

The two men were standing at the Kuerig machine, waiting for the coffee to finish drizzling. As expected, the bodyguard stepped in between them to guard his boss as Breck approached, but when Khodorovsky saw Breck's badge, he smiled.

"You must be local law enforcement, yes?"

"Sheriff of Quandary County, Breck Dyer."

Khodorovsky nodded like the encounter was not only expected but long overdue. "Just call me Anatoli. All my friends do. And it is much less to form for your mouth."

Breck turned to face the bodyguard. The dude was a beast. Protein shakes or steroids? Probably a little bit of both.

"And you are . . . ?"

"This is Aleksandr. He works for me—security specialist. I never travel without him. Especially to your Wild West. Say hello, Aleks."

But Aleks did not say hello.

"Don't be offended. He's just a deep thinker. How can I be of help to you, Sheriff Breck Dyer?"

"I have some questions for your bodyguard."

"His English is so-so. But I am happy to provide translate."

It sounded like both of their English was so-so. Breck glanced around the lobby. The after-conference chatter was in full swing. The lobby seating was full, people were hanging around the fireplace, and a line was forming for the Kuerig. Apparently, everyone knew how to operate that little machine but him.

"Let's find a quiet corner to chat," Breck said.

"It is quiet in my suite. Come."

Khodorovsky took his coffee cup and headed straight for the elevators and pressed the button on the wall. Aleks followed on his heels, and they both stepped into the first one that opened. Where was Jenny? The good thing about the crowded lobby was that it *was* crowded—plenty of eyewitnesses. Breck casually patted his pockets to make sure his cell phone was still there. And his cuffs. And his .44 Special.

"Sheriff Breck Dyer?" Leaning out, Khodorovsky held the elevator door open. "Hop on in here."

This was why he got the big bucks.

Breck got in the elevator, and Aleks pressed the third-floor button. They rode up in awkward silence while Khodorovsky sipped his coffee, and then the door slid open again. To the left, Breck knew, was the Asbjorns' suite. But the men turned right, and he followed them down a private corridor that dead-ended at an arched doorway. A sign read Presidential Suite. There was a small sofa in an alcove for waiting visitors, soft wall sconce lights, and White House style Roman columns on each side of the door.

"This is us." Khodorovsky took out a Hyatt hotel key card. It looked just like the one Jansen Asbjorn had been carrying in his wallet. Bright red, with white lettering. The size of a credit card.

Similar to the Asbjorn's suite, the room was large and open. But instead of rustic lodge furnishings, there were white marble tiles and oriental rugs.

"I take it you're not from around here?" Breck asked.

"Just a little corner of the world we call Moscow."

"What do you do in Moscow?"

Khodorovsky sank onto a plush couch and indicated that Breck should sit on the couch across from him.

"Aleks, crank up that fireplace, would you? Make our guest comfortable. Once the sun goes down, it gets a little chilly, yes?"

The bodyguard went to a digital thermostat fixed on the wall and hit a couple of buttons until a perfect row of orange flames flickered in the hearth. Khodorovsky smiled. He seemed entirely at ease.

"I am an investor."

"You here for the conference?" Breck asked.

"Oh, yes. Cryptocurrency is fascinating to me."

"Do you invest in it?"

Khodorovsky took a sip of his coffee. "No."

In his peripheral vision, Breck kept track of the bodyguard. For such a big guy, he was pretty lithe. One second he was at the thermostat—the next, he was opening a kitchen cabinet, then suddenly, he was standing right next to Breck, looming like a waiter, presenting a crystal platter full of cheese and olives.

"Aleks has so many talents. I am quite lucky to have him." Khodorovksy's eyes went to his bodyguard. "Did they teach you how to serve hors d'oeuvres at SVU, Aleks?"

SVU? That was the new KGB. It was clear that Khodorovsky knew why Breck was there and wasn't afraid to show his hand. There was even a little twinkle in his eye like he was a cat playing with a mouse, and Breck was the mouse.

But Breck could play games, too.

"Are you looking forward to Jansen Asbjorn's session?" he asked. "I hear he's scheduled to speak on the dangers of investing in cryptocurrency. How dangerous can it be?"

Taking the cheese platter back to the kitchen, Aleks returned and stood near the fireplace. There was a row of ornate candles on each end of the mantle—just like the ones in the Asbjorn's suite.

"Very dangerous," Khodorovsky said. "But Aleks is looking forward to it, especially. He has great interest in what they call crypto-mining. He won't shut up about it. How do you feel about mines, sheriff?"

He wasn't even trying to be subtle now. Breck reached into his back pocket and took out the screenshot from Tya's office. Khodorovsky leaned forward to see.

"That's you, Aleks. Look! You are on candid camera."

But Aleks did not look.

"Did you know Jansen Asbjorn is missing?" Breck asked. "He and his wife were staying here, in this very hotel. That's her in the Quandary Ski Resort lobby. You're looking at a still frame from the security video."

Khodorovsky examined it closer.

"She must be sleepwalker. She is wearing her PJs. Perhaps her husband is sleepwalker, as well, and merely wandered away. Scientific studies demonstrate people wake up in strange places."

"Like the Keystone Mine?" Breck asked.

Aleks was still standing by the fireplace like a statue, but he didn't flinch at the comment. Breck folded up the piece of paper and put it back in his pocket. He had done what he came to do. Meet the men who murdered Jansen Asbjorn and let them know they were in the crosshairs of the investigation. He didn't need to press the issue to the breaking point. Not here, not now.

Breck stood and went to the door. Anatoli Khodorovsky called after him.

"Are you leaving, Sheriff?"

Looking around the room one last time, Breck spotted a bottle of vodka on the counter near the cheese and olives. Smirnoff. What was this, a bad James Bond movie? Russians, the KGB, a dead man in a mine shaft, and a bottle of cheap vodka.

"Hedda Asbjorn was kidnapped and held hostage in her suite. She managed to escape and ran across the street for help. Your bodyguard Aleks followed her into the lobby of the ski resort, which makes him a person of interest. I'll be in touch."

CHAPTER 20

Vodka Under The Bridge

Standing inside the elevator, Breck wiped his palms on his pants. Sweaty hands. Pathetic. He had been in tight situations before, but in Quandary, they were few and far between, and maybe that was the problem. Working a small town's misdemeanors was a far cry from big city felonies. Was he getting soft?

The elevator settled on the main floor, and Breck headed into the lobby.

Ding, ding, ding. Someone was ringing the hell out of the little silver desk bell. Some crypto millennial in need of fresh towels? Nope, it was Jenny.

"Breck! You were supposed to wait until I got here. I was worried you were dead in a mine shaft. Don't you answer your phone?" She grabbed the bell and dropped it in a wastebasket. "And where's the desk jockey? I didn't know what room you were in or where to even start. I've been standing here this whole time, crapping bricks."

Breck pulled out his cell phone. The battery was dead. Oops.

"Did you bring me a coffee?"

"No, I didn't bring you *coffee.*" Seeing he was okay, she started to relax. "So did you talk to the bad guys, or what?"

"Yeah. Those are our kidnappers, guaranteed." He noticed the black camera bag with the shoulder strap. "You got it. Did Danny give you any grief?"

Jenny's face softened.

"No. Not really."

"Seriously? The last time I borrowed it, I didn't get it back to him for a month, and he was ticked."

It looked like she had something on her mind.

"You all right?"

"Yeah, I'm fine," Jenny said. "There's some other stuff going on at the brewery. I'll tell you about it later."

They rode the elevator up to the third floor, turned left, and walked down the carpeted hallway to the Asbjorns' suite. The yellow crime scene tape was still in place, a big X across the doorway. Breck pulled it down and swiped the spare key card, and the door unlocked.

"Here. I found this in the back of your Jeep."

Jenny set the camera bag down and took off a small backpack. It contained a basic crime scene kit—another roll of police tape, latex gloves, and fingerprint powder. While Breck began dusting the front door for prints, she took out the camera.

"How do you get this lens cap off?" she muttered.

Once she figured it out, Jenny went around the room, snapping photos. The documents on the dining table, the bloody candlestick, the chairs where Hedda and Jansen had been duct-taped.

"Hey, would you Google the name Anatoli Khodorovsky?" Breck asked.

"Is that the the guy from the ski resort lobby?"

"No, that was his bodyguard, Aleks. Anatoli Khodorovsky is a Russian businessman here for the conference, and he's the mastermind behind all this. And guess what? Both of them are staying in the Presidential Suite. Right here on the same floor."

Jenny knelt to get a close-up of the candlestick. *Click, click.*

"You find any fingerprints on that door?" she asked.

"Yeah. A few decent ones."

Breck lifted the powdered fingerprints off the door using strips of special adhesive tape and carefully placed them in the backpack. But he knew the prints may or may not belong to the Russians—they could belong to the Asbjorns, or the manager, or a maid for that matter. Were they going to find anything incriminating? Probably not. If Khodorovsky wasn't joking, then Aleks was a trained SVU agent. That meant the guy was neck-deep in foreign ops, intel, and good old fashioned espionage. He could wipe fingerprints just as easily as he could wipe the Hyatt surveillance video.

"Anatoli what-ski?" Setting down the camera, Jenny pulled out her phone.

"Khodorovsky."

"How do you spell that?"

"Just like it sounds."

Breck went over to the dining table to look at the bloody paperwork again. There were unmistakable red fingerprints all over a signature page. Probably

Jansen's. It was pretty clear what had happened. Sign this paper, or go for a little drive to the Keystone Mine.

"Why Anatoli, you rich red Russkie." Jenny scrolled on her phone. "It says he's a major stockholder in the Aeroflot Group. Tell me something. Would you chuck a Norwegian down a mine shaft when you're worth five billion?"

"Everybody needs a hobby."

"Not me. I'd be sitting in a beach chair in Hawaii working on my tan, twenty-four-seven, three sixty-five. I wouldn't move a muscle until someone scraped my raisin ass out of that chair with a spatula. Five billion dollars!"

On the document, there were two places for people to sign, but only one person had. Was it some kind of purchase agreement? Breck frowned. The handwriting was almost indecipherable, and it was in a foreign language. However, enough of the consonants and vowels were similar to English that it could easily be Anatoli Khodorovsky's signature.

Jenny came over while she skimmed through an article on her phone.

"Hey, check this out. Spain filed money laundering charges against him and handed the case over to Russian authorities, but after a little legal back and forth, they dropped the charges. I guess when you're a Russian oligarch, high crimes and misdemeanors are just vodka under the bridge."

Breck got out a plastic evidence bag and put the document inside for safekeeping. He needed someone to translate it into English. It would shed some light on what had led to Jansen's murder, but what they needed was a firsthand account, and Hedda could give it to them. All she had to do was point the finger at Aleks and Anatoli, and they could arrest them before they slipped out of the country.

"I wonder if Hedda is ready to talk?"

"Either way, we need to tell her her husband is dead. She needs to know."

Breck knew that wasn't going to be easy. Jenny said Hedda didn't trust them and didn't even want to set foot inside the Sheriff's Office. Why? Did she think they had something to do with Jansen's murder? Hopefully, Tya had talked her down by now and convinced her they were the good guys.

"I bet Tya can translate this document." Breck held up the evidence bag. "But it can wait until tomorrow. Before we call it a day, I want to dust that Hyatt keycard you found in Jansen's wallet and run those prints as soon as possible."

Jenny yawned.

"Why don't you do that solo," she said. "Can you drop me off at Safeway? I can walk home. My fridge is empty, except for a moldy Subway sandwich. Did you know those things sprout if you forget about them long enough?"

She put the lens cap back on the camera and carefully tucked the whole thing in its carry bag. Then she glanced up with an odd look on her face.

"What's wrong?"

"You should talk to Danny."

"Why? Is he worried I'm going to break his precious camera?"

"Just go talk to him."

CHAPTER 21

Sea Of Japan

It was a cold walk home from Safeway, but there was something about the autumn air that was nostalgic even in the dark. The smell of crisp pine, the soft chatter of river water churning over smooth stones. Bare aspen branches creaking in the breeze.

Jenny was born and raised in Denver. These were the same smells and sounds of family day trips in the mountains when she was a kid. Yellow leaves and a picnic basket. Her mom and dad hiked slowly up the trail to St. Mary's glacier while she and her sister Natalie ran ahead so they could slide down the snowfield before lunch. Even after a long hot summer, the glacier never melted, and in the sun, it was slushy, and her pants got soaked.

Becoming a cop had been a childhood dream. Whether she was busting heroin dealers downtown, or chasing away loitering vehicles at the airport's curbside, it never got old. When the chance arose, Jenny even took horseback riding lessons and signed up for the mounted patrol, and spent an entire summer riding around Civic Center Park like Wyatt Earp—the chick version.

Jenny didn't get on a horse very often these days, but ever since Johnny Tibbs saw her ride, during the cartel investigation the previous summer, his cheesy flirt talk doubled. So, it was no surprise he left a voicemail.

"Yellow, Jennifer." On the phone, he always said *yellow* instead of *hello*. It was pretty lame. "Hope you got a fancy dress in your closet, 'cause I got an extra ticket to the ProRodeo Hall of Fame this weekend. Big fundraiser, champagne, rubbing elbows, you know the drill. I'd love to have you on my arm. Think about it. Call you later."

Hooping her wrists through the plastic Safeway bag handles, Jenny put her cell phone in her pocket and dug out her house keys. She unlocked the front door to her rental cottage and flipped on the lights. It was cold inside. She always turned down the furnace when she went to work. She could barely pay her rent half the time, and getting a high utility bill in the mail was an extra kick in the nuts.

The ProRodeo Hall of Fame was in Colorado Springs. That was a three hour drive, and a long time to be alone with Johnny Tibbs in a pickup truck. She knew he had a stack of western CDs in the armrest. Sons of the Pioneers. Michael Martin Murphy. Flying W Wranglers. She could only listen to *Cool Water* so many times before she lost her mind. But it would mean free food and a reason to put on some makeup.

Setting the bags on the table, Jenny took off her fleece jacket. It had been a brisk walk. In the low forties, maybe. She loved autumn, it was her favorite time of the year, and she wished it lasted longer, but she knew winter was right around the corner. If they made it to Halloween without a major snowstorm, it would be shocking.

Frozen meals went in the freezer, coconut water and yogurt in the fridge.

The cantaloupe at the grocery store had looked too good to pass up, so she bought one. The thing had gotten mighty heavy on the long walk home, and she almost laid it on the side of the road for the magpies to fight over. Taking a kitchen knife, one of the big ones, Jenny sliced it open on a cutting board. She ate a few pieces and put the rest of the cantaloupe in a bowl.

Grabbing a carton of coconut water, she headed over to the couch, sat down, and unlaced her boots. She loved coconut water. If the Flying W Wranglers sang a song about cool coconut water, maybe she would be more impressed.

The mail was all advertisements and bills. Ten dollars off an oil change. Subway coupons. She flipped through the envelopes, hoping to see a winning notice from Publishers Clearing House. But the only letter was from her landlord—the rent was overdue. Again.

"Cool water."

Even if she wanted to go with Tibbs to the fundraiser, she didn't have a fancy enough dress. She had a couple in her closet, leftover from her college days. But the last time she tried one on, it was a wee bit too tight. How much did dresses cost these days? Jenny got on her phone and started to shop online. Her bank account was scraping bottom, and, naturally, everything that caught her eye cost way too much.

She turned on the TV for background noise. There wasn't much on this time of night, just the news and a MASH rerun. She almost shut it off, but it was the episode where Henry got sent home. It was like watching a car wreck because she knew what was coming at the end. Radar O'Reilly walked into the operating room, and Trapper yelled at him to put on a mask, but Radar didn't. He slowly recited a message and could barely get the words out. *Lieutenant Colonel Henry Blake's plane went down in the Sea of Japan. It spun in. There were no survivors.* Jenny felt a lump in her throat every time. She wanted to cry.

"Freakin' MASH. I hate this show."

She grabbed the remote control and shut off the television. It wasn't true, of course. Jenny had seen every episode a thousand times.

She started looking at dresses again and put one in her online shopping cart, but sighed and deleted it. What did Johnny say about the Park County Sheriff's Office? Was he kidding, or were they hiring? She checked their website, and, sure enough, they were advertising for a deputy sheriff position. The pay range was a little vague, but the low end was more than what she was getting in Quandary.

What would Breck do if she took a job somewhere else? Could he even afford to hire a replacement? The pay was lousy with no raise in sight. It would have to be some pimple-faced kid, fresh from POST certification.

Jenny turned the TV back on. Another episode of MASH was starting. She cranked up the volume. While humming along to that classic opening tune, "Suicide Is Painless," she texted Johnny Tibbs.

Count me in for the rodeo thing.

Going back for the bowl of cantaloupe, Jenny settled onto the couch and popped a chunk in her mouth. She wished she had a hamburger instead, but if she was ever going to fit in that old college dress, this was how it happened.

CHAPTER 22

Jack-O-Lanterns

It was either a sappy episode of MASH or the doom and gloom of the Denver news.

Matthews chose the news.

Road rage on C-470 ended in a shotgun blast. Some kid brought cannabis-infused lollipops in his lunchbox. A bicyclist got paralyzed by a hit and run. It held his interest until they cut to a little brunette correspondent girl at a pumpkin carving workshop, getting Jack-O-Lantern how-to tips from someone called Grampa Willy. The old-timer got sidetracked on memories of orange circus-peanut candy. Finally, the girl sent it back to the studio anchors where the weatherman chimed in with freeze warnings across the metro, so drain those sprinkler systems and cover your garden plants with plastic.

Matthews checked the other channel. Still MASH. He went back to the news. With any luck, there would be a skyscraper on fire when they got back from commercial.

Was that the doorbell? At this hour?

Matthews put the television on mute.

It rang again. *Bing bong. Bing bong.*

The leather recliner squeaked when he got up. He parted the curtains to see who was out there. It was Chief Maxwell Waters, Alma's finest. And the man looked flustered.

"Max? Kind of late, buddy. What's on your mind?"

"I thought you said I was gonna win this election in a landslide."

"You will."

"People hate me. They keep tearing down my signs. I've been knocking on doors all afternoon and got egg on my vehicle twice. I had to run it through a car wash before the paint got ruined, but the nearest one is all the way out in Frisco. Why isn't there a damn car wash in this town? You know what? It ain't worth it. I've got a good job already, so remind me, why am I doing this again?"

Matthews knew it was true. The residents of Quandary rarely drove up the canyon to Alma unless they wanted a speeding ticket. Waters was too aggressive at his job, and everyone knew it, but he was the only one running against Breck, so Matthews needed to keep him focused.

"Tell you what. Drop by City Hall tomorrow, and we'll go over talking points for the debate. I've got all kinds of dirt on Breck. That guy is going down in flames, and you're the one who's gonna shoot him down."

The only reason Waters was running at all was that Matthews talked him into it. Breck had been a thorn in his side for far too long. But the office of sheriff was only up for re-election every four years, so having Waters chicken out now wasn't an option.

"Don't forget. You're in it to win it, Max." Matthews guided him right back down the flagstones, to his car. "Why don't you take advantage of the late hour and go knock down some of Breck's signs."

Chief Waters laughed bitterly. "Good one."

Of course, Matthews wasn't kidding. He knew some senior high school stoners who lived down the block. He had been paying them to skateboard around town, vandalizing Johnny Tibbs' mayor signs, and he could pay them to destroy Breck's signs, too, if Waters didn't have the gumption. But it was better not to chide the man at the moment, given his ego was in such a frazzled condition, and he might just walk away from the entire election if Matthews pushed him too far.

"What am I going to say at the debate?" Waters asked.

"You say Breck is weak on crime—that's your mantra. Then you go for the kill and remind everyone the DA is investigating him for corruption. Remember that drug cartel from Mexico that came through here? That was his baby. His side gig to make a quick buck. This town has gone down the tubes, and you're the only one who can fix it."

Waters got inside his car and hooked an elbow out the open window.

"I don't know if that's gonna work," he muttered. "What if Breck solves that Keystone Mine murder before the vote? No one will believe he's weak on crime if he arrests someone."

Waters started the engine and put it into gear, but Matthews reached out and gripped his arm.

"What are you talking about?"

Waters raised his eyebrows.

"You don't know?" Another bitter laugh. "The sheriff doesn't even keep the city mayor informed when there's a murder investigation. Maybe I can use that on stage."

"Max! What the hell are you talking about?"

"Some fella turned up dead in the bottom of a mine shaft. I heard that red-head gal on the radio the night it happened. 'Breck, Breck, come in, Breck.' But I guess he had his radio off that night." Waters' face lit up. "Maybe I can use that on stage, too—incompetent sheriff, incommunicado in an emergency. Can't be reached, can't be trusted. Vote Maxwell Waters for Sheriff of Quandary County."

Headlights were coming up the street. It was Aspen's used and abused Corolla clunker. Matthews knew the sound of that rotten muffler a mile away.

"Here comes my daughter," he said. "Drop by my office tomorrow, got it? We need to talk."

And he needed to talk to Breck. Cuss him out. Was it so hard to inform the mayor what was going on in his own town?

Waters drove away as Aspen pulled into the driveway. Landscape lights lined the concrete pad, and when she got out, Matthews could see on her face that she was angry. But Aspen was always mad at him these days, so that was no surprise. The surprise was that she had come to visit him at all.

He braced for the inevitable outrage.

"Ptarmigan?" That was her childhood nickname. "Did you bring us a free pizza for a late-night snack? Daddy's tum-tum is empty."

"It's inhumane!" Aspen looked just as frazzled as Waters had. "It's animal cruelty! We need to shut this guy down, daddy."

"What are you talking about, ptarmigan? Who do we need to shut down?"

How come he had to keep asking everyone what they were talking about?

"There's a kill buyer at the fairgrounds. He buys horses at the auction to sell for slaughter. But he's running a scam, daddy. He cranks up the price first, on his fake horse rescue website. We need to call Sheriff Dyer right away. There's no time to waste. He's driving them to Mexico if no one coughs up a thousand bucks per horse!"

Well, well, well. His daughter wasn't there to fight about college or her Volkswagen Beetle. This wasn't a blame game house call. Apsen needed his help—score one for Poppa Matthews.

"Let's go inside, and I'll make you a cup of hot chocolate. You can tell me all about it. Don't worry, ptarmigan. We'll nail this guy."

Aspen was breathing hard, like a bull facing a matador, but when he said that, her face relaxed. She even smiled for a split second.

Bingo—the big break Matthews needed. The route back into his daughter's good graces. If he helped take down this kill buyer at the fairgrounds, everything would be okay again. Maybe he could even talk her into moving back into her old bedroom again, and they could eat brunch together at the Blue Moose. He knew what she would order. French toast with powdered sugar instead of syrup, and the latest market-driven flavor of cappuccino. English toffee yack, or hazel something-or-other. That's what she always used to get before things went south between them. There was a farmer's market in the Safeway parking lot. They could even buy some big orange pumpkins and carve Jack-O-Lanterns for Halloween.

CHAPTER 23

All This Election Talk

While her father made hot chocolate in the microwave, Aspen sat on a stool at the kitchen island and typed in the Bachelor's website, *Save All The Pretty Horses*. Just typing in the URL made her fingers recoil.

"Buy innocent, healthy horses for a hundred bucks, sell them for a thousand. Hey, all you bleeding hearts out there. Here's your chance to 'save' them from slaughter." Aspen could barely sit still. "Who could even pretend this is morally acceptable?"

Matthews set a mug of hot cocoa in front of her. "Extra marshmallows."

But she was too frustrated to touch it.

"What kind of sicko does this? It makes me want to hurl."

She showed him the website. The Blue River Horse Rescue. Photos of all the horses available for "adoption." The dun gelding was among them, staring at the camera with his coal-black eyes. The site had a contact page, linked to an email account, but no physical address. That was smart. The Bachelor was keeping the location secret. In case someone went over there in the middle of the night and opened all the gates.

"Let's find out where this guy lives," Aspen said.

"Can I take a look?" Her father gently took the phone out of her hand and scrolled through the horse photos. "Who is this joker?"

"I never caught his name, just his bid number." Aspen wished she had asked the auctioneer, or the lady with the awful bangs seated in the next row down, or the concession guy who sold the nachos. Someone at the fairgrounds knew who he was, but the moment had passed. "There was a magnetic sign on his pickup truck. It said Blue River Horse Rescue. I couldn't find anything about it online, not even a Better Business Bureau review or a Facebook page. It can't be legit. Have you heard of it?"

"No, but I bet he lives outside the city limits. He could be anywhere in the county. He's got to have at least a couple acres, to keep those horses on."

What time was it? The day had gone by in a blur, and at this point, it was way after business hours, so the Sheriff's Office would be closed.

"Do you have Sheriff Dyer's home number?" she asked. "We need to call him. Right now."

She looked at her father, expecting him to whip out his phone and dial. But he frowned.

"Let's just think about this first, okay, honey? What I see here is a horse rescue website. It even claims to be a legally registered non-profit organization. These prices are listed as suggested donations, to help the rescue cover operating expenses."

Now it was her turn to frown.

"That's a front. He told me himself, if they don't sell in two weeks, he's trucking them across the border to a rendering plant, for *slaughter*. That isn't what an animal rescue does. They find them forever homes. Not turn them into chorizo."

She looked closely at her father. She got that he was the mayor. He had to act professional and objective. But it was so obvious what was going on here!

"We need to call the sheriff," she said again. "He can open an investigation. Expose this for what it is."

The microwave beeped. Her father got off his stool to make himself a hot chocolate.

"I'll be honest. It doesn't sound like anything illegal is going on here." He took out the Swiss Miss and stirred some into his cup. "Dyer can't do anything if there isn't a law being broken."

Aspen couldn't believe it. "We have to make a report, at least!"

Matthews sprinkled in some marshmallows and took a sip. "Ow, that's hot."

"Daddy! Why don't you want to call Sheriff Dyer?"

"No laws are being broken, number one. And number two, the sheriff is hip-deep in a murder investigation. That's not public knowledge, which is why I didn't tell you sooner. We don't want to throw something at him right now, like this, that's not a life or death priority. He only has one deputy, and they're spread pretty thin as it is. Make sense?"

"But it *is* life or death." Aspen felt her blood starting to boil again. And then a shiver, as she looked at the photo of the dun gelding. Those eyes! He knew he was on Death Row.

"He ships those horses in two weeks, you said?" Matthews thought for a second. "Then we have time. Let's give the sheriff some leeway for a few days. I know it's hard to sit still, but we have to. For now."

Aspen's mind raced.

"What about Mr. Tibbs?"

"Johnny?" Matthews smiled like it was an odd suggestion. "What about him?"

"He owns the biggest horse ranch in the county. He has plenty of pasture to keep all those horses. Maybe we can ask him to help?"

Matthews nodded, chewing it over. Aspen leaned forward, counting on a green light, a hell yeah, let's do this thing.

But instead, he gave her his classic Father Knows Best face. She knew that look. It was the same look he gave her when he said she had to drop out of CU and enroll in Quandary Community College. And the same look he gave her when he told her they had to sell the Volkswagen Beetle.

"I hate to say this, but Johnny Tibbs isn't going to buy those horses or let them stay at his ranch for free. He's a tightwad." Matthews blew the steam off his hot chocolate. "Besides, and I hate to say this, too, but I heard he ships his used-up trail horses to Mexico. He's probably on a first-name basis with this kill buyer. I would not be surprised."

Feeling blindsided, Aspen got up and paced the kitchen. This was a crisis! Her father said he could help but kept shooting down every suggestion she had.

"What can we do, then?" she asked. "What about calling Chief Waters? Maybe he can help."

"Sorry, honey. It's out of his jurisdiction. He's just a small-town cop an hour away in Alma." Matthews held up a finger like he just got an idea. "But I'll tell you what I can do. I'll get the city council to pass an ordinance outlawing the sale of horses for slaughter. The county fairgrounds are just outside of town, but still inside the Quandary city limits, technically speaking."

Aspen sighed. "It's already illegal, daddy. That's half the reason this guy set up a fake rescue. The other half is to make a big fat pile of money."

Matthews held up the bag of marshmallows. "Need some more?"

Aspen looked at her cup on the countertop. The marshmallows had melted. She hadn't even touched it. Hot chocolate? That had been her favorite thing to drink on a chilly night—when she was a kid. Now, she liked vanilla cappuccinos and caramel lattes, but of course, she wasn't going to say that out loud. Not here, not now. Despite everything, he was still her daddy, and this was his way of trying to show he cared.

"The council can do something, trust me," Matthews told her, kindly. "Next time we meet, we'll think of something."

"When do you meet?"

"Second Tuesday in November. That's in just a few short weeks, right after the big election. And when I get re-elected as mayor, the first thing I'll do is allocate city funds to stop this guy."

Aspen's face fell. "That'll be too late."

Coming over, Matthews hugged her.

"Sorry, honey. We may not be able to save these poor ponies. But we'll stop this whole racket one day, for good." He kissed her on the forehead.

She wiggled free. Aspen didn't want a hug. She wanted results.

"Why can't we just call Breck? I don't understand. He's a good person. He'll do the right thing."

Her father sighed, but it was his politician sigh. Aspen was way too familiar with that emittance.

"You know what?" he said. "I've endorsed Chief Waters for sheriff, and it's looking good that he'll win. He's the kind of guy who won't stand for a fake horse rescue. Breck, on the other hand, obviously doesn't care. Otherwise, he would have shut this down a long time ago. Tell you what. Once I get re-elected, and once Waters gets in as sheriff, we'll be a force to reckon with. Plus, how would you like a high-paying job with the Sheriff's Office? Waters will be hiring new deputies and a dispatcher. You could run that radio, easy, and it comes with a real paycheck. Quit the pizza place, buy a new car. Shoot, why don't you move back in? I haven't touched your room. It's just like you left it. I know that tiny studio apartment is expensive, and to be honest, it's pretty much a dump. You deserve better."

Wait a minute. Aspen suddenly realized what was going on. All this election talk. He was spinning the whole situation. He was spinning her whole life! None of it had anything to do with saving horses.

"You don't want to call Breck because you want him to *lose*. And you don't want to call Johnny Tibbs because you want him to *lose*."

Aspen marched to the sink and dumped her hot cocoa down the drain.

"Ptarmigan! That's ridiculous."

"You know what, daddy? I trust Sheriff Dyer with my life."

Breck *had* saved her life before. Literally. What had Chief Waters ever done besides give her a parking ticket in front of the Alma ice cream shop and a lecture on how simple it was to put a nickel into a coin-operated parking meter? As for Johnny Tibbs, the only thing she really knew about him was his generous job offer to tie mud knots on his trail horses. That, and the fact he was running against her dad for mayor.

Aspen grabbed her phone and car keys and slammed the front door on her way out.

CHAPTER 24

Fellesferie

When the floodlights came on, the entire perimeter of Tya's mountainside home lit up like an A-Bomb just went off. So did her bedroom, even though it was on the second floor and the curtains were closed.

It was late, and she was lying in bed with her laptop, reading *Aftenposten* and sipping white wine. But those were motion lights, which meant one thing. Sven. Wasn't he supposed to be in Oslo through Halloween? Unless his little hussie kicked him to the curb. One of these days, Tya knew he would come crawling home, begging her to take him back. But she was nobody's fool, and had a speech rehearsed and ready to go, capped off with a fingernail face-rake for dramatic flair.

She slammed the laptop.

Putting on a silk robe and fuzzy slippers, Tya shuffled out of the bedroom, down the hallway, and looked out the balcony window. From there, she had a clear view of the entire parking area, and the A-Bomb light left no place to hide.

But it was empty.

So was the long private driveway. She looked for those familiar Hummer headlights, winding through the dark pine, but there was nothing. At least, as far as she could tell. The driveway was long, stretching at least a quarter mile down to the entry gate, with many twists and turns. He probably freaked when he saw her SUV in the garage and turned around. After all, Tya had been living in the ski resort apartment for the past six months.

Unless it wasn't Sven at all.

Maybe a deer triggered the motion lights. Or worse, a bear?

Tya's blood ran cold. She had nearly gotten mauled in her own kitchen, once upon a time. It happened on a hot summer day. She opened the patio doors to let the breeze in and went into the kitchen to get a glass of wine. The next thing she knew, a full-grown momma bear walked right in. Looking for food, it knocked over the trash can and smashed the pantry to pieces, and Tya dashed through the garage to escape. She felt lucky to get out of there alive. The bear reeked of decay and death—what a horrible smell. She would never forget that odor. And she would never forget to shut the patio doors, either—and lock them.

The motion lights went off, and everything was dark again.

Going further down the hall, Tya peeked in the guest room.

The bed was empty.

"Hedda?" She flipped on the light switch. "Are you in here? Where are you?"

She checked the bathroom and the closet, but Hedda Asbjorn was gone.

Tya's blood ran cold again. Something had triggered the motion lights. Or someone. What if it was the kidnapper? Had he broken into the house and taken Hedda captive again? The man from the ski resort. Tya could remember his eyes. They were stone cold.

Heart pounding, she held her breath, hoping it wasn't him. And in the silence, Tya heard someone else breathing. Short, quick gasps. Hyperventilating. It was coming from beneath the bed. Lifting the bed skirt, Tya peered underneath and saw Hedda, teeth chattering, skin white as a ghost.

"It's okay. It's just me. Come on out of there."

Tya forced a smile and held out her hand.

Hedda crawled out from under the bed, clutching a steak knife.

"Let's just relax and breathe, all right?" Tya gently took the knife away. "You are safe. There's nothing to worry about whatsoever."

"Someone's out there," Hedda whispered, trembling. "Is it them?"

"No, just a deer or a fox. It happens frequently. That's part of living in the mountains." She continued to hold Hedda's hand. "You should be used to that, living on Skogsøya. Don't you have foxes on the island?"

"Just squirrels."

Tya was trying to get her talking about something, anything, to calm her down.

"That makes sense. I guess it's too small an island to support anything bigger than that. Remember when Sven and I stayed there for *fellesferie*? For the whole month of July, the four of us sat on the pier, watching sea eagles dive for fish—when it wasn't raining. And you made delicious shrimp sandwiches for lunch almost every day. Mayonnaise and just a squirt of fresh lemon. I miss that."

But Hedda wasn't able to make the leap from night sweat terror to shrimp sandwich reminiscence. Tears filled her eyes, and she began to sob.

"They're going to kill me. They're going to break in here and kill us both. Oh, please, God."

"No, that's not true." But another pang of fear shot through Tya's stomach. She didn't see any deer or fox or bear or squirrels, or any wildlife whatsoever, in the floodlights. "I'm going to heat some water. Make us each a cup of chamomile tea. Lay down under the covers, okay? I'll be right back."

But Tya didn't go to the kitchen. She went back into her bedroom, into the walk-in closet. On a shelf below her jewelry box, there was a drawer. In the drawer was a gun case, with her .45 Magnum tucked inside. She counted out six bullets from a box of ammo, opened the cylinder, and fed one into each chamber.

"Can you shoot that?"

It was Hedda. Too afraid to be alone.

"Yes." Tya showed her the revolver. "Can you tell me what's going on?"

Hedda wiped her eyes with a Kleenex.

"I am so worried. Jansen refused to sign. They took him away, and maybe they separated us to scare him into signing, but I can sign, I *will* sign, I don't care anymore. I want this to be over. I want to see Jansen again."

"Sign what?"

"I've said too much. If I talk to anyone or the American police, I will never see Jansen again. That is what they said."

The look on her face was awful.

"Does this have something to do with the conference?" Tya asked. "Or Bear Coin? They're holding him for ransom, aren't they?"

But Hedda was done talking. She crawled into Tya's bed and pulled the covers over her head.

Finally, the poor woman was starting to open up about what happened. Tya's first impulse was to call Breck, but it was late. It could wait for the morning.

Hedda's husband was the founder and CEO of a cryptocurrency exchange called Bear Coin Capital. It was the largest crypto exchange in Norway, and the Asbjorns were filthy rich. Billions of kroner. They owned an expensive home in Oslo, another in Bergen, and an entire island off the south coast they used for a summer holiday getaway during *fellesferie*. That had to be what was going on here. Someone wanted to cash in on their success and tracked them all the way to Quandary, Colorado—a tiny ski town in the middle of the Rocky Mountains.

Instead of unloading the gun and putting it back in its case in the drawer in the closet, Tya set the Magnum on the night table, fully loaded, right where she could grab it.

CHAPTER 25

Peace Pipe

Breck was on autopilot. The little digital clock on the dashboard read midnight, and his mind kept drifting from the dead man in the Keystone Mine to the south face of Annapurna to crawling in bed when he finally got home. But he couldn't close his eyes yet.

It was a solid half hour's drive from the Sheriff's Office to his cabin. And to get there, he had to drive up the long canyon road, and, at the moment, it felt like it was never going to end. If the Jeep swerved off the edge, it was a three-hundred-foot drop into a rocky ravine and the river below. There were no guardrails, and no cell service, even if he survived the fall and tried to call for help, so the best thing was not to take the plunge in the first place.

Breck rubbed his eyes and slapped his cheek.

"Wake up, amigo."

At least he had some fingerprints to use. Besides the ones on the hotel door, he lifted a nice clean set from Jansen Asbjorn's Hyatt key card—the one Cash found in the mine. Breck emailed all the fingerprints to a friend in the Department of Homeland Security who would forward them to INTERPOL. It was a long shot, but if Anatoli Khodorovsky had gotten arrested in Spain, his prints were on file somewhere. Good chance his bodyguard's were on file, too, given his penchant for misdeeds.

Europe was eight hours ahead of Colorado, and it was already breakfast over there, so maybe he would hear back by the time he woke up. Breck hoped so. Without some kind of proof, the Russians could mosey on down to Denver International Airport, hop a plane back to Moscow, and then the proof wouldn't matter.

Kyle's helmet was lying on the passenger seat. He had dropped by the brewery on his way home, and Danny told him what happened. It sounded like Nickie still blamed him for her husband's death.

Breck ran his fingers over the cold plastic.

"Sorry, Kyle."

The stars were out. Orion, the Big Dipper, Cassiopeia, Pegasus, the Seven Sisters. All revolving around the North Star like a pinwheel.

At such a high elevation in the Himalayas, with zero light pollution, the stars were so bright and distinct they were stunning. On Annapurna, Breck and Kyle had taken along a tent, sleeping bags, and foam pads to insulate them from the snow while they slept. It was a monster route, and they were climbing in "alpine style"—just the two of them, minimal gear, fast and light. In the 1950s, when people were climbing the highest peaks in the world for the first time, entire teams laid siege to the mountain. It was a completely different mentality. They brought tons of gear and relied on porters to haul it. They didn't climb, they conquered. It wasn't art, it was war.

Over rehydrated noodles, Kyle joked about the wood-fired pizza they ate in Kathmandu. As soon as they finished the route, that restaurant was the first place he wanted to go. Freeze-dried meals got old quick.

The days they spent in base camp were long and lazy. They slept a lot. The last thing Breck wanted was to risk high altitude sickness, or hypoxia, or fluid in the lungs or brain. So they took time to get acclimated, letting their bodies adjust to the atmospheric pressure and the oxygen content in the air, before the ascent.

Breck unzipped the tent and went outside. He sat in a camp chair and rubbed sunscreen on his face. The sun was scorching hot on the glacier. Using binoculars, he studied the south face of Annapurna. He could easily see their route. It was the direct line, bottom to top, right up the middle.

"Conditions won't get any better than this, and monsoon season is right around the corner," Breck said. "Tomorrow morning, let's get started before the sun comes up. I'm totally stoked."

He glanced at Kyle, who was lying in the tent, reading a book. Gaston Rébuffat, *Starlight and Storm*. Breck loaned it to him for inspiration, since Rébuffat had been on the Annapurna first ascent team, back in the day.

"What chapter are you in?"

"The one where he climbs the Matterhorn." Kyle held up the book cover. "This dude looks like Lyle Lovett. Look at that face. Only a mother could love it."

"Yeah."

Breck set the binoculars down and closed his eyes, visualizing himself balanced on his front-points on a steep wall of ice. Extreme exposure. The abyss pulling at his mind and body.

You were his mentor. You should have kept a closer eye on him, on everything he did. On every knot he tied, and every move he made. This is on you, Breck. You killed him.

He would never forget Nickie's words, the last time he saw her. Ten years hadn't done anything to soften the sting.

Was she right?

The monsoon season had started earlier than predicted. A surprise snowstorm rolled over Annapurna while they were climbing the mountain, and it was raging chaos. Visibility dropped to zero, and they started making blind rappels. There were only two options: either keep descending and hope they made it to the glacier or hole up and wait it out.

Spindrift poured over them. Breck cringed. The sting of snow crystals peppered his face, filled his mouth and hood and sleeves. It was beyond freezing. He traversed beneath a granite outcrop and started chopping ice. But Kyle was freaked. He wanted down.

"We gotta get off this mountain."

"Too dangerous. Help me chop a ledge. We'll sleep here until the weather clears."

"What about avalanches?" Kyle yelled in the wind. "The whole tent is gonna get swept off the face."

"If we set it up beneath this outcrop, we'll be safe, even if something cuts loose. Too risky to rappel in these conditions."

"No way, man. I'm going down."

"Wait. Hold on."

"See you at the bottom."

He watched Kyle lean back, put his weight on the rope, and the anchor blew. He was gone in an instant. There was nothing Breck could do.

He should call Nickie. Explain what happened, what went wrong.

But Breck had tried that a decade ago, and she refused to talk or listen, or even let him attend the memorial. She even turned him away at the door of the church in Boulder, where the service was held. Shut the door in his face. Feeling lost and alone with his grief, Breck wandered across the street to a gas station and bought his first pack of cigarettes. American Spirits. There was an Indian chief on the front of the package, smoking a peace pipe. That's what drew his eye to the cigarettes in the first place because that's what he wanted. Peace.

What did that feel like?

CHAPTER 26

Deal With It

The sun was up, but it was a chilly morning for a bike ride.

Coasting to a stop, Jenny hopped off and leaned her mountain bike against the dumpster. Her rental cottage was so close to the Sheriff's Office she could have walked to work, but she was training for the Oktoberfest bike race. If she had time later in the day, she wanted to ride up the canyon and back down again, but with a murder investigation in full throttle, she knew that was a long shot.

Oktoberfest was the Quandary Brewery's annual beer-swilling German-vibe festival. Danny rented a big white canvas tent for the parking lot, and they had all kinds of fun competitions, like yodeling. Jenny was horrendous at yodeling, so she didn't even try, but she rocked at Hammerschlagen—pounding nails into a tree stump with a sledgehammer.

This year her goal was to own the bike race. The top prize was five hundred dollars. That would buy a ton of breakfast burritos at the Blue Moose. Those things were tasty as hell but cost twelve bucks each.

After she unlocked the Sheriff's Office, Jenny kicked open the door.

"Wakey, wakey."

But Breck wasn't there. She was expecting to find him sprawled on the jail cell cot. Glancing back outside, she realized his Jeep wasn't in the parking lot. He must have made the long drive home last night. When he dropped her off at Safeway, she made him promise to stop by the brewery after he dusted the hotel card for fingerprints. Poor Breck! He had no idea what he was walking into.

Did Danny give him the helmet? How did it go down? She was curious, but should she ask? *Hey, Breck, did you get your dead friend's brain bucket? You know, the guy who fell to his death on a Himalayan mountain? His widow left it with Danny since she hates your guts and doesn't even wanna look you in the eye.* Yeah. Sensitive subject.

The Sheriff's Office was an icebox. It was about that time of the year, time to fire up the big potbelly stove. The building was an old stone church from the 1800s. No ducts, no furnace. Just that potbelly, but it was on the wrong side of the room, just a little too far from her desk. This year, she planned to buy a space heater to keep her feet warm while she was typing, answering phones, or playing Candy Crush on her phone. The crime rate seemed to drop with the temperature, and the winter could be pretty boring. If she had a squad car, she could at least spend the slow days catching speeders.

But this week wasn't boring at all. A dead guy in a mine shaft. A kidnap victim who escaped from her captors. Russian bad guys.

"And phone messages. Lucky me."

Jenny grabbed a pen and a notepad and pushed the playback button.

"This is Jamey Frederick, Breck's attorney. I've been trying to call him, but his cell is off, and his landline just rings. Can someone tell him to call me? Soon? An investigator with the DA's office stopped by my office, and . . ." her voice was quavery. "Let's just say, he told me they have a witness. Someone who informed the governor that, last year, Breck partnered with a drug cartel. This is bad. Very bad. Someone call me, okay?"

Jenny looked at the clock. Where was Breck? He usually got there at eight o'clock sharp. It was almost nine.

There were more messages.

"Hello? It's Aspen. Aspen Matthews, the mayor's daughter." The girl sounded furious. "I want to report a scam and animal abuse. And illegal things. It's happening at the fairgrounds, and it's really important. Here's my cell number—"

Jenny wrote it down, and even though Aspen was dead serious, Jenny couldn't help but smile. The mayor's daughter, Aspen. She was a good kid. Trusting. Honest. Truthful. Not like her father at all. What was that old adage? The apple doesn't fall far from the tree? Well, in this case, the apple fell from the tree, rolled across the field, and jumped the creek.

A third message.

"Good morning, Breck. This is John McMurray, at DHS. I ran those prints from the key card up the food chain, and they came back hot. Anatoli Khodorovsky. Call me."

"Holy shiz." Jumping up, Jenny looked out the window at the cars driving up and down Main Street. No Jeep. "Come on, Breck, buddy, where are you? We gotta go."

She dialed his cell phone, but it went straight to voicemail. His cabin was far enough away from town that it rarely got a signal unless the sun, moon, and planets were all aligned correctly, so she tried his landline. *Ring, ring, ring.* Whatever. She slammed down the phone.

Jenny carried a 9mm Luger handgun. She took out the magazine and went to the gun cabinet to get the spray oil and wipe it down. She hadn't fired it for awhile. Not since the last time she took Tya to the gun range for target practice.

"Handcuffs. Gonna need those."

Clipping a pair to her belt, she dashed back to the window. She could see up the street, past the Blue Moose and the brewery, to where the canyon road began. There were yellow leaves all over the blacktop. But still no Jeep.

Pulling up the Quandary Ski Resort website, Jenny clicked on the crypto-currency conference link. The day's schedule popped onto the screen.

9:00 – Economic Risks
10:00 – Blockchain Technology and Risk Management
11:00 – Cryptomining—A Risky Business?
12:00 – Lunch Break
1:00 – Currency or Asset? Or Risky Investment?

"The only thing that isn't risky is lunch," Jenny muttered.

Arresting Khodorovsky would be risky, too, depending on whether or not his sidekick with the chiseled physique would intervene or not. From the sound of it, they had the oligarch's fingerprints on Jansen's key card, but they had nothing on the bodyguard. Would he just sit back and watch as they arrested his boss, or would he put up a fight? Pull a gun?

Jenny was pumped. It was going to be a big day. Things could go very right or very wrong.

"What up, commie?" She head-banged the air, then dropped to the floor and sent the trash can flying with a foot-sweep. It rolled against the jail cell with a clang. "That's how your junk is gonna feel. Deal with it."

"Deputy O'Hara?" someone said.

The linoleum was gritty. She jumped up and wiped her palms on her pants. A man was standing in the doorway, dressed in a dark suit and carrying a briefcase.

"How can I help you, sir?" Jenny felt stupid. Whoever he was, he didn't look convinced that she could be helpful. "And yes, I am Deputy O'Hara."

"District Attorney Investigator Reuben Dempsey. If you have a moment, I was hoping to interview you."

"About?"

"The DA received an accusation against Sheriff Dyer regarding his involvement with a Mexican drug cartel and their plan to grow and distribute illegal cannabis in the county. If true, those are some serious allegations."

"They aren't true. He's innocent, and in fact, Breck and I took down the cannabis operation ourselves. Didn't you get the memo?"

He opened his briefcase and pulled out a digital voice recorder.

"Let's get started, shall we?"

Jenny glanced out the window again. Where the hell was Breck? The Economic Risks session was starting at any moment. They needed to get down there and make an arrest before the Russians bolted for the airport. Would she have to bike to the ski resort and do it herself?

But first, she had to deal with this yahoo.

CHAPTER 27

Door Number Six

There were only ten rooms at the Continental Divide Motel and Campground.

The motel itself was a small, flat-topped building with vending machines out front. Anyone driving by on the highway between Quandary and Frisco could easily mistake it for a rest area restroom facility. And many people did, which was how the owner lured in half his business.

Despite the limited amount of motel rooms, the cash cow was the camping area behind the building. People paid top dollar to park their RVs there for the summer while they spent their free time four-wheeling in the mountains or shopping in the nearby tourist towns. But this late in the year, the camping season was over, and the whole place was a ghost town.

Only one car was parked out front of the motel—a little Ford Focus with a Budget Rental sticker in the window. Aspen Matthews knew it was her mom's, so she parked her Corolla right next to it.

As soon as she got out, she crinkled her nose. There was a small concrete swimming pool behind the motel. Even though Aspen couldn't see it, she could smell it. It was a natural hot springs pool, and it smelled putrid—like rotten eggs.

She knocked on Door Number Six.

"Mom, it's me. Rise and shine."

After a long minute, the door creaked open, and Valerie Matthews appeared in the doorway, blinking in the morning sunshine, like it was the brightest thing she'd ever seen in her forty-seven years on the planet, then took a big sip from a plastic cup.

"Aspen, honey. Let me fix you a mimosa."

Valerie led the way to a little kitchenette counter, which must have doubled as a baby changing station by the previous paying guests. It had that distinct chemical smell that only baby wipes had. Aspen nearly gagged. What was worse? The sulfur hot springs swimming stench, or baby butt fog? But her mom didn't seem to notice or care and filled a second plastic cup with champagne and orange juice and refilled her own, too.

"I'll pass."

But Valerie looked mischievous and held it out towards Aspen. "You're twenty-one now. It's legal. Don't let your mother drink alone."

"No, thank you."

"More for me, then."

Carrying both cups to the queen-sized bed, Valerie crawled in, somehow managing not to spill either one and wiggled her legs beneath the comforter. Once she settled into place, she took a test taste from both cups.

"This one is too orange juicy. Can you bring the champy over here, honey?"

"Mom, can you listen? I need your advice." Aspen took the offending cup from her mother and set it on the nightstand. Valerie cradled the other one close to her chest, frowning deeply, when Aspen reached for it. "I left a message at the Sheriff's Office last night, but I haven't heard back yet, and maybe they have a bigger crime to focus on, so maybe they're too busy, but who knows? I can't wait. We gotta do something right now. I tried talking to daddy, but—"

Valerie waved at her to stop.

"Honey bunny. Slow down. There's no talking to daddy. You should know that by now." Her eyes were glazed from the alcohol. "You think it was bad he pulled you out of CU? You think it was bad he hawked your Beetle for a buck? Well, let me tell you something. He sold my SUV, too. The Lincoln Navigator! You know that was my baby. And the house, Aspen. My house. *Our* house. The bank evicted me. I was going to get a room at the Hyatt, a nice suite to live in, something respectable, something appropriate for my age and station in this crappy life. But it was booked solid, thanks to that stupid conference, so I wound up here, drowning my sorrows in this dump, and yes, I know it smells like diaper doody."

Aspen used to think divorce was just two people who fell out of love and were better off apart. Not anymore. Divorce was ugly, and it didn't end once the papers were signed. Money. College. Vehicles. Housing. Yet all the trouble seemed to come from only one direction. Her father! It was so obvious now. He was an egomaniac. All he cared about was being mayor.

Valerie held up her mimosa, toasting the day.

"Now, what's new on your end?"

What was there to say? Everything felt wrong like the whole world was off-kilter. Perhaps her mom had the right idea, after all. Mimosas might be the only way to cope. But then an image appeared in her mind's eye—the dun gelding. Cooped up in the horse trailer, packed in like a sardine, eyes wide with terror, and a one-way ticket to his doom. Dog food? Glue factory? Meat bits on a frozen pizza?

"Mom, I was at the fairgrounds, at the horse auction, and I found out there is a guy who bids on all the horses no one wants. He lists them on a fake horse rescue website and hikes up the price, and if no one buys them, he takes them to a slaughterhouse. He bought a batch of poor horses on the spot while I was watching." Aspen sat on the edge of the bed and gripped her mother's hand. "There may not be anything we can do to help ourselves right now, but we can help those poor horses. Daddy won't listen, and the sheriff has bigger things on his plate. What do we do?"

Valerie's bleary face eased into a soft smile. A proud smile.

"You inspire me, daughter. All this garbage coming down like rain but look at you. You're not consumed with self-pity or bitterness. You're worried about the welfare of other living creatures. Creatures who can't defend themselves."

Setting her mimosa on the nightstand, next to the other drink, Valerie gave Aspen a warm hug. Then she swung her legs out of the covers, went to the front wall, and tore open the curtains. Morning sunlight streamed in.

"So, Seneca won't help? Then go over his head."

"How? He's the mayor."

"He's *only* the mayor." Her eyes seemed clear now. The mimosa glaze was gone. "Did you know there is a Colorado state senator in this dinky little town, of all places, at this very moment? That's big news. It made the front page of the newspaper, and that's your answer. Her name is Dana Stayne. She's at the ski resort attending that kooky computer conference. Go over there right now. Talk to her. She's an animal advocate, and illegal horse slaughter will stop her dead in her tracks."

CHAPTER 28

Preaching To The Choir

A bank of burnt tobacco smog rolled into the Sheriff's Office.
Jenny hated that smell.

Pausing before he came inside, Breck took a final drag and then flicked the cigarette at the dumpster. She cringed when she saw how awful he looked. Hair mussed, face unshaven. Same clothes from the night before, but now they were wrinkled and creased. He must have slept in them—or else he hadn't slept, which seemed more likely, gauging by the dark bags under his eyes.

The District Attorney investigator shut off his audio recorder. "Thank you for your statement, deputy."

Breck's eyes narrowed when he saw who it was.

"Get what you need, Dumpsey?"

"It's *Dempsey*." Putting the recorder into his briefcase, the investigator got to his feet and shook his head as he walked past Breck. When he got to the door, he glanced back and smirked. "Our office received your written statement, Sheriff Dyer. Now that we have your deputy's statement, we can make a more educated assessment of the situation. We'll be in touch."

They locked eyes, but neither one said anything for a long moment. Jenny hurried around her desk and got in between them before Breck could say anything stupid.

"Everyone's just doing their job, aren't we?" she said. "Thank you for stopping by, Investigator Dempsey. Have a great day, and enjoy your weekend."

As soon as he left, Jenny punched Breck in the arm.

"What did I do?" he asked.

"You don't mouth off to that guy, of all people."

"Didn't say a thing."

She looked him over, disgusted.

"I thought you quit smoking? What happened?"

Breck didn't offer an explanation, but he didn't have to. She knew the answer.

"You talk to Danny?"

Ignoring her, Breck crossed the room to check the coffee pot. It was just dregs and had been sitting on the burner for too long, but that didn't stop him. He got a *Ski Quandary!* mug out of the wash rack and filled it to the brim. Reaching in the fridge, he pulled out the half and half carton, but it was empty.

"Damn it. We're out of cream."

"This will brighten your day," Jenny said. "Your buddy at DHS called. The prints on the hotel card are Khodorovsky's. We've got him dead to rights. Let's go clap the bracelets on that freak."

Her pep talk worked. Before she was even done talking, Breck tossed the carton in the trash and pulled out his car keys.

"Let's roll."

But Jenny pointed at the restroom door. "Why don't you clean yourself up first, Pig-Pen. It's called a comb. Buy one."

Breck chuckled, but it was forced. He took a long sip of lousy coffee, watching her over the rim, but then his eyes lost focus, and his gaze drifted— the thousand-yard stare. Jenny felt terrible for him. Everything that could go wrong was going wrong. Dead friend, angry widow. The mayor's lies, and the DA's spies.

The investigator had drilled her with questions for hours. Where had Breck been the whole time? She could guess. Sitting in a deck chair at his cabin, smoking those smelly cigs, one after another, before he finally remembered he had a job to do and made the long drive down the canyon.

"You want to know what I told Dempsey?" she asked.

Breck turned and poured his coffee in the sink. "Tastes like motor oil."

"I told him the truth."

"I know you did."

"This is a witch hunt." She crossed her arms. "Mayor Dingleberry is their secret witness. There's no mystery about that. They want to take you down and take your badge, so play it cool, okay? Don't fall for their crap."

"I need caffeine."

"There's a can of Red Bull in the fridge."

"I hate that stuff."

"Your lawyer called, by the way. That girl is worried. Dempsey dropped by her office and gave her a scare, too. How old is she anyway? Sounds like she's twelve on the phone."

"It doesn't matter what fairy tale Matthews tells the DA. If they're being honest and dig deep enough, they'll find out who conspired with the drug cartel. And it wasn't me."

"Preaching to the choir." Jenny gave him a thumbs up. "Now go wash up. Seriously. We're walking into an international finance conference to arrest a Russian oligarch in a ten thousand dollar suit. We should look a little respectable. Do you have any fresh clothes?"

"No."

But, to her surprise, Breck went into the bathroom and closed the door. She heard him turn on the faucet and yank some paper towels out of the metal box hanging on the wall.

While he was getting cleaned up, Jenny checked the clock. High noon. It was lunch break at the conference. Better to wait until the next session started and everyone was in their seats. That was the time to pounce. Arresting Khodorovsky in a room full of people would be the safest bet. His bodyguard wouldn't try anything with so many witnesses. But if they tried to corner him in a hallway or a quiet room, Aleks might get violent. Why run the risk?

After getting grilled by the DA's investigator all morning long, Jenny's mouth was dry. She went to the fridge. That Red Bull wasn't going to drink itself.

How long have you worked for Sheriff Dyer? How well do you really know him? Every question Dempsey asked felt like a trap, and she thought long and hard before she opened her mouth. Jenny kept it short and sweet—yes, no, I don't recollect. But those types of answers didn't go over so well. He got pretty tenacious, kept trying to throw her off guard. *The Quandary County Sheriff's Office is on the brink of financial collapse. I get it. All those cartel operatives, rolling in cash. Why not tap into that? Just a little bit? There are a lot of inconvenient truths here, deputy. You don't need to go down with the ship. Unless you're in on it. Are you in on it?*

The bathroom door swung open, and Breck came out. He had washed his face and fixed his hair.

"Much better," Jenny said. "Have you eaten anything today?"

"No."

"Then let's swing by Subway. I don't want to bust Khodorovsky on an empty stomach. My treat."

CHAPTER 29

Auto-Smile

"Time to digest what you've heard. Soak it in." The speaker was an Asian millennial stereotype, with dark-framed eyeglasses and a polka dot shirt emblazoned with the words: *What's In Your Wallet?* "You've got five minutes to interface with your break-out groups, then find a seat, and we'll land this plane."

Everyone in the conference hall stirred and stood.

Senator Dana Stayne was immediately cornered by a social media tech lord named Ziggy Mars, a thirty-something overgrown kid, who had spent the entire week lobbying for political favors.

"No risk, no reward." Ziggy had created FaceWorld, a social media rocket ship. "I bought a cool mil in Bear Coin, just because I liked the way it rolled off my tongue. *Bear Coin.* Jansen Asbjorn is a brand-concept genius. I thought he was supposed to be speaking today. What happened?"

Stayne's face went into auto-smile. She didn't think about what expression she needed to make anymore. Her facial muscle memory was hardwired to her political self-awareness. Ziggy Mars. What a joke. Everyone knew he changed his name when his company hit the stratosphere—and he got astronomically rich. It was painfully obvious that Mars was a David Bowie wannabe. He even co-opted an English accent to sell the image, even though he was a hundred percent Portland. All that was missing was a red lightning bolt painted on his face.

"Good question. You know as much as I do. Perhaps he flew back to Norway at the last moment to pop some champagne with his CFO. After all, Bear Coin's worth has been jagging upwards recently. It will soon be the number one altcoin at this rate."

"Indeed." Mars seemed impressed. "If you're paying attention, that means you have a stake in Bear Coin, too. How much did you buy in for? Did you go big or small? Are you an Ursa Major . . . or an Ursa Minor?"

It was no surprise that a man who named himself Ziggy Mars liked to pepper his conversations with references to constellations and planetary pathways. It was one of his many irritating eccentricities. But Stayne knew that part of politics was dancing to other people's tunes—as long as they were useful.

How about some star talk of her own? Toss the fool a bone.

"Some people believe that since the Little Bear is smaller than the Big Bear, it must be less important." Auto-smile. "But, the Little Bear's got the North Star by the balls."

"Absolutely brilliant!" Ziggy Mars applauded. "Very Bowie."

Stayne wanted to walk away so bad. He was just an overpaid socialite whose only value was his campaign donations. Didn't he realize he was the North Star in this metaphor? He may be rich, but he wasn't as major a player as he thought.

Anatoli Khodorovsky elbowed in between them.

"Did you know there is a hound in the stars, in the night sky, that wants to devour the other constellations?" he asked. "In Russia, we call him Simargl, but the goddess Zorya holds him back with a chain. If he got loose, it would be the end of the world."

Mars blinked and grinned, but it was obvious he wasn't sure what either one of them were talking about.

"Speaking of devouring, I smell Tex Mex."

He excused himself and made a beeline for the taco bar.

"Good timing," Stayne said. "The Red Planet was getting on my nerves."

"You are most welcome."

She didn't need an auto-smile with Khodorovsky. Their relationship went way beyond platitudes and pleasantries. Much like the stars above, they operated on an entirely different plane of existence than everyone else in the room.

"Even though the man is an idiot, his question is valid," she said. "Where is Jansen? He was on the schedule."

"Jansen will not be on any more schedules, I'm afraid. Our situation has . . . changed."

Stayne scowled. "What does that mean?"

Khodorovsky threw a deliberate glance at his bodyguard, Aleks, who was standing watch nearby.

"Jansen is feeling, how do you say, down in the pit."

"Do you mean, down in the dumps? That's the idiom. It means feeling melancholy. Depressed. Is he sad about our . . . situation?"

Khodorovsky shrugged. "My English is a little hit and miss. But I believe 'pit' is the right word."

She leaned close to speak in a lower voice, so close that their noses nearly touched.

"Tell me the *situation* is stable, regardless of how Jansen feels about it."

He shrugged.

"Let us simply say, the hound has wiggled loose of his chain."

The word games were getting out of hand, but there were too many people standing around them to talk freely. Worse still, Ziggy Mars was coming back, carrying a taco in one hand and a bottle of beer in the other. But a brown-haired girl in her twenties got there first.

"Senator Stayne? My name is Aspen Matthews, and I hate to interrupt, but I have to talk to you about something extremely important and extremely urgent."

Better than another chat with the Red Planet. Auto-smile.

"I'm all ears, Ms. Matthews." The name took a second to register. "Wait, are you related to Mayor Seneca Matthews?"

The girl nodded, rather crisply.

"He is my father. But I'm here on my own since he won't listen. There is a man in this county running an illegal, inhumane operation. He buys cheap auction horses and drives them to Mexico to get slaughtered. He's a kill buyer! He also runs a fake rescue and tries to sell them first. We can't let him get away with it, but there's barely any time before he takes them south, and I am begging you, Senator Stayne, to intervene. Please. Before it's too late."

The session host got back on stage and spoke into the microphone. "One-minute warning. Please wrap it up, and find your seats."

Ah, such innocence, such naivete. It was almost moving. Stayne put her hand on Aspen's shoulder.

"*This* is why I ran for office in the first place, Ms. Matthews, to use politics to change the world. A voice for the voiceless. It can only happen if someone has the courage to take a stand and ask for help. I will help you."

She snapped her fingers. One of her aides swept in from the shadows. It was Brenda, her right hand. Brenda was a gaunt woman that always wore lipstick that was way too red for her skin tone. But Stayne liked it. It was a bold power color. Ambitious.

"Brenda. Take Ms. Matthews to the lobby, write down her contact information, and listen closely to every word she says." She turned back to Aspen. "The conference is about to start again, I'm afraid. Go with my aid, tell her everything you just told me."

Tears formed in the girl's eyes.

"Thank you, Senator. Thank you."

Hope. That was what Stayne trafficked in. Even if it didn't go a step farther than a conversation and a leaky tear duct. Auto-smile. Brenda led the girl through the conference hall, out of sight and out of mind.

Of course, Stayne also trafficked in other things. Some of which were less noble, but far more profitable.

Khodorovsky had vanished, but now he was back, carrying a taco in a napkin.

"We should talk, Anatoli."

"I love talking."

"There is an alpine hut at the top of the chairlift, with a café inside. Meet me there as soon as this is over."

Stayne began walking toward her seat but stopped as soon as she heard Sheriff Breckenridge Dyer's voice.

"Anatoli Khodorovsky, I am placing you under arrest."

She spun around. What did he just say?

Khodorovsky's bodyguard swept in, but Deputy O'Hara leaped in front of him with a David versus Goliath look on her face that would have made Stayne laugh—if it was happening to anyone else in the room.

"What have I done to deserve American arrest?" Khodorovsky tossed his taco in a trash can and held out his wrists. "Too much charm? Or too much good looks?"

"You are under arrest for the murder of Jansen Asbjorn."

CHAPTER 30

Brokenhearted Savior

The Blue Moose served breakfast food all day. Matthews sat by himself at a table in an empty booth. He could hear voices in the next booth over. It was a family from Kansas, making memories over eggs and pancakes, laughing over hash-browns. A waitress brought him a cup of ice water and some silverware.

"You ready to order, or do you need a minute to look over the menu?"

"I'm waiting for someone."

"Okay, I'll check back later."

Matthews picked up a butter knife. In the reflection on the narrow blade, he could see his own eye, staring back at him.

Was it so long ago? His daughter, seated across from him, in the very same booth he was sitting in now, raving about the French toast. As a joke, he always cut off a corner of whatever he ordered and offered it to her, but Aspen always refused. One bite of something else would throw off her taste-buds and ruin her meal.

"She hates me." He was speaking to the butter knife eye. "What are you looking at?"

Were things simpler when they lived in Vail? Before politics? That was where Aspen was born. Matthews was in real estate back then, and he was pretty good at it. Every time he saw his face plastered on a "Home Sold" yard sign or a street bench at the bus stop, it made him feel like he was inching his way to the top, and there was no better place to sell residential homes than a prosperous ski village. Until the economy tanked—thanks to an epic failure of low-interest home loans by the ham-handed federal government. And greedy banks. And greedy realtors. Of course, he could count himself in that category if he was honest. How many bad loans did he push to make that seven percent commission?

Overnight, Matthews' paychecks stopped rolling in. He knew he had to make a bold move, so he sold their multi-million dollar home and moved the family to a mere one-million-dollar home in Quandary. The appearance of prosperity was important, and it was possible since things cost much less there than they did in Vail. But it was still expensive. Life was expensive. Needing a new gig, Matthews decided to run for mayor of Quandary. What better platform for a candidate to run on than a reality check from a former realty guru? So Matthews painted himself as a brokenhearted savior, who understood the community's desperation, its frustration with government failure—and it worked.

A text came in on his phone.

Running late. Writing a speeding ticket. Thirty-five in a thirty, I can't let that slide. Go ahead and order. Get me a southwest omelet, extra bacon.

Chief Waters. When was he going to learn the art of politics? Writing speeding tickets a couple of weeks out from a countywide election for the office of sheriff? How stupid was this guy?

Matthews tried to catch the waitress, but the Kansas family flagged her down first. The dad handed her a cell phone and asked her to take a family photo.

The last family photo the Matthews took was at Elitch's, down in Denver. He handed his cell phone to a stranger while they posed in front of the roller coaster. How many years ago was that? Aspen was probably fifteen, sixteen. Was it her birthday? He couldn't remember. The picture was hanging on the wall back in his office at City Hall. That day, Valerie had been mad at him for something. She had those rock hard eyes, and the moment was frozen in time.

Matthews' phone rang. It was Senator Stayne.

"Hi, Dana. I'm still working on that Kevin Costner thing. He's on set somewhere in Bucharest, and his agent won't let him near a phone. That's Hollywood for ya. How's the conference going?"

"Your county sheriff stormed the conference hall and arrested Anatoli Khodorovsky in front of everyone."

"What? When did this happen?"

"Two seconds ago. Anatoli is one of the richest men in Russia, and I know him personally. He's an honest businessman. To be perfectly candid, he was *this close* to financing a crypto-mine prospecting facility right here in Quandary, but that's not going to happen now, is it? Breckenridge Dyer must think he's the big fish in this pathetic little pond, but he just swam into very deep water. And pissed off the wrong shark."

To win the mayoral election, Matthews needed the senator's endorsement, not her wrath. Not now! He may not have a movie star's scalp to offer her, but he could certainly give her Breck's.

"Don't worry, senator. I'll shut him down."

"Whatever you do, it better be quick."

The line went dead.

What could he do, really? Yell at Breck? Threaten to slash his budget? Again? It was pretty much nonexistent as it was. Besides, Breck never listened to a word of advice Matthews had ever given him. He was incorrigible. Defiant.

Why not do . . . nothing?

Give him enough rope, and Breck would hang himself. After all, Khodorovsky was a top tier stockholder in the Aeroflot Group, Russia's monolithic, iconic airline service. Who in their right mind would think he had anything to do with a murder in a tiny Rocky Mountain town? Whatever bizarre train of events led Breck to this monumentally quixotic apprehension didn't matter. It didn't pass the smell test.

At least, that's how he could spin it.

Maybe it was time to drop by the Quandary Herald. Explain how irrational Breck was to the editor—arresting a wealthy Russian oligarch in a room overflowing with business and political leaders? The man *was* going to invest millions. Boost the town's economy. How many other potential investors were being chased off in the process?

Matthews picked up the butter knife again. Was this metal blade a window to the soul? Or a tool of the trade? Because slicing through Breck's bull was as easy as a hot knife through butter.

One uncomfortable fact loomed in the dim recesses of Matthews' mind. The Bear Coin bigwig was dead. The most likely explanation was an accident—the man simply tripped and fell down a mine shaft. Maybe mine exploration was the guy's hobby. Worst case scenario, someone murdered him, and Khodorovsky was somehow involved. But even if that was true, what difference would it make? By the time the guy went to trial, Breck would have already lost in the court of public opinion and lost the election.

Goodbye, Sheriff Breckenridge Dyer. Hello, Sheriff Maxwell Waters.

Speak of the devil. The front door opened, and Chief Waters came inside the Blue Moose, spotted Matthews, and sat down, out of breath like he'd run a marathon.

"Where's my omelet?"

Utter Nonsense

Holding Khodorovsky's hand, Jenny pressed his fingers onto an ink pad, and then onto a white paper form.

"Where I come from when a redhead beauty takes my hand, I buy her a martini."

"Martinis are gross."

She gave him a paper towel and a squirt of hand sanitizer so he could clean his hands. Then she handed him an eight-by-ten piece of paper with his name and a prisoner identification number and lined him up against the wall.

"What is this?" he asked.

"Perp card."

"Am I a perp?"

"I don't give these to just anybody."

The printer was broken, so Jenny had to write the information out with a ballpoint pen. While she powered up Danny's camera and took off the lens cap, Khodorovsky examined the paper, and her girly-swoop lettering, with a look of amusement. It irritated her that half the equipment in the Sheriff's Office was crap. With a major arrest like Khodorovsky, with all the international attention that was sure to follow, would it put Quandary County on the fed's radar and impress the boys upstairs enough to give them some freaking grant money? Jenny had applied online about a hundred times, but all they got was a big fat pile of nothing so far.

She took a step back to get him into the frame.

"Say piroshki."

After she snapped a few photos, Jenny yanked the paper out of his hand, wadded it, and threw it in the wastebasket.

"Don't I get a phone call? My lawyer is in Moscow, and it will take him several days just to get here. Sooner I call, sooner he comes, sooner we resolve this nonsense."

"It's after hours in Mother Russia. No one's going to answer the phone right now."

Taking him by the arm, Jenny led him into the jail cell and locked him inside. Khodorovsky held his wrists out through the bars, and she uncuffed him.

"Where did the real sheriff go? I do not see him."

"I am a real sheriff."

Heading back to her desk, Jenny put away the fingerprint supplies. Breck was outside on his phone. Somehow the governor had heard about the arrest already, and instead of calling to say congratulations, he was chewing Breck out. It didn't make sense. Why was he mad? They had a suspect and evidence directly linking him to the scene of the crime.

"I see your boss through the window," Khodorovksy said, pointing. "He does not look so happy."

"Can you sit down and be quiet, please?"

"Who is he speaking to? Perhaps I can help. I have friends in high places. I golf with president of United States. He is my BFF. We collude all the time."

Jenny unholstered her Luger 9mm and put it in the desk drawer. This guy thought he was funny and charming and completely in control, but he wasn't. Behind the smooth talk and the billion-dollar bank account, the man was a killer. Or, more likely, his bodyguard did all the dirty work. But at the very least, they now had a little breathing room to close the case. It was a simple truth—when someone got locked in jail, they couldn't flee the country.

"I forget. What is your bodyguard's name? Albert?"

"Aleksandr. But call him Aleks. He likes Aleks."

"I'll keep that in mind."

"Your name tag says Deputy Sheriff O'Hara. But what do you like to be called?"

"Deputy Sheriff O'Hara."

Images of the Keystone Mine kept coming to mind. The shoe in the mud. The dark wood timbers holding up the tunnel. Borrowing Cash's super bright flashlight, the ThruNite TN12, and shining it down the pit on turbo mode. Jansen Asbjorn, face down and a hundred percent dead. She'd never forget the moment Breck rolled him over, and his intestines sprung out. Just like those prank peanut cans, full of fake snakes.

"Remind me again, Deputy Sheriff O'Hara. What am I being accused of? One minute I am eating Tex Mex, the next I am in a tiny jail cell."

"We are charging you with the abduction and murder of Jansen Asbjorn."

He smiled slowly.

"Just because he missed his conference session doesn't mean he is dead. Maybe he drove to Garden of Gods for tourist walk."

"Oh, we found his body. And we found hard evidence that you did it."

Jenny expected Khodorovsky to get defensive, but his smile only grew broader.

"What evidence?"

When she didn't reply, his eyes drifted around the room. The stone walls, the potbelly stove. The small, colorful stained glass window above Breck's desk.

"Are you police or preachers?"

Whenever she stopped and thought about it, Jenny felt a little guilty. This used to be a place that ministered to lost souls, according to the principles of the Holy Scriptures. Now it was a place that processed lost souls, according to the principles of the United States justice system. But then, there was a time and place for everything, right? That was in the Bible, too. A time for war and a time for peace. A time to mourn and a time to dance.

Right now, it was time to mess with this guy's mind.

Jenny walked over to the evidence locker, next to the coffee machine. She rapped her knuckles on it.

"Guess what I found in the Keystone Mine? Jansen's hotel key card. You left perfect little fingerprints on it. You know what I'm talking about? The access card to the room where you beat Jansen senseless. The same room where you duct-taped his wife to a chair and made her watch. I found that key card in the mine, in a wallet, near the body. Right where you killed him."

Khodorovsky waved his hand like he could wave away what she was saying.

"I don't know in whose sick mind such a thought could be formulated. Such thinking is paranoid."

"You got sloppy, and you got busted."

Jenny knew he wasn't going to admit to anything, not now, not ever. At least they had solid proof of his involvement, enough to press charges. Maybe now, Hedda Asbjorn could trust them enough to make a formal statement and identify her abductors. That's how they would get Aleks and cinch the noose on Anatoli.

"When my lawyer arrives, and this misunderstanding is cleared up, I promise I will not hold it against you. I buy you martini then. Do you have a pretty dress?"

Khodorovsky was arrogant. So completely assured of himself. Just like Johnny Tibbs in that regard. Both men were full of themselves, and both men had hit on her, and both asked if she had a pretty dress. Was she supposed to be flattered? Or was she just an idiot magnet?

"What were you trying to get Jansen to sign?" Jenny asked.

"Sign?"

"Yeah, that document on the dining table. Whatever it is, it had to be pretty important to kill the man over."

"This is utter nonsense."

"I'm guessing money. It's always money, isn't it? But you're already a billionaire, so what's the deal?"

"It is difficult to imagine nonsense on a bigger scale than this. Please disregard these issues and don't think about this anymore again."

CHAPTER 32

Need-To-Know Classified

While he was out in the parking lot, getting grilled by Governor Loopenhicker over the phone, Breck spotted a vehicle parked down the street. Dark blue Suburban. In October, the tourist season was in a lull, and there weren't too many cars parked on Main Street that he didn't recognize.

"Do you understand what I'm saying, Sheriff Dyer?" the governor asked.

"I understand how it might look to someone who doesn't know the situation," Breck said.

"I don't think *you* understand the situation. The Fifth Judicial District Attorney has opened an investigation to determine whether you collaborated with a drug cartel to sell illegal cannabis in Quandary County. He's trying to make a case against you, Breck. You hear me? This is serious business. And now I found out you've arrested an elite Russian businessman at that cryptocurrency deal. Based on what, exactly? A fingerprint on a hotel key card?"

Breck was done explaining. He had said the same thing over and over, and Loopenhicker didn't seem to be listening. It was like he would rather argue than hear a logical assessment of the truth.

"Tell me something," Breck said. "Who is feeding you all this information? Because all you had to do was call and ask me."

"I'm calling you now! And it doesn't matter who told me what because what I see here is a pattern. Procedural improprieties, lack of communication, piss poor professionalism. Whether or not you're guilty of anything shady, the end result is the same. People are losing faith in your ability to execute your official duties."

Up the street, the Suburban pulled away from the curb and sped away. The doors never opened or shut, and no one got in or out, so the driver must have been sitting inside this whole time. Watching.

"Let me ask you straight up," the governor said. "Did you collaborate with that drug cartel?"

"No."

"I want to believe you. But if you didn't, then who did? And whoever it was, got away free and clear . . . right under your nose."

Loopenhicker paused, and neither one of them spoke for a long moment.

"I'm this close to asking you to step down, Breck. Right or wrong, guilty or innocent. You've got an optics problem at the very least, and maybe what your county needs is new blood."

"See, that's the problem. Someone is out for blood. Mine. If the DA is investigating me, fine, let him investigate. I have nothing to hide, but I'm not going to step down because of dirty politics."

Loopenhicker cleared his throat.

"Listen to me, Breck. Think of me as a friendly colleague, looking out for your best interests. But the DA? He's your adversary in this process. I hope you have a decent lawyer."

The Sheriff's Office door creaked open, and Jenny poked her head outside. Breck could tell she was nervous about interrupting, but he waved her over.

"I appreciate the call, and your concern, governor."

"This isn't concern. It's a warning shot across your bow, sheriff."

Click. Call over. Breck jammed the phone in his coat pocket and rubbed his eyes. What he wouldn't give to drag his lawn chair to the lakeshore by his cabin and jab a worm onto a hook, fling it in the water, and wait all day for nothing to happen. Was there even a single trout swimming around in that water? Probably not.

"Hey," Jenny said. She closed the door behind her. "The manager at the Hyatt Residence Club just called. Zachary."

"And?"

"He says some dude is demanding to get into the Asbjorn's room. Claims to be with a government agency of some kind, but Zachary felt a bad vibe, so he called us."

"Okay, I'll go check it out." Breck took out his keys.

"Can I go instead? Please don't leave me here with this clown."

"I thought you hated driving a stick shift."

"Only at night. Driving during the day is . . . tolerable."

Breck tried to smile, but he had too much on his mind. Like, where was Aleks?

"Lock the door after I leave. I think I spotted Aleks in a dark blue Suburban, parked up the street, staking out the office."

"You sure it was him?"

"Just a gut feeling."

He got in the Jeep and drove across town. The clouds were thick and hung so low the mountaintops were lost in a fog. Was it going to rain again? He needed new windshield wipers, bad. All they did was streak and smear, but the closest auto parts store was in Frisco, and he didn't have time to make a special trip just for wipers. Of course, his lawyer lived in Frisco. When was his next appointment?

"Oops. Was I supposed to call her back?"

It completely slipped his mind. Jamey Frederick had left a message on the answering machine, and Jenny said she sounded super stressed. The DA was hounding her, too.

"Good times."

On his way to the Hyatt, Breck saw political signs all along the roadside. *Matthews For Mayor. Waters For Sheriff. Tibbs For Mayor.* Someone had vandalized Johnny's signs with black magic markers. Mustaches, eye patches, and four-letter words.

Rental cars filled the Hyatt's parking lot, thanks to the cryptocurrency conference, but Breck found a place to park the Jeep and headed inside. Beneath the portico, he passed a jet black Dodge Challenger with its hazards flashing. The valet looked irritated. He wasn't the only one. There was a face-off at the front desk. Zachary was having an animated conversation with another man, who had both hands on the countertop like he was about to lunge over at any second.

"What's going on here?" Breck asked.

"You the county cop?"

"What do you want with my crime scene?"

"Officer Billy James, USCIS. You and I need to talk."

He looked slick: leather motorcycle jacket, bald head like Bruce Willis, blue-tinted sunglasses notched in his collar, and a Bluetooth in his ear. He was also wearing a shoulder holster. Breck could spot it a mile away, the way his jacket hung. The man whipped out a black wallet with a gold badge inside—United States Citizenship and Immigration Services.

"The kid won't let me in the room." Billy James glared at Zachary, then turned his intense gaze onto Breck. "Talk some sense into him, or I'm going to bring in the feds and rock your little world."

"What does Customs want with my crime scene?"

A squiggly vein pulsed above the man's eyebrow.

"What crime scene? Listen to me. This is need-to-know classified, but I can tell you this much. I'm here for a Norwegian staying in this hotel. Name is Jansen Asbjorn. He wants to claim asylum, and, quite frankly, his life is in danger. So the sooner I find him, the better this looks for you."

"He's dead."

"What?" James stuttered and looked unconvinced. "You're yanking my f'n chain. That's a sick joke, you small-town hick. Where's my guy?"

"Have a nice day."

Breck walked over to the Keurig machine, but Billy James ran over to intercept him. He held up his hands and waved them like they were little white flags, and he was surrendering.

"Sorry, buddy. High stakes, high pressure. Didn't mean to be rude."

Dark roast coffee pod. Put it in the machine, just like Aleks had done. If a Russian thug could figure it out, then so could he. Breck pushed the silver start button, but nothing happened.

"This piece of junk."

He looked around for Zachary, but the reception desk was vacant. He was probably hiding in the hotel office, like a turtle in his shell, waiting until they left.

"The water reservoir is empty," James said. "You gotta put water in it first."

"What? Forget it."

Breck yanked the coffee pod back out and threw it in the wastebasket. Why couldn't they just have a regular coffee maker? When was this fad going to be over? At least the 7-Eleven was right down the street.

"Why was Jansen seeking asylum?" he asked. "I've got a suspect in custody, but it sure would be nice to know what's going on."

James looked stunned.

"Why *was* he . . . ? Oh, damn. You're for real. Dead? Who did it? Who do you have?"

"A Russian businessman. He was attending the same conference where Asbjorn was speaking."

"Don't tell me it's Anatoli Khodorovsky?"

Now it was Breck's turn to be stunned.

"You know him?"

"Un-frickin'-believable. I have to make a phone call." James put a finger to his Bluetooth and marched across the lobby for some privacy.

CHAPTER 33

Hazard Lights

USCIS Officer Billy James huddled in the far corner of the room, on his Bluetooth. Talking to his boss, and that guy's boss, and maybe even *that* guy's boss, depending on the reason Jansen Asbjorn had claimed asylum with the United States Customs and Immigration Services.

Breck heard the electronic *bong* of the elevator door as it slid open. He couldn't see the door from where he was standing, and after a few seconds, he caught the dull metallic *shush* as it slid closed again. But no one walked around the corner into the lobby.

According to the hotel records, both Anatoli Khodorovsky and Aleksandr Medved were registered guests in the Presidential Suite. That could have been Aleks, just then, in the elevator. That could have been him, earlier in the dark blue Suburban, keeping an eye on the Sheriff's Office.

Billy James wandered back, looking shaken. Beads of perspiration covered the entire globe of his smooth bald head.

"What's your name again?" He wiped his scalp with the back of his hand.

"Sheriff Breck Dyer."

"Breck. That's a badass name."

"You all right?"

"Yeah, I'm rock solid."

Hunching over, James put his hands on his knees and vomited. It spattered all over the expensive oriental lobby carpet.

"Why don't you sit down for a second?" Breck said.

He ushered him towards a lobby chair, and James sank down, eyes closed tight.

"Must have eaten some bad sushi. My head is swimming, man."

"You stationed in Denver?"

"Hell, no. I'm from DC. Flew in this morning—bloody Mary and sushi in first class. But I get that every time I fly anywhere, so it's gotta be food poisoning. Ah, my head is killing me."

"You've got altitude sickness, amigo."

Breck went over to the front desk and rang the little silver bell a few times. The office door cracked open. Zachary peered out of his hideaway.

"Yes?"

"Clean up on Aisle Four."

Careful not to step in the man's regurgitation, Breck helped Billy James get to his feet, but he was too wobbly to stand, so Breck hoisted him over his shoulder and carried him out the lobby doors. The Dodge Challenger was still parked under the portico, hazard lights flashing. Was there a metaphor in there somewhere?

"Forget about your race car. Take an Uber back down to Denver. Drink some water and eat some ibuprofen. Come back in the morning, and I'll take you to the hospital to see the body. You can tell me what's really going on."

"Where's his wife? Hedda Asbjorn. Is she dead, too?"

"No, Hedda is safe. She's recuperating at a friend's home."

"Then she's not safe. Take me to her right now."

Breck leaned down and dumped him on the car hood.

"The elevation here in Quandary is 9600 feet. Your symptoms will go away if you lose some altitude, and take a day to acclimate."

But Officer James shook his head.

"I ain't going nowhere. Take me to Hedda Asbjorn."

Then he wretched again, all over the hood.

Breck took a step back, out of the splatter zone, but he still got some sushi on his boots. Billy James was a lowlander. His body needed to adjust to the altitude or his symptoms could get worse. Tya's home was another thousand feet higher, and that was where Hedda was staying. There was no way this guy was going to make it.

"Tell you what. I'll bring her to you. Let's find someplace for you to lie down." Breck hooked a thumb over his shoulder. "How about here?"

"The boss-man booked me a room at that little ramshackle piss hole on the highway. He likes to see me suffer."

Breck wiped the tip of his boot on the Challenger's front tire.

"I can tell."

"Naw, man. I rented these wheels on my own dime. Got off the plane, went to the car counter, and the boss-man had me driving some kind of Pinto wannabe chick-mobile, and I'm like, I don't think so. Homey don't play that."

James dug his car keys out and rolled off the hood but sank straight to the asphalt. Kneeling, Breck picked up the keys, and picked him up, too, and stuffed him in the passenger seat.

"I can drive my own car."

"Sure thing."

Breck got behind the wheel and pushed the start button.

The Challenger was fast, and the suspension hugged the road like a NAS-CAR track. They blew past the Starbucks and Safeway and out onto the open highway. Breck glanced at the speedometer. Whoops. He backed off the gas pedal. It purred like a kitty cat at eighty. Good thing they weren't passing through Alma. Waters would go bananas if he caught Breck speeding in a civilian vehicle.

"What room are you staying in?"

"Lucky Number Seven."

When they arrived at the Continental Divide Motel and Campground, Breck nosed the car into the parking space in front of his room.

"Maybe I will lie down for a bit."

Taking his keys, James clawed his way out of the car and tried to unlock his motel room, but went sideways, and Breck grabbed him by the arm.

While they were standing there, another vehicle pulled into the motel parking lot. Valerie Matthews was at the wheel. It was strange to see her driving a little rental car instead of her fancy Lincoln Navigator. Parking right next to the Challenger, she got out with a Safeway bag full of orange juice and Swiss Rolls in one hand and a champagne bottle in the other.

"Sheriff, what are you doing here?" She watched Billy James struggle to stand. "Conducting a sobriety test?"

Breck smiled, looking at the champagne.

"Are you going to need one, too?"

"No. But I'm not dumb enough to drink and drive, thank you very much." But Valerie wasn't being defensive. She even smiled back. "Would you like a mimosa?"

"No, thanks. I'm on duty."

She kept smiling. "Maybe another time?"

"Maybe."

James finally got his door unlocked and stumbled inside onto the bed. Breck followed him in. He spotted a cup by the sink, so he filled it with cold water and set it on the nightstand.

"Drink that."

But Billy James curled up into a ball, on the bed, facing the wall.

"The room is spinning like crazy, and I've got a killer headache. This sucks."
Breck sat down in an old avocado-green recliner. It was time to get some
answers.

"Let me see if I got this straight. Jansen Asbjorn owns a Norwegian cryptocurrency exchange called Bear Coin. He flies to Quandary for the conference,
rents a suite at the Hyatt, and so does Anatoli Khodorovsky, a Russian billionaire. Anatoli, and his bodyguard Aleks, follow the Asbjorns into their room one
evening. They want him to sign a document of some kind. So they tie them up
and beat Jansen with a candlestick. But Jansen doesn't sign. So they drive him
up to the Keystone Mine, where they dump his body in a pit so deep it won't be
found. The Russians clean out his wallet but somehow miss his hotel key card.
When they get back to the Hyatt to work on Hedda, Khodorovsky can't get in
the door. No key card. Meanwhile, Hedda wiggles free from the duct tape, waits
until they leave, then runs across the street to the Quandary Ski Resort for help.
Aleks chases her, but she gets away."

James rolled over to face Breck. The mattress creaked under his weight.

"What else you got?"

Breck continued.

"The Asbjorns knew they were in danger before they ever came to Quandary. That's why Jansen set up a secret meeting with a Customs officer, on US
soil, to claim protective asylum. Correct? But that officer shows up too late. So
the big question is, what did Jansen have that Khodorovsky wanted so bad?"

Billy James grinned.

"My motel neighbor's got a crush on you. Did you see that?"

"Valerie? She's the mayor's wife," Breck said. "Ex-wife."

"How long they been divorced?"

"I don't know. Three years."

"If she asked me over for a mimosa, I wouldn't say no."

Breck got up and went for the door.

"Sweet dreams. I'll be back in the morning."

He opened the door, but Billy James sat up.

"Hey, wait a second." His skin looked even worse, perspiration rolling like
raindrops. He picked up the cup and drank the whole thing. "Khodorovsky's
bodyguard, Aleksandr Medved. He's dangerous. Don't let Hedda Asbjorn out
of your sight."

CHAPTER 34

Mr. Lawyer

"Holy crap, Breck. Tell me that's my new squad car!"

Jenny cupped her hands over her mouth.

A cold rain was starting to fall. It hissed on the hot hood, and the sushi vomit, caked-on like concrete, began to dissolve and streak. Breck handed her the keys to the Challenger.

"Yep."

"You're lying, but I don't care."

Leaving her gawking at the vehicle, Breck went inside the Sheriff's Office to check on their prisoner.

"I want my lawyer," Khodorovsky said. "This is America. You are legally obligated to give me a phone call."

There were several extra desks around the room, where all the other deputies used to sit—back in the old days, when Breck could afford other deputies. He unlocked the jail door and led Khodorovsky to one, with a telephone on it.

"One call. Keep it short. Five minutes tops."

"Give me privacy."

When he didn't move, Khodorovsky leaned in front of the phone, so Breck couldn't see what number he was dialing.

"Yes, hello, Mr. Lawyer. It is me, your favorite client. Did you know I have been arrested? Charged with murder. Apparently, they have evidence—fingerprints on a hotel card. They say I dropped it in a mine shaft, somewhere in these beautiful Colorado Rockies. Such an absurd allegation. I believe it is in our best interest to properly analyze this hotel key card, yes?"

He winked at Breck and then lapsed into Russian.

Even though it was a language he didn't understand, Breck was sure he heard Hedda's name. Anatoli kept talking and talking. Was he dragging the conversation out just to enjoy his full five minutes of freedom? Oh, well. The man was entitled to a phone call.

Breck spotted a newspaper on his desk. The Quandary Herald. Jenny must have put it there on purpose. Was that Waters and Matthews on the front page? He went over and skimmed the story. *You gotta be kidding.* It was a nasty political smear, implying he had locked up the one man who was going to save Quandary's economy with a big-budget investment. That was a joke. It was obvious that Khodorovsky was only in town for one reason—and it wasn't a new business startup plan.

The front door opened, and Jenny walked in, grinning from ear to ear.

"I took it to the top of Red Mountain Pass. All I can smell is hot brakes. Man, that thing is fast." She set the keys to the Challenger on his desk. "Who owns it, for real?"

Breck glanced at Khodorovsky, but the Russian was busy on the phone and wasn't paying attention to them.

"A Customs officer. He showed up at the Hyatt, looking for the Asbjorns." He kept his voice low. "They were going to claim asylum."

Jenny's happy grin faded away.

"Asylum?" she whispered. "That means they were too afraid for their lives to return to Norway. Gee, I wonder why."

Khodorovsky hung up the phone and turned around to face them. He had a twinkle in his eye.

"All done."

Taking him by the arm, Jenny guided him back into the jail cell and slammed the door. *Clank.*

"So that was your lawyer?" she asked.

"Mr. Lawyer, yes."

"So, when shall we expect Mr. Lawyer to show up?"

"I shall let it be a surprise."

Snapping her fingers, Jenny walked back to her desk and shuffled through all the paperwork and food wrappers until she uncovered a notepad she used for phone messages.

"Breck, I forgot to tell you something. Aspen Matthews called and left a voicemail. She wants to report some kind of scam at the fairgrounds. Here's her cell number. Oh, and did you ever touch base with your attorney?"

"Not yet."

He took the message pad and flipped through it. Besides Aspen and Jamey Frederick's messages, there were a dozen complaints about the newspaper. Jenny's handwriting was hard to read, but apparently, some people thought he screwed over the town. *Nice move, Matthews.*

"Don't people realize there are two sides to every story?" Breck muttered.

Speaking of two sides to every story, Anatoli's phone conversation just now, who was he really talking to? His lawyer—or his bodyguard? Or someone in Moscow with an even longer reach?

"I can't even think about calling all these people back right now." Breck tossed the message pad on his desk. "Do you have Tya's phone number?"

"Yeah."

"Call and make sure she's okay and that Hedda's okay, and tell her I'm on my way over."

"Um, okay . . . should we be worried?"

Breck glanced at Khodorovsky. The oligarch was stretched out on his cot, humming, as if he didn't have a care in the world. If that wasn't his lawyer on the phone. . . .

"Call Tya, right now."

Dashing outside, Breck slid into the Challenger, jammed the accelerator to the floor, and shot out of the parking lot like a bolt of lightning. He had a bad feeling in his gut. What if the Russians decided Hedda Asbjorn was better off dead? Aleks could have figured out she was staying with Tya. That wouldn't be hard to do, not for a former SVU agent. The two women could be in danger, especially now that Khodorovsky was behind bars. Hedda was the only witness to Jansen's murder, and without her testimony, Khodorovsky would walk.

The rain was falling steadily, but that didn't slow Breck down.

Zipping through Quandary, past the ski resort, he turned onto the long dirt road that led to Tya's mountainside mansion. Hopefully, Jenny had gotten through. He checked his cell phone, but there was no signal. Quandary's cell service was unbelievably worthless.

The road wound through the forest for several miles before it dead-ended at the gate to Tya's property. Skidding to a stop, Breck rolled the car window down and pushed the talk button on the call box.

"Hello? Tya? Are you home? It's me, Sheriff Dyer."

Static.

The more he thought about it, the more Breck became convinced there was no lawyer on the other end of that phone call. Aleks was Mr. Lawyer. Did Khodorovsky instruct him to kill Hedda? The conversation had been in

Russian. It would have been so easy to do that, even with Breck and Jenny standing two feet away.

Suddenly, Tya's voice came over the speaker.

"Hi, Breck. Everything is fine here. Jenny called me on the landline and said you were going to drop by. Do you want to come up to the house? We're about to eat supper. Shrimp sandwiches. You're welcome to join us."

Oh, thank God. Relief washed over him, and he rested his forehead on the leather steering wheel. Maybe he was wrong. Maybe Anatoli had actually spoken to his lawyer after all. But better safe than sorry.

"Breck? You still there?"

"I am. Thanks for the invitation, but I better not. I recently had a bad run-in with another man's sushi, so I'm steering clear of seafood for the time being."

"Okay, but you're going to miss out on a fantastic meal. And we'll miss your company."

"Hey, Tya. Can you bring Hedda down to the Sheriff's Office tomorrow? If she's willing to talk about what happened, I'd like to get her official statement on record. And can you let her know there is a Customs and Immigration officer in town who wants to meet her? She'll know what that's about."

"Will do. She's still pretty upset, but we'll be there. First thing in the morning."

Breck started to roll up the window but stopped. That uneasy feeling started creeping back. He stared down the road, but as far as he could tell, in the hazy rain and fading sunlight, it was empty. His mind went back to the dark blue Suburban, parked down the street, during his conversation with the governor.

Breck hit the call button again.

"Hey, Tya? I'm going to park down here, all night, okay? I want to watch the road, just to be safe."

"Is that necessary? No one can get through that gate."

"Just to be safe," he repeated.

"You bet. Hey, have you heard anything yet, from the kidnappers? Have they made a ransom call?"

Breck cringed. He wasn't going to say anything over the intercom. But it was time to tell Hedda that her husband was dead and bring her to the morgue to ID the body.

"I can't say anything right now, but I will explain everything in the morning."

"Okay. Good night, Breck."

He rolled up the window and spun the Challenger around, so he had a clear line of sight down the dirt road. It would be easy to spot headlights coming, in the darkness.

He kept the engine idling, and the heater on full blast. Raindrops pattered the windshield, and a few fat snowflakes swirled down, too, and dissolved on the glass. He turned on the wipers.

If only he had brought along a thermos of coffee and something to eat, but there had been no time for that, and Breck certainly wasn't going to impose on Tya, given the circumstances. Too bad his cell didn't work, or he could call High Country Pizza for a roadside delivery. He checked the console and the dashboard compartments, hoping Billy James kept snacks in the car, but there was nothing. Not even a stick of gum.

It was going to be a long night.

CHAPTER 35

Ain't My High

The landline rang. It jarred Tya out of a deep sleep, and she tore off the bed comforter and flipped on a lamp. She checked the caller ID before answering. It was the ski resort.

"Hello?"

"Mrs. Tordenskjold, it's Cash. Did I wake you?"

It was 2:00 A.M.

"That's okay. What's wrong?"

"The security alarm went off here at the resort—top floor. Someone just broke into your apartment. Somehow they snuck up there and kicked in the door. You want me to call the cops?"

Her apartment? Tya rubbed the sleep out of her eyes. A burglary? She did have all kinds of high-end artwork there, plus a wall safe with her most expensive jewelry, hidden behind the Edvard Munch painting. The bronze eagle sculpture was worth half a million dollars alone. Not to mention all the wine.

"No, don't call the sheriff. He has more important things to worry about right now. Did you see who did it?"

"No. But whoever it was, they knew how to avoid all the cameras. Like a ninja."

After she separated from Sven and began living in the apartment, Tya installed a security camera in the stairwell, and the hallway leading to her apartment, since she was a little nervous living all alone. Not getting caught on film took skill.

Or else it took foreknowledge. What if . . . what if it was Sven? He certainly knew the layout and where all the cameras in the building were. Tya started to get angry but checked herself. Sven had called a few days ago, demanding the keys to their condo in Vail, but Tya told him to kiss-off. The keys were in the apartment wall-safe. Did he waltz in there and just take them? What else did he take? If he took any of the wine to booze up his little skank, Tya was going to go ballistic.

"I want to see for myself," she said. "I'm coming down there right now."

After she threw on some clothes and grabbed her purse, Tya tiptoed down the hallway. She paused at the guest bedroom and listened. Snoring. Hedda had finally fallen asleep. All it took to settle her nerves was a good dinner, a silly movie, and a half bottle of Chardonnay.

Speaking of wine, Tya knew precisely how many bottles were in the wine cooler at the apartment. The exact count. If one were missing, she would know it.

As quietly as she could, Tya dashed downstairs and pulled her SUV out of the garage. The motion lights clicked on and flooded the whole area with dazzling light. At the bottom of the long winding driveway, she pushed the button on her visor that opened the entry gate and pulled onto the main road.

A sports car was idling in the shadows, with its running lights on, covered with a thin layer of wet snow. Was that Breck? Where was his Jeep? She pulled up next to the Challenger and rolled down her window. He rolled his down, too.

"Everything okay?"

"Yeah, nothing to worry about," Tya said. "I need to shoot down to the ski resort for a little while."

But Breck looked concerned.

"Everything okay?" he repeated.

"Sven stopped by the resort. I need to go straighten something out."

Behind them, the front gate slid closed with a clank.

"Is Hedda with you?"

"No, she's in bed, sound asleep. Be back before you know it."

"Okay, I'll be here."

Tya sped down the road, tires splashing through the slush. It was good to see a little snow in the air. That meant ski season was almost here. She flipped her headlights on bright. At night, in the narrow LED beam, the road to town felt like a never-ending tunnel through the forest. She had to stay alert for wildlife in case a deer darted out of the trees. She wished Sven would dart out of the trees. She'd hit the accelerator. Was he stealing the condo keys and her wine to plow a ho-bag in Vail? They weren't even divorced yet! Technically speaking.

When she reached the resort, she parked beneath the awning at the entrance, where it was dry. She left the engine running and raced into the lobby.

Cash was manning the reception desk, and from the look on his face, he thought he was going to get fired.

"I'm sorry, Mrs. Torkenskjold. I don't know how anyone could have broke in. I had my eyes glued to the camera feeds, pretty much the whole time."

"Relax, Cash. This wasn't a random burglary."

She took the elevator up to the top floor. Sure enough, the apartment door was wide open. The door jamb splintered. Tya went inside and removed the Munch painting that covered the wall safe and spun the dial. She should have changed the combination six months ago like she changed the lock on the apartment door. Why hadn't she done that?

To her surprise, the keys to the condo in Vail were still inside, hanging on a little eye hook. She frowned but felt relieved. Closing the safe, Tya went and checked the wine cooler, counting the bottles one by one. Nothing was missing.

"That's weird." She turned and looked around. "Sven? Are you here?"

But the apartment was empty. The eagle sculpture was untouched. The jewelry was still in its box. Every other piece of art in the room was where it should be.

But she did spot something that shouldn't be there—a bottle of vodka in the trash can. She reached in and retrieved it. Smirnoff. It was empty.

"How did this get here?"

The first thought that came to mind was Cash. What if he let himself into her apartment when she wasn't around? Watched HBO on the big screen? Drank a little vodka? It was the perfect hideaway from the real world, and as the manager, he had a master key to every door in the resort. But even if the vodka bottle was Cash's, why would he kick in the door? It didn't make any sense.

Taking the bottle with her, Tya rode the elevator to the ground floor, marched to the reception desk, and waved the Smirnoff.

"You're busted, pal."

"What? I don't drink that junk. Ain't my high."

She smelled his breath. No liquor.

"All right, you're off the hook. Call a repairman as soon as the sun comes up. I have something important to do tomorrow, off-site, and I won't have time to take care of it myself. Get that door fixed, okay?"

"You want me to call the cops, or what?"

"No, I'll let the sheriff know what happened."

"You got it, boss."

CHAPTER 36

Predictable

Even though he was six-foot-four and cut like a stone, Aleks had mastered the art of contortion into small spaces. There were times he had to worm his way through an industrial air duct or crawl into a storm drain. One time, to sneak into London, he zipped himself inside an airport suitcase and remained there for hours, all the while holding a very deadly vile of Polonium-210. Very uncomfortable.

The floorboards behind the front seats of the Land Rover were carpeted and smelled like spring flowers. A little heating vent, hidden under the driver's seat and designed to keep the back seat passengers' feet warm, was puffing warm air directly at his face. It was nice because his nose was cold from standing outside for so long. To be cautious, he had parked his Suburban behind the 7-Eleven, walked down to the ski resort, and after he broke into the third floor apartment to set off the alarm, went back outside and waited behind a pine tree, shivering in the darkness, until the Land Rover drove up to the entrance.

Getting inside was simple. She had left the doors unlocked.

As if the Tordenskjold woman was trying to make his job as easy as possible, she kept the radio blaring. Aleks could clear his throat, or hum along to the music, or sigh without fear of being heard. He even chuckled out loud as he recalled cramming into a filthy little two-door Yugo in Czechia the previous winter. Perhaps he should retire and join the circus.

The Land Rover slowed, and the music stopped. Aleks felt cold air as Tya rolled down her window.

"Hi, Breck. Are you staying warm out here? Can I bring you a blanket or a pillow?"

Aleks couldn't make out what the sheriff was saying. Something self-deprecating and stoic.

"Okay. See you when the sun comes up. I guess that's not too far away. Bye!"

Then the window slid shut, and the SUV rolled forward. Aleks could feel the angle of the road getting steeper. Suddenly, a very bright light shined through all the windows. It was the woman's home security floodlights. Aleks had triggered those himself the other night, sneaking through the forest trees. But it did not matter because once she parked inside the garage, no one could see what would happen next.

He listened to the buzz of the garage door descending.

It was time.

Aleks sat up. Just to add a little fear factor, he waited until she felt his breath on her neck and looked in the rearview mirror. That was a fun game to play.

He seized Tya's long blonde hair with one hand. She screamed and thrashed but couldn't go anywhere, as he reached around the headrest, hooked his other arm around her throat, and began his famous Anaconda Death Squeeze. The woman gagged and coughed and used her little fists to beat on his forearm, but of course, it was no more irritating than a mosquito's bite.

When she went limp, Aleks released his grip and got out of the SUV.

A row of fluorescent bulbs on the ceiling illuminated the entire garage, and he looked around to assess where he was. It was a three-car garage, and there were some rich people's toys. An ATV, a couple of snowmobiles. Milk crates full of old hobbies and old computers. A shiny Harley Davidson motorcycle.

Aleks spotted a security panel on the wall. Little yellow LEDs indicated the exterior motion lights had been activated, and another one lit up the moment he opened the door to go inside the house, but no alarm went off. Perfect.

Once his eyes adjusted to the darkness, Aleks could tell he was standing in a laundry room. Across from the washer and dryer was a big bench for people to sit and tie their shoes. It was dark in the house, but there were small nightlights here and there. Aleks walked through an archway, into a kitchen aglow with blue digital displays. He paused at the chopping block and considered taking a long serrated bread knife. Those kinds of knives reminded him of old war movies, where field doctors amputated limbs with similar tools. He had done that himself, once or twice, though he was no doctor.

One of the steak knives in the set was missing. Aleks opened the dishwasher, but it was empty, and so was the sink. Everything in this tidy little kitchen had its place and purpose. He smiled. Hedda Asbjorn was quivering in her bedroom with that little steak knife. This was fun, yes?

He spotted a landline telephone. Pop went the cord.

Aleks moved without making a sound. Through the living room shadows. Up the carpeted staircase. He paused on the balcony landing to look out the big bay windows. This spot was where the Torkenskjold woman often stood, her watchtower, to look out over her kingdom. When Aleks accidentally triggered the motion lights earlier that week, she had appeared at that very window, looking to the left and right. She never saw him.

Down below, the motion lights kicked on again. The Land Rover shot out of the garage in reverse and banged into a landscape boulder, denting its bumper.

Aleks frowned. He should have given her delicate little neck an extra Anaconda Squeeze.

The vehicle raced away, kicking up gravel, all the way down the steep driveway. The Tordenskjold woman was driving erratically. Aleks watched her red taillights flicker through the misty trees until they vanished.

A floorboard creaked.

Smiling, Aleks turned to look, but the hallway was empty. He jiggled the guest bedroom doorknob. It was locked. He took a step back and kicked it open on the first try. He saw Hedda Asbjorn trying to crawl under the bed, so he grabbed her ankles, dragged her out screaming, and swatted the steak knife out of her hand.

"Please! Don't!"

With a concrete grip, Aleks parked her on the bed. Tears flowed, and her jaw trembled. So predictable.

"Where is Jansen?" Hedda asked. "Please, tell me he is okay. Please!"

It was clear the sheriff had not informed her that her husband was deceased. Good. What else would she reveal? Aleks stared at her. Sometimes, looming was far more effective than words. It created a sense of suspense that people responded to favorably.

Hedda gripped the bed covers, twisting the fabric into a knot.

"I will sign, okay?" she whispered. "I will sign."

That was what he wanted to hear. But unfortunately, the legal document was in the sheriff's possession now. The last time he saw it, it was sitting on the dining table in the Asbjorn's room the night he and Anatoli took her husband away. When they returned, after dropping the unlucky man into the pit, deep in the Keystone Mine, the Asbjorn's hotel door would not open. Anatoli was so angry when he realized they had abandoned the hotel key card by accident. In the mine, when they cleaned out Jansen's wallet, they took every useful thing— cash, credit cards, ID, and key card. Unfortunately, the key card looked remarkably similar to a Safeway grocery store discount card. Both were solid red, with white letters. They only realized their error when they tried swiping the Safeway card to unlock the Asbjorn's suite.

But Anatoli couldn't blame him for the mistake. It wasn't Aleks's fault. Anatoli was the one who sorted through Jansen's wallet, while Aleks flung the man down the mine shaft. If nothing else, it was a good reminder to study the English language better.

Aleks put his hands on Hedda's shoulders and looked her in the eye.

"Have you cooperated with police?"

He dug his thumbs into her clavicles, making her wince.

"No!" She whimpered. "You told me not to, and I haven't told them anything. Please, let Jansen go."

"You will deny Mr. Khodorovsky was involved in your abduction, first thing tomorrow. Or I will kill your husband. He is alive, no matter what anyone tells you. Understand?"

"Yes, I understand."

He heard the distant sound of tires screeching. That would be the sheriff.

CHAPTER 37

Panicked

"Lock the doors and do not get out until I say it's safe."

"Hurry, Breck . . . she's upstairs . . . and. . . ."

But Tya could barely get the words out. It hurt to speak. She was sitting in the passenger seat of the Challenger, holding her throat.

"Just lock the doors."

Breck drew his Rossi .44 Special revolver and got out of the car. He knelt by the hood for a moment, squinting in the floodlights. Sleet and snow were falling all around him, and fog engulfed the entire house.

Tya's garage was wide open, and he could see black tire chirp-marks on the concrete where she stomped the gas pedal to the floor.

Dashing inside, Breck made a quick sweep to make sure Aleks wasn't hiding in the garage clutter, and then pushed open the laundry room door and shined his flashlight inside the house, gun up. He held his breath for a second, listening.

But the house was silent.

After a quick check behind the door, Breck moved through the kitchen into the living room. Couches, curtains, closets. There were plenty of places to hide. But he couldn't waste too much time. Time was critical, and it was ticking away fast. At that very moment, Aleks was searching the house himself, on a mission to finish what he started.

Breck needed backup. He almost pulled out his phone, but of course, there was no cell service here. He spotted a landline, but the Russian had ripped the cord from the outlet. It was ruined. Even if he could somehow reach Jenny, it wasn't like she could jump in an extra patrol car and race up there. She could relay a message to the State Patrol, or hell's bells, call Chief Waters and tell him to put down the doughnut.

Where was Aleks? The guy was dangerous. He nearly choked Tya to death, and he killed Jansen Asbjorn, but not before he took a candlestick to the man's facial features. It was brutal and sadistic. What would he do to Hedda if he got the opportunity?

With no time to lose, Breck hustled up the stairs, shining his flashlight in the hallway.

The guest room. A bootprint was on the door. Breck was expecting either a fight or a dead body, but all he found was Hedda Asbjorn, pale but unharmed, sitting on the edge of her bed.

"Where is he?" Breck asked.

No response.

After clearing the closet and checking under the bed, Breck ran up the hall-way and flipped on the master bedroom lights, but it was empty, so he went back to the bay window. The house motion lights outside were still blazing, and he surveilled the parking area, the landscape boulders, the hillside, and the forest, but no one was out there, except Tya in the passenger seat of the Dodge Challenger.

"We need to go." He held out his hand, but Hedda didn't take it. "It's not safe. They know you're here."

Grabbing her hand, he pulled her downstairs and flipped on every light switch he encountered in the process. He noticed the patio doors that led to the back deck were open. The big wooden deck was only a stone's throw from the dark forest. Aleks was gone. Or was he?

They had to get out of there.

As soon as Tya saw them coming, she unlocked the car doors. Breck helped Hedda into the back, and then slid into the driver's seat. The car was still idling, with the windshield wipers on high, swishing at the wet snowflakes swirling in the foggy mist. Too bad it was just a fancy airport rental and not a cop car. There was no CB or siren or satellite computer system. All they could do now was drive. Breck put it into gear, hooked the wheel, and punched it.

Tya reached back and gripped Hedda's knee. "Are you okay?"

Her voice was raw.

Hedda blinked.

"Yes, thank you. I appreciate your concern."

It was an odd, formal response. Breck glanced in the rearview mirror. She was staring off into space.

Tya gave up on Hedda and turned back around.

"I'm so stupid." Her words came out in whispery pieces. "I had a gun . . . the whole time . . . in my purse . . . but I panicked."

"You're not stupid. You're alive."

It was no small thing. Tya *was* alive, and so was Hedda. If Breck had gotten there a few seconds later, Aleks would have gotten to her first and killed her. Right? That's the whole reason Aleks was there—tying up loose ends. Aleks hid in Tya's SUV to access the property, choked her out, and went inside to murder Hedda Asbjorn so she couldn't identify her kidnappers.

As they sped downhill, Breck checked the rearview mirror again.

One problem with that theory: Hedda hadn't been killed. Yet Aleks had already come and gone by the time Breck got there, with time to kill her, or at least do some serious tracheal damage. But there was no evidence of a struggle. The woman was fine. Scared, but fine.

They reached the security gate at the base of the driveway. It had been smashed open. Tya had been running on adrenaline and terror, and in the throes of a near-death experience, hit the gas instead of the brakes. She plowed right through the gate, sped across the road, nearly clipping the Challenger, and crashed into a tree. Thank God for airbags.

Heading back to town, Breck drove as fast as he could, but visibility was low and he had to be careful. The tires slid in the slush when he went around tight corners, and the road was long and windy. Finally, once they lost enough elevation, they broke out of the bad weather and he hit the gas pedal.

"Hedda? There is a United States Customs and Immigration Services officer waiting for you," Breck said. "He's here to grant you asylum. You're safe now."

But she shook her head.

"No, I do not want to claim asylum. Please, no."

"I thought that's what you wanted? Your husband set this whole thing up before he was. . . ."

Tya had nodded off in the silence, but hearing their conversation, she woke up and rubbed her eyes. It was dawn, and the sky to the east was starting to change color.

"No, I don't want to talk to that officer or anyone," Hedda told him. "I just want to go home. And I want to see Jan again."

"You will," Tya said. "I promise."

She gave Breck a side-look, obviously expecting him to chime in and make the same promise.

"Mrs. Asbjorn?" Breck hated delivering news like this, but it was always best to just say it quickly. Like pulling off the proverbial Band-Aid. "I am sorry to tell you this, but your husband, Jansen Asbjorn, is dead."

CHAPTER 38

Bigger Man

The moment Brittany spotted Johnny Tibbs' cowboy hat bobbing up City Hall's concrete stairs, she yanked out her phone and put it on video mode, so she could live stream what was about to happen. But in her excitement, she dropped it on the tile floor, just as he walked in the door, and to her horror, the screen shattered.

It was a six hundred dollar iPhone.

"Please, God, no!"

"It's okay, girl, I ain't mad at you. Where is he?"

Tibbs stormed past her desk and tore open the mayor's door. But Matthews was already on his feet, on the far side of the desk, brandishing a letter opener for self-defense.

"Yeah, you better be scared, you little shit stain." Tibbs was fuming. His eyes fell to the letter opener. He burst out laughing and called over his shoulder to Brittany. "He thought I was coming in, guns blazing, to put him down like a diseased heifer in heat. Tell me you got that on film?"

"I dropped my phone," she moaned. "It's broken."

But Tibbs didn't care. He pointed a finger at Matthews.

"I caught those kids drawing mustaches on my signs, and they 'fessed up and said it was you. I knew it all along. You think you can play dirty, Matthews?"

"Settle down, Johnny. If all you got is kids playing around with campaign yard signs, it's going to make you look like a whiny bastard when you lose the election. Sour grapes, buckaroo. Get over it."

Tibbs slammed his palm on the desk. Matthews bristled and gripped the letter opener even tighter.

"Every single one of my wranglers got an absentee ballot in the mail to-day . . . which they never requested. How is it that the mayor box is already checked? Right next to *your* name?"

Matthews laughed, but it was more like a nervous hyena coughing up a lung.

Brittany stood in the doorway, transfixed. How could she break her phone at a moment like this? She tapped the screen on her phone repeatedly, but it didn't light up. It was ruined.

"This would have gone viral."

But they didn't hear her.

Brittany had a channel on YouTube, with over fifty thousand subscribers, called *Brittany the Beauty Guru*. The money she made from it covered the cost of her season ski pass, so it was well worth her time. She tested all kinds of newly released makeup products and demonstrated application techniques with eyeliner, lipstick, hairstyles, and stuff like that.

But her channel wasn't all style tips and tutorials.

Once in a while, she got lucky when something insane happened, and she got it on video. Like the time a moose wandered into Safeway. Brittany was in the produce section picking out sprouts and basil. When she turned around, she discovered a moose standing right beside her, cropping at the cilantro. People slunk down the cereal aisle and hid behind the avocados, but not her. She got out her iPhone and hit the live stream, and by the next day, her channel was trending. Hashtag, moose selfie.

A mayoral candidate beat down would have been pure clickbait.

"You accusing me of election fraud already, cowboy? It must be sad know-ing you ain't got the votes, so here you are trying to poison the outcome before a single ballot has been counted. Take it up with the county election supervisor."

Tibbs guffawed.

"You mean Linda? How does that filly still got a job? I seem to recall that you lost the vote four years ago, by a *hair* . . . but you wouldn't concede and demanded a recount. Wasn't she the one who magically discovered 963 ballots in the trunk of her own car? They all said 'Matthews,' and that's how you won."

"I'll tell you how she's still got a job. It's called an elected office, and ap-parently, everyone in Quandary likes Linda enough to keep her around. That's how it works. And that's how I'm going to win because everyone in town knows you're an arrogant redneck, and nobody wants to hand you the reins."

Johnny started to circle the desk.

"Funny how Linda managed to win the bid on that luxury home," he growled. "Less than a week after she found those votes. For *half* of what it was worth. It's like she made a backroom real estate deal or something."

Moving to keep the desk between them, Matthews smirked.

"It's called a foreclosure."

"A foreclosure that wasn't even listed publicly. Yeah, I checked. That's some shady wheeling and dealing, Matthews, and it's all gonna shake out in the wash. Your number is up, pard."

Having said what he came to say, Johnny Tibbs exited the building.

Brittany watched his cowboy hat bob back down the concrete stairs and float out to the parking lot, and he was gone like a tumbleweed in the wind. What a cruel twist of fate! What did she do to deserve this? All she needed to do was hit the record button. It was that simple.

"Brittany!" Matthews dropped into his chair, trying to catch his breath. "You saw that crazy hick prick. He's out of control. Call Sheriff Dyer, tell him to drop whatever pointless thing he's doing, and get over here. I'm filing an assault charge, and you're my star witness."

"But, sir, Johnny didn't touch you."

"He took a swing at me. You saw it."

"You were the one holding a weapon."

Matthews looked at his hand, then casually slid the letter opener into his desk drawer. He raised his finger like he was going to say more but gave up.

"You know what? I'm taking the high road. I won't turn him in. I'm the bigger man here."

But Brittany wasn't listening anymore. She went back to her desk, cradling her six hundred dollar iPhone like a dead puppy.

CHAPTER 39

Blue Line Special

"Just you and me again, *Krasny.*" Khodorovsky smiled at Jenny, though his eyes were on her auburn ponytail. "You know what *krasny* means?"

"You know what 'death penalty' means?"

"*Krasny* means red in Russian. Interesting factoid—it has same root word as word *krasivy*, which means beautiful."

"Good thing you're rich because your lady skills are poor."

"I'm going to miss our jailhouse conversations, *Krasny.*"

Picking up the landline, Jenny dialed the Quandary Brewery. She was getting cabin fever, cooped up in the Sheriff's Office with this guy. She needed to talk to someone normal.

"Danny? It's me. Can I order a burger and fries? And is there any chance you can deliver? I've got a suspect in custody, and I can't leave."

The brewery served the best hamburgers in town, and Danny only charged her five bucks as a cop courtesy. The Blue Line Special. That was a lot cheaper than a Blue Moose burrito and a whole lot tastier than the yogurt waiting for her in the fridge.

"Yeah, I want cheese. Who wouldn't want cheese?" She hung up.

Was it lunchtime already? The morning had blown by in a whirlwind. When Breck returned to the office, he brought Hedda Asbjorn, Tya Tordenskjold, and a crazy tale about a Russian stowaway in her Land Rover. Tya had gotten a good look at her attacker in the rearview mirror, and of course, it was Aleks. She recognized him from the ski resort, when he chased Hedda into the lobby in her pajamas and socks.

Meanwhile, Hedda was in a state of wide-eyed denial. Chattering to herself, she kept repeating, over and over, that *Jansen is fine, it isn't true, Jansen is fine.* Breck tried to get a formal statement on record about the kidnapping, but couldn't get through to her, so he took them both to the hospital. Tya needed to see a doctor. Her neck had severe bruises. As for the Asbjorn widow, it was time to identify the body. Good luck with that. Even so, Jenny wished she could have gone along with them because babysitting Russian oligarchs wasn't as fun as it sounded.

She stepped outside into the parking lot to wait for Danny.

The gray clouds had lifted and drifted, leaving all the mountain tops covered in fresh white autumn snow. From summit to timberline, the snow stretched down the slopes. Autumn was almost over. Hopefully, this case was almost over, too. They had Khodorovsky in jail, and Hedda was safe. The US-CIS officer would whisk her back to DC, and they had Jansen's Hyatt key card in the evidence locker. All they needed now was to catch Aleks.

It looked like a little Lego speck from this distance, but she could see the Keystone Mine from the Sheriff's Office parking lot. Shiny tin shacks twinkled like stars on the ridge below the summit of Red Mountain. It was pretty in the snow and sunshine.

Of course, the inside of the mine was very different. Dank, cold tunnels, and rotting timbers. Poor Jansen. What a place to give up the ghost. And poor Hedda, she was devastated. She must have really loved her husband. Not everyone could say that about their spouse. Just look at Tya and Sven, and Matthews and Valerie. Johnny Tibbs was divorced, too. Why was finding love such a difficult thing in this world?

Jamey Frederick, Breck's lawyer, had called the Sheriff's Office that morning, just after he left for the hospital. More bad news. An attorney from Monterrey, Mexico, had visited her office in Frisco. He demanded that Breck should be extradited to stand trial in Mexico for murdering one of their fine upstanding citizens, a man named Alphonso Zorrero. Jenny felt a flutter in her stomach. Zorrero. He was the cartel commander who shot up the town last year and tried to kill them both. But the attorney had his facts wrong. It wasn't Breck who put a bullet in his brainpan. It was her.

"Chin up, girl." Jenny dug out a five-dollar bill from her pants pocket. "Always look on the bright side of life."

She couldn't wait until Khodorovsky was long gone, and things got back to normal. It was just a matter of time until he got transferred to an actual prison, somewhere else in the state, like the Super Max in Florence. A lot of big-time criminals were locked up inside those walls. The Unabomber. Timothy McVeigh. What if Khodorovsky got shivved by El Chapo?

Food for thought.

Speaking of food, she spotted Danny's pickup coming down the street. It was a dark green Ram with big mudflaps and a toolbox in the bed. There were some silver kegs stacked in there, too. Danny spent half his week delivering beer to restaurants and bars all along I-70.

He parked and jumped out of the cab with a square Styrofoam container and a newspaper tucked under his arm.

"Perfect timing, I'm starving."

"I put extra fries in there."

"I love me some fries."

"I know you do. Have you seen the paper today?"

"Nope."

It was the Quandary Herald. The paper had a pretentious byline: *Defying the Darkness that Destroys Democracy.* All they ever printed was salacious gossip and biased political commentary. Why pay money for that kind of garbage when she could get it on the internet for free?

Danny held it up so she could see the front page. There was a giant full-color photo of Seneca Matthews and Chief Maxwell Waters. Waters had his arm around the mayor's shoulder, buddy style.

"Another Dire Day in Dyer's West World." Jenny opened the Styrofoam container and ate some french fries. "I can't wait to read it. I love riveting literature."

"Where's Brecky?" Danny walked to the front door of the building and shoved it open. "You in there, brother?"

But Breck wasn't inside. Only Khodorovsky, watching from his cot like a curious Siberian varmint.

"Who is your brother?"

"Ignore him," Jenny said, walking past Danny. She took her food to her desk, while he plopped down in Breck's swivel chair and immediately started going through the drawers in his desk.

"You done with my camera?"

"Not yet. Can we keep it a little longer?"

"Just don't let Breck touch it."

He kept rummaging through the desk.

"It's not in there," Jenny told him. "It's in the evidence locker. Safe and sound."

But Danny didn't stop. After a minute, she realized he wasn't looking for his camera or anything in particular. He was just shuffling papers around, randomly moving items from one drawer to the next. Breck was going to be ticked.

Jenny almost gave him a lecture but held her tongue. Danny was just being Danny. Besides, he had just brought her lunch, and he didn't have to do that. Why jeopardize future lunch deliveries over a bit of brotherly condescension?

She took a bite of the hamburger. Cheese dripped on her desk, and she mopped it up with a french fry.

It was tempting to ask how it went with the helmet. Surely, they had a heart to heart when Breck swung by the brewery to get it. Right? Probably not. There was too much machismo swirling between the Dyer brothers to get past awkward pleasantries. She could guess how it went down. *Here's the helmet. Thanks. Bye.* Maybe it wasn't her place to ask. And perhaps it was best not to say anything in front of this communist freak show, anyhow. Khodorovsky was listening to every word they said and drinking it all in.

Danny slammed Breck's desk drawers and stood up like he was about to leave.

"Is there a Russian Roulette convention?"

"No. Why do you ask?"

"I saw another Boris at the brewery."

Jenny wiped her mouth with a napkin.

"What does this guy look like?"

"Ripped."

"When? Today?"

"Yesterday."

"Why was he there? Was he acting suspicious?"

"The guy ordered a hamburger and then took it out to his Suburban."

Walking to the window, Jenny studied Main Street. Late season tourists were going in and out of the art gallery and the Blue Moose. A few cars were parked along the curb. From where she was standing, she had a good view of the brewery parking lot, too. So Aleks *was* driving a Suburban. Breck was right.

CHAPTER 40

Secret Life Raft

There wasn't a clue, not a glove, boot, ice ax, or anything that might indicate where Kyle might have fallen. No matter how long he searched the icy glacier, Breck couldn't find him. To make matters worse, the numbing pain in his feet was getting worse by the moment. Finally, it became too much to continue. It was like walking on broken glass. When he pulled off his boots, his heart skipped a beat. All his toes had turned black and blue.

It took days to worm across the glacier, crawling on his hands and knees. Every inch felt like a mile. When he finally returned to base camp, he stared at the satellite phone. The last thing he wanted to do was tell Nikki her husband was dead.

And the last thing he had wanted to do was tell Hedda her husband was dead.

As Breck pulled back the plastic sheet, exposing Jansen Asbjorn's body, she went white and collapsed. Her breath came in short gasps. He could still hear Nickie gasping for breath, thousands of miles away, on the other end of that phone. At least Hedda had some closure, right here, right now. Nickie had no way to say goodbye. Not for ten long years. Ten years of questions and second guesses and what if's. Mainly, what if Breck had died and Kyle had come home instead?

"I'm very sorry, Mrs. Asbjorn."

Breck put his hand on the poor woman's shoulder.

"Jan . . ." she whispered. "Why didn't you just . . . sign?"

Sign those Norwegian documents? What if he had? Perhaps Khodorovsky would have thanked him for his time and flew back to Moscow a richer man.

Or else he would have shoved Jansen down that mine shaft anyway and killed Hedda, too. Bear Coin was a high-profile multimillion-dollar enterprise. Simply transferring its ownership to a Russian businessman wouldn't go unnoticed. Or unchallenged, once the Asbjorns spoke with lawyers and federal authorities back home in Norway.

"Do you want to call someone?" Breck asked. "A family member?"

"They said if I cooperated with the American authorities, they would kill Jan. I said nothing. But they did it anyway."

Her face creased with heartbreak and tears slid down her cheeks. It was hard to watch. Breck hated to ask questions at a time like this, but he needed answers.

"I know it's a lot to process, but please tell me what happened, Hedda. Anatoli Khodorovsky is sitting in a jail cell right now, but I need you to cooperate with us, to put him away for good."

Seeing a box of tissue on a nearby counter, Breck handed it to her.

Suddenly, Hedda became strangely calm. She took a tissue and wiped her nose and cheeks, and looked at Breck in a way she hadn't before. Was it trust? Or nothing to lose?

"The Russians aren't after Bear Coin Capital."

"What *are* they after?"

Hedda caressed her husband's hair, and squeezed his cold hand.

"I want to claim asylum, please."

Breck wanted to ask more. But there was a balancing act when it came to questioning a grieving widow, and he had pushed too far already. It was time to take her to meet the Customs and Immigration Officer Billy James—presuming the guy hadn't keeled over from pulmonary edema by now.

Respectfully, Breck covered Jansen Asbjorn's body with the plastic shroud.

"Let's go claim asylum," he said.

Offering his arm for support, Breck led Hedda down the hallway, past the reception desk, and into the parking lot. He had Billy James' business card in his wallet, with his cell number on it. After he helped Hedda into the car, he leaned on the hood and dialed.

"Go for Billy James."

That was how he answered his phone? The guy was a joke, but Breck didn't have the energy to care.

"I've got Hedda Asbjorn with me right now, and she is ready to claim asylum."

"What are you waiting for? Bring her over. And bring my car. There better not be a scratch on it, or you're paying for the repairs."

"Listen. I don't care how you speak to me, but you better be professional with this poor lady. Her husband was brutally murdered while you were eating sushi."

"Wait! Hold on! Dyer, you there? Don't you hang up on me."

Breck sighed.

"What is it?"

"I ran out of Pepto. Can you drop by a store on the way over? And ginger ale. And a big bottle of Advil. My head is still pounding like crazy. I'll pay you back. I'm good for it."

"Anything else?"

"Naw, that'll do."

As Breck jammed the phone in his pocket, Tya came out of the hospital, wearing a foam neck brace. Her eyes were bright and she even gave him a wave as she crossed the parking lot.

"What did the doc say?" he asked.

"No permanent damage to the larynx or esophagus." Her voice still sounded raw. "I'm just going to be talking like this until my throat heals. How is Hedda holding up? I should have been there, in the morgue."

"No, you needed to get checked over. You had your airway cut off until you lost consciousness, remember?"

Tya peered through the windshield. Hedda was in the backseat, her head in her hands.

"What is wrong with this world?"

Good question. Breck put his hand in his pocket, around the package of American Spirit cigarettes, but he didn't take it out. He just held onto it, like a secret life raft.

"I'm going to take her to meet that Immigration officer now. She's ready to claim asylum. Maybe we'll get some answers. Hey, can you translate a Norwegian document I found in their suite? It's in the evidence locker back at the office. I can bring it to you later."

"Sure. You know where to find me." Tya poked at the neck brace. "This thing itches."

"You don't need it."

She undid the Velcro strap and removed it from her neck.

"Can you drop me off at the ski resort? I need to lie down, and I don't want to go back to the house. Ever."

"I don't blame you." Breck let go of the American Spirits and pulled out the car keys instead. "I'll get the guy who did this. Okay?"

Tya gently touched her throat and smiled.

"Okay."

CHAPTER 41

Mission Accomplished

At the Continental Divide Motel, Breck knocked on lucky Number Seven.
"It's open!"

Pushing open the door, he walked straight into a tangy cloud of stink. Billy James was lying on the bed, exactly where he had been lying the day before, and the trash can by the bed was brimming with yellow puke.

"Hedda Asbjorn is sitting in the car. If you think I'm bringing her in this hellhole, you're out of your mind." Breck propped open the door for circulation. "Get your ass out of that bed."

"No, I can't move." Billy groaned. "Did you bring me what I asked?"

Breck raised his eyebrows.

"Oh, you were serious?"

"Yeah, I'm serious."

There was an empty Pepto-Bismol bottle on the nightstand. Oh, well. Things had been too crazy to even think about running personal errands for this guy. Breck pushed open the motel room curtains, swept a wad of dirty towels off the recliner, and kicked them under the bed.

"All right, I'll see if she wants to come in."

He went back out to the Challenger.

"The man from Immigration is inside, but I've got to warn you. He's ill, and it's not a pretty sight in there. Would you like to come back another time?"

"No, I want to claim asylum right now."

So be it. Breck led her inside the motel room.

"Hedda Asbjorn, meet Customs and Immigration Officer Billy James."

Billy tried to sit up but immediately swooned and collapsed back on the mattress.

"I'm gonna sue Delta and the damn sushi company, and I'm gonna be a rich man, my friends. Filthy rich."

"Money isn't everything," Hedda muttered.

From the doorway, Breck had a good view of both the parking lot and the highway. If Aleks was following them, he was keeping his distance. Breck hadn't even seen the blue Suburban—not since he first spotted it, near the Sheriff's Office.

Beside the Challenger, there were only two vehicles parked at the motel. One was Valerie Matthews' rental, and the other was Aspen Matthews' clunker.

Billy James noticed Breck's posture and got serious. Holding his stomach with one hand, he pushed himself upright with the other. While his leather jacket was hanging on a coat hanger, he was still wearing the same clothes as before, and must have slept in them, too. Everything was wrinkled and stained.

"Something's got your radar buzzing. What is it?"

"We had a situation last night. Mrs. Asbjorn was nearly assaulted, and the suspect got away."

"You kidding me? I thought you had her in a secure location? This lady is a key witness in an international investigation. I'm talking the CIA, White House, and Seal Team Six."

Breck frowned.

"What do you mean?"

"Wish I could let you in, amigo. But this whole case is need-to-know, and you don't need to know."

A dark SUV sped past the motel on the highway, but it went by too fast. It could have been a Suburban, or it could have been a Ford Explorer, or something else entirely. There were too many SUVs on the road these days.

"Hedda?" Breck looked her in the eye. "What did the Russians want you to sign?"

"Don't answer that!" Billy wagged a finger. "You're in my custody now, and my responsibility. This sheriff has done his duty, poorly I might add, and his services are no longer required."

"As long as she's in this county, her safety *is* my responsibility. Besides, I've got a big stake in all this. I am conducting an investigation into the death of her husband, and she is the key witness. You can't shut me out."

"We won't be in your county much longer, pal. Give me the keys to my car, and then get out."

Billy James got out of bed, but he was lightheaded and stumbled across the room, grabbing the mini-fridge for balance. Breck stepped around him, for one final appeal. From the beginning, Hedda had been reluctant to talk. She had been in shock and she had been intimidated, stalked and threatened, and only now was she finally starting to trust him—but the clock was ticking.

"Please, Hedda," Breck said. "Tell me the truth. Why did the Russians kill Jansen and kidnap you if this wasn't about Bear Coin Capital?"

She stared out the window bleakly.

"They want Skogsøya."

"This conversation is over." Billy James grabbed Breck by the sleeve and hauled him into the parking lot, slamming the door behind them. "Game over, Barney Fife. Take a hike."

"I will. When I know she's safe."

"She's safe with me."

In the next motel room, Breck saw the curtains part. Aspen and Valerie's faces appeared behind the glass.

Breck lowered his voice.

"The man who tried to assault her last night? It was Khodorovsky's bodyguard, Aleks. The guy is violent and unpredictable. Until I have him behind bars, Mrs. Asbjorn is not safe. Whatever he wants, she has it."

Billy smiled confidently.

"I have an E4 black belt in Krav Maga. But if it puts your mind at ease to know my itinerary, I'll be driving her down to Denver first thing in the morning. Next stop, DC. But right now, I have a heap of paperwork and phone calls to make. Boss-man wants an update." He patted Breck on the shoulder, like a faithful dog. "Mission accomplished. Go home."

He held out his hand, expectantly.

Breck gave him the keys to the Challenger.

Billy James wobbled back into his motel room and slammed the door, and with that, Breck found himself standing alone in the asphalt parking lot of the Continental Divide Motel without a vehicle. His Jeep was still parked at the Hyatt Residence Club. How was he going to get back to the office? Jenny only had a mountain bike to putter around on.

"Sheriff Dyer?"

It was Aspen.

"Hey."

"Is everything all right?"

"Yep."

She came out of her mother's motel room, carrying a backpack on one shoulder.

"I'm heading off to class."

"Yeah?"

"Business Management 101. Kind of lame. I should be taking real classes in Boulder right now."

Breck suddenly remembered she had left a message at the Sheriff's Office.

"Oh, Aspen. I'm sorry I never got a chance to return your call. It's been busy."

She looked around the parking lot and then jingled her car keys.

"Are you stranded? Need a ride?"

"Sure."

He got into the passenger seat of her Corolla, and she drove towards town. The car had a strong odor—old pizza. Above the blur of passing pine trees, Breck stared at the snowy mountains all around them. What did Hedda say? Skogsøya? What did that mean?

"Sorry," Aspen said. "The heater is broken in this thing."

"The heater in my Jeep doesn't work, either." He smiled. "So, tell me about this scam at the fairgrounds."

Her knuckles turned white as she clenched the steering wheel.

"Oh, buddy. Don't get me started. . . ."

CHAPTER 42

Chess Game

Riding the chairlift at sunset felt like a zen moment—floating in the quiet calm, beneath a beautiful orange sky and fresh snow on the slopes.

Matthews wished he had someone with him to share the moment. Like his daughter. Or his ex-wife. Valerie might even melt a little and thread her arm through his and kiss his cheek like she used to when they first got married. Of course, that would never happen again. Not at this stage in the game.

But what about Tya? Maybe with the help of a little white wine?

Another time, perhaps.

This chairlift ride was a business trip. Matthews was going to the alpine hut to meet Senator Dana Stayne, and the only way to get there was the chairlift.

Building a café on the ridge above the ski slopes was Tya's idea after a ski trip to Chamonix. Alpine huts were all over the Alps. Some of them were simple small emergency shelters, but a lot were comfortable buildings with cafés inside. Having one in Quandary gave the town a European vibe, which Matthews thought was perfect. As mayor, it certainly had his stamp of approval. Anything to bring in more tourists and keep the money flowing was good for the city. And any excuse to spend time with Tya was a bonus. Too bad he wasn't going to meet her now—that girl was smoking hot, and he knew there was tension between her and Sven. If they got separated, she was fair game.

As soon as the bench dipped near the ground, Matthews jumped and ducked. Dismounting from the chair lift was a dicey game of dash or die. More than one sorry sucker got clocked in the back of the skull simply trying to get off the ride. It was a significant liability issue. An enclosed gondola would solve that problem. Why not ask Tya to dinner to discuss the issue? Over a bottle of white wine?

Matthews spotted Stayne through the café windows.

"How did she beat me up here?"

Even though he had left City Hall extra early to make the rendezvous, the senator was already there, waiting for him. It was the psychology of power. Whoever showed up second showed up late, and he hated that feeling.

He went inside, and took off his stocking cap and gloves. It had been a chilly ride up the mountain. Another reason for a gondola.

"Dana, have you tried the spice cake yet? It's amazing."

She waved him into a chair as if he needed permission to sit in her presence. That was irritating.

"Look at the sunset. Quite a view from up here." He unbuttoned his overcoat and sat down with as much dignity as he could muster. "Most people don't get to see the sunset from the summit of a twelve thousand foot mountaintop."

"Breck Dyer. I want him gone."

"I'm working on it, trust me. Have you seen the front page of the Quandary Herald this week?"

"I saw it. That was a smart move, Seneca."

Matthews kept a straight face, but inside he was dancing. She called him *Seneca*. She had never called him that before. The Ice Queen was warming up.

"We have less than two weeks until the election," she said. "A lot can happen in two weeks."

"Indeed."

"We need more ammunition to take Dyer down. What else do you have?"

"Debate dirt. Chief Waters will drop some bombs, and Breck will get booed off the stage. I'm coaching Max on what to say. And get this—I know the moderator, Mike Jameson. He thinks I walk on water, so I'll get the questions beforehand, and Breck won't know what hit him. There's not a chance in hell Dyer gets re-elected."

The senator's expression was flat. She didn't seem impressed.

"If you want to lock this election down, you need to make a big move."

"I agree."

What was she expecting? The Quandary Herald *was* his big move.

"Anatoli Khodorovsky."

Matthews arched an eyebrow. "Yes?"

"He needs to be released immediately. Put pressure on Dyer. Heavy pressure."

"I don't know. If Breck has evidence this man is involved in a murder, he can't just let him go. It's out of my hands. I can get the newspaper to write up another article, but that's the best I can do."

The Ice Queen reached across the table and put her hand on his. It took all he had not to wriggle away. Her little cucumber fingers sent ice through his veins.

"Listen to me. There is a bigger picture. A much bigger picture. Anatoli needs to be released immediately."

"What is the bigger picture?"

"Anatoli is a friend of mine, and I guarantee he had nothing to do with that man's murder. He is innocent. But he is also an international businessman, with many responsibilities to attend to in Russia. He simply can *not* remain locked inside a backwoods county jail." She retracted her frigid digits. "Did you know your ex-wife is filing a civil suit against you?"

"Yes, I do."

No, he did not. But he wasn't going to say that out loud. It would be just like Valerie to sue him out of spite.

"Litigation costs a fortune, Seneca. I'm not telling you anything you don't already know. But I can help."

Was a United States senator offering to help him fight his ex-wife? Financially? Why? Suddenly, Matthews felt like a pawn in a chess game.

"Get Anatoli out of prison. Make that your number one priority." She smiled again—an unsettling Ice Queen smile. "You're going to have fun telling everyone how a rich uncle bought you a boatload of Bear Coin. Just don't tell them I'm the uncle."

Up until a moment ago, he thought this whole situation was about a county election. But she was just using him, and his local petty squabbles, to get what she wanted. Which was what? A rich Russian businessman out of prison?

CHAPTER 43

While She Drowned

Aspen only had enough money to put in a half-tank of gas and hoped it would get her through until payday. And if she didn't get the heater fixed in the Crapolla soon, full winter ski gear would be a requirement, just to get behind the wheel.

"Why is everything so expensive?"

Unlocking the door to her apartment, Aspen went inside and threw her backpack on the sofa. It was a one-room studio, and the whole thing was smaller than her bedroom at her dad's house on Eyrie Road.

The Business Management course was a night class. It was two hours long and ran right through the dinner hour. People always brought snacks. Tonight had been pure torture. The tattooed emo, who sat in the back row, packed in a Zip-lock full of microwaved tater tots, and as soon as he opened the baggie, the smell filled the entire classroom. Aspen's mouth watered the whole time.

She rifled through the pantry, but there were only ramen noodles and peanut butter.

Quandary Community College. What a joke. What a joke her life was turning out to be. All her dad cared about was cinching his re-election. Her mom sat around chugging mimosas in a motel room. Between delivering pizza and writing boring essays, there wasn't much to do except lay on the sofa and wonder how she could rise above her circumstances. Go to school, they said. Get a career, they said. How was she supposed to do that with a degree from QCC?

Getting out her purse, Aspen counted how much cash she had left. It wasn't much. She was not in the mood for anything in her pantry. It was tempting to drive to High Country Pizza, even though this was her day off, and see if anyone had ordered a pizza and then forgot to pick it up. She could always eat cheaply at the Subway in Frisco, but it was a ten-minute drive in the wrong direction, and she didn't want to waste the fuel.

"Okay, ramen. I guess it's you and me."

Aspen turned on the stove and put a pot of water on the heater coil. Then there was a knock on the door.

"Hey, girl! We're coming in."

It was Adria and Fauna, two of her old roommates from CU, down in Boulder, with a six-pack of Mike's Hard Lemonade and a bottle of peach schnapps. They walked in and looked around, not even trying to hide their disgust.

"Look at this place," Adria said. "Don't tell me you live here."

"Look at this table," Fauna said. "Nasty."

She set the alcohol on the kitchen table. The table was mustard yellow, round and wobbly, and must have been built in the 1960s by a blind man. But for five bucks, it was a thrift shop score.

Aspen grinned.

"What are you two doing here?"

"Saving the day," Fauna said and hugged her. "It sucks that your dad cut you off."

"I can handle it."

"We texted like a million times. Did you get any of them?"

"No. My phone's on the fritz."

That was a lie. It wasn't on the fritz. Aspen just couldn't pay her phone bill. It was such a weird feeling not having a working phone. She felt cut off from the rest of the planet. At least she had the laptop. Her neighbor had WiFi and was kind enough to give her the password, so at least she could get on social media. Adria had sent her a message on Facebook earlier in the day, asking for her address. Now she knew why.

"I wish I knew you were coming," Aspen said. "I just got back from class, and I've got a paper to write."

"Give some nerd ten bucks to write it for you," Adria said.

She cracked open a hard lemonade and handed it to Aspen. Fauna opened one, too, and they all clinked bottles, just like old times.

Seeing her friends again stirred up all kinds of emotions. Joy, regret, hope, despair. It was such a nice thing to know somebody cared enough to drive up I-70 to see how she was doing. Aspen felt like her life stopped the moment she quit CU. She had only attended classes for her freshman year, but it was the best year of her life.

"What classes are you taking?" Aspen asked. "Got to be better than Business 101."

"I'm taking Film Studies this semester," Fauna said. "I wanna make award-winning investigative documentaries, and change the world through film. Werner Herzog is amazing. His tonality and framing are insane. My dad just bought me a Nikon D850 with a macro lens."

Aspen felt her heart sink a little. The girls meant well, but this was already spiraling somewhere she didn't want to go. Setting down her bottle of hard lemonade, Aspen grabbed her laptop and brought up *Save All The Pretty Horses*.

"Check this out. There's a fake horse rescue operating in Quandary County. I'm going to bust this thing wide open." She scrolled through the photos. The dun gelding was right there, black eyes staring through the computer screen, right into her soul. "The dude who runs it is a kill buyer. You know what that means?"

"No, what does that mean?" Adria asked.

"The guy buys horses at an auction and then sells them to a slaughterhouse."

"No way. That's wrong."

The girls scooted their chairs around so they could see better.

"Your dad's the mayor still, right?" Fauna asked. "Get him to do something."

"He won't do jack. But I'm going over his head. I've already told Dana Stayne about it. We had a face to face meeting."

"You mean, the senator?"

"Correct."

"That's crazy." Adria snapped her fingers, and turned to Fauna. "Maybe you should do a documentary about it? You've got the eye for it."

Then she poked Fauna in the eye.

"Ow!"

The next thing Aspen knew, the two girls were rolling on the floor, fighting. Hard lemonade went everywhere.

"Hey! What are you guys doing?"

Fists flew, hair got pulled, and then they rolled into the kitchen table, knocking it over. The peach schnapps hit the floor, and so did the laptop—keyboard letters scattered like marbles.

"What the hell?" Aspen shouted.

She had forgotten. When she was living in the dorm at CU, this sort of thing happened constantly. Drunken catfights. Fingernails and shin kicks. Usually, it was over a boy, but almost anything could send the girls into a frenzy when they had alcohol in their systems.

Aspen sank to the kitchen floor. Her laptop was ruined. Even if she could snap the keys back into place, half of them shot under the stove. Aspen relied on that thing for class, and she needed it for social media, too, especially without a working cell phone.

Brittany was going to laugh when she heard this. It was a lousy week for personal electronics.

But what was she supposed to do now?

Aspen threw it into the trash can, and then went to the stove. The water was boiling. Ignoring all the yelling and fighting, she opened a package of Ramen and submerged the block of dried noodles with a spoon, holding it underwater while it drowned—while she drowned.

CHAPTER 44

Darkest Before The Dawn

Shutting off the engine, Aspen put her head on the steering wheel and closed her eyes. She was parked in the parking lot at the Continental Divide Motel, between her mother's Ford Focus and her new neighbor's Dodge Challenger.

She had left her college friends passed out, drunk, in her apartment. Fauna was on the couch, her eyes swollen shut, and her forearms crisscrossed with red scratch marks. Adria had crawled into the bathroom before she finally went down in a puddle of peach schnapps and pee.

It was a bitter irony. Those girls were waltzing their way through their sophomore year at CU, Aspen's dream school. Her destiny. The giant granite slabs of the Flatirons rose above the campus like totems of achievement, a life path that was no longer hers to take for granted. The only thing rising above Quandary community college was an old Jiffy Lube sign they never took down.

"I hope they're gone when I get back."

Through the cracked windshield of the Corolla, she stared at Room Number Six. The metal numeral on the door was barely attached. Instead of fixing it properly, the manager had used yellow thumbtacks to hold it in place. How sad was that?

Life was sad. It could sure throw some cruel twists, too. Is this what was waiting for Aspen in a couple of decades? Living in a dumpy motel room, divorced, broke, and drowning her sorrows with mimosas? Aspen was already broke, but she had no intention of sliding down this existential slope any further.

"Things always seem darkest before the dawn."

Wasn't that a line from a country song?

She was going to Google it and find out—just as soon as she could pay her cell phone bill. It was time to turn her life around. Starting with the dun gelding.

Aspen kicked open the car door, ready to kick the world's ass, but it bounced back and slammed into her shin. Her car keys went flying and disappeared beneath her mom's rental car.

"Oh, come on!"

Kneeling on the pavement, Aspen tried to retrieve them, but of course, they had landed in the dead center of the vehicle, just out of reach. Did she do something to make the universe angry? Because everything seemed to be going wrong. Murphy's Law was supposed to be a silly saying, but it seemed pretty real at the moment.

Giving up on the keys, Aspen limped to her mother's door and almost knocked but noticed the next door over was open just a crack. Room Number Seven. It sounded like someone was smashing furniture. They must be having a worse day than she was.

Suddenly, the door to Room Number Eight opened, and a woman dashed out onto the sidewalk and ran straight towards her.

"Help me, please! Help!"

She was whispering, but Aspen immediately knew she was afraid for her life.

"What's wrong?"

"There is a murderer next door. My name is Hedda Asbjorn. I want to call the sheriff, please!"

A piece of furniture splintered inside Room Number Seven, and the woman cringed. She was white as a sheet. Aspen dashed towards the Corolla and reached in her pocket for the keys, but they weren't there. They were under the Ford Focus!

"You gotta be kidding me."

She ran to her mother's motel room, and, thankfully, found the door unlocked. As soon as both of them were safely inside, Aspen latched the deadbolt and drew the curtains tight.

Valerie was lying on the bed with her forearm resting over her eyes.

"Honey, is that you?"

"Yes, mom. Where's the phone?" Going to the dresser, Aspen grabbed the landline, but the receiver was broken and dangled by the wires like a dead rooster. "What happened to the phone?"

Valerie moaned but didn't answer the question. They could easily hear the noises next door, and then something hit the wall, causing the headboard to wobble. Valerie banged a fist against the floral wallpaper.

"Knock it off, over there!"

"Mom, give me your cell phone."

Aspen spotted her mother's purse on the dresser, hidden behind a row of empty champagne bottles. She rooted through it, pulling out makeup and a coin purse and wadded Kleenex, and all kinds of odds and ends. But no phone. Aspen dumped the whole thing upside down, but it wasn't there.

"Your father's lawyer called. Seneca is filing a countersuit. Somehow, he heard that I am suing, so he sicked his attorney on me." Valerie pointed at the broken telephone. "The man was a jackass, and I do not abide jackasses."

Aspen put her hands on her hips.

"Mom! Where is your cell phone?"

"Where's *your* cell phone? I've been trying to call you all day."

"I can't pay my phone bill, okay? I'm broke."

"Well, join the club." Valerie suddenly realized Hedda was in the room. "Who are you?"

The racket next door stopped.

The silence was eerie.

Hedda pressed her index finger to her lips to shush them. She dropped to the floor and tried to slither under the bed, but the gap was too small. Then she raced into the bathroom, and they heard her draw back the shower curtain and climb into the tub.

"Did you already say what's going on?" Valerie rubbed her eyes and sat up. "Tell me again. I'm listening now."

Gripping her mother by the arm, Aspen leaned close and whispered in her ear.

"We need to call Sheriff Breck. I think something bad is happening next door. This woman is freaked out, and so am I."

"It's somewhere in this bed, I think."

Aspen flung the pillows and tore off the blankets and sheets, but didn't find the cell phone. She tried the nightstand, but there was only a Gideon Bible and an old Yellow Pages phone book in the drawer.

"I hope I didn't drop it at the ice machine," Valerie whispered. The seriousness of the situation was starting to register, and she crab-crawled around the carpet, checking beneath each piece of furniture.

A shadow appeared on the curtain. Someone was walking past their room but stopped right outside the window. Aspen's pulse was pounding. She held her breath and stared at the shadow, willing whomever it was just to keep on moving.

After a moment, the shadow disappeared. Was it the motel manager? Did he hear all the commotion?

Resuming her search, Aspen ripped the cushion off the corner recliner and spotted her mother's phone, lying among bits of stale popcorn and sticky pennies.

"I found it!"

She punched 9-1-1.

"Sheriff's Office, this is Deputy O'Hara. How can I help you?"

"This is Aspen Matthews. I'm at my mom's motel, and there's something scary happening. A lady is here, and she's terrified. Hedda. She said her name was Hedda, something."

"The Continental Divide, right? Aspen, tell me which room you're in."

"Number Six. We're in Room Number Six. Please get here as fast as you can. Some guy just walked past the window . . . holy crap, he's back."

Aspen felt her heart sink. The shadow had returned.

"Lock the door and don't let him in," Jenny said. "We're on the way right now. We'll be there very soon. Just hang tight, Aspen."

"He's trying to look between the curtains, but I don't think he can see in."

Aspen's hands were trembling. The phone slipped out of her hands and landed on the floor, but Valerie snatched it up. She hit the hang-up button, punched a few numbers, and pressed it to her ear.

"Mom, what are you doing?"

The doorknob rattled.

"Seneca? It's me! I just want to say goodbye just in case we don't make it. Someone is trying to break into my motel room." Valerie pinched Aspen by the sleeve and dragged her towards the bathroom while she talked. "What? For the love of God, shut up about your idiot lawyer!"

CHAPTER 45

Getting Real

The speedometer ticked ninety the whole way. Whenever Breck drove that fast, he was nervous the soft top was going to rip off the Jeep and disappear in the night sky like a bat out of hell. The canvas was ancient, but somehow it held on.

Jenny was in the passenger seat, with her head between her knees, like they were on an airplane that was about to crash into the ocean.

"Hang on!"

Yanking his foot off the accelerator, Breck mashed the brake, and the Jeep skidded to a stop in the parking lot of the Continental Divide Motel. The smell of burnt rubber filled the air.

Jenny sat up and unbuckled her seat belt.

"We're too late!" she shouted.

The door to Room Number Six was hanging off its hinges.

They both jumped out and drew their guns. Breck went right, and Jenny went left. Aspen's Corolla, Valerie's Ford Focus, and Billy James's Dodge Challenger were all parked in a row, but other than that, the lot was empty. The manager drove a minivan, but he must have locked up for the night and gone home.

Just as they approached the doorway, Aspen peered out, holding a bottle of champagne like a club.

"Sheriff? Is he gone?"

Breck shined his flashlight at her, making her squint.

"Aspen, are you hurt?"

"No, I'm okay. You got here just in time. Whoever it was ran off."

"Where did he go?"

"I don't know. We all hid in the bathroom and locked the door. I heard someone break in and start tearing things apart. When he rattled the bathroom doorknob, I thought we were all dead." Aspen's voice was quivering. She tried to let go of the bottle, but her fingers wouldn't unclinch. She stared at her own hand like it was an alien. "But when we heard your siren. . . ."

Stepping past her, Breck tried the light switch but it didn't work, so he shined his flashlight around the motel room. The whole place was trashed, but he didn't see Aleks.

"Where is Hedda Asbjorn?"

"Inside the tub. My mom's in there, too."

He breathed a sigh of relief. Both Valerie and Hedda were safe. Aspen was safe. If they had arrived at the motel even one minute later, the situation might have been very different. But with Aleks still on the loose, all three of them were still in danger.

"Go back into the bathroom, and lock the door again. I'll let you know when it's safe to come out."

He raced back outside into the parking lot. Jenny was busy shining her flashlight inside the car windows, in case Aleks was hiding in any of the vehicles. Waving her over, Breck pointed at Room Number Seven.

"This is Billy James's room," he whispered.

After a silent countdown, he kicked open Billy's door and flipped on the light switch. It worked, and a desk lamp, lying on the carpet, clicked on. The room was a wreck. Mattress cockeyed, dresser on its side. A broken television. Billy's suitcase was upside-down, and his clothes were scattered all over the place. The last time Breck was in there, it smelled like puke, and the guy was so dizzy he couldn't see straight. But Billy James wasn't going to see anything anymore. He was on the floor, eyes bulging, blue in the face.

Breck knelt and checked for a pulse.

The man's neck was raw with abrasions.

"Jenny. Call an ambulance."

"Is he alive?"

"No. But call them anyway. And get the State Patrol up here, too. We're going to need some help."

Poor Billy. Getting choked to death was a rough way to go. And Tya, too— Aleks nearly choked her to death. The guy was a sociopath, and they needed to hunt him down before he could hurt anyone else.

Outside, car tires started kicking up gravel. It was too soon for the State Patrol to arrive. Breck ran back outside and saw a Suburban shoot around the motel and onto the highway.

Jenny dropped her phone and drew her Luger, but it was too late.

"Shit on a shingle!" she growled. "He was parked behind the building this whole time!"

Reaching inside the Jeep, Breck grabbed the CB mic.

"State Patrol, this is Sheriff Dyer. Be on the lookout for a late model Chevrolet Suburban, dark blue, southbound from the Continental Divide Motel. Consider the suspect armed and dangerous. Code 3."

The radio chirped.

"Lose another one, Dyer?" It was Chief Maxwell Waters. He was always listening to radio transmissions because he didn't have anything better to do.

Breck pushed the call button again.

"Be advised. An ambulance is en route. 10-53."

"You and your *Starsky and Hutch* ten codes," Waters radioed. "Just talk plain, and maybe I'll come help."

Breck dropped the mic on the driver's seat. He wasn't in the mood to trade barbs with Waters.

"You want to go after Aleks?" Jenny asked.

"Let the staties run him down. Our priority is Aspen, Valerie, and Hedda."

"I'll check on them."

While she went inside, Breck holstered his revolver and walked to the edge of the road. He heard distant police sirens and saw faraway flashing lights from both ends of the highway. The State Patrol was coming from Frisco, and the ambulance was coming from Quandary. But the first vehicle on the scene was none of those. It was Mayor Matthews in his BMW.

"Where's Aspen? Valerie? Are they okay?"

He left his car door open and ran towards the motel, but Breck intercepted him.

"Hold on. Jenny is speaking with them now, getting answers. Wait out here with me."

Matthews tried to push past him, but Breck stiff-armed him in the chest.

"I said, wait."

"Get out of my way."

But Breck wouldn't let him pass.

"This is a crime scene, and the suspect is still on the loose. Aspen and Valerie are safe, and you can see them in a minute, but right now, you'll just be a distraction. Let Jenny do her job."

Matthews glared at him but took a step back. He pressed his hands to his face and sagged against the Jeep fender. A State Patrol car shot by the motel, siren piercing. A second one raced into the parking lot and skidded to a stop. A trooper jumped out, and Breck pointed at Billy James's room.

"There's a Customs and Immigration officer down inside. He's dead. You want to help me secure the scene?"

"Sure, Breck."

While the trooper went inside to survey the situation, the blood drained from Matthews' face.

"Another murder? The man in the mine, and now. . . ." He turned to Breck, his eyes a little softer than before. "Val called me to say goodbye. She thought they were going to get killed. What happened?"

"I don't know why, but I know who."

Matthews frowned.

"Don't tell me you still think Khodorovsky is behind all this? You need to let him out of jail because you've got the wrong guy, obviously."

"This was Khodorovsky's bodyguard."

"What? That doesn't make sense. Why would his bodyguard go on a murder spree in Quandary? I've got it on good authority Khodorovsky is innocent, so something else is going on here. It has to be."

Breck leaned against the bumper, next to him. "Why do you say that?"

But Matthews cupped his hands over his face and stopped talking.

Breck studied him. Was he holding back tears? Or was he stressed about something else entirely? The man was always dabbling in something shady, and it wouldn't be a surprise if he knew more than he was going to admit. But now, everything was getting real for him. Too real. And maybe that's what it would take to get him to break.

Breck put his hand on the mayor's shoulder. It was a genuine gesture, but he felt Matthews tense up.

"This isn't a game," Breck said. "This guy was going to hurt Aspen and Valerie. Talk to me, Seneca."

"Don't call me that." His jaw clenched. "I want to see my daughter."

CHAPTER 46

Friends Or Enemies?

Standing at the kitchen sink in his home, Matthews filled the electric kettle with tap water. Behind him, in the living room, Aspen and Valerie were both curled up beneath a big fleece blanket on the couch. The television was on. It was an episode of MASH. Every time Matthews turned on the TV, that stupid show was on. But it was mindless escapism, and that's what his daughter and ex-wife needed right now. They were both staring at the screen, watching silly slapstick humor, and a never-ending stream of corny jokes.

The last thing they needed to see was the ten o'clock news. Some freelancer with a camera caught the police radio chatter and trailed the State Patrol to the motel. If the guy hadn't sold the footage to a Denver news station by now, then he was an idiot.

After switching on the kettle, Matthews rooted through the pantry for the Swiss Miss and marshmallows. That cheap motel. Valerie should have known better than to rent a room in that dump. The old guy who owned the motel was going to wake up to a massive lawsuit. Matthews was going to fix this. He was going to fix everything.

"Ptarmigan? Mommy says you can't pay your phone bill. I'll take care of it, okay?"

Aspen turned and gave him a hollow smile.

Breck was convinced the assailant at the motel was Khodorovsky's body-guard Aleks. That was insane. What purpose would that serve? His daughter told him they were sheltering a frightened woman named Hedda when it happened. That would be Hedda Asbjorn, wife of the newly deceased Bear Coin mogul. Whoever his murderer was, they must have come back for her. So why not shake down the local riff-raff? The tweakers. The junkies. That's where Matthews would have started. It was probably some low-life who thought kidnapping a rich guy would be easy money, and drugs were an expensive habit.

But what if Breck was right? If that was true, and Khodorovsky was pulling the strings, then why in the world would Dana Stayne vouch for him?

"Dad?"

Matthews looked up. "Yes, ptarmigan?"

"I don't want hot chocolate."

"You sure?"

"Put on a pot of coffee instead."

He turned off the electric kettle and got out the coffee grounds and a paper filter. She was trying so hard to act like an adult. Too tough to drink a little cocoa. Well, good for her—she shouldn't let this situation beat her down. The Matthews family weren't cowards. They were fighters.

He watched Aspen return to the couch and snuggle up with Valerie again. She was just a little girl! And Valerie? A middle-aged, mimosa guzzling drunk. They were a threat to nobody. Why would anyone want to hurt them?

Matthews felt his phone vibrating in his shirt pocket. He checked the caller ID. The Ice Queen. He jogged quietly upstairs and went into the bedroom before he answered.

"Good evening, Dana."

"Are we friends or enemies, Seneca?"

Every time they spoke, she skipped the small talk and went right for the kill. He wasn't quite sure how to respond, but he was sure she was about to throw down an ultimatum. This wasn't a welfare check. It was about cementing loyalty and ferreting out weaknesses.

"Friends."

"Then prove it to me."

Matthews peeked out the bedroom curtains. He had a clear view up and down Eyrie Road, but it was hard to see much in the darkness. The neighborhood Home Owners Association had decreed that bright bulbs were light pollution, so they put low-watt bulbs in all the street lamps. As a result, any cars parked along the curb were in the shadows. He spotted a vehicle across the street. It could belong to a neighbor, but Matthews' spidey senses were tingling.

"Breck thinks Anatoli Khodorovsky sent his bodyguard to murder the Asbjorn woman tonight," he said. "My daughter and wife were in that room. Are you a hundred percent certain this Russian is on the up and up? I need to know what's going on if I'm going to put my neck on the line."

There was a long silence. Matthews swallowed. It was the moment of truth.

"There are two paths for you to choose from," she said. "You can get Anatoli out of jail and get re-elected. Overnight, you'll get rich in Bear Coin and pay off your debts. You can put your daughter back in CU, buy her a nice car, and pay off your wife's mortgage and have plenty leftover for family brunches at the Blue Moose."

"I like that option."

"Or, you *don't* get Anatoli out of jail, and you *won't* get re-elected. I'll endorse Johnny Tibbs and give him the key to your closet—the one with all the skeletons in it. Not only won't you be mayor, but by this time next year, you'll be in prison."

"Prison?" Matthews frowned. "I haven't done anything illegal."

"I hear the DA's office is investigating Breck Dyer for corruption. They believe he was working hand in hand with the Los Equis drug cartel last year to profit from the sale of illegal drugs in Quandary County. They think he was the one who coordinated the cultivation of an illegal grow field in the mountains off Boreal Pass Road." Stayne sighed melodramatically. "If the DA learns that you were the one who had Zorrero on speed dial, things will go very differently."

Pulling the curtains tight, Matthews started searching his bedroom. He needed to search his office next. Was there a hidden camera or a microphone? How did she know so much about his life?

"As for me, I happen to have the *governor* on speed dial," Stayne added. "Now, when I call him, do I tell him I am endorsing Seneca Matthews for mayor of Quandary? Or Johnny Tibbs?"

Matthews could feel those cold cucumber fingers seizing his scrotum, and she wasn't even standing in the room.

"We are friends, Dana. Good friends. I'm happy to pull some strings and get Mr. Khodorovsky released. Give me twenty-four hours."

"Good. Let's not speak of this again."

She disconnected.

Was it true Khodorovsky's bodyguard killed Jansen Asbjorn in the Keystone Mine? Was it true he killed a Customs officer at the Continental Divide Motel? Was it true they almost took out his family in the process? It could all be true, but the only truth that mattered at the moment was that he might lose the election, his family, his bank account, and his freedom—if he didn't play along.

"What is truth?" Matthews muttered.

Heading downstairs, he nearly bumped into Aspen in the kitchen.

"Where did you go, dad?"

"Sorry, honey. I had to run upstairs for a moment."

She opened a cabinet and stood on her tiptoes but couldn't reach the mugs. Matthews gently took her by the shoulders and pointed her towards the living room.

"Here, let me do that. I'll bring it to you. You want cream and sugar?"

"Yeah, both."

"Okay, go sit down. It will just take a second."

She slowly shuffled back into the living room and got under the fleece blanket. Valerie was asleep, and Aspen closed her eyes and dropped off, too. Matthews wished he could crawl in there, one big happy family, but it wouldn't go over so well. Both of them had good reasons to hate him. And yet, here they were, all three of them, under the same roof again.

He wished the moment would last forever. But it wouldn't. Soon, he would go back upstairs, crawl into an empty bed, and chug some NyQuil. Without that cherry-flavored nectar, he'd lay awake all night long and worry about the long list of things he needed to do to survive another day. But that was what life was about, wasn't it?

Survival.

CHAPTER 47

Little Annoying Bugs

Breck cut the engine, and the Jeep shuddered to a standstill. The Sheriff's Office looked ghostly in the moonlight. Overhead, some of the clouds had broken apart, and the Big Dipper was easy to spot. Using it as a pointer, he found the North Star.

True north.

Just a pinprick in the darkness.

The ambulance had taken Billy James's body back to the hospital. There was barely room in the morgue for another body, but what else could they do? Put him in the walk-in cooler at the brewery? Danny wouldn't like that. And neither would the health inspector.

Breck glanced over at Hedda. She was strapped into the passenger seat, gazing out the window at nothing in particular. Jenny was in the back of the Jeep, cramped on the tiny bench seat.

"We need to find a secure location," he said.

"There's not too many options." Jenny leaned forward. "I guess Tya's house isn't exactly a safe spot anymore. And she can't bunk in the office, can she? Not with you-know-who inside."

"Nope."

"Well, we can rule out the motel. And she can't go back to the Hyatt. Not with that freakshow, Aleks, on the loose."

Breck itched his cheek. He needed a shave.

"I wonder if Tya has fixed her apartment door yet?" he said.

Jenny got out her cell phone.

"Let me text her and ask."

Breck took out his cell phone, too. "You do that. I need to call Customs and tell them what went down."

He pushed open his door and slid out onto the pavement. A light wind was blowing, so he zipped up his jacket. It was downright chilly. A few leaves fell from nowhere and landed on the hood while he scrolled through his contacts. Major Jonathan McMurray, Department of Homeland Security. Customs and Immigration was a wing of the department, somewhere in the mix. He would know what to do. Breck dialed, but it was two hours later in Washington DC, and long after business hours. What was he going to do—leave a message? *Officer down, call me back in the morning, and I'll give you the deets.*

"Come on, pick up."

Breck began to pace around the parking lot to keep warm.

McMurray was a Military Assistant to the Homeland Security Secretary. Breck had met the man a few years earlier. A Hollywood movie company was filming a boxcar chase scene along some railroad tracks in Quandary County, and they hired McMurray as an on-set firearms consultant. It was some kind of James Bond type of flick. Both of them owned a .44 Special revolver and instantly bonded.

It rang several more times, but just before it went to voicemail, McMurray answered.

"Hello? Breck? I've got about thirty seconds before I head into a meeting. What's up?"

"I have bad news. A Customs and Immigration officer was killed tonight."

"What? In Quandary?" McMurray's voice became tense. "Don't tell me it was Billy James?"

Breck was shocked. There had to be hundreds of employees at Homeland. "Yeah. Did you know him?"

"Are you certain he's dead? It would take some serious firepower to take Billy out."

"Sorry, John. I'm the one who found him."

It sounded like he put his hand over the receiver and talked to someone else for a moment.

"Breck? Billy James was running an op for me. He was supposed to bring in a man named Jansen Asbjorn and his wife, Hedda Asbjorn. They were planning to claim political asylum. But when he arrived in Quandary, Billy called to tell me Jansen was dead. Now, Billy's dead, too? What's the wife's status?"

"She's safe."

"Alright. Listen. I'm hopping on a plane first thing tomorrow morning. I will personally escort Mrs. Asbjorn back to DC. Keep her safe until I arrive."

It felt like the temperature was dropping. Breck shivered. It was tempting to light a cigarette, but he knew Jenny wouldn't like that. He walked over to the front window of the Sheriff's Office, and looked inside. Khodorovsky was in his cell, stretched out beneath a blanket, as if he didn't have a care in the world.

"Remember those fingerprints I sent you?" Breck asked. "You said they were Anatoli Khodorovsky's. Well, those prints connect him directly to Jansen Asbjorn's murder, and I arrested him for it. But his bodyguard, Aleksandr Medved, is still on the loose. He's the one who killed Billy."

"Holy hell." McMurray hesitated like he wanted to say more. "This is big, Breck. I'll brief you in person when I see you. I don't want to say any more over an open line. Please, don't let Khodorovsky out of your sight, and keep Mrs. Asbjorn safe until I get there."

"Will do."

Breck put his phone back in his pocket and returned to the Jeep. He unzipped the rear panel, so Jenny wouldn't have to squirm over the driver's seat to get out. Hedda was still sitting quietly, staring off into space. After yet another near-death Aleks experience, she had gone silent again. Who could blame her?

Once Jenny jumped onto the pavement, Breck zipped the panel closed, so they could talk privately.

"What did Tya say?" he asked.

"Her apartment door is still broken. A repairman is coming by tomorrow, but Tya is too freaked out to stay there by herself. And she doesn't want to go home, either. Not until she gets better security installed at both places."

"That's smart."

As they talked, Breck glanced up and down Main Street. *Where are you, Aleks?* He could be anywhere, waiting for the right moment to attack. He could be sitting in his Suburban, watching them through binoculars, or staking out the ski resort or Tya's house. He could be holed up in the Presidential Suite back at the Hyatt or on his way to the airport in Denver, hoping to sneak out of the country before he got flagged on a watch list. It was anybody's guess.

"What did Customs have to say?" Jenny asked.

"Major John McMurray will be flying here tomorrow, to escort Hedda back to DC to process her asylum request."

"That name sounds familiar."

"He's the same guy who left a message the other day about the fingerprints on the Asbjorn's Hyatt keycard."

"Well, good. This will all be over soon." Jenny yawned. "As for tonight, Tya asked if she could crash at my place. She's on her way over now. Hedda might as well stay with me, too. You heading home?"

"No, I'll sleep here tonight and keep an eye on Anatoli."

"Before you get in your jammies, would you bring over a couple of spare cots?"

Jenny opened the passenger door, and helped Hedda slide out of the Jeep. Breck was expecting a snarky comment about stepping stools, or how he should install a ladder for short people, but Jenny didn't say anything. Taking Hedda by the hand, she began to lead her down the sidewalk to her cottage.

"I'll bring those cots over in a few minutes," Breck called.

"Don't take too long. It's way past bedtime."

It was a decent plan. Since Jenny's rental cottage was only two blocks away, he could run down there if Aleks tried to attack Hedda in the middle of the night. And if Aleks tried to break into the Sheriff's Office to spring Anatoli, Breck could call Jenny for backup.

He unlocked the Sheriff's Office and went inside.

"I saw you out there, talking on your phone," the Russian said, ripping off his blanket and sitting up. He looked irritated. "I hope you were consulting with your lawyer."

"Why is that?"

"You have detained an innocent man, and I am nervous to think what kind of repercussions will strike you as sheriff."

Extra cots were stacked in the second jail cell, behind a pile of split wood they used for the potbelly stove. He was going to have to tie them on the roof of the Jeep, but it was a short drive. Choosing two, Breck starting for the door but noticed the little red light on the answering machine was blinking. He set the cots on the floor beside his desk.

"I have powerful associates who will not allow this miscarriage of justice to go unpunished." Khodorovsky rapped his knuckles on the bars. "And, of course, I will file a lawsuit against you for wrongful imprisonment."

Breck pressed the play button. It was just a couple of complaints about the newspaper story again. Nothing worth saving. As he hit the delete button, there was a knock on the door.

"Perhaps that is one of my associates now," Khodorovsky said.

Breck frowned. No lawyer would be knocking on the door at this hour. Would Aleks be so bold as to knock on the Sheriff's Office's front door? Maybe. Breck drew his revolver and went to the window, but it wasn't Aleks—it was Tya. Her Land Rover was parked next to his Jeep. The whole front end was crumpled, from crashing into the tree at the end of her driveway.

He put the gun back in its holster and opened the door.

"Hey."

"Hi, Breck. I was on my way to Jenny's place, so I thought I'd stop by and say hello. See how you're holding up. She said another person got killed at the motel. Strangled. Was it the same guy who attacked me?"

"Yes, it was."

The color went out of her cheeks.

"Would you like to sit down for a minute?" he asked.

"Okay."

Breck offered her a chair at Jenny's desk. He didn't want to tell Tya the details and hoped she didn't ask too many questions. Her neck was still bruised. Aleks probably meant to choke her to death that night in her garage.

"I'm sorry you don't feel safe enough to sleep in your own bed tonight," he said. "But we'll get this guy. This will be over soon, I promise."

Tya smiled weakly.

"I've got a construction crew coming to the ski resort tomorrow. They're going to install an entirely new door—made out of steel instead of wood. Plus, more security cameras and a panic room. That place will be safer than Fort Knox. After that, they're going to put in a new alarm system in my house, too."

"That's good," Breck said.

In his cell, Khodorovsky was listening to every word they said. He spotted a spider crawling up the back wall, went over, and slapped it flat.

"Little annoying bugs get squashed."

"Just ignore him . . . that's what I do." Breck smiled to put her at ease. "Since you're here already, would you mind looking at that Norwegian document I was telling you about? It won't take long."

"Okay."

He went to the evidence locker and spun the dial until it clicked. He took out the blood-smudged paper from the Asbjorn's suite and set it on the desk in front of her.

"Can you tell me what this is?"

Tya studied it for a moment.

"It's a real estate purchase agreement. Proof of sale."

"For Bear Coin Capital?"

"No, for Skogsøya. It's a little island that Jansen and Hedda own, off the south coast of Norway. They go there every summer. Skogsøya translates to Forest Island."

"An island?"

"I've been there," Tya said. "It's very nice. Lots of trees, a beautiful house on the shore. Sauna, swimming pool, tennis courts. You can watch sea eagles diving for fish from the pier. They even have a helipad and a private helicopter to take them back and forth from the mainland. It's very peaceful."

That didn't make sense. A wealthy Russian oligarch could easily afford to purchase a private island anywhere in the world. Why would Anatoli want the Asbjorn's summer getaway so bad that he was willing to track them to a little ski town in the Colorado Rockies? And kill for it?

CHAPTER 48

Giddy Up

Jenny rooted around in her fridge. The light bulb had blown a long time ago, and she never got around to replacing it, so all the organic items hiding in the rear had taken on a life of their own. It was a jungle back there.

"Do you like yogurt?"

Didn't she just go to the grocery store the other day? If Jenny had known she was going to have overnight guests, she would have loaded up on frozen pizzas instead of yogurt.

"I do have a frozen meal left if you want it. Don't let the brand name spook you. Hungry Man—but it works for hungry ladies, too."

She looked at Hedda, hoping for a smile. But Hedda was seated silently at the kitchen table, her eyes drifting across the tabletop. It was covered in loose mail and coupon clippings, empty coconut water cartons, and a pile of wadded Subway sandwich wrappers. Jenny's laptop was buried in there, too, but Hedda spotted it.

"May I use your computer?"

"Sure."

That was the first coherent sentence she had managed to say since the motel. On the walk over from the Sheriff's Office, Jenny tried chatting but didn't get more than a yes or no response. Why didn't the Russians just leave this poor woman alone?

When Breck dropped off the cots, he informed Hedda that McMurray was coming to take her back to DC. She seemed relieved. Jenny was looking forward to his arrival, too. Not having to worry about guarding Mrs. Asbjorn night and day would be a big thing off their plate. Then they could focus on hunting down Aleks and putting him behind bars. It would be helpful if another local police agency could lend a hand, hunting him down. Too bad Chief Waters was such a flaming turd. The State Patrol was spread too thin to do more than they already had, and unfortunately, quite a few of them were turds, as well.

Tya was curled up on the couch, watching some reality show about the Coast Guard in Alaska. A helicopter hovered over a capsized boat, lowering a diver into the ocean on a cable. Jenny went over and gave her a yogurt.

"That would be one sweet job."

But Tya was zoned out. She must be exhausted, too, with all the crazy crap going on. Now that she had translated the Norwegian document, they knew it was a real estate purchase agreement, between the Asbjorns and Khodorovsky, regarding their summer getaway island. Maybe Hedda would be willing to open up a little, and talk about it, now that she was safe and help was on its way. Couldn't hurt to try.

Jenny went back into the kitchen and sat at the table.

"What's so special about your island?"

Hedda shook her head sadly.

"Why didn't you just sign, Jan?" she mumbled.

Jenny squeezed her forearm.

"Listen. We've got Khodorovsky locked up, and tomorrow you'll be on an airplane to Homeland Security headquarters. It's all over."

Hedda's eyes got watery. She had cried many times off and on, ever since she appeared in the ski resort lobby. That seemed like a long time ago, but it wasn't.

"It's okay to talk about it," Jenny said. "The more we know, the more we can help."

"I am not sure why they want Skogsøya so badly. But I can't even think about that now. The Russians are the least of my problems. Look."

She showed Jenny her email page on the laptop. There were dozens of new messages, with unpleasant subject lines.

Show Me The Money!

$@!% Thief.

I Will Sue You.

The list went on, and it didn't get better. Jenny frowned.

"What's going on?"

"All these emails are from Bear Coin investors. Everyone is frustrated with Jansen. No one can access their cryptocurrency."

"Why not?"

Hedda covered her eyes and slumped in her chair.

"Bear Coin has $190 million in cold storage," she whispered. "But only Jansen had the access key."

"I'm not sure I understand. Where's the key? Was it in his pocket? I don't remember seeing a key chain in his personal effects."

"It's not a real key." Hedda's lips quivered. "It is a digital key—a series of passwords. Everyone's cryptocurrency is being held in a cold wallet, in cyberspace. Jansen had it memorized so that hackers couldn't break in. He is the only one who knows . . . knew. . . ."

The doorbell rang.

It was showtime.

Jenny jumped up, and cautiously approached the front door. Breck had already come and gone. Was it Aleks? Who else would it be? If he had been surveilling the Sheriff's Office, in the shadows, watching and waiting, it would have been simple to trail them to her rental cottage. Why didn't she ask Breck to drive around the block a few times and sneak Hedda in the back door? How stupid was that?

Jenny was still wearing her belt holster, and put her palm on the pistol grip and checked the peephole, but all she saw was a cowboy hat. Frickin' Johnny Tibbs.

She opened the door.

"What's up, Johnny?"

He looked her up and down.

"I thought you'd be in that little black dress by now. We gotta run, or we'll miss the hors d'oeuvres."

It took her a second to figure out what he was talking about, but then it hit her: the ProRodeo Hall of Fame fundraiser. Oops.

"Was that tonight?" she asked.

"Throw on that dress and some ruby red lipstick, and let's roll."

"Sorry, cowboy. I've got company. You're going to have to cut cattle all by yourself tonight."

"I love steak, and I love steak puns. That's why you're coming with me." He looked past her shoulder and saw Hedda at the kitchen table and Tya on the couch watching television. "Send your friends home. You can do girls' night anytime."

Stepping outside onto the doormat, Jenny eased the door halfway shut. His shiny Ford F-350 pickup truck was idling by the curb. A couple of cars drove by, and some teenagers were walking down the sidewalk towards Starbucks, staring at their cell phones. Other than that, Main Street was quiet. Maybe Aleks wasn't out there after all. Maybe he was on a jet plane headed for Moscow.

"Look, Johnny. I can't breakaway. We've got a serious situation going down, and I'm on the clock until it's resolved."

"What could be more important than steak with Johnny Tibbs? Besides, you're too cute to stay home on a Friday night."

Jenny smiled and brushed back some stray strands of red hair. He was full of it, but it was still nice to hear.

"Giddy up and get off my porch."

CHAPTER 49

A Favor To Ask

"Time to fatten the turkeys. Gobble up!"

In the morning sunshine, Luke Roberts throttled the Bobcat skid steer, dumping a thousand-pound bale of grass hay in the mud. Two dozen hungry horses were watching nervously and waited until he drove the noisy machine back through the pasture gate before they moved in to eat.

The skid steer had a special three-pronged spear attachment so he could jab the hay and transport it from the barn to the pasture without breaking a sweat. He used to buy sixty-pound square bales from a guy in Westcliffe, a hundred miles away, and spend a full day loading hundreds of them by hand onto a flatbed trailer, then another full day stacking them in his hay barn, bale by bale. It was a back-breaking chore, and he hated it. So one day, he bought the old skid steer for next to nothing, off a no-name father and sons construction company that went belly up. Luke paid full price for the spear attachment at the feed store, but it was worth every penny.

Plus, the skid steer ran on diesel fuel, and Luke loved the smell of diesel fumes. His pickup was diesel, too. Only a city slicker would drive a pickup truck that ran on standard gasoline.

Luke lived in an old 1970's mobile home in a narrow mountain valley. He chose the spot because, number one, no other soul lived within a ten-mile radius. And number two, it had everything he needed to keep horses on-site without having to do much work—like the old wooden cattle pen. Some vaquero hammered it together a hundred years ago, and it was still standing. Also, a creek ran through the valley, so horses could drink all they wanted, and he didn't have to invest in a water tank—one less thing to buy.

Luke parked the skid steer and headed inside his mobile home.

He buttered some bread, peeled off the plastic from some fake cheese slices, and fired up the stovetop. It was grilled cheese time. Now the question was, did he have any of those jalapeño flavored Cheetos left?

Before he could find out, Luke saw a flash. Sunlight reflected off a car window. Someone was driving up the dirt road. *His* dirt road. Didn't they see the No Trespassing signs? Probably some old couple made a wrong turn onto his property, looking for autumn colors. Happened every fall. People were stupid.

Luke Roberts grabbed his deer rifle. He had no intention of shooting anyone. He just liked to give the oldies a scare. But to his surprise, it wasn't senior citizens. Two women in a fancy Audi parked in front of his mobile home and got out. Both had short hairspray hairdos, pantsuits with silk blouses, and expensive-looking sunglasses.

"You look like Jehovah's Witnesses. Turn that car around and get the hell out of here."

"Mr. Roberts? How do you do?" One of the ladies was older than the other. She didn't even blink at his deer rifle. "My name is Dana Stayne, and I am a Colorado state senator. Your representative in Congress."

Luke shouldered the rifle and hooked a thumb in his belt loop.

"You here to ask for my vote? I don't vote for nobody, never."

Stayne didn't try for a handshake or even take off her sunglasses to be polite. "So, this is the Blue River Horse Rescue."

"Maybe."

Luke was shocked. He never told anyone his address. If someone bought one of the horses from his *Save All The Pretty Horses* website, he trailered the animal to the county fairgrounds as a meeting point. He didn't want any animal-loving crusader to find out where all the horses were kept and turn them loose. Or worse, set up a picket line at his front gate and post updates on their social media pages.

"You like money, don't you?" she asked.

"Maybe."

The senator snapped her fingers, but they didn't make any noise—like rubbing two dill pickles together on a hot summer day. The other one, a skinny woman with bright red lipstick, instantly produced an envelope. She held it out like bait on a hook. It was full of hundred dollar bills.

"For you, Mr. Roberts."

The senator spoke in a no-nonsense tone, but it was hard not to smile. This was the second time someone had waved an envelope full of money under his nose this week. First, those girls at the auction, and now a state senator. And it was the second time Luke turned it down.

"I don't take government handouts."

"Think of it as a friendly gesture. And, as your friend, I have a favor to ask."

"I don't do favors."

This was taking forever. Most conversations Luke had were over in seconds. His grilled cheese was going to be burnt to hell.

Stayne took off her sunglasses.

"You're a kill buyer, Luke. You call this a horse rescue? I call it a front. When you signed up as a non-profit organization with the federal government, you committed tax fraud. But I understand—everyone's got to make a living. Relax. I'm not here to bust you. I'm here to help. What if the sheriff comes after you? What if he gets an anonymous tip from a concerned citizen? I happen to know you're on his radar. Wouldn't it be nice to have someone in a high position of power to protect you from going to jail?"

The woman was bold, given the fact he was holding a rifle. Luke grinned.

"And let me guess. You're that person?"

She grinned back.

"I am."

But Luke's smile faded away as he thought about what she was saying. Fraud? Jail? If the sheriff started poking around and asking questions, then maybe he did need some help.

He took the envelope and flipped through the bills.

"What kind of favor?"

CHAPTER 50

Another Trap

Tya was lying on a cot in Jenny's living room when she got a text from Cash.
It's a work zone over here. Construction crew arrived. They brought loads of wires, cameras, lumber, and steel.

That made her feel a whole lot better. Plus, a private security company from Denver was on their way up I-70 and should arrive soon. They would post guards in the lobby, night and day. All these things added up to a small fortune, but who said money couldn't buy peace of mind?

Tya set her phone down and yawned.

"Get any sleep?" Jenny asked from the couch.

"Not a wink."

"Me, either."

"How many episodes of the Alaska Coast Guard show did we watch?"

"Every single one."

Crossing the room, Jenny peeked into the bedroom to check on Hedda, then tiptoed to the kitchen and started making coffee. Watching her, Tya smiled. Jenny was wearing a gunbelt over her pajamas—her Luger was on her hip. The girl was an animal. If the Russian bodyguard had tried to break into the cottage, he would have had a fight on his hands. But he hadn't. The night had passed quietly, and now the sun was shining.

Tya began to feel like everything was going to be okay.

"I'm going to head over to the ski resort. There's a construction crew over there, working on my apartment, and I want to make sure they're doing it right."

Jenny looked skeptical.

"Well, I need to stay here with Hedda. You sure you want to go alone?"

"It'll be okay." Then she felt butterflies in her stomach. "Would you mind checking the backseat of my Land Rover?"

Jenny gave her a travel mug full of fresh coffee and searched her SUV to make sure no one was hiding inside. Tya wondered if she would ever jump into the front seat again, without looking over her shoulder. Probably not.

When she arrived at the ski resort, Cash stared at her with the most remorseful eyes she had ever seen.

"Mrs. Tordenskjold? I'm so glad you're okay. I want to apologize for everything."

"It wasn't your fault."

"I should have seen the dude. I don't know how he got by me." His eyes focused on her neck and the bruises. "I'll never smoke weed again."

"The guy who did this was no amateur. Trust me, he could have snuck past Chuck Norris."

While they were watching TV, Jenny had explained that the guy who attacked her was a Russian with hardcore military training. How crazy was that? It was straight out of a spy novel. He broke into her apartment, set off the alarm, and lured her to the ski resort. While she went inside, he crawled into the backseat of her SUV and hid there the whole time.

While she listened to the radio.

While she rolled down her window and chatted with Breck.

While she opened the big iron gate that protected her driveway.

He had remained unseen and unnoticed until she parked the Land Rover in her garage and shut off the engine.

Tya dipped her hand inside her purse. It was reassuring to feel the cold steel of the .45 Magnum. If anyone ever attacked her again, she wouldn't hesitate to use it.

"I'm heading upstairs to check on the construction crew," she said. "Call me as soon as the security team gets here, okay?"

Still looking morose, Cash sank into the chair behind the reception desk.

"By the way, Mr. Tordenskjold is here."

"What?" Tya turned and looked around. "Where?"

"The alpine hut. He said he would wait for you in the café."

Sven was in town? This could only be about one thing—divorce papers. Oh, well. Might as well get this over with.

Walking past the elevators, she headed down the hallway towards the other side of the building, which faced the ski slopes. Voices carried from the conference hall. The arrest of Anatoli Khodorovsky and Jansen Asbjorn's death hadn't put a damper on anyone's interest in cryptocurrency.

As soon as she got outside, Tya put on her sunglasses. It was good to see a little snow on the slopes. It almost put her in the mood for skiing. But her enthusiasm waned because she knew Sven was going to fight her over the ski resort. It was a big moneymaker, and he wasn't going to simply walk away and let her keep it.

But when she got to the chairlift, Tya didn't get on.

She gently touched her throat.

The memory was fresh—regaining consciousness, her vision blurry and her throat on fire. Throwing the Land Rover into reverse and speeding out of the garage. Her neck still hurt from the man's grip and the whiplash from wrecking her SUV.

Now a Customs and Immigration officer was dead, too. What was going on in Quandary? Tya wondered what Sven would say when he heard all this? When he learned Jansen Asbjorn had been murdered? When he saw the bruises on her neck?

Sounds like it's been a rough week. Let's get divorced.

The chairlift continued to hum overhead.

Forget it. She wasn't going to walk into another trap—not today.

Stone-Cold Politician

It was well into the afternoon. Major John McMurray, and whatever muscle he was bringing from DHS, hadn't shown yet. Breck was getting antsy. Whenever he tried calling McMurray, he got an automated message explaining how the cell phone number Breck was trying to reach was unavailable. Jenny kept texting him, wondering if the cavalry had arrived yet, but the answer was always no. She was going just as stir crazy as he was.

The landline rang.

"Sheriff's Office. This is Breck."

"This is Foreign Minister Sergei Lavrov, at the Consulate General of the Russian Federation. I understand you have arrested Anatoli Khodorovsky. Release him immediately."

"Wrong number."

Breck hung up.

Where was McMurray and his team? The day was slipping away.

After staying awake all night and skipping breakfast, Breck knew he had to eat something. It was tempting to dial the brewery and order a cheeseburger, but that would require a conversation with his younger brother. The first thing out of Danny's mouth would be: *Where's my camera?* But Breck had a feeling that he might need it again before this investigation was over.

From his jail cell cot, Khodorovsky was staring at the stained glass window in the wall above Breck's desk. It depicted a pale white dove hovering against a rich blue background, with a yellow cross glowing in the middle.

"What does the dove represent?"

"You hungry?" Ignoring him, Breck peeled a magnet advertisement off the door of the kitchenette fridge. High Country Pizza. "I hope you like pepperoni."

Outside, a car door slammed.

Finally. It had to be DHS.

Breck hurried to the window, but all he saw in the parking lot was a silver BMW. Then, Mayor Matthews barreled through the front door, and he didn't look happy.

"You gotta be kidding me. Why is this man still locked up?"

"Because he's a murder suspect."

Matthews went to the cell and looked Khodorovsky over.

"Dammit, Dyer. This man has been wearing the same clothes for a week." He waved his hand in front of his nose. "And he's ripe. Even prisoners deserve clean clothes and a shower. This is a county jail, not a gulag."

Slowly sitting up, Khodorovsky studied Matthews. "Who are you?"

"Mayor Seneca Matthews. I run this town."

Breck drummed his fingers on the desk. Where was DHS?

"Do you even know who this is?" Matthews shook his head in disbelief. "You didn't slap the cuffs on a local pickpocket, Dyer. This gentleman was at the crypto conference for a reason, and he's got some mighty deep pockets. He was going to invest in Quandary, for crying out loud. You think he will now? After what you've put him through? And his lawyer is going to go ballistic when he hears about these third world accommodations."

Groaning, Khodorovsky got to his feet and held his back awkwardly.

"May I have a simple glass of water?" He looked at Matthews with doe-eyes. "Or a bowl of porridge? Please help."

"Look at this poor guy!"

"This poor guy should take an acting class," Breck said.

After Matthews stewed for a moment, he came close and tried to put his hand on Breck's shoulder.

"Breck, buddy. I'm trying to save you from a heap of litigation. You're already under investigation for corruption. The DA is building his case against you right now, and when he springs it on you, you're going to wish you had nothing else on your plate to distract you. It'll take everything you got to keep your job and stay out of jail yourself."

Matthews never called Breck by his first name. It was always Dyer this or Dyer that.

"Did you come here for a reason?" Breck asked.

"I came to tell you . . . thank you." A pause. "Did you hear me?"

"Yeah. And I'm waiting for the punchline."

"I'm serious. My ex-wife and daughter are safe because of you."

That almost sounded legit, the way he said it. What was the game here?

Crossing the room, Matthews slid his hands in his pockets and gazed out the window at the passing cars. It was a long, awkward silence. When he finally turned around, his face had softened into a mix of regret, frustration, and relief.

"Listen. Forget about everything I just said. I've got your back."

"Are you feeling all right?"

"I'm sick of Dana Stayne jacking me around. She says if I do what she says, she'll endorse me. Yeah, well, screw that. And you know what else? The DA doesn't have anything on you. At least nothing he can prove."

Had the man lost his mind? Breck was struggling to compute what he was hearing. For the past four years, ever since Matthews became mayor, he had nothing to offer Breck but scorn.

"So what are you trying to say?"

"Nothing. That's it."

Matthews pulled out his car keys and grinned, but it was a war-weary smile. His footsteps echoed as he walked towards the front door.

"Watch out for Senator Stayne. She wants your badge."

"Hold on." Breck eyed him suspiciously. "Explain."

Matthews checked to see if Khodorovsky was listening, which he was.

"She wants you to cut him loose."

"Why?"

"I don't know," Matthews said. "But she's trying to bully *me* into putting pressure on *you*. My guess? If you release this guy, she'll claim you're colluding with the Russians. I think it has to do with the sanctuary policy thing."

Ah, that made sense. Not too long ago, Stayne had tried to convince the governor to declare Colorado a sanctuary state, to give criminal illegal aliens safe harbor from federal ICE agents. It was all optics, a ruse to get more votes by playing off of people's compassion for immigrants, but it was dangerous logic. Violent crimes would go unprosecuted, and bad guys released out of political stupidity. Breck wrote an op-ed for the Denver Post, taking a vocal stand against it. Many other county sheriffs followed his lead, and then the governor caved, and that ticked Stayne off. So, was that it? She had a grudge to settle?

"Valerie and Aspen," Breck said. "Doing okay?"

"Yeah, they're recovering at my place."

"Thanks for the heads up."

"Sure," Matthews said. "I still owe you big for keeping my family safe."

"No problem."

Matthews cast a glance at the jail cell.

"You got proof he killed Jansen Asbjorn?"

"Yep," Breck said.

"Is it rock solid?"

"We've got his fingerprints on the Asbjorns' hotel key card, and a Norwegian real estate document, for motive."

Matthews thought for a moment. "You got that stuff somewhere safe?"

"Right here in the evidence locker."

"What about Jansen's wife? Got her somewhere safe, too?"

"Of course."

Matthews thumbed through his key ring. His car's ignition key was black, with a silver BMW logo on it, and several buttons. He pushed the auto-start.

"All right, Breck. I better run."

He went outside and drove away.

What just happened? The man was a stone-cold politician. But, maybe he had an actual heart locked away, deep inside that granite façade, and Breck had just caught a rare glimpse, like Bigfoot in the woods.

The landline rang again. He went over to the desk and grabbed it.

"Sheriff's Office."

"Breck? John McMurray."

"Weren't you supposed to be here by now?"

The line went silent. He could hear other voices in the background, papers shuffling, and phones ringing.

"John?"

"Yeah, I'm still here." The Major sounded off-kilter. "And I'm still *here* . . . in DC."

Breck frowned.

"What's the deal?"

"I'm getting some heat. I've been told to sit tight."

"You're not coming to pick up Hedda Asbjorn?" As soon as he said it, he heard Khodorovsky snicker. "She needs federal protection. We still have a Russian hitman on the loose."

"I know that. But my hands are tied right now—department politics. Someone is stalling me, and I don't know who or why yet. But I'll find out. You just keep that woman safe."

Breck carried the phone as far as the cord would stretch. He didn't want Anatoli to hear any more than he already had.

"I found out why Khodorovsky killed Jansen. He's after their private island, Skogsøya. Does that make sense to you?"

"Yes, it does. I can't say much over an open line, but I can tell you this. The CIA has been monitoring Skogsøya all summer. Somehow, GPS signals are jammed around that area, and some other suspicious activity is setting off serious alarm bells with Homeland." McMurray's voice was tense. "Sit tight, Breck. I'll get to Quandary as soon as I can."

As soon as Breck hung up, the telephone rang again. Now what?

CHAPTER 52

Where Are Those Clowns?

Jenny had to go into the bathroom and close the door, just to get a break from Hedda's stress-chatter. It was driving her crazy.

"I need a vacation."

Turning on the faucet, Jenny soaked a rag with hot water and blotted her face. Emails had been streaming in all day long, one after another, and they were all from angry Bear Coin investors locked out of their accounts. No condolences. Not one "sorry for your loss." It was all about the Benjamins. And now, between getting kidnapped, her husband's murder, and $190 million lost in cyberspace, the woman had reached her breaking point. Poor Hedda, God love her, but she simply couldn't stop talking.

"Deputy Jenny?"

Break time was over. Jenny opened the bathroom door.

"Yes?"

"More emails. They're making threats now. It's horrible!"

"Okay, let's take a look."

They sat down together at the kitchen table, and Hedda began reading the messages out loud. She had to translate some that were written in Norwegian, but Jenny was surprised to see how many were in English. Even more surprising, she recognized some of the names.

"Hey, that's a famous Hollywood actor." She tapped the screen. "He's in all those *Pirates of the Caribbean* movies. Have you seen them?"

"No," Hedda said.

"There's another one! The cute guy from *That '70s Show*." When Hedda shrugged, Jenny shrugged, too. "I guess it's a sad commentary on how much Netflix I watch."

As they scrolled through the emails, she spotted another familiar name. Colorado State Senator Dana Stayne. Twenty million dollars were sitting in her Bear Coin account—and she wanted it bad.

Tears started slipping out of Hedda's eyes, but then a light went off in her mind.

"I think Jansen may have written down the access codes on a piece of paper."

"You think? Or are you sure?"

"When we came here to the USA, we knew we were going to claim asylum. It was part of the plan. We were never going to return to Norway, so we brought many important things in our luggage. Mementos, photos, jewelry. But we kept all our most important papers together in one place . . . Jansen's briefcase. Inside is our cash money, national ID cards, and passports. Things like that. The codes must be in that briefcase. Where else would they be?"

Numbers and letter sequences were an easy thing to forget, but Jenny was having trouble believing that the CEO of a cryptocurrency company would rely on pen and paper for anything. It was so old-school.

"I keep all my passwords on my cell phone. That way, if I forget one, I can easily look it up."

But Hedda shook her head firmly.

"Jan was always worried about hackers. He would never keep the codes on any electronic device. He was very adamant about that." She jumped up and grabbed her coat. "We have to go to the Hyatt, right now. The briefcase is on the top shelf in the bedroom closet. Please. Let's go!"

Jenny felt lightheaded from lack of sleep. All she wanted to do was curl up on the couch and snooze, but that wasn't going to happen anytime soon.

"I wish we could run over to the hotel right now, Hedda, but we can't."

"Why not?"

"Number one, I don't have wheels. Number two, the Department of Homeland Security is supposed to be here at any moment. And number three, I guarantee that Aleks is sitting outside, waiting for us to let our guard down."

She tried texting Breck again for the hundredth time.

Where are those clowns?

But all he texted back was a frowny face.

"We need to find Jan's access codes!" Hedda threw her coat on the floor. "None of the investors will ever be able to get their money back without those codes."

"I still don't get it. Why are the Russians doing all this? What's so special about your private island?"

"I have absolutely no idea."

It was gloomy in the apartment. Jenny wanted to open the curtains and let in some afternoon sunshine, but Aleks could be sitting in a tree with a sniper rifle. It wasn't worth the risk. Not so close to the finish line. But Jenny's optimism was fading fast. What if DHS didn't get there for another day or two? A week? A month?

She grabbed her phone and sent Breck another text.

Running low on food and toilet paper, and SANITY.

Breck wrote back.

Hang in there. By the way, the horse trader just called. Wants to confess to tax fraud. Claims the fake horse rescue was Tibbs' idea. Guy is paranoid. Only place he'll meet is Starbucks. Heading over there now.

Jenny shook her head as she typed.

Johnny Tibbs? That's bogus.

There was no way Johnny was involved in a kill buyer scheme. He may be a hundred percent ego, but he would never get involved in a racket like that. The man lived by the cowboy honor code. Doing something shady wasn't in his wheelhouse.

Hedda crawled onto the couch and pulled a blanket over her head.

Jenny sat next to her.

"I'm sorry. I know you're frustrated, and you have every right to be."

The remote control for the television was lying on the coffee table. Jenny took it and flipped on Netflix again. There were way too many true crime shows and kidnapping movies in the universe. Maybe a cartoon? But before she could pick a show to watch, her cell phone rang. It was Tya.

"Hey, Jenny. How are you doing?"

"Cooped up and going crazy. How about you?"

"The construction crew is done. My apartment has a brand new steel door, and they converted the spare bedroom into a panic room. There's cameras everywhere, and the private security team arrived, too. Do you want to bring Hedda over here? It's the safest place in Colorado."

"You kidding? You're a lifesaver!"

CHAPTER 53

Weirdo

The barista set a tall paper cup with a plastic lid on the service counter and pointed at Breck.

"Coffee for the sheriff."

"Thanks."

He already knew it was going to need a massive amount of cream to be drinkable. The coffee at Starbucks was always too bitter. He grabbed a pitcher of cream off the counter and took it with him to an empty table by the window, with a good view of the street.

Was Luke Roberts going to show? The guy was all nerves on the phone. When Breck invited him to the Sheriff's Office, he raved how Johnny's boys were tailing him everywhere he went, and he didn't want to get a beat down in the police parking lot. Apparently, he wasn't afraid of a beat down in the Starbucks parking lot.

Not the sharpest knife in the drawer.

As he waited, Breck watched a pickup truck park on the street. It had the Tibbs Ranch logo on the door. Two of Tibbs' wranglers got out and came inside the coffee shop, laughing loud over some crass cattle joke.

"That's what *she* mooed!" one said.

They got in line and ordered a dozen cups of dark roast to go. All black, full caffeine. It was obvious they were making a coffee run for the other guys back at the ranch headquarters. The barista put all the cups into cardboard carriers, and the two wranglers jumped into their pickup and drove away. They weren't there to beat up Luke Roberts.

Breck's cell phone rang. He checked the caller ID, but it wasn't Luke or Jenny. It was his lawyer, Jamey Frederick.

"Hi, Jamey. Sorry I haven't had a chance to call you back."

"Things keep getting worse. The DA's investigator, Dempsey? He came by my office with a formal request for the Sheriff's Office budget. They want to see how all the discretionary funds are spent. He wasn't very nice about it, either." She sounded stressed. "They also subpoenaed your bank account to see how it corresponds."

"They want to know if I'm skimming?" Breck wanted to laugh. "Our budget is so low—there's nothing to skim. But if that's all they want, I can email the budget to you this weekend."

"Sorry," Jamey said. "I feel like all I ever have for you is bad news."

"It's okay. You're just doing your job."

"Ummmm. . . ."

"What is it?"

"I hate even to ask, Sheriff Dyer. But . . . can you pay your bill soon? The lease on this office suite is way past due, and I'm barely scraping by. You're my only client right now. Did I mention they cut off my electricity yesterday?"

"I'll get a check in the mail today."

"Can I swing by and pick it up instead? I can be there in ten minutes."

Breck looked around the coffee shop. No horse trader. Luke Roberts was jerking him around for some reason. It wasn't hard to imagine why. He was probably making a break for the state line with a trailer full of horses destined for Mexico at that very moment.

"Sure, Jamey. Meet me at the Sheriff's Office."

Breck hung up and took a long sip from his coffee cup. He could extend an olive branch to Chief Waters, tell him to be on the lookout for the Blue River Horse Rescue truck and trailer. If Roberts was heading south to Mexico, he would have to drive right through Alma.

Breck was just about to get up and leave when Luke Roberts' pickup truck rolled to a stop outside. He wasn't making a break for it, after all.

Luke got out of the cab, carrying a manila envelope. He paused and scraped his boots along the edge of the curb to clean off the horse manure. Breck hoped this guy wasn't telling the truth. He liked Johnny—sort of. If nothing else, Tibbs was a red-blooded American and believed in the Constitution of the United States. He was also a solid presence on the city council. More than once, he kept Matthews from going too far overboard on some issue. Yet, on the other hand, Tibbs was obnoxious. He always tried to make Breck look like a dope in front of Jenny and then capitalize on his own machismo to ask her out on a date.

Luke Roberts came inside the Starbucks and strutted straight towards him, waving the envelope in the air.

"Sheriff Dyer!" he shouted.

Everyone in the coffee shop stopped what they were doing.

Breck pointed at an empty chair.

"Saved you a seat."

"I will not break bread with the likes of you." Luke waved the envelope again. "You can count me out of your horse rescue scheme. I want no part of it, no matter how much you pay me. You, sir, are a dirty cop. Good day!"

He flung the envelope on the table and hustled out the door before Breck could say anything. He jumped in his truck and sped off, pitching dark diesel fumes into the sky.

What the hell was that?

Breck looked around. Starbucks was unnaturally silent. The only sound was the sputter of the milk frothing machine. The barista and the other customers were staring at him, waiting to see how he would respond.

"Your guess is as good as mine," he said.

Opening the envelope, Breck looked inside. It was empty, except for a single one-dollar bill. The All-Seeing Eye on the back of the bill had been circled in black Sharpie ink.

He went to the counter.

"Can I get another cup of coffee?"

"Sure, Sheriff." The barista's name tag said Alexa. "Who was that weirdo?"

"Trust me. You don't even want to know."

Whatever hijinks Luke was cooking up, the timing couldn't have been worse. With Anatoli in jail, Hedda at Jenny's, and DHS on the way, this was a complete waste of time. Oh well, he would settle up with Luke Roberts later. The man may have driven away, but Breck knew every corner of Quandary County—and he knew where Luke lived. In that mobile home at the base of Grizzly Peak, with No Trespassing signs tacked on every tree trunk in sight. Luke wasn't the only lonely crackpot hiding in a remote corner of the Rocky Mountains. But he was Breck's lonely crackpot.

His phone buzzed. Another text from Jenny.

Are you done yet?

Leaving soon.

Come pick us up. Tya's apartment is now officially fixed and fortified. Hedda will be safer there. And before we drop her off at Tya's, we need to swing by the Hyatt.

What's at the hotel? he replied.

Tell you when I see you. And let's order a pizza. We're both sick of yogurt.

Breck grabbed his coffee, topped it off with cream, and headed for the door. First things first. Hopefully, cutting a check for his lawyer wouldn't take too long.

CHAPTER 54

Russian Spycraft

"Pull over."

Senator Dana Stayne always rode in the backseat of her SUV, like she would in a limo. Her driver, Jackson Hong, looked like a young reincarnation of Bruce Lee, and he had martial arts skills. There was no room in her entourage for males, as a general rule. Men were leeches. Men were narcissists. Anything a man could do, a woman could do better. But unfortunately, she had to admit that biology did eclipse ideology when it came down to one particular reality—brute force, which was why Hong was the only exception to her entourage rule. Plus, he was Asian. Nothing worse than white males. There were way too many of those in the world of politics.

As a state senator, Dana traveled widely, and there were times a sense of security could not be completely ensured. Such as her private meetings with Anatoli Khodorovsky and his bodyguard. In Russia, conflicts frequently got resolved with either poison or a shove out a seven-story window, and those two were capable of anything. So why take a chance?

Jackson Hong eased the vehicle to a stop beside the 7-Eleven. It was a red brick building with a sign in the window that advertised a *Free Slurpee With Gas Purchase*. Dana stared at a row of wooden pallets heaped high with bags of ice melt along the front wall. Winter wasn't there yet, but the convenience store was ready to cash in. She could admire that type of foresight. Even the Coors-swilling, Powerball buying, blue-collar, salt of the earth, urchins of society needed to de-ice their driveways.

There was a Post Office mailbox by the sidewalk.

"Take this, and draw an X on the front of that mailbox."

Dana pulled a piece of white chalk out of her purse and gave it to Brenda, her ever-present, heavily lipsticked aid. The young lady didn't question the order. It only took a second, and she was back inside the vehicle.

"Mr. Hong, drive around the block."

He sped away. Dana only felt comfortable in big cities with big people and big consequences for every big decision. She hated small towns like this. The Blue River Bank. Quandary City Hall. High Country Pizza. She could barely stand looking out the window. Heaven forbid they take a wrong turn through a residential neighborhood. What would they find? Rocking chairs? Roosters? American flags? Burning crosses?

If it weren't for the cryptocurrency conference, she wouldn't even know Quandary was on the map, or who Seneca Matthews was, or who Breck Dyer was. But before she ever traveled anywhere, Dana always did her homework. It was essential to know who was who, what was what, and, more importantly, everyone's dirty little secrets.

Jackson turned onto Main Street.

They passed the Sheriff's Office. An old clunky Jeep was parked out front, next to a little green sedan. *That* was where Anatoli Khodorovsky was locked up? It looked like an old church. The only reason she even knew it was the Sheriff's Office at all was the gold star logo stenciled on the front door. Was this even a real town? It felt like a Clint Eastwood film set.

"Mr. Hong? Turn around, and take us back."

A grocery store was up ahead—something called a Safeway. Jackson turned into the parking lot, spun around, and shot back out onto Main Street. As they drove past the Sheriff's Office again, Dana saw Sheriff Dyer lock the front door and climb into the Jeep, while a young woman got into the green sedan and drove away.

Perfect timing.

As soon as they returned to the 7-Eleven, Aleks was waiting by the mailbox. He had a small paper sack in his hand, with a liquor bottle inside. What, was he pretending to be a wino? Russian spycraft was so cartoonish—but she didn't dare say that out loud.

As they pulled up to the curb, Dana rolled down her window and held out a ten-dollar bill.

"Here, Mr. Homeless Man," she said, loud enough for anyone to hear. "Buy yourself a hot meal."

Aleks came over and took the bill. On the back was a yellow sticky note, with a phone number.

"That's the number for a local idiot. He is no longer useful."

"I understand," he said.

A *useful idiot* was a classic foreign intelligence term—a designation for people who were not aware that they were being manipulated. Aleks would know exactly what it meant.

"One more thing," Stayne said. "There is an evidence locker inside the Sheriff's Office. Jansen Asbjorn's Hyatt key card is inside. So is the purchase agreement for Skogsøya. The sheriff just left the building, and I can't hold back DHS much longer. It's now or never."

Aleks put the ten-dollar bill in his pocket and took a swig from his bottle. Dana spotted the label. Smirnoff vodka. How gauche.

"When you see him, tell Anatoli we've got a major problem. When Jansen died, he took the secret access codes for Bear Coin to the grave. I can't access my twenty million."

Aleks shrugged.

"Not our problem."

"It will be your problem if I don't get my money."

It was time to cut bait on this Bear Coin mess. The moment she could access her account, she would transfer that money into cold hard cash and drop it in a bank account in Panama or Switzerland. The whole reason she had invested in Bear Coin in the first place was because cryptocurrency was untraceable. Regular bank accounts, even off-shore, were traceable—if someone had the resources to dig deep enough. The last thing she wanted was to be at the receiving end of a House investigative committee, or worse, a Special Counsel probe into her finances. But at this point, it was a risk she needed to take.

Some truck driver with a giant Slurpee came out of the 7-Eleven and stared at them as he crossed the parking lot. Dana took out another ten-dollar bill.

"Don't spend this on drugs, young man," she shouted and rolled up the window.

Jackson Hong hit the gas pedal.

As the chair for the Committee on Foreign Investment in the United States, Dana had the power to approve significant deals between private US companies and foreign countries. The whole point of the committee was to make sure enemy players didn't get their hands on anything compromising the interests of the United States. There was an entire list of no-nos: nuclear, IT, military, and space.

One day, Anatoli Khodorovsky approached her in secret. He said the Aeroflot Group wanted to buy a cutting edge GPS company in Vermont. But GPS was on the list of no-nos. Dana had no idea what they wanted the technology for, clearly something shady, but it was better not to ask too many questions. Not when they were willing to slip her twenty million dollars in cryptocurrency. But with Bear Coin frozen, she might as well have done it for free.

Dana didn't do anything for free.

"Senator?"

It was Brenda.

"What is it?"

"I uploaded the video to YouTube. It's ready."

Besides being an excellent videographer, the best thing about Brenda was that she was quiet and invisible. It was easy to forget that she was sitting there. Breck Dyer certainly hadn't noticed her at the coffee shop, filming the whole encounter with Luke Roberts. Could it have been any easier to set this guy up? No wonder he was under scrutiny by the DA's office for something he didn't do.

"Push play."

"Yes, ma'am."

The title of the video was *Corrupt Colorado Sheriff Caught In The Act*. It was only thirty seconds long, which was plenty of time to do damage. Breck Dyer at the Quandary Starbucks, holding a manila envelope while Luke Roberts accused him of fraud. It was perfect.

Dana's cell phone buzzed. It was Mayor Matthews.

"Seneca."

"Hello, Dana. Are you ready to endorse me for mayor?"

The man was shameless. But he had provided useful information. And now Aleks knew that information, as well. Once the Hyatt key card and the real estate agreement were no longer inside the evidence locker at the Sheriff's Office, the case against Anatoli would have no teeth—except for Hedda Asbjorn's testimony. But that was an easy fix, too.

"We are friends, Seneca. That's what friends do."

CHAPTER 55

Investigative Journalist

Working at High Country Pizza was ruining Aspen's love for pepperoni. When she first bought the Corolla, the interior smelled like dog butt. The first thing she invested in was a pine tree air freshener to hang on the rearview mirror. It worked, until she got the High Country job.

No amount of air fresheners could kill off the clinging stench of delivery pizza.

Every time Aspen opened the door, it hit her like a slap in the face. Every time she walked into class, the other students made bets on what kind of pizza she delivered last, based on the scent of her contrail.

Parking at the Hyatt Residence Club curbside entrance, Aspen left the engine running. The valet was never happy to see her, and he waved his hands and yelled for her to park way out in the lot. But she didn't plan on walking that far because the pizza would get cold before she ever delivered it, and she needed hot pizza to make decent tips.

Besides, the valet was just some part-time prick who hated his job. Aspen hated hers, too, but the difference was she kept her frustration bottled up deep, deep inside. Why make everyone around her miserable? This moment was just a blip on the radar, as far as she was concerned. It wasn't going to last forever. At some point, her High Country days would all be a forgotten memory, a stepping stone to something bigger and better. At least, that's what Aspen told herself. Otherwise, why get out of bed in the morning?

The manager, Zachary, was sitting at the reception desk and watched her come in.

"Who is it for?" he asked.

"Sheriff Breck." Aspen looked around the lobby. "Have you seen him?"

"Hold on." Zachary picked up a telephone and dialed. "Sheriff? Did you order a pizza?"

A couple of people were sitting in the lobby chairs by the fireplace, typing on laptops. Aspen recognized one of them from the cryptocurrency conference—Ziggy Mars. He was one of the richest men on the planet, thanks to FaceWorld. Maybe a year ago, Aspen would have been excited to meet him, but she was sick of social media. Especially FaceWorld. It was nothing but people arguing politics or moms posting pictures of their kids. Plus, it was depressing to see what her old friends at CU were doing on the weekends. Fauna and Adria were constantly attending parties at local pubs, indie film festivals, and concerts at Red Rocks. What was she going to do, post a selfie with a double pepperoni?

Zachary hung up the phone.

"He's on his way down. You can wait by the elevator."

"Okay, thanks."

Aspen carried the box around the corner and waited. It didn't take long. The door dinged, and Breck stepped out and handed her a twenty-dollar bill.

"Keep the change," he said.

She put the money in her back pocket.

"Sheriff? Any news on that horse rescue scam? Are you going to bust the guy?"

"Well, I spoke to Luke Roberts earlier today, and something about him seems off."

"Is that his name? Luke Roberts?" Aspen smiled grimly. The Bachelor.

"Tell you what, I'm in the middle of a murder investigation, but I can head out there in a couple of days to check on those horses. If any one of them looks abused or malnourished, I'll confiscate the whole herd on the spot."

"A couple of days? That may be too late. What if he decides to load them onto a trailer tomorrow?"

"Sorry, Aspen. I've got to get back upstairs. Thanks for the pizza."

Breck pushed the elevator button, and when the door slid open he stepped inside and pushed a button on the wall. But before the door closed, he nodded appreciatively.

"You should really think about a career in law enforcement, Aspen. A police detective, or the FBI, or something. You've got the knack for it and a good heart."

The door closed, and she was alone again.

Waiting for a couple of days was unacceptable. Something had to be done immediately. Right now. Why didn't anyone else see how important this was? Lives were at stake. Horse lives!

Racing through the lobby, Aspen jumped back in her car. Her hands were trembling. It was a mixture of anger at the grumpy valet, frustration with her own meaty perfume, and a gut-wrenching fear that while Sheriff Breck was bogged down with other priorities, the kill buyer would roll out of town like a thief in the night.

What was she going to do?

Horse stealing was a hanging offense, but the First Amendment protected investigative journalism—even if it meant a little trespassing. What if she snuck onto the property, like a rogue freelance reporter, and videoed the horse herd? Like all those abused pet commercials with skinny cats and dogs in cages. She could set up a fundraiser page. Call it, *Rescue the Rescue Horses.* If she explained how the animals would wind up in a bottle of Elmer's Pegamento, and if enough people saw it, the fundraiser would go viral and raise enough money to save them all.

But the Blue River Horse Rescue website didn't reveal its street address. How was she going to find the place? Breck seemed to know where it was located, but she couldn't ask him for that information without revealing her plan.

She needed to stop and think. Pulling into the 7-Eleven, Aspen got out her phone and Googled the rescue. Nothing helpful. Come on, where was this guy keeping the horses? Who else might know?

The auctioneer. He seemed familiar with the kill buyer, gauging by how he ran the bidding at the auction. The fairgrounds weren't too far away, so Aspen sped right over, parked her car, and walked around—but she didn't see a soul. No one was in the outdoor arena, the grandstands were empty, and the indoor arena was locked.

Aspen spotted a poster stapled to a fence post, listing all the upcoming events for the season. The next auction wasn't for a few more weeks. So much for that idea.

What about the vet? There was only one equine veterinarian in Quandary, and didn't the Bachelor say something about calling him for a Coggins certificate? The vet *had* to know where Luke Roberts' fake horse rescue was located! If she explained the situation, maybe he would tell her the address.

Aspen was about to look up his number when the Blue River Horse Rescue pickup rattled across the dirt parking lot. Aspen's first impulse was to run back to her car and follow him home. But as she watched, he pulled around behind the grandstands and parked. Was he trying to avoid prying eyes?

"You can't hide from me."

Dashing along the fence line, Aspen wanted to find a good position to see what the Bachelor, Luke Roberts, was up to now. Whatever it was, it was something illegal, no doubt. And she was about to get it all on film. Too bad Brittany wasn't there—she could have live-streamed this on her Beauty Guru YouTube channel, and all her subscribers would see it.

A dark blue Suburban appeared and drove straight over to Luke's truck.

Aspen got out her phone and hit record.

"This is Aspen Matthews, investigative journalist," she whispered. "I am at the Quandary County fairgrounds, and I'm about to bust the Blue River Horse Rescue dude. I believe his rescue is a cover story for a horse slaughter pipeline from Colorado to Mexico. Who is Mr. Luke Roberts meeting? A cohort in crime? Let's find out, shall we?"

A tall man with big biceps got out of the Suburban, went around the pickup to the driver's side window, and leaned inside to talk. A loud pop made Aspen jump. What was that? A firecracker?

The big bicep guy went back to his Suburban, got in, and sped away.

"Holy crap." Aspen kept recording and walked quickly towards the pickup. The closer she got, the more her pulse pounded. "Hello? Mr. Roberts?"

CHAPTER 56

No One Deserves That

While Jenny scrolled crime scene tape around the Blue River Horse Rescue pickup truck, Breck examined the cab. The driver's side window was down. Luke Roberts was hunched sideways over the gear shift, a blackened bullet hole in his left temple. His straw cowboy hat was on the floorboards, with red blood sprayed across the brim.

Breck walked back to his Jeep.

Aspen Matthews was sitting inside, with the door wide open, her cheeks streaked with eyeliner. He opened the glove box. It was full of old Subway napkins. He gave one to her, and she blotted her eyes.

"How are you feeling?"

Breck knew the girl was in shock and didn't expect a coherent answer, but to his surprise, Aspen seemed to snap out of it. Reaching into her pocket, she took out her phone and brought up a video.

"I got it all on film."

"You did?"

"I was standing over there by a fence post. I wasn't sure what was happening when they first drove up. I thought I could catch the guy doing something illegal. I didn't know. . . ."

She tried to push play, but her hands trembled, so she just handed the phone to Breck. Sure enough, the entire encounter was right there, in high definition, and there was no doubt about what he was watching. The Suburban drove up. Aleks got out and leaned in Luke's window. Boom.

"I'm going to need to borrow your phone, okay?" Breck said. "We'll download that video as evidence, and you'll get it back soon. I promise."

Aspen sniffed and blew her nose in the napkin. Breck didn't quite know what to say. Between the motel and the fairgrounds, she had two close calls with Aleks. Did she realize how close she had come to being harmed or killed?

"Sorry you had to see such a terrible thing."

"No one deserves that," she mumbled. "Not even . . . oh, boy."

"Not even Luke Roberts."

Breck quietly slipped away and went over to join Jenny at the pickup. She had finished cordoning off the vehicle with tape and was busy taking photos of the truck interior with her cell phone since Danny's camera was back at the office.

He showed her the video. Her jaw fell open, and they watched it again.

"Let's go arrest this commie freak!"

"Tell me something," Breck said. "Why did Aleks kill this guy?"

"I don't know. Luke Roberts doesn't strike me as the cryptocurrency type."

He leaned inside the pickup cab. Dirty Wranglers, three-day scruff. There were grease stains on Luke's vest and a George Strait cassette sticking out of the dashboard radio. A bag of jalapeño flavored Cheetos was on the floor, beside a pile of crushed Coors cans.

"Me, either."

On Aspen's phone, Breck scrolled through the video again and paused on an image of the Suburban's front bumper.

"Hey, check it out," he said. "You can read his license plate. I'm going to hop on the radio and put out a BOLO before he gets too far."

"I'll call Aspen's parents. They need to know."

Breck sighed. That was all he needed. Mayor Matthews showing up at another crime scene. Oh, well. It was the right thing to do. Aspen was the man's daughter, and she had just witnessed a murder. She needed family support at a time like this.

Heading back to the Jeep, Breck got on the CB and let the State Patrol know what was going on. He gave them the make, model, and license plate number. There was no way Aleks was going to get away now unless he ditched the vehicle. But why would he do that? He had no idea there had been a witness when he shot Luke Roberts. If he realized Aspen was standing there, filming the whole thing, she wouldn't be alive to talk about it.

Breck hung up the CB and smiled softly.

"We'll catch this guy."

"Good. But, what about the horses?" Aspen asked. "They're all alone at some secret location, and they need hay and water. Someone has to feed them."

"I know where Luke lives, and I know just who to call—Johnny Tibbs. They're going to be fine, Aspen."

He heard sirens. It was the ambulance from the medical center. As soon as it came to a stop, two nurses pulled a stretcher out of the back. Another body for the morgue. Did they even have room for another one? Jansen Asbjorn, Billy James, and now Luke Roberts.

Another vehicle came rumbling across the dirt parking lot. The Quandary Herald editor was a wiry guy with jet black eyelashes and short white hair, poking straight out like a porcupine. He got out of his car and walked over to the Jeep, extending his cell phone like it was a microphone.

"Any comments, sheriff? For the record?"

"One gunshot victim. Male. Deceased. That is all."

"I see there is a Blue River Horse Rescue sign on the vehicle's door," the editor said. "Was it Luke Roberts?"

"Before we release his identity, the victim's family needs to be notified." Jenny crossed her arms. "You know the drill."

When it came to the Quandary Herald, Breck didn't feel like oversharing. Especially after they ran that front page Matthews-Waters political smear campaign, how could they call that news? No one at the paper even called him to balance out the story or interview him for a response. And now, here was a dead man in a pickup truck at the fairgrounds. It was going to make for another spicy headline.

"What is your connection to the horse rescue, sheriff? Were you in cahoots with Luke Roberts, profiting off the rescue scam?"

"No."

"Why in the freaking world would you even say something like that?" Jenny asked.

The editor whipped his phone back and forth, aiming it at Breck and then at Jenny, like he was in the middle of a knife fight.

"Have you seen the video yet?" he asked.

Breck frowned.

"What video?"

"A new video was just posted on YouTube. A tipster called it in to the Quandary Herald, maybe a half-hour ago. It shows you and Luke Roberts arguing at Starbucks, and Mr. Roberts accused you of being a dirty cop. He says you are running a horse rescue scheme."

"You gotta be kidding me." Jenny spun around and walked away, muttering. "One guess which mayor was the tipster."

But the editor wasn't interested in her quips and commentary. He was focusing on Breck, like a coyote focusing on a jackrabbit.

"Only one week until the election, and the sheriff's debate is tomorrow night. People want to know the truth. And if Luke Roberts was just murdered, then you have some serious explaining to do."

Now it was starting to make sense. Breck couldn't figure out what Luke's coffee shop shanghai was all about and almost forgot about it, with everything else going on. He was being framed.

Play-Doh

"Slow down, Seneca!"

Valerie always yelled when she was stressed. She yelled when she wasn't, too.

On a normal day, Matthews might yell back, but instead, he tuned her out. His mind was so full of hypothetical horror scenarios, and the dirt parking lot at the Quandary County fairgrounds so full of potholes that he needed total concentration and both hands on the wheel to keep from wrecking.

"There she is! I see my baby!"

Valerie unclipped her seat belt before the BMW finished skidding to a stop. In a rolling cloud of dust, she shoved the door open and leaped outside.

Gripping the steering wheel, Matthews took a couple of deep breaths. He watched his ex-wife race towards their daughter and throw her arms around her. Aspen was okay. But she had been in the wrong place at the wrong time. Again. First, the motel, now the fairgrounds.

The girl was supposed to be living a normal sophomore lifestyle: classes, jobs, boys, and parties. A twinge of guilt zipped through his gut. He shouldn't have pulled her out of the university in Boulder because none of this would have happened.

The hard truth was, his bank account had bottomed out—but things were starting to change.

Just before he got the call about Aspen from Deputy O'Hara, he got a call from Dana Stayne. He had done his part, and now she was doing hers. She promised to open a Bear Coin account in his name and top it off with two million dollars. Next week, she said, so hang tight. Apparently, at the moment, there was some kind of computer glitch at Bear Coin, but once it got resolved, he would be sitting pretty.

Through the windshield, he watched Aspen and Valerie hold each other, swaying, crying. O'Hara was standing there, like a security guard. Why didn't she give them some privacy?

Poor Aspen. She needed a new lease on life. When the money came in, the first thing he planned to do was get her back into a real university—Ivy League this time. Even if he had to slick some palms to get her accepted. Yale, Harvard, it didn't matter. Those schools were the gateways to all the elite career fields. New York law firms. Hollywood. Washington DC. *Aspen Matthews, state senator.* That had a nice ring to it. And she wouldn't get there with a degree in Environmental Whining from a party school in Boulder. There were far more important climates to change.

Out of the corner of his eye, Matthews spotted Breck talking to the newspaper editor, over by the ambulance. Was he gunning for a front-page article of his own? Time to put a stop to that. Matthews unclipped his seat belt, got out of the BMW, and jogged towards them.

"Another murder in Quandary?" Ginning up sound bites was his bread and butter. "I'm still mayor of this town, and on my watch, I expect our citizens to feel safe. That means I expect my sheriff to keep them safe."

The editor swung his cell phone towards him, recording audio.

"I understand it was a local cowboy this time," Matthews continued. "What happened? Bar fight? Drug deal? I thought the city council was paying you to patrol our streets, Dyer."

Breck gave him a sour look.

What? Couldn't he appreciate the concept of media spin?

"We need to talk," Breck said.

Matthews pointed at the editor's phone, which he was waving beneath their noses.

"Then talk."

Breck did not look pleased. Did he think they were buddies now? Because they weren't.

"The world is watching, sheriff," Matthews continued. "And the election is right around the corner. If you want to keep your job, grab the bull by the horns."

It was obvious that Breck wanted to walk away, but he held his ground.

"A man was just shot in the head. We have a positive ID of the killer, based on an eyewitness who filmed the entire incident on a cell phone. I gave State

Patrol a description of the man and his vehicle. Big strong Russian guy. Ring any bells?"

"A Russian . . . ?"

Matthews trailed off.

Was he serious? Wait a minute.

When O'Hara called, all she said was Aspen had witnessed a crime at the fairgrounds. A murder. But if the killer was Khodorovsky's bodyguard and his daughter saw the whole thing, then she was in danger. Just like Hedda Asbjorn. And Tya Tordenskjold. And Billy James. And Jansen Asbjorn.

This was bad. Very bad.

He looked over his shoulder. Valerie had their daughter wrapped in her arms, and the girl was sobbing. Even though she was safe, a dark cloud descended on him.

Dana wanted her Russian buddy out of jail and threatened to flip the DA scandal onto him if he didn't do what she asked. Everyone knew she played hardball, so Matthews did what he was told. He worked Breck like Play-Doh to discover what they had on Khodorovsky—a key card and a Norwegian real estate agreement. Big deal. What could Dana possibly do with that info? Any sane person would tell the man's lawyer, so he could know the extent of the evidence, and begin poking holes in the legal case. But it was starting to look like the Russians were poking holes in people's heads. And the Ice Queen, Senator Dana Stayne, was right there in the middle of it all.

Somehow, he was too.

"Pardon me. I need to check on my daughter."

He went over and put his arms around his family, broken as it was, and held them. Aspen's hair smelled like pizza. Valerie reeked of alcohol and was so badly shaken up, she couldn't talk.

"Daddy?"

Aspen looked up at him with those familiar, beautiful, blue, innocent eyes. She looked so young. Was she twenty-one years old? Or twelve?

"It's okay, ptarmigan."

"I saw what happened, daddy."

"What were you doing here in the first place?"

"Trying to expose Luke Roberts as a fraud."

Who was she talking about? Matthews glanced at the pickup, behind all that yellow tape. The sign on the door said Blue River Horse Rescue. Ah, yes. The horse slaughter situation. That seemed like a million years ago.

"Maybe someone else had the same idea," he suggested, even though he knew it wasn't true. Why spook her with the truth? "It was probably an animal rights vigilante."

Aspen wiggled free of the group hug.

"I saw the guy, daddy. He looked like a bodybuilder. I got it all on video."

"Video?"

A cold shiver ran through Matthews' body. Not only did Aspen witness the murder, she filmed it, too? If Aleks found out. . . .

"Well, whoever did it, he won't get far. Sheriff Dyer put out an APB, and the State Patrol is out there looking for him. I'll bring Chief Waters in on this, too. But for now, both of you should stay at my house until the man is in custody. You'll be safe there."

"Safe?" Valerie had that deer in the headlights look. "We aren't safe anywhere in this town. We should leave Quandary until this is all over. My sister still lives in Fort Collins. Aspen and I can stay there."

"Don't go. Please? There's nothing to worry about. I can protect you."

The words tumbled out confidently. But could he? Matthews would talk to Dana. Make it clear his family was off-limits. He wasn't sure what kind of relationship the senator had with the oligarch, and he didn't want to know. But she was a powerful ally, with a long reach.

Matthews took Aspen's hand and Valerie's hand.

"You're both safe with me."

CHAPTER 58

Zephyr

The sun was going down.

Wadding all the crime scene tape into a crinkly ball, Breck looked around for a trash can or a dumpster. The fairgrounds seemed so quiet now. The ambulance transported Luke Roberts' body back to the morgue, a tow truck hauled his pickup to a county storage yard, the Matthews clan went home, the newspaper editor was gone, and it was down to just Breck and Jenny, making a final sweep of the area.

"There's one over there," Jenny said.

She pointed at a green metal barrel by the outdoor arena.

Breck walked over and dropped the ball of yellow tape inside. The barrel smelled like old Coors and nacho cheese, and it was overflowing with garbage. Not only was it a trash can, but also a spittoon. Everything was coated in tobacco juice and sunflower seeds. Yummy.

The parking lot lights began to buzz and then flickered on. The fixtures contained big mercury vapor bulbs that cast a harsh purple glare.

"That Bad Sheriff YouTube video was a total set-up," Jenny said.

Breck was quiet. There was something about all this he couldn't understand.

"So who made the video and why?" he asked.

"To make you look like a corrupt cop, so you'll lose the election."

"Having a man killed so I'll lose my badge. That's pretty hardcore, don't you think? Can you imagine Matthews or Waters doing that?"

"Those two may be idiots, but they're not murderers."

"What about Anatoli? As payback for locking him in jail."

"The dude *is* a killer. But would he go to all that trouble to make a YouTube video to ruin your reputation? His modus operandi isn't character assassination. It's just plain old assassination."

Since they were near the outdoor arena, she climbed the wooden fence and sat on the top rail. Breck climbed up, too, and they sat quietly for several minutes. The sky was getting darker and darker, and faint stars began to twinkle.

"Aspen sure is having a bad week." Jenny sighed. "When I was her age, my biggest worry was finding the right shade of concealer to cover my acne."

"If we have time tomorrow, let's give the girl her phone back. Good excuse to make sure she's dealing with everything okay."

"A house call at the Matthews place? The fun never ends." An old tenpenny nail was sticking out of a board. She wiggled it, but it didn't come out of the wood. "So the big debate with Maxy Waters. You psyched yet?"

"Can't wait. You psyched for your big date with Johnny Tibbs?"

"That was last night. I forgot about it until the cowboy showed up at my front door, wondering why I wasn't dolled up and ready for steak."

Breck softly laughed.

"You missed out on some riveting conversation, I'm sure."

"I missed out on a *Cool Water* sing along." She tried wiggling the nail again, and this time it came out of the board. "You know, we shouldn't be sitting here. Not with Aleks on the loose. We should be hunting his evil ass down."

"True."

They jumped onto the ground and walked back to the Jeep. Breck glanced around one last time. Were they missing anything? Why did he always feel two steps behind?

He got in the driver's seat and started the engine. As they drove back to the office, they listened to the CB chatter. The State Patrol hadn't found anything yet, but that only meant Aleks hadn't driven down I-70. He was probably still in Quandary, biding his time. Maybe he was even stalking Hedda again.

At a stoplight, they watched some high school kids skateboarding circles around a patch of *Tibbs For Mayor* signs. One of them had a black marker and began drawing a mustache on Johnny's face.

Breck checked his cell phone. No new messages.

"Let's stop by the office. Maybe DHS left us a voicemail on the machine."

"I wonder how Hedda is coping?" Jenny shook her head slowly. "What a mess. Remind me never to invest in cryptocurrency."

They had dropped her off at the ski resort earlier, as soon as Aspen called to report Luke Roberts' death. The Hyatt had been a big let down. Jansen's briefcase only contained the Asbjorns' marriage certificate, ID cards, passports, and their cash. Hedda had combed through everything, but Jansen hadn't written down the Bear Coin access codes after all.

The light turned green, and Breck turned onto Main Street. He drove slowly past the tourist shops, paying attention to every vehicle parked alongside the curb, hoping to spot the dark blue Suburban.

When they reached the Sheriff's Office, Jenny leaned forward, eyes wide.

"Oh, you gotta be kidding me!"

The front door was wide open, and the frame splintered.

Luke Roberts' death—was it just a distraction for a jailbreak? As soon as Breck parked, they both drew their guns and rushed inside the building, but Khodorovsky was still locked in his jail cell.

"Hello, officers of the law. I missed your lovely faces," he said. "You won't believe it. To my great shock, a big gust of wind blew open the door. What you call a zebra?"

Breck cleared the bathroom while Jenny checked the storage room. But Aleks wasn't there. No one was, except Khodorovsky—and he appeared to be having fun.

"Zephyr." He snapped his fingers. "That is the word."

Jenny holstered her Luger and frowned.

"Stop acting like you don't know English, you douche."

Opening the tactical closet, Breck began counting everything. Shotguns, rifles, handguns, flak jackets, helmets, handcuffs.

"Did he take anything?"

"No."

"Then why did he kick in the door?" Jenny wondered.

It was a good question. Breck looked around the room again. The spare key to the jail was inside his desk. If Aleks had wanted to, he could have easily let Anatoli out. Maybe this was a little demonstration to prove that he could come or go as he pleased.

"Update," Khodorovsky announced. "My lawyer will arrive at Denver International Airport at 7 A.M. flight tomorrow morning. I expect he will arrive on this very spot at approximately 11 A.M., Mountain Time, depending on traffic . . . and how long the line is at Krispy Kreme. You know how it goes. If hot sign is on, line wraps around building."

Jenny walked over and grabbed the bars.

"Aleks broke in here just to tell you that?"

Breck examined the front door. The frame and latch were ruined. It wasn't going to close without being repaired. That meant one of them needed to stick around the office at all times until they could get it fixed. Divide and conquer. Bravo, Aleks.

"So why didn't you try and escape?" Jenny asked.

Anatoli shrugged.

"Why would I do that? I travel to USA all the time. If I escape your little prison now and jet back to Moscow, I cannot return without much red tape." He laid down on his cot and got comfortable. "Besides, I will be set free tomorrow. Legally."

"Ain't gonna happen," Jenny said. "Did you forget we arrested you for the murder of Jansen Asbjorn? You haven't even been arraigned yet. You can't get out on bail until you go to court."

"So you say. But you have locked me up without proof. Only the word of a distraught Norwegian lady with major financial problems. Perhaps she will lose her nerve and no longer testify."

Jenny's eyebrows shot up.

"No proof? You forget something? We have evidence. Your fingerprints are on the hotel key card, dummy. Not to mention the Forest Island document. Jansen's blood, your signature. You should have put a bow on it and signed it *Santa Claus*."

Breck went over and stood next to her so that he could look Khodorovsky in the eye. The Russian was acting more arrogant than usual. This felt like theater. A game. What was he up to?

"Evidence?" Khodorovsky clapped his hands. "Show me this evidence."

Breck and Jenny both turned to look at the evidence locker at the same time. It was open. Aleks must have used a crowbar.

CHAPTER 59

Invisible Pistol

Danny backed his Ram pickup right up to the Sheriff's Office doorway. The bed was filled with hand tools, extension cords, a big table saw, and several sticks of lumber. Breck and Jenny were standing in the parking lot, waiting for him to arrive. Breck grabbed a board and started to pull it out as soon as Danny parked, but his younger brother waved him away.

"I've got this, Brecky. Go be a cop, or whatever it is you do."

"Maybe I will."

"Where's my camera?"

"You'll get it back. When we're done with this case."

Jenny cringed. The only way Danny was going to get his camera back was in an alternate universe. It had been locked inside the evidence locker for safe-keeping. Now it was gone, along with all the crime scene photos they had taken, and the key card and the real estate agreement, too. She wondered why Breck didn't just tell Danny the truth. Was he secretly hoping to recover the camera if they tracked Aleks down? That was a big if.

"Well, I want it back right now," Danny said. "I'm going to publish a coffee table book full of mountain photos, and I need to shoot the autumn leaves before they're all dead and gone. Like your career."

"Coffee table? Leaves?" Breck was irritated. "Sounds pretty gay."

"You're the homo, so shut up, and give me my damn camera back."

Breck dropped the board he was carrying, and it clattered on the cold asphalt.

"You know what? You're on your own."

After he went inside the Sheriff's Office, Danny knelt and picked up the board. He glanced in Jenny's direction, smirking, but never made eye contact.

"What a loser," he said. "Been like that since he was born."

Ah, brothers. Half of what came out of Danny's mouth was guaranteed to be condescending, sarcastic, or both. But when it came to fixing things, whether it was wrenching an engine or sawing a two-by-four, his manual skills outweighed his smack talk.

At first, Breck didn't want to call him, but Jenny talked him into it. With such a high-profile prisoner inside the jail cell, it would have been a royal waste of time to search the internet for a random contractor and hope he could squeeze them in at the last minute. A royal waste of money, too. Danny never charged them a dime whenever he helped out.

The sky was gunmetal gray and the wind cut like a knife. Jenny was wearing her thick marshmallow down jacket. Danny was only wearing a plaid flannel shirt, but he didn't even seem fazed.

"I wish you would have brought us piping hot cheeseburgers," she said.

"Blame it on Brecky. He didn't ask." Unzipping a canvas tool bag, Danny pulled out an electric drill and buzzed it in the air a few times. "I'll have this door on its hinges again in no time. You can thank me later."

His yellow beard had been getting bushier all summer, and it was much longer than it had been, even a month ago. It had officially crossed the line from Jeremiah Johnson into Taliban territory.

"Good luck getting on an airplane." She pointed at his chin. "Are you going full ZZ Top on us, or what?"

He raked his fingers through it a couple of times.

"All the cool kids are doing it."

"Yeah. That's what I was thinking."

Both the Dyer brothers were easy to torment. Jenny had so much to work with, given Danny's blazing ego and Breck's quiet insecurities.

But, as soon as the thought crossed her mind, she felt guilty for even thinking it. Watching a climbing partner rappel to his death would mess anyone up. Add to that, the district attorney's investigation, and now a YouTube video depicting him as a horse scam ringleader. Maybe Breck had a good reason to be nursing those quiet insecurities.

Jenny rested her palm on her pistol grip, and her eyes roved the street. She had been doing that ever since they got back to the office and found the door kicked in. It was anybody's guess where Aleks was, and she wasn't going to let her guard down for one second, given the psycho's penchant for surprise attacks.

"If I'm going to repair this door, you're kind of in the way."

Danny was staring at her, waiting for her to move.

"Yeah, yeah, yeah."

Stepping out of the doorway, Jenny began to pace around the parking lot. Was she overthinking the situation? Aleks wasn't going to attack her or Breck. Not now. He already got what he came for—the Asbjorns' Hyatt suite key card, and the Norwegian real estate purchase agreement. Danny's camera, too.

Kneeling in the doorway, Danny began prying out the broken door jamb. The wood cracked as he pulled on it.

"This isn't going to be easy. The whole door frame is jacked up. I'm going to have to re-frame the entire thing."

"Sounds like a hoot." Jenny squeezed past him. "I'll leave ya to it."

Once she got inside, she headed for the fridge and grabbed a can of Red Bull, went and sat on the corner of Breck's desk, and took a couple swigs. She could feel the caffeine coursing into her system. Jenny's heart began to beat faster, and she suddenly wanted to punch someone. Breck was busy typing the crime scene report for the fairgrounds murder and didn't even glance at her. She hit him in the shoulder.

"You think Anatoli's lawyer is coming tomorrow?" she asked.

No answer.

Type, type, type.

Jenny glared at Khodorovsky, who had a smug smile on his face. It was unreal. All their evidence was gone. The only thing they had against him now was Hedda Asbjorn's testimony. Khodorovsky knew that, too. It wouldn't be a surprise if Hedda was next on his list of *Things to Go Bye-Bye*. But now that Tya installed all the new security features at her apartment, Aleks was going to be in for a surprise.

The phone rang. Jenny plucked up the receiver.

"Deputy O'Hara speaking."

"This is Mayor Matthews. Put Dyer on."

"He's busy. Can I take a message?"

Breck mouthed the words, *Who are you talking to?*

She twirled her finger at her temple, making the universal coo-coo symbol.

"Someone leaked the YouTube video to the Denver news stations," Matthews told her.

"*Someone?* Meaning you?"

"Listen to me, deputy." He was mad. "The moment Dyer gets voted out of office, you're out of a job, too. Think about *that*. And good luck finding a new one, because every time you put out a resumé across the great state of Colorado—hell, anywhere in the West—or anywhere at all, even the moon, I'll make sure to write such a glowing reference you'll be radioactive. You might as well file for unemployment because you won't be getting employed anytime soon. You hear me?"

"All I hear is bull shiz, squishing in my ears."

"Tell Dyer he needs to recuse himself from this Luke Roberts' investigation. The video implicates him. Period."

Jenny started to hang up. She wanted to, bad, but she didn't want to give Matthews the satisfaction of having the last word.

"You're dreaming if you think Breck is stepping down."

"Yes, he is. We can let Chief Waters take over the sheriff's department until all this gets resolved. He's a highly respected police officer with years on the force, and—"

"Waters?" She scoffed. "The extent of his investigative prowess is deciphering parking meters. All he does is whine about jurisdiction every time we get within a stone's throw of his rinky-dink town, so don't talk to me about respect. And speaking of jurisdiction, you're the mayor of Quandary, and you don't have any say over the county Sheriff's Office."

Jenny slammed down the phone. She drew an invisible pistol from an invisible hip holster and put an invisible bullet through her skull. It was a little macabre, given the nature of Luke Roberts' untimely demise, but Breck thought it was funny and smiled.

It was good to see him smile.

CHAPTER 60

Freedom

The next morning, Breck was standing in the doorway, fiddling with the new brass deadbolt, when a limo pulled up to the curb. The driver leaped out to get the door for an older gentleman who looked like he was in his eighties. Stringy white hair. He leaned on a cane for support. Every step was slow and rickety, and crossing the parking lot took so long that Breck wondered if he should get the man a wheelchair.

It was 11 A.M. sharp, and that meant one thing—Mr. Lawyer.

"Sheriff Dyer?" As expected, the man had a thick Russian accent.

"Yes?"

"I am Konstantin Veselnitskaya, Mr. Khodorovsky's attorney. You must release my client immediately unless you can produce physical evidence linking him to a crime. Can you?"

There it was. The circle was complete.

"Come on inside."

Breck held the door open and led him to an empty chair beside his desk. Across the room, Jenny was warming her hands at the potbelly stove. Judging by the look on her face, she knew exactly what was happening.

The man adjusted his eyeglasses and looked around the room, studying the Sheriff's Office—the vaulted timber ceiling, the woodstove, and the antique jail cell. His eyes lingered on the evidence locker, hanging off its hinges, before finally settling on Khodorovsky.

"Do you have proof of my client's culpability, sheriff?"

"You have great timing," Breck said. "Someone broke into the Sheriff's Office last night and stole all the evidence. Imagine that."

"So, you have no legal standing to detain him. Release him this instant."

All of Khodorovsky's clothes were wrinkled. Except for his suit coat, which had been hanging up on a wall peg the entire week. He carefully slid his arms in the sleeves and stood at the cell door expectantly.

"Konstantin! You made it. You bring me Krispy Kreme?"

"Glad to see you still have your sense of humor, Mr. Khodorovsky. No pastries, but I did bring you freedom."

The old man produced a sheaf of documents and set them on Breck's desk. The cover sheet had the name of a Moscow law firm, a formal demand for his client's release, and a declaration of intent to sue for false imprisonment and lack of evidence. Breck started to flip through it, but it was page after page of legal mumbo jumbo, mostly Russian.

Ring, ring, ring.

The Sheriff's Office landline. It had been ringing like crazy all morning long. The Russian consulate foreign minister kept calling, claiming diplomatic immunity, even though Khodorovsky wasn't a diplomat. Reporters from the Denver Post and the New York Times were desperate for a comment. They must have reached out to Governor Loopenhicker for a comment, too, because he was furious about the bad press and called to make sure Breck knew exactly how furious he was.

The one person Breck hoped would call didn't—Major McMurray.

Jenny shook her head in disbelief as Breck opened his desk drawer and took out the jail cell key, but what else could they do? As soon as he unlocked the heavy iron door and swung it open, Khodorovsky strutted out with a triumphant smile.

"It's been real, and it's been fun." He clapped Breck on the shoulder. "But I wouldn't say real fun."

Using his cane for balance, Konstantin hobbled out the door without another word, but Khodorovsky didn't appear eager to leave.

"Best of luck with your re-election, Sheriff."

Breck tossed the key back into his desk drawer. Why was everything in his desk in the wrong place? It was like someone deliberately disorganized each drawer.

"You may have gotten out on a technicality, but Aleks is a wanted man. If he tries to get on your jet plane, we'll be right there on the tarmac, and I'll arrest him for murder, and you for complicity."

"I'm not leaving town. In fact, perhaps I shall come watch the big debate. Tonight, yes? I sincerely hope they will be serving popcorn." Khodorovsky held out his hand for a handshake, but Breck ignored it. "I hope you find the real killer, Sheriff. This little town has a big problem with crime. It is unfortunate."

The Russian headed outside, and Breck and Jenny followed him into the parking lot. The limo was still idling by the curb, and as soon as the driver saw them, he opened the back door. Konstantin was already in the backseat.

Khodorovsky hunched his shoulders against the bitter breeze, but he smiled. "Ah, I have missed the fresh air."

"Don't get used to it," Jenny said. "We know you killed Jansen Asbjorn, and Billy James, and Luke Roberts. I'm sure Aleks did your dirty deeds, but you're up to your commie nips in innocent blood."

"I'm going to miss you, *Krasny.*" Khodorovsky patted his jacket pockets, but they were empty. He glanced at Breck, hopefully. "This calls for a cigarette, yes?"

Breck pulled out the package of American Spirits and shook one out. But instead of giving it to him, Breck popped it in his own mouth.

"No hard feelings," Khodorovsky said, with a laugh. "Take care of yourselves, my friends."

And with that, he slid into the backseat next to Mr. Lawyer, and the vehicle slowly pulled away. They watched it drive down the block, turn the corner, and disappear. Before he could light it, Jenny snatched the cigarette out of his mouth and crumpled it into tobacco crumbs.

"Where the hell is DHS?" she growled.

Inside the Sheriff's Office, the phone was ringing.

"He's not getting away that easy." Breck took out his Jeep keys. "We still need a formal statement from Hedda. If we can get her to identify Anatoli and Aleks as the ones who assaulted her and Jansen at the Hyatt, we can put him right back in jail and his lawyer won't have any reason to complain."

"Well, what are we waiting for?"

CHAPTER 61

Sales Pitch

M etal clunked and whirred, and the new steel door swung open like a bank vault.

"Welcome to my fortress," Tya said.

"We barely got past your new security team down there," Jenny told her, as she walked inside. "Had to flash our badges just to get on the elevator."

"Yeah, there's no sneaking past those guys."

Breck looked around the apartment. She wasn't kidding. It felt like a fortress. The windows had been replaced with bulletproof glass. The guest room door was gone, and in its place was a chrome-plated sliding panel that looked a lot like an elevator—the panic room. Extra security cameras were mounted everywhere.

"Where is Hedda?" he asked.

Tya pointed at the white leather sofa. Hedda huddled beneath a blanket. All Breck could see was her socks—just like the first time he saw her. She had been sitting on that same couch, wrapped in that same blanket and scared out of mind.

Jenny knelt down by the couch.

"Are you okay?"

Hedda groaned.

"Let's talk in the other room," Tya said, and led them into the kitchen.

Several *Ski Quandary!* mugs were sitting on the kitchen island, half-full of cold coffee, near a ceramic dish filled with Norwegian gingersnap cookies. Something caught Jenny's eye—a used napkin with a smear of bright red lipstick.

"Did we miss the party?"

"A senator dropped by to express her condolences to Hedda about Jansen's death." As she talked, Tya put the mugs into the dishwasher. "You just missed her. She left a few minutes ago."

"Don't tell me it was Dana Stayne?" Breck asked.

"Yeah. How did you know?"

Jenny's face fell.

"The other day, Hedda realized something was wrong with the entire Bear Coin cryptocurrency website. No one can get in, and no one is happy about it. When Jansen died, he took the secret access codes to the grave. Which means everyone who invested in Bear Coin now owns a big fat pile of nothing."

"Okay . . . ?" Tya glanced at Breck, still confused.

"Dana Stayne had twenty million dollars in a Bear Coin account," Jenny said.

Breck glanced back at the sofa. This was unbelievable. No wonder Hedda was hiding under that blanket! Stayne must have said something threatening, and left the woman terrified.

"Tya, tell me exactly what happened."

By the look on her face, it was obvious Tya felt like she did something wrong.

"I got a call that the senator was in the lobby, and wanted to speak privately with Hedda, to offer her condolences. So I told the security guys to bring her up to the apartment. The senator had one of her aides with her, too. We had coffee and cookies. Stayne told Hedda how sorry she was to hear about Jansen. It seemed legit. Before she left, she gave Hedda a long hug and whispered something in her ear. I just thought it was a heart to heart talk because Hedda has been crying ever since."

It was a heart to heart, but not in a good way.

Breck went back into the living room and knelt by the sofa.

"Hedda? It's Sheriff Dyer. I know you're going through a lot right now, but Deputy O'Hara and I would like to speak with you."

No response.

"I know Senator Stayne threatened you. But, it's important that you give us a formal statement about who abducted you and Jansen. We need to hear it from you. Please. If you don't, the men who did this are going to leave town and get away with his murder."

The blanket began to quiver.

Breck hated pushing so hard, but there was no other choice. But before he could say anything else, Jenny tapped him on the shoulder.

"We're losing track of time," she said. "The debate is going to start soon."

What were the chances the Russians were outside, sitting in the limo sipping vodka, waiting for him to leave the building? Khodorovsky knew all about the debate. He even made a joke about attending. If they wanted an opportunity to force Hedda to sign the Forest Island real estate agreement, this was it.

"I'm not going. Aleks and Anatoli are out there somewhere."

"The new security detail won't let either one of those freakshows get near the apartment, and I'll be right here the whole time. Hedda couldn't be in a safer place." Jenny put her arm around Tya's shoulder, buddy style. "Besides, this girl can shoot a hole in a Coke can at fifty paces. Trained her myself. We've got this."

Tya's cell phone was lying on the fireplace mantle. It buzzed. A text came in. When she read the message, her face clouded over.

"What is it?" Jenny asked.

"That piece of . . . Sven."

"Isn't he in the Alps?"

"No, he's back in town." Tya clacked her fingernails on the mantle. They were manicured with an expensive white glaze, and they sounded like a snare drum at a military parade. "He wants me to sign divorce papers."

"Sorry to hear that," Breck said.

"I'm not."

Given Hedda's fragile emotional state, he wondered how long it would take until she calmed down enough for a formal interview. But Jenny wasn't done with her sales pitch.

"Breck, I know the last thing you want to do right now is argue politics with Max Waters. But if you don't win this election, we're both out of a job. And do you really think Quandary County will be safer with that goofus in charge?"

CHAPTER 62

Philistine

The only place that sold pizza in Frisco was Little Caesars, or as Aspen liked to call it, Little Seizures. She smiled whenever she said it that way. Nicknames were fun. Besides, they had a bad reputation for pre-cooked half-price heat-lamp specials. As a result, whenever anyone craved a decent pepperoni pie, they called High Country Pizza in Quandary for delivery.

Aspen flipped on her turn signal and pulled into a small, run-down strip mall. Half the store spaces had *For Lease* signs in the empty windows. All that was left was a tanning salon and the Law Offices of Hoyt, Hoyt, and Frederick. The leathery looking lady who ran the tanning salon never ordered pizza, but the attorneys were regulars. Well, attorney. Every time Aspen delivered pizza to their office, she only saw one person working—Jamey Frederick.

It was, apparently, a one-woman show with no office staff or receptionist.

Aspen never saw Hoyt or Hoyt and secretly wondered if they even existed. Just for kicks, she liked to concoct imaginary storylines about the Hoyts. Her most creative tale was that the Hoyts were conjoined twins named Hem and Haw. Hem had a monocle in his right eye, and Haw had a monocle in his left eye, and they lived in a secret room behind a faux filing cabinet that slid to the side at the push of a button. However, the hidden doorway behind the filing cabinet was too narrow for them to walk through without shuffling sideways, and they always argued about who went first.

"Medium cheese." Aspen set the pizza box on the reception counter while Jamey rifled through her purse for cash. "How come you never order any toppings? Personally, I'm sick of pepperonis, but the veggies are always fresh. My favorite combo is spinach, onions, and sun-dried tomatoes. Shredded mozzarella, no cheddar. You should try it sometime."

"If I'm being honest, it's the cheapest thing on the menu, and I'm flat broke."

"Really? But you're a lawyer."

"Are you kidding me? Number one, we barely have any clients besides divorces and DUIs. And number two, I'm drowning in student loan debt, and I'm never getting out, which is why I can't tip more than a measly buck. Sorry about that."

It was a nine dollar pizza, and Jamey gave her a ten-dollar bill. She must have been hungry, because she immediately pulled out a slice of pizza and took a bite. Hot marinara sauce dripped onto the counter.

"No big deal, I get it." Aspen looked around the tiny office. "So I have a question. Where are Hoyt and Hoyt? I never see them."

Jamey chuckled, a little sarcastically, and shook her head.

"Don't ask."

The place seemed dimly lit, and Aspen suddenly realized why. None of the lights in the office were on. The only illumination was coming through the windows, but it was a dull, gloomy light, because the sky was overcast. There were even a few snow flurries in the air.

"It's getting dark in here," Aspen said. "You want me to flip on the light switch?"

Jamey blushed.

"They cut off my electricity the other day. I'm lucky the tanning salon lets me use their WiFi. Otherwise, I'd be screwed."

"My neighbor lets me use his WiFi, too," Aspen said. "Hey, it could be worse. Do you have to rely on your dad to cover your cell phone bill?"

"That *does* sound worse."

Aspen smiled. She liked Jamey. They could probably be friends if they spent time together. And it would be nice to have another friend, besides just Brittany. Seeing Adria and Fauna had made her miss the dorm life in Boulder—for about ten minutes. Seeing them drunk and fighting was a wakeup call. That was not Aspen's world anymore. She had moved on.

"Hey, I have another question. If I wanted to start a horse rescue, is there anything special I need to do, legally speaking?"

Jamey took a napkin and blotted the surface grease off the pizza.

"You'll want to register a business name and probably launch it as a non-profit organization. That way, you can accept donations legally and write off all expenses. You'll need a tax exemption identification number, and I can help you draft a mission statement. Then you'll need a board of directors—a board chair, vice chair, treasurer and a secretary."

As she spoke, Aspen felt her heart sink a little. That sounded like a massive can of worms. Her eyes drifted to the filing cabinet against the back wall. What would Hem and Haw say?

"So, are you too busy with DUI's and divorces to help me start a horse rescue?"

"Nope. Either everyone is happily married or sober as a nun because I'm down to one client right now. It's a government corruption case."

"That sounds interesting."

"I'm starting to think this poor guy is getting railroaded."

"Still sounds interesting."

Finishing off her first slice, Jamey picked up a second piece of pizza and gave her a weak smile.

"Do you ever feel like David versus Goliath, but your little slingshot doesn't work very well?"

Aspen knew the feeling. She could still picture Luke Roberts' snide face when he outbid her on the dun gelding. The Bachelor and his snarky comments. The twinkle in his eye when he told her she had to cough up a thousand bucks or the horse was going to the slaughterhouse.

"Just keep fighting," she told Jamey. "You never know what can happen."

Suddenly, Aspen felt sick to her stomach. Luke Roberts, her Philistine, was lying on a slab in the county morgue. It was one thing to wish sweet revenge upon your opponent. It was quite another to see them get shot in the head right in front of you.

CHAPTER 63

Is This Thing On?

There were so many vehicles at the fairgrounds, Breck almost gave up looking for a spot. It was tempting to turn around and keep driving, back to the ski resort. Politics was such a waste of time. But, as he was making one final pass around the building, some generous fool threw it into reverse and vacated a parking space right by the entrance.

"Well, that sucks. Now I have to go inside."

Breck pulled in and cut the engine. At least he didn't see Aleks's Suburban or Anatoli's limousine in the parking lot. But, everyone else in the county had made it, by the look of things.

The *Corrupt Colorado Sheriff Caught In The Act* YouTube video already had five thousand views, even though the entire county only had about a thousand residents. There was a long string of comments on the video page, but it was all trolls, and Breck refused to read them. Surely, sooner or later this dark cloud would pass and things would go back to normal. Right?

A news van with one of the Denver channel logos was circling, searching for a place to park. It had a satellite dish on the roof. Everyone in Denver was going to see this.

"Perfect."

He held his hand flat for a second—only a slight tremble. Public speaking was the worst, let alone debating political issues in front of God and the whole wide world. But, if he didn't defend his reputation, who would?

Taking a deep breath, Breck finally went inside the indoor arena. Not many open seats. He had never seen the stadium seating packed out like this before. The building was buzzing with the sound of a thousand conversations, as everyone tried to talk louder than the people around them and louder than the '80s rock music playing on the loudspeakers. Bon Jovi's *Blaze of Glory* was blaring. It was a nice little number about going down in flames.

A rotund man appeared and shook Breck's hand. It was Mike Jameson, owner of Mikey's Bikeys bike shop, and council member less-than-extraordinaire.

"Sheriff Dyer? I was worried you might not show. Let me escort you onto the stage. We're about to get started."

"Sure, Mike. Lead the way."

The stage, built out of plywood and two-by-fours, was right in the middle of the arena. The edges were decorated with patriotic paper ribbons and miniature American flags. Chief Waters was already up there, standing behind one of the podiums.

"Don't trip on all those wires," Mike mentioned. "I told the boys to drill holes in the stage floor and run it all underneath, but no one listens to me."

The audience was full of familiar faces, some good, some bad. Both Matthews and Johnny Tibbs were working the crowd, shaking hands and hobnobbing for votes—in just a few days, they would be standing on that very same stage. Someone with a sense of humor had scheduled the mayoral debate for Halloween, and it was guaranteed to be a night of horrors.

Might as well get this over with.

Breck climbed onto the platform, and Waters waltzed over with a disingenuous handshake.

"Time for a new career path, Dyer. I hear Krispy Kreme is hiring."

"Good. That's my dream job."

Sure enough, there were electrical cords and microphone cables laying everywhere, taped to the plywood floor. Careful not to trip, Breck went and stood behind his podium to get a feel for it. The spotlights were bright, and it was hard to see the crowd without squinting. The Denver news crew was nearby, setting up their video cameras on tripods. Breck grit his teeth. They never covered Quandary. The only reason they were filming was because of that stupid YouTube video.

"Good evening! Everyone take your seats, and we'll get started." Mike Jameson stepped into the spotlight, in between the podiums. He tapped his microphone a couple of times, and people cringed at the sound. "Is this thing on?"

As people found their seats, Breck noticed someone familiar at the concession stand. He shielded his eyes from the spotlight. Holy Moses. It was Anatoli Khodorovsky. He was buying a carton of yellow popcorn. And if that wasn't enough brazen behavior to digest for one day, the Russian oligarch walked over and sat down in the front row—right in between Mayor Seneca Matthews and Senator Dana Stayne.

Mike Jameson tapped his mic again.

Boom, boom, boom.

"Welcome to the official Quandary County sheriff candidate forum. I am the debate moderator for the evening, and my name is Mike Jameson. What a rowdy crowd! Are you ready to rumble?"

Who did Mike think he was, a referee at a boxing match?

"On my right, incumbent Breckenridge 'Breck' Dyer has been sheriff of Quandary County for a solid four-year run. Plagued by scandal and accusations, can he convince enough voters that he should keep his badge? On my left, challenger Maxwell Waters, currently chief of police in Alma. Today, these two gentlemen will debate finances, arrest records, staffing choices, and their plans for the office if elected. Let me hear you say, oh yeah!"

No one said *oh yeah*. There was a general smattering of applause, but the loudest voice came from the hot dog vendor, who announced he was all out of spicy mustard.

"Please be courteous and turn off your cell phones." Mike wiped his forehead with a Kleenex. "I know it's cold outside, but it is hot as an oven up here. Can someone turn the building thermostat down, please? Thank you."

He stepped off the stage and took a seat at a folding table. While he shuffled some papers around, Breck pulled out his cell phone and pumped up the ringer volume to high. He crossed his fingers, hoping for an emergency call. Maybe someone would be kind enough to drive off the canyon road heading up Red Mountain Pass and take the three hundred-foot plunge into the ravine. Then Breck could politely excuse himself.

CHAPTER 64

Pleased As Punch

"Question for Sheriff Dyer. What do you believe are the most important job priorities facing the Quandary County Sheriff's Office today?"

Breck leaned forward, barely able to hear the question. There was an audio monitor beside his podium, which was supposed to amplify everything, but it was on the fritz. The only sound coming out was a steady hiss of static.

"Can you repeat the question?"

"Job priorities," Mike said. "What the most important job priorities?"

"Keeping citizens safe is my number one priority. My office has worked tirelessly to address the important issues facing our community. For example, compared to last year, the county has seen a significant reduction in illegal drug use."

Breck squinted in the spotlight. The bleachers were a haze of bobbing, blurry faces. Some people clapped.

"I want to acknowledge Deputy Jenny O'Hara, who has been a tremendous asset," he continued. "As everyone probably knows, the city of Quandary does not employ its own city police department, so the city council signs a contract with the county Sheriff's Office, and we provide street patrol services."

Across the stage, standing at his podium, Chief Waters was making a show out of yawning. Big open mouth. Stretch those arms. Smack those lips. But Breck soldiered on.

"The main problem we face is a severely decimated budget. This is because the city council has cut the funding and only pays the Sheriff's Office a bare minimum. In addition to that, federal funds are tight. Putting it simply, we need money to be effective."

That was a good spiel. It sounded professional, and it was honest. Hopefully, people would respond to that. He nodded at Mike Jameson to let him know he was finished.

"Response from Chief Waters," Mike said, using his best movie trailer voice.

Waters slid an index card out of his pocket and sneaked it onto his podium. Breck wanted to cry foul, but he didn't. They said no notes were allowed at the debate—otherwise, he would have brought some of his own.

"Three dead bodies. In the space of one week. You call that safety?" Waters leveled an accusing finger. "We all know what Dyer's tireless work has produced. You can even watch how he operates on YouTube. Everyone seen the video yet?"

A posse of teenaged boys immediately began to boo and throw paper cups. Breck knew those punks. They all lived on Eyrie Road near Matthews' house. In fact, they were the skateboarders who had been drawing mustaches on Johnny Tibbs' mayor signs.

"That's just the tip of the iceburg," Waters said. "The district attorney has been investigating Dyer for corruption. Shame on this man! And shame on you if you plan on voting for him."

Breck looked to Mike Jameson for a signal that it was okay to respond, but Mike had his head down, flipping through his list of scripted questions. He threw another softball to Waters.

"Tell us how you would do things differently if you get elected, Chief Waters."

"First, a Norwegian spelunker died in the Keystone mine. Then, a government official from Washington DC got murdered at the Continental Divide Motel." Waters leaned into the microphone. "Dyer will say the Sheriff's Office is too understaffed to provide coverage for the county. Too incompetent, I'd say."

"We *are* understaffed," Breck said. "And that wasn't a Norwegian spelunker. It was—"

But Mike cut him off.

"Let him finish, sir."

"What about Luke Roberts?" Waters was reading straight off his index card now. "It was true the man ran a fradulent horse rescue. When the horses didn't sell, he sold them to a slaughterhouse. That was bad, but it gets worse. Thanks to that YouTube video, we learned that Sheriff Dyer was the head honcho and Roberts was just a pawn in his game. And then, mere hours after he exposed the truth in public, poor Luke Roberts got shot in the head, right outside this very building. Who can explain that?"

The audience erupted.

Some people shouted at Breck, others shouted at Waters. While Mike Jameson pleaded with everyone to settle down, Waters grabbed the microphone off his podium, and began prancing around the stage.

"You hear Dyer locked up a billionaire, too? The only crime the man committed was trying to save our economy. We could have afforded a new cell phone tower, but not now!" He spoke so loud the speakers rattled. "Breck is running Quandary into the ground. Vote Maxwell Waters for Sheriff of Quandary!"

He dropped his mic on the floor, rapper style, and walked off stage.

Breck had been gripping the edges of his podium so hard that his knuckles were white. He unclamped and flexed his fingers. That was brutal. When did Max Waters become so vicious? He basically accused Breck of murder! Whoever had written the speech on his index card had done their research, and they were insidious. The sad part was, people might actually believe the accusations.

"Four more years! Four more years!"

Breck looked up. It was his brother, Danny, chanting. More than one person joined in, including Johnny Tibbs and all his wranglers. That was nice to see.

Mike tapped the microphone.

Boom, boom, boom.

"Closing statement, Chief Waters?" But Waters had disappeared, so Mike turned to Breck. "Closing statement, Sheriff Dyer?"

Anatoli Khodorovsky, Mayor Matthews, and Senator Stayne. The unholy trinity. Seated side by side in the front row, looking pleased as punch. It was like they orchestrated the whole thing. And maybe they did. These people were lethal—literally and politically. Jansen Asbjorn died over the sale of a mysterious Norwegian island. Billy James was murdered before he could grant the only witness safe asylum. And Luke Roberts was killed to destroy Breck's credibility, lose the election, and lose his career in law enforcement.

"I stand by my record," Breck said. "You all know Jenny and me, and we are working hard to provide high-quality public service to the community. Thank you for your support."

But a line had already begun to form at the concession stand, and it didn't seem like anyone was listening at that point. Did it matter?

CHAPTER 65

Blast From The Past

Getting into his Jeep, Breck fired up the engine and backed out of his parking space. But he didn't drive to the ski resort, or to his cabin for a quiet escape, or even the 7-Eleven to buy cigarettes. He circled around the fairgrounds, driving slowly.

There was still unfinished business.

As people streamed into the parking lot, looking for their vehicles, Breck was looking for a vehicle, too, and he spotted it idling near the holding pens with its running lights on—Khodorovsky's limousine. The driver was sitting on the hood, sipping booze from a silver flask. His cell phone must have rung, because he took it out of his pocket and answered. After a quick chat, he screwed the lid on his flask, got into the driver's seat, and drove the limousine towards the arena entrance.

"Go get your boss."

Breck parked far enough away that he could watch them without being seen. The driver got out and stood by the back door like a Marine at attention. After a few minutes, Khodorovsky came out and got in the back seat.

"Now, go get Aleks."

Once they pulled onto the main road, Breck gave the limo a little headstart before he began to tail them. With Hedda safe inside Tya's fortress apartment, the conference over, and DHS on their way, why would Anatoli risk sticking around Quandary? But Breck wasn't going to let the Russians get away clean. At the very least, he could arrest Aleks for assaulting Tya.

But instead of a secret rendezvous, or a high speed highway chase, the limo went straight to the Hyatt Residence Club.

Breck eased into a parking spot with a good view of the entrance. The limo eased to a stop under the portico, and the hotel valet rushed over to open the back door. Anatoli emerged, palmed the valet a greenback, and strolled confidently into the lobby.

Where are you Aleks? Packing your bags inside the Presidential Suite? Or lurking somewhere else? Like the ski resort?

He texted Jenny.

Everything okay?

She wrote back.

Fine and dandy. The french chef sent up a crazy good meal. I just ate snails for the first time in my life. How was the debate?

I made Bon Jovi proud.

What does that mean? Was Bon Jovi there?!

Breck almost wasted time looking for the flame emoticon, but instead scrolled through his phone contacts. Nickie Oberland. He held his finger over the call button, floating, hesitating.

Long before he had even dreamed about the Himalayas, Breck spent the weekends rock climbing with Kyle. Back then, Nickie had been a flight attendant with Frontier Airlines. She loved her job. She got to see new places, and traveling was her passion. But after Kyle disappeared, she took a desk job at the private jet terminal at DIA, and Breck could guess why. Nothing worse for a grieving widow than spending night after night in random hotel rooms, alone with her thoughts.

He pushed *dial* and held his breath. It rang a couple of times.

"Hello?" Nickie's voice was a blast from the past.

"Nickie. It's me." He cleared his throat. "Don't hang up. Please."

Silence.

"I have his helmet. Thank you. Danny gave it to me. . . ."

Silence.

What could he say? There was so much that needed to be said, but he couldn't seem to find the right words.

"Hey, Nickie? There's a Russian jet parked at your FBO. I don't know the tail number, but. . . ."

He wanted to ask other kinds of questions. How have you been? Are you remarried? Or dating someone new? Kids? Family? Maybe she was doing better these days, but the way Danny described their conversation at the brewery, the pain was still raw.

"Yeah, I know which one it is. I'm looking at it right now."

Breck sat up straight.

"Okay, great. Have you spoken with the pilots? Do you know their flight plan?"

"No, but they just did a walk around inspection. Probably means they'll be leaving soon."

Nickie sighed, but she didn't hang up. That was good. At least she was talking. It had been ten years since they had spoken last, back at the memorial. That final moment was ingrained in Breck's memory—the look in her eye as she shut the church door in his face.

"Why do you . . ." but Nickie trailed off. "Why didn't you . . . ?"

"Can I see you sometime?"

Silence.

He held his breath.

Still silence.

"Thanks for your help, Nickie."

The line went dead.

Even though winter was in the air, sweat was dripping down his face. Breck unzipped both his jacket and the Jeep window. The stress of the debate and the stress of the phone call—it was all taking its toll. He stuck his head out the window and took a couple gulps of cool, crisp air.

Another text came in. It was from Jenny again.

Where are you?

Hyatt. Stakeout. Starving.

Sounds like fun. I'll be right over. Snails are gone, but I can stop by the 7-Eleven. What do you want?

Large coffee. Two creams. Microwave burrito.

About ten minutes later, she opened the passenger door and got inside the Jeep. She was carrying a white plastic sack and two coffees in a cardboard carry-container.

"Frick, it's cold out there." She handed him a Styrofoam cup. "Why is your window down? Roll it up and turn on the heat. My toes are frozen. Aren't yours?"

She cringed as soon as she said it.

"Sorry. I forgot. You don't have toes anymore?"

"I still have some toe nubs."

"Toe nubs? Oh, God."

"Did Danny tell you?"

"Maybe. Yeah." She looked down at his boots as if she had x-ray vision. "I can't believe you lost your toes in the Himalayan Mountains. That's crazy. You're lucky you survived."

She cringed again.

"Sorry. I heard about your friend, Kyle. Shut up, Jenny. Drink your coffee, Jenny."

She took a long sip from her cup and then propped it between her knees so she could sort through the plastic bag. It was full of candy bars, corn nuts, a can of Coke, and a carton of coconut water. Snacks for the stakeout. There was a burrito inside, too. She carefully handed it to him.

"It's super hot. I think I left it in the microwave a little too long."

The wrapper was blazing hot, so Breck set it on the dashboard to cool off while Jenny ripped open one of the Kit Kat bars and took a bite. She pointed at the limo, still idling beneath the portico.

"Are we going to bust these evil Russian pricks before they skip town?"

"That's the plan," he said. "Anatoli's private jet is sitting on the tarmac in Denver, and the pilots are getting ready to take off, but there's no way he'll leave his boy Aleks behind."

The neon red Hyatt Residence Club sign flickered and began to glow against the gray sky. A few random snowflakes pattered across the windshield. Breck leaned forward and studied the third floor. All the curtains in the Presidential Suite windows were drawn. What were they doing up there? Taking a pre-flight siesta?

"How is Hedda?" Breck decided to unwrap the burrito. Steam rolled out of the foil. "Did you get her to talk?"

"Yep. I recorded her formal statement. We can officially arrest Anatoli again."

"How long did you cook this in the microwave?"

"I don't remember."

He set it back on the dashboard.

Suddenly, the limo slowly pulled forward and parked. The driver got out, sipping his flask, and went inside the building. At almost the same time, Breck got a text from Nickie.

Those Russian pilots just got into a taxi with their overnight bags. Heading to a hotel.

Breck sighed, and unbuckled his seatbelt.

"They're not going anywhere."

"Why don't we run inside and arrest Anatoli right now?" Jenny asked. "If Aleks is in there, we'll get them both."

"Something about all this feels wrong. I could have sworn they were going to make a run for it." Breck glanced around the parking lot. There were several SUVs, but he didn't see the Suburban. "I want to see Aleks with my own eyes before we make a move. Otherwise, he'll be in the wind."

"Well, I hope we can wrap this up tonight. Oktoberfest is tomorrow. I've been riding my bike all summer, and I'm finally in decent shape." She punched the air a couple times. "Gonna win that bike race."

CHAPTER 66

Danny's Wearing Lederhosen

After a long night of Kit Kat bars and coffee, Jenny couldn't fight it anymore. She fell asleep with the sunrise and didn't wake up until Breck nudged her.

"What time is it?"

"You don't want to know," Breck said.

"Anything new to report?"

"Aleks never showed his face, and Khodorovsky never left the hotel."

The sun was directly overhead, and it was warm outside. Breck had his window down to let in some fresh air. It looked like a downright pleasant day. There were even birds chirping. Then Jenny heard something else—rubber wheels humming on the asphalt.

"You gotta be kidding me."

Suddenly alert, she unzipped her window.

Reaching outside, Jenny toggled the big side mirror on the passenger side so she could see behind the vehicle. Two bicycles zoomed by on the street, and they were flying. The riders were both girls, one with a brown ponytail and one with a blonde ponytail, flopping behind their helmets. Jenny recognized them. It was Aspen Matthews and Brittany Chisolm from City Hall.

"Go! Go! Go!" Aspen shouted.

"Big money!" Brittany shouted back. "I need a new iPhone!"

In a matter of seconds, Jenny lost sight of them, but then more bikers pedaled past, hot on their heels, panting and shouting. The Oktoberfest bike race.

Breck yawned and rubbed his eyes.

"Sorry to wake you, but it's my turn for a nap."

He pulled a lever and the driver's seat reclined.

Bad guy surveillance took patience, but Jenny was running out of patience. How many times did she ride her bike up and down the canyon training for the race? All for nothing. Except that her calves were cut like stone now, and if she could ever afford to buy a decent dress, she'd look good and know it. But she sure could have used that prize money.

"I bet Danny's wearing lederhosen." Jenny kicked at a pile of candy wrappers on the floorboards. "And I guarantee he's got that charcoal grill going in the parking lot. You know, the big one he welded out of an oil drum. How many bratwursts can he fit on that, do you think?"

But Breck was already asleep.

The Presidential Suite windows. The curtains parted and then fluttered closed again. Were they watching the Russians, or were the Russians watching them?

Breck's cell phone buzzed, and his eyes flicked open. As soon as he saw the caller ID, he levered the driver's seat back upright and cleared his throat.

"It's McMurray." He hit the answer button. "John? Tell me you've got good news."

Jenny perked up and tried to listen in on the conversation, but she could barely hear the man's voice coming through the little speaker in Breck's phone. *Buzz, buzz, buzz.* Like a bee trapped in a tin can.

"Khodorovsky is still here in Quandary. We're sitting on his hotel now. . . . Fantastic. Thanks. See you soon."

He hung up the phone and slapped the steering wheel.

"Hot damn."

"What is it?" Jenny asked. "Is he coming, or what?"

"Yeah." Breck stretched his arms and arched his back. Joints cracked and popped. "McMurray's bringing a whole strike team. He's also working on a federal injunction to ground the jet, and a search warrant, as part of the investigation into Billy James' murder."

"Took him long enough. But better late than never."

Breck glanced at her and smiled. But then it slowly faded away.

"I've been trying to figure something out," he said. "McMurray said he was getting flak from above, right? He was supposed to be here days ago, but someone threw a wrench in the works. Someone higher up the ladder."

"Maybe it was just standard bureaucratic BS."

"I didn't get that vibe." Breck hooked his arms over the steering wheel and stared at the third floor for the millionth time. "What do we know about Dana Stayne?"

"We know she's got twenty million dollars sitting in a Bear Coin cold wallet . . . which she can't touch."

"She also came to watch the sheriff debate and sat with Mayor Matthews and Anatoli Khodorovsky."

"Let's see what the internet has to say." Jenny got on her phone and Googled the senator's name. "Hey, check this out. Dana Stayne is the chair of some kind of senate committee on foreign affairs. She could have sway over DHS. Maybe she's playing her own little game of thrones?"

Breck drummed his fingers on the dashboard.

"What if she calls Anatoli and warns him DHS is on the way?"

"Good," Jenny said. "It'll draw him out. At the very least, we can detain him for questioning."

Breck drummed his fingers again.

"I'm worried about Hedda."

"Why? She's in lock-down. The apartment is like a castle now. Plus, Tya's packing a .45 Magnum, and even Aleks will think twice with that bad boy pointed in his fat face."

But Jenny could tell Breck wasn't convinced. He turned around, trying to get a look at the ski resort. From where they were parked, they had a decent view of the building.

"There's something about all this I don't like. Can you walk across the street and check on them?"

She wiggled her cell phone.

"We can always call."

"I'd feel better knowing you're right there if something goes wrong."

CHAPTER 67

I'll Be Back

Aspen was late to work, but she didn't care. She was too happy. Five hundred dollars! And a blue ribbon that said *winner*.

When was the last time she felt like a winner? That warm gooey feeling of being a loser sure was a familiar feeling—losing out on a real degree from a real college, losing out on her Volkswagen Beetle, that she had loved so much, and losing out on family meals at the dining table, night after night, day after day, with both a mom and a dad who loved each other.

The blue velvet ribbon dangled around her neck. Of course, as soon as she got to High Country Pizza, it was going in the trunk, so it didn't wind up smelling like pepperoni. Her duffel bag was back there. It had her bike helmet and cycling clothes, a water bottle, and some leftover carbohydrate gels. That was how she won the race: hydration and quick calories. Everyone else loaded up on bratwursts covered in sauerkraut and Grey Poupon before the race started. Bad move. Heavy food was slow to digest and weighed a ton in the ol' gut. How many brats did Cash pound down? And he wondered why he came in last! Hey, if people wanted to sabotage their own success, who was she to stop them?

Parking by the curb, Aspen zipped her ribbon and prize money inside the duffel bag, slammed the trunk, and dashed inside. The high school kid holding down the fort looked frazzled.

"Where have you been?" he muttered. "The front desk at the Continental Divide Motel. They called in an order a half-hour ago. Hurry!"

He handed her a lukewarm pizza box. That meant the tip would be lousy, but since she just won five hundred smackers, it didn't sting quite as bad as it might have.

Aspen carried the pizza outside, fired up the Crapolla again, and hit the gas. Pretty soon, she was out of town, flying down the open road.

Five. Hundred. Bucks.

She knew exactly what she was going to do with it, too. Seed money for the rescue. Running a business would cost way more than five hundred, but it was the jump-start she needed.

Once her shift was over, Aspen was going straight back to the brewery to pick up her bicycle, and celebrate her victory. Brittany was still there, waiting for her to come back, drinking beer and playing Hammerschlagen with some of the young wranglers from the Tibbs ranch. Aspen couldn't wait to share her plans with all those bike race losers. Even the Tibbs wranglers could appreciate a horse rescue, right? How could they not?

The first order of business was to think of a name. A bunch of sing-song names ran through Aspen's mind, but nothing stuck.

Stable Homes.

Pony Paradise.

How about *Pretty Horse Safe Haven?* But riffing off of Luke Roberts' *Save All The Pretty Horses* website might seem a little insensitive. The man had been murdered, after all.

Perhaps something official. *The Quandary County Horse Rescue.* That had a strong vibe. It might be smart to go with something like that to help with future fundraising. Rich people with gigantic bank accounts might be more inclined to open their pocketbooks if she chose a respectable name. If she got too cutesy, they might think it was a joke.

As she drove into the motel parking lot, Aspen spotted her mother's car. The Ford Focus rental. Once the shock of the Customs officer's shooting had worn off, Valerie moved back into the motel. It was the only place she could afford, and she had no interest in staying at the house on Eyrie Road in such close quarters with her ex-husband. Some things were never going to change.

A quick hello wouldn't hurt. She parked outside of Room Number Six, and knocked on the door. The old fart who owned the motel was going to be mad the pizza was cold, but Aspen was too excited to tell her mom about the prize money and her big plans.

Valerie appeared, with a warm smile and a can of Diet Coke in her hand. No mimosa? There wasn't even any alcohol on her breath, and she looked more clear-eyed than Aspen had seen her in a long time.

"Guess what, mom? I won the bike race!"

"Congratulations, honey! That's fantastic. Come on inside, and tell me all about it."

"I can't. I'm working. Gotta drop a pizza off at the front desk. But I'll be right back and tell you all about it. And . . . I want to tell you what I've decided to do with my life."

"Give me a hint before you go."

Aspen felt a rush of pride.

"I'm going to start my own horse rescue. It's going to be a non-profit organization, run on donations and grants and stuff like that. I've even got a lawyer who will help me with all the legal aspects."

"What about college?"

"I can do both. A basic business degree will help me run the rescue, too." Aspen walked back to her car, and grinned. "I've got to deliver this to the front desk, then I'll come back. This will only take a sec."

"I'm proud of you, honey."

"Thanks, mom! I love you."

"See you soon."

Aspen got in the driver's seat, and sped down to the office. At this point, she knew what was about to happen. Cold pizza, half-hour late, no tip. But that was okay. She was on top of the world, and nothing could spoil her day.

"Hello?" She went inside the office.

The owner was eating an egg salad sandwich and watching an old rerun of *Cops* on an ancient television. He must have gotten too hungry, waiting for her to show up, and made a sandwich. Was he going to yell at her?

"Sorry, I'm so late."

"Oh, I didn't order it," he said. "Some fella in the campground, in Spot Number Nineteen. You can't miss him. He's the only one back there."

Jumping back in her car, Aspen drove around the building. As she passed Room Number Six, Valerie waved from her doorway.

Aspen honked and mouthed, *I'll be back.*

Sure enough, the whole campground was empty except for a single vehicle—an old wood-paneled Cherokee. It looked just like Cash's truck, but it couldn't be him. When she left the brewery, Cash was still there, making excuses about why he came in last at the bike race. Once upon a time, Aspen and Cash had dated, but that had been a big mistake. Ah, the memories.

Pulling up next to the Cherokee, she rolled down her window and waved at the man sitting in the driver's seat.

"Did you order a pizza?"

"Yes. Pizza. How much?"

The man opened the door and got out. Tall, muscular, and handsome. He looked familiar, but Aspen couldn't quite place him. Had the guy ordered pizza before?

"Ten bucks," she said. "You know what? My ex-boyfriend drives a Cherokee just like this."

"Just like this?"

"Yep. Say, that's a neat accent. Where are you from?"

He smiled, but it was a little creepy.

"Moscow."

CHAPTER 68

Give The Man An Oscar

Thunder echoed off the snowy mountain tops.

As the afternoon crawled by, Breck watched thick gray clouds roll in, and the temperature dropped like a stone. The nice sunny weather had come and gone. Ice cold raindrops began to tap on the canvas soft top.

He couldn't figure it out.

Why were the Russians still in town?

Their schemes had fallen apart, and surely Khodorovsky knew the clock was ticking. With DHS on the way, even his high powered attorney wouldn't be able to keep him from being detained. Not with Hedda's testimony on record.

And yet the limo was still in the parking lot.

"If it was me, I'd be on a plane for Moscow."

The battery must have died in the digital clock that was Velcroed to the dashboard. What a little piece of crap. It only cost a couple of bucks at the auto parts shop, and it was cheap in every sense of the word. Breck ripped it off and stuffed it in the 7-Eleven sack. It was full of trash now—the greasy burrito foil, numerous Kit Kat wrappers, empty coffee cups, and Coke cans.

Beneath the hotel portico, the automatic doors swished open, and Anatoli strolled out and lit a cigarette. He smoked and yukked it up with the valet for a few minutes, then he flicked the butt and went back inside. The dude was bold—no question about that.

Breck checked his phone. Jenny was in Tya's apartment. Everything must be normal, because she texted a photo of her supper.

Grilled lamb chops with charred eggplant salsa.

Breck spent a few minutes scrolling through his emoticons, looking for something clever, before he gave up. There were too many of those little cartoon things.

It was getting later and later, and McMurray had gone radio silent once again. It sure would be nice to know their ETA, or if his team had canceled their flight altogether. At least Hedda was safe in Tya's apartment, and Breck felt a lot better knowing Jenny was personally standing guard.

He doublechecked his handcuffs and .44 Special revolver were still where they should be, and rested his hand on the door handle. Waiting on DHS was feeling more and more like a false hope. With Hedda's formal statement, it was tempting to just go up to the Presidential Suite and arrest Khodorovsky and Aleks, if he was in there. But going in alone was risky. He had no idea who was in the suite, or what kind of firepower they had, or how aggressive they might react. Judging by how they treated Jansen Asbjorn, Billy James, and Luke Roberts, there was good reason to think things would go sideways.

"Good times."

Then Jenny sent him another text.

Cash called to report his Cherokee got stolen during the bike race. Who would want to steal that old clunker?

Breck shook his head. That was the least of his worries.

The CB crackled.

"Sheriff Dyer, you copy?"

"This is Breck."

"State Trooper Norwood. I've got a Chevy Suburban that matches your BOLO description."

"Really? Where?"

"The Quandary Ski Resort. It's sitting in the parking lot."

Breck twisted around and tried to get a look at the resort, but rainwater was trickling down the rear window, and everything was just a blur. Did Aleks ditch his SUV? Right across the street? That could only mean one thing—Hedda.

"10-4. I'll be right over."

But before he could turn the key in the ignition, he heard tires squealing.

A car whipped into the Hyatt parking lot. Its headlights were bright blue LEDs, and Breck held his hand over his eyes to block the light. It was a BMW— and not just any BMW.

"Oh, great."

Slamming on his brakes, Matthews skidded to a stop, blocking in several other cars. He jumped out and raced towards the Jeep, banging on Breck's door frantically.

"Open up! I need to talk to you right now. Come on, hurry!"

Breck unzipped his window. "What do you want?"

"They . . . they took my baby girl. They have Aspen."

"Who took her? Who are we talking about?"

Squinting in the rain, Matthews pointed at the Hyatt.

"The Russians! Khodorovsky. He called me a couple minutes ago. He said you were parked down here in the Hyatt lot, and I was supposed to tell you that . . . if you didn't. . . ."

He was either out of breath or else having a panic attack. He bent over by the fender and dry retched. Was this some kind of trick? Anatoli was full of them, and Matthews was, too. In fact, he was such a skilled showman he could have won an Emmy Award for some of his performances.

"Get out of here," Breck said.

"No! I'm not lying." Matthews gripped the window frame. "Please. Help her. Please. I'll do anything."

Forget the Emmy. Give the man an Oscar.

"Get in."

Matthews ran around and climbed into the passenger seat. He was dripping wet, and his hands were trembling.

"Tell me what happened."

"His bodyguard kidnapped my daughter. She was out delivering pizza, and he grabbed her, and took her to the Keystone Mine. If I don't bring Hedda Asbjorn to the hotel, the bastard is going to set off a stick of dynamite and cave in the mine. Aspen will be buried alive! Khodorovsky told me you were parked right here. I'm supposed to tell you something: *The fuse burns at forty-six seconds per foot.* What the hell does that mean?"

"Slow down. Take a breath."

Matthews was talking a mile a minute. Breck had never seen him act this way. Was it possible he was telling the truth? Did he get in over his head?

Breck looked up at the Hyatt.

"Forty-six seconds per foot?"

"He said you would know exactly what that meant."

Down in the mine where they recovered Jansen Asbjorn's body, Breck remembered seeing a wooden crate lying in the dirt. It was an old dynamite box, with those very words stenciled in black paint: *Fuse Rate, forty-six seconds per foot.* Khodorovsky wanted Breck to know he was serious.

"Have you tried calling Aspen's cell phone?"

"Of course, I did. No answer. So I called High Country Pizza. They said she never came back from a delivery at the Continental Divide Motel. Then I called Valerie. . . ." Matthews swallowed hard and looked at Breck with absolute sincerity in his eyes. "He said we have until sundown. That's it. Please. Help."

With the rain and low clouds, it was hard to tell where the sun was in the sky, but the light was fading fast. The mine was a solid hour's drive all by itself, all the way up the canyon, near Red Mountain Pass. Even if Breck complied and gave Anatoli what he wanted, how was Aleks supposed to hear about it? There was no cell signal at the mine. Unless he was just going to kill the girl regardless.

"What do we do?" Matthews asked. "What does Hedda Asbjorn have to do with this?"

"Get out, go home. Wait for me to call."

"Not a chance in hell."

Matthews put on his seat belt.

Whatever the truth of the matter was, Breck wasn't going to gamble with anyone's life. Not Hedda's, and not Aspen's. They had to get up to that mine and rescue her—and there wasn't a moment to lose. There wasn't even enough time to go across the street, ride the elevator up to Tya's apartment, and explain it all to Jenny. A phone call would have to do, and it had to be quick before they drove out of cell range.

Breck backed the Jeep out of the parking space, careful not to hit the BMW. If this was Alma, Matthews would get a parking ticket and a lecture. Where was Chief Waters when you needed him?

As they sped by the ski resort, Breck dialed Jenny's number.

"Breck, what's up?" she asked. "The lamb chops are all gone, buddy."

"Anatoli's making his move."

"Did he split for Denver?"

"No, worse. Aleks kidnapped Aspen Matthews while she was delivering pizza at the Continental Divide Motel. I'm heading up to the Keystone Mine right now. That's where he took her."

"What? Why? If they hurt that girl—"

"Anatoli is trying to work out a trade—Aspen for Hedda. That's what this is all about." Breck put the windshield wipers on high. The rain was coming down hard now. "By the way, the State Patrol just found Aleks's Suburban right there, at the ski resort. He must have ditched it and switched vehicles. Give them a call and tell them what's going on."

"I will."

Breck turned on the light bar and siren and blasted through the stoplights.

He made a hard turn onto Main Street, and headed past the tourist shops on the way to the canyon. As they sped past the Quandary Brewery, it was obvious Oktoberfest was still in full swing despite the rain. A crowd was packed inside the big white circus tent in the parking lot, playing games, drinking beer, and eating bratwursts and potato salad.

"Breck, that mine is a death trap." Jenny sounded worried. "You shouldn't go in there alone. Come pick me up."

The cell connection was getting spotty already. The rain always made it worse.

"This could all be smoke and mirrors," he said. "But if they really do have Aspen at the mine, I can't turn back now. Besides, I'm not alone . . . I've got Mayor Matthews with me."

"Holy frick balls."

They entered the canyon, the phone beeped, and the conversation was over.

CHAPTER 69

My Little Ptarmigan

Breck glanced at Matthews. He looked like he wanted to puke. It could be the fear for his daughter, the fear of losing the election, or the fear of driving off the canyon road and cascading three hundred feet into the bottom of a ravine. Or all of the above. Either way, Breck handed him the 7-Eleven trash sack.

"If you have to hurl, use this."

As they gained elevation, the rain changed into snow, just like it did when he sat outside of Tya's front gate, in Billy James's Dodge Challenger. But, at this time of year, it always did that—rain low, snow high. The problem was, the access road leading to the Keystone Mine was a bumpy, rutted, four-wheel-drive road on a good day. In wet, snowy weather, it would be a mud-fest. Bad conditions wouldn't stop the Jeep, but it would certainly slow them down. Hopefully, Aleks wasn't in a hurry to do anything stupid.

But Aleks liked to do stupid things. And in the span of a week, he had been a busy boy. Assault, breaking and entering, menace, and murder. He was sadistic, too. Choking Tya to within an inch of her life. Terrorizing Valerie, Aspen, and Hedda in their motel room. Now, he kidnapped Aspen, even though her father, the good mayor of Quandary, had entertained some kind of secret alliance with his boss, Anatoli Khodorovsky—the mastermind behind everything.

Oh, what a tangled web we weave.

Breck glanced at Matthews again.

"Don't worry. I won't let anything happen to your daughter."

"You're optimistic." Matthews was staring into the 7-Eleven sack. "I guess you have to be. It's your job."

The road curved and curved back. Breck downshifted, and the whole Jeep rocked with the force of each turn. The asphalt was slick. The tires squealed. When the road finally straightened out, he punched the gas pedal. The speedometer needle bounced up to forty, fifty, sixty, then seventy. They were out of the canyon now, and the pine trees went by in a blur.

Matthews wiped his eyes.

"Listen, I want you to know—"

But Breck was done playing games.

"What? That you're working with the Russians? Tell me something—how did Aleks know where I kept the evidence against Anatoli? I told you exactly what we had and exactly where it was. You knew, and you told them. Don't lie to me."

Matthews wadded up the 7-Eleven sack and tossed it behind the seats. He stared out the window.

"No. I didn't tell the Russians." His voice was flat. "I told Dana Stayne. She's the one who wanted Anatoli out of jail. She wanted those charges dropped. Not me."

"What did *you* want?"

"I wanted to pay my debts. Provide for my family. I wanted her endorsement for mayor, and I didn't want her to turn her fury on me." Matthews turned to face Breck. "Dana threatened to flip the DA's investigation onto me, instead of you, if I didn't help get Khodorovsky out of jail. So, yeah . . . I walked in that Sheriff's Office and found out what evidence you had on him. I told Dana Stayne—state senator of Colorado, chairman of the Committee on Foreign Investment in the United States, and the most soulless whore I've ever gotten into bed with. Politically speaking."

There it was. The truth. Breck wished he had a tape recorder.

Matthews cleared his throat and looked back out the window.

"And my daughter? She may not live to see another day. My baby girl. My little ptarmigan. And it's all my fault."

The windshield wipers swished like a metronome. They passed the General Merchandise, but the lights were off. The clerk must have shut the place down and gone home. Breck checked the gas gauge, but of course, it was broken. When was the last time he filled up? That was all he needed now—to run out of gas in the middle of a hostage crisis.

The road began to wind, zigzagging up a steep grade. These were the final switchbacks heading up to Red Mountain Pass. The snowflakes kept getting thicker, so thick it was hard to see where the edge of the road was. When they reached the top of the pass, Breck mashed the brakes and angled off the asphalt onto a narrow dirt road. This was it—the turnoff to the Keystone Mine.

"Look," Breck said, pointing to fresh tire tracks in the snow.

It had to be Aleks. Who else would be driving to the mine in a blizzard?

"I'm going to kill this guy." Matthews was starting to look alive again. Even a little wild, like a caged cat. "She's my only child. She's all I got."

Breck gunned it, and they bumped and jostled up the mountainside.

They were in the clouds now, and the fog was dense. Breck turned on his headlights, but the bulbs were dull and barely did any good. At first, pine branches raked the sides of the Jeep, but as they got higher, the forest began to thin. They were approaching timberline. Lightning cracked and everything went white for just a second.

Granite rocks.

Wilted tundra.

Old, dilapidated buildings.

The Keystone Mine.

Ore cart rails stretched into a rectangular opening cut in the mountain, and Cash's stolen Cherokee was parked right next to it, with snow and mud caked around its wheel wells.

"Do you see her?" Matthews leaned forward. "Where is she?"

But Breck didn't see anyone. He parked behind the Cherokee, and twisted the squelch dial on the CB a couple of times.

"State Patrol, come in."

No response. The radio wasn't picking up anything.

"Anybody reading this transmission?"

But there was only static.

Matthews jumped out of the Jeep and tore at the Cherokee's doors, calling for his daughter. But the doors were locked. He wiped the snow off the windows and cupped his hands to see inside the vehicle, but it was too dark.

"Hold on. I've got a flashlight."

Breck came over and shined a light in the vehicle's windows, but the Cherokee was empty. Except for a pizza box in the backseat. As soon as Matthews saw it, he turned pale.

"Oh, my God."

Hail pellets began to fall from the sky, rattling the old tin roofs around them. Breck zipped up his jacket. Matthews wasn't wearing a coat, and his sweater was soaked from the rain in the Hyatt parking lot. He started shivering.

"What do we do?" he asked.

In his flashlight beam, Breck saw two pairs of footprints in the snow, one big and one small. They led from the Cherokee, along the ore cart rails, straight into the mine tunnel. Breck checked his revolver to make sure it was loaded.

"Stay here. I'm going into the mine."

CHAPTER 70

Stay Frosty

In the rain and twilight, all Jenny could see through the window in Tya's apartment was the flash of the State Patrol car in the parking lot below. Blue and red strobe lights.

Her cell phone rang.

"Deputy O'Hara? We found an abandoned vehicle."

It was the State Patrol dispatcher, a black woman in her fifties appropriately named Jade. She spoke like a robot. Jenny bumped into her once, standing in line at the Subway in Frisco. Long painted fingernails, dead fish eyes, and the lady was bleak.

"Way ahead of you," Jenny said. "Chevy Suburban."

"No. Another one. This is a white 1986 Toyota Corolla, abandoned at the campground. Front door was open, keys in the ignition. The car is registered to Aspen Matthews."

Jenny felt a chill. This was really happening. It wasn't a wild goose chase.

"The mayor's daughter. She's our missing girl."

"Troopers interviewed the motel owner. He said a man with a foreign accent borrowed his landline to order a pizza from High Country. Mid-thirties, tall, muscular."

"That's our primary suspect in a string of murders."

"One more thing," Jade said. "In the vehicle, the officers found a Quandary County evidence bag lying in the driver's seat. The seal is broken. It contains a red swipe-style plastic card. It says, Hyatt Residence Club."

"Are you kidding me?"

"I don't kid."

The Asbjorn's key card. Aleks left it behind. Why?

"Did they find a legal document?" Jenny asked. "Written in Norwegian. Bloody fingerprints."

"No."

It didn't matter. Hedda formally identified the Russians as her attackers, and the key card was the hard proof they needed to connect Anatoli to the crime scene. Mr. Lawyer couldn't save him now.

"Jade! Send all your troopers straight to the Hyatt in Quandary. I'm right across the street at the ski resort, and I'm heading over there right now to make an arrest. I need all the backup you can spare."

"I can divert the boys from the speed trap on I-70, but it'll take twenty minutes for them to arrive. Trooper Norwood is at your location."

"I'll grab Norwood, but we'll wait in the Hyatt lobby until the others arrive. This is a major bust."

Grabbing her fleece jacket, Jenny reached around to make sure her handcuffs were still where they should be, clipped on her belt. The Luger was in its holster— time to nail this commie prick. But first, she had to get out of the apartment.

"Tya! How do I get this thing open?"

Jenny couldn't figure out the new steel entry door. Instead of a doorknob, there was a keypad, and she had no idea what the code was.

Racing over, Tya typed in a number sequence as fast as she could, but the metal door didn't open. It made buzzing sounds, and little red lights flashed. Muttering, Tya tried again, and kept reentering numbers until the door unlocked and swung open.

Deciding against the elevator, Jenny took the stairwell. The sound of her boots echoed the whole way down. When she reached the ground floor, she rammed the door open and found herself in the hallway near the food court. The tables were filled with conference-goers eating dinner, and the noise of the door was so loud, many people twisted around, startled. But Jenny ignored the looks and ran towards the lobby.

Two private security guards, dressed in gray suits and sunglasses, were posted beside the elevator.

"We've got a situation across the street. Stay frosty, fellas!"

When she ran by the reception desk, Cash waved to catch her attention.

"Hey, deputy! Did you find my Cherokee yet?"

Before he had finished the sentence, Jenny was in the parking lot. She pulled up the collar on her jacket. The rain was ice cold. Across the street, the glowing red letters of the Hyatt sign seemed to float in the darkness.

She ran towards the State Patrol car, still parked in the lot, lights flashing. Trooper Norwood was sitting inside, typing up a report on the Suburban. He was a quiet young man with a stern face, who took his job very seriously. Jenny knew him. She knew all the staties.

He rolled down his window.

"Did you get a call from dispatch?" She was out of breath. "Jade?"

"Yes, ma'am."

"Let's roll." Jenny jumped in the passenger seat. "But no lights and no siren. We don't want to spook this guy."

"Yes, ma'am."

It only took a minute to drive across the street to the Hyatt, and as they circled through the parking lot, Jenny pointed out Khodorovsky's limousine. It was still sitting in the special Presidential Suite parking space.

"Keep an eye on that thing. It's the getaway vehicle." He pulled into the portico, long enough for her to hop out. "Our suspect is a Russian oligarch by the name of Anatoli Khodorovsky. He may not be alone, so consider him dangerous. The hotel has security monitors, so that's where I'll be. The moment the other troopers arrive, meet me in the lobby, and we'll arrest him."

"Yes, ma'am."

As she surveyed the rest of the parking lot, Jenny noticed Matthews' BMW blocking an aisle way. Some poor guy was standing there, jingling his keys in the rain. His car was boxed in. If this were a normal day, she would have dialed a tow truck without hesitation. Watching Matthews' precious BMW get towed away would have been a high point of her career. But this wasn't a normal day.

As usual, Zachary was seated behind the reception desk, sipping on a can of Sprite.

"Can I help you?"

Jenny made a quick survey of the lobby, but didn't see Khodorovsky. She didn't see anyone. The conference was over and the Hyatt had emptied out.

"Have the Russians in the Presidential Suite come down yet? Or are they still in their room?"

"I can't say." He shrugged. "I haven't seen them if that's what you're asking."

"Yes, that's what I'm asking." Jenny was on edge. She took a deep breath to calm her nerves. "Listen. The State Patrol is on the way. When they get here, we're going to arrest Khodorovsky. If the dude doesn't respond to a neighborly knock, I'll need a key card so we can get into his suite."

A miserable look crossed Zachary's face, but he opened his wallet and produced a plastic card.

"The boss is not going to be happy."

"He'll get over it." Grabbing it out of his hand, Jenny tucked it in her back pocket. "Where are your security monitors? I want to make sure Khodorovsky doesn't sneak out the back door."

Spinning around in his swivel desk chair, Zachary gave the office door a shove with his toe. It swung open. Jenny waited for him to lead the way inside, but he didn't get out of his chair.

"Do you know how much a cleaning crew charges for a crime scene?" he asked. "When there is blood all over the place, it's called a biohazard. They had to wear hazmat suits. The boss blew a gasket when he saw the bill."

"I'm pretty sure the Asbjorns didn't sign up for the experience."

She circled around the reception desk and went into the office. The entire row of flat-screen monitors mounted on the wall was nothing but static.

"Hey, Zach Attack. Get in here and turn these on."

Zachary took a long sip of Sprite before he got out of his chair. When he came inside the room and saw the static, his face scrunched up.

"What are you waiting for?" she asked. "Turn these things on."

"They are on."

He flipped a few switches, but nothing changed. Not one screen so much as flickered. Pushing him out of the way, Jenny tried flipping the switches herself. On, off. On, off. Then she peered behind the row of monitors and saw all the cables were sliced clean. A pair of wire cutters were even lying on the carpet.

"Good job, numb-nuts." She flicked the can of Sprite in Zachary's hand. "Somebody snuck past you while you were tossing a whiz."

"That's impossible." But he said it without much force. He rubbed his eyes. "Listen. Managing this place isn't as glamorous as it seems. My boss hates me, the pay sucks, and I basically work twenty-four seven. I can't sit here at this desk every waking second, can I?"

As he was complaining, Jenny heard the wail of police sirens.

"I told them no sirens!"

She ran back out into the lobby, just as Norwood led a half-dozen State Patrol troopers through the front entrance, in their flat-brimmed hats. They looked like a platoon of Marines. One of them handed her the open evidence bag they found in Aspen's Corolla, with the Asbjorns' key card in it.

"Deputy? Who are we taking in, and why?"

"Our suspect is Anatoli Khodorovsky, and I'm formally charging him with the murder of Jansen Asbjorn, a Norwegian who died this past week. But he is also connected to two other murders."

Leading the way, she charged up the stairwell to the third floor and banged on the Presidential Suite door. The troopers drew their guns, but nothing happened. No one opened the door. Jenny didn't hear any sounds of commotion inside, but that didn't mean anything. Khodorovsky could be waiting inside with an AK-47.

Jenny took out the master key card that Zachary had given her, and swiped the lock. The door clicked, and the little LED turned green.

"Sheriff's Office!" She drew her Luger and kicked open the door. "Freeze and get on the ground!"

The elderly Russian attorney, Konstantin Veselnitskaya, was sitting on the couch with his cane in his lap and merely raised his hands. He was alone.

"My client is innocent, deputy."

Jenny swung her gun around the big open room. It appeared to be empty. But was it?

"Turn this place upside down. Check the closets, bathrooms, under the beds. If Anatoli is hiding inside a roll of toilet paper, I want to know."

Going to the far wall, she yanked open the curtains, in case Anatoli was hiding behind the drapes, but he wasn't there. Through the glass, blots of wet snow were beginning to fall from the sky. The weather was getting bad. The pavement down below was turning into slush, and all the cars in the parking lot were white.

Except for the limo, because it was gone.

CHAPTER 71

Three Kilometers Of Distance

Tya was sitting on the white leather sofa next to Hedda, sipping a flute of Chardonnay.

"Mrs. Tordenskjold? Are you okay?"

The voice came from the intercom mounted on the wall. It was the leader of her new security detail—the blonde guy with the buzz cut. Even though he was kind of cute, he had a rough ex-military vibe about him that was a turn-off. Sven would go insane if she started dating again. That was an interesting thought. Once this whole crazy ordeal was over, and things went back to normal, it might be worth it to ask the guy out to dinner—just for a social media photo op. Tag Sven, and let the magic begin.

Tya went to the panel and pushed the talk button.

"Yes, I am fine. Why do you ask?"

"The motion sensor in your panic room was triggered. Did you retreat inside? Did an intruder break in?"

She glanced over at the panic room. Everything was quiet. The sliding steel door was wide open and ready for business. If anyone did break in, all she had to do was run inside and push a big red button, and it would seal out any danger until help arrived. But Tya hadn't gone inside, and Hedda was still camped out on the sofa.

"No, everything is fine in here. Should I be concerned?"

"Probably just a malfunction, but it would be a good idea if I could inspect the panic room. If it's a problem with the wiring, that's an easy fix. Or if it's a mouse, I can trap it. May I enter the premises, ma'am?"

Blonde Buzz Cut was standing right outside her door. Tya could see him on a brand new flat screen monitor, bolted to the wall, right next to the loudspeaker.

It was comforting to have such a high-end professional team at the resort. Their services didn't come cheap, but after nearly getting choked to death, this was no time to skimp, and peace of mind was priceless.

The company was called Bridge Head Private Security. All the guards wore gray dress suits with pocket squares, and dark sunglasses, with handguns in shoulder holsters. They kept a van stationed in the parking lot with satellite surveillance equipment, and they even had a drone with night vision technology. There was no way that man, Aleks, was going to get past them.

What a relief. If Senator Dana Stayne hadn't recommended them, Tya would have had to rely on budget rent-a-cops from the Yellow Pages.

Why was Breck so suspicious of the woman? The senator had been nothing but kind and compassionate with Hedda. Was it politics?

"Sure. Come on in."

It was funny how easy it was to push the right buttons when there was no pressure. The thick metal door unlocked with a clang and swung open. Tya gave Blonde Buzz Cut her best Instagram smile, but instead of entering the apartment, the man remained in the hallway, standing like a statue.

"Aren't you coming inside?"

Anatoli Khodorovsky appeared in the doorway, holding a pistol.

"He is not, but I am."

From the sofa, Hedda screamed.

What was going on? Taking a step back, Tya's mind reeled, trying to take in what was happening, and connect the dots. She remembered this guy. He was behind bars in the Sheriff's Office just the other day. He squished a spider on the wall. How did he get out of jail? How did he get by the security detail? And why was Blonde Buzz Cut just standing there? Tya wanted to yell at him. *Do something!* But fear shot through her veins, her mind clouded over, and she felt paralyzed.

Khodorovsky handed the security guard a roll of hundred dollar bills.

"Not necessary, sir."

"Think of it as bonus for job well done," Anatoli told him. "Now, return yourself to downstairs lobby and alert me immediately if police arrive."

"But our cover is blown, sir." He indicated Tya and Hedda. "I can stay and help you clean this up."

Khodorovsky chuckled.

"Not necessary."

He swung the door shut.

"Do not move, girls." He held the gun at his waist, waving it around casually. "First one to run for panic room gets extra special treatment. Not to worry, however, as we can resolve this situation quite peacefully. We can all go our separate ways, healthy and whole. You would like that, yes?"

Grabbing Tya by the arm, Khodorovsky shoved her roughly onto the sofa. Hedda hadn't moved, except to pull the blanket over her head.

After he tucked the pistol in his belt, the Russian oligarch reached into his suit coat pocket and produced a piece of paper and a pen. He set them on the coffee table.

"Now, let us get to business at hand. Mrs. Asbjorn, I require two things. A signature and the passwords to access Bear Coin. Rumor has it there are two hundred million dollars out there in cyberspace, waiting to be claimed. Might as well be me, yes?"

Tya stared at the paper. It was the legal document. The same one that Breck had asked her to translate. The Skogsøya real estate agreement.

Without further prodding, Hedda emerged from her cocoon, took the pen, and signed her name on the black line to finalize the sale.

"Very good." Khodorovsky smiled. "This is so easy when everyone cooperates."

Tya's heartbeat was pounding like crazy. Her purse was sitting on the coffee table. The .45 Magnum was inside. Should she grab it?

Khodorovsky folded up the real estate agreement and tucked it back inside his suit coat. Spotting Tya's laptop, he walked over to her desk and clicked the mouse to wake up the screen.

"Mrs. Asbjorn, would you join me, please? I need those pesky passwords."

Tya reached over and gripped Hedda's hand. It had been a major discussion topic over JB's escargot the night before. Jansen's passwords were a mystery, and Hedda simply didn't know what they were. What was the Russian going to do when he realized she couldn't provide them? Tya's eyes went back to her purse.

"Mrs. Asbjorn?" Khodorovsky snapped his fingers. "Come. Sit. Type."

Shaking like a leaf, Hedda did what she was told. She went and sat down in front of the computer.

"It will take a few minutes to . . . to. . . ." Her voice cracked. "To log in to the account."

"Please, do."

Anatoli walked over to the large bronze eagle sculpture. He ran his finger along one of the wingtips.

"Majestic. Deadly. There are no raptors quite like the bald eagle. Their eyesight is what is most impressive, you would agree?" He was talking to Tya. "Did you know they can see a tiny little field mouse from three kilometers of distance? Tiny little mouse is simply going about business, searching for next meal. Hello, piece of corn, where are you? Then, boom! Tiny little mouse *is* the next meal."

During the summer holiday they spent together at Skogsøya, Tya and Hedda spent many lazy days sitting on the pier in lounge chairs, watching sea eagles dive for fish. Tya loved talking about the latest Per Petterson novel or the new ballet performance at the Oslo Opera House, and so did Hedda. But Sven and Jansen preferred to argue politics. After spending so much time in the United States, Sven had grown to appreciate the benefits of a capitalist economy, but Jansen berated him for not thinking globally. When it got too heated, Tya would beg them to change the subject. She hated politics. She just wanted to be happy. To have friends and pleasant conversations about culture and books and skiing, and never stop to worry about all the horrible things that happened in the world, none of which they had any control over, anyhow.

"Mrs. Asbjorn? Tell me you find piece of corn?"

Tears began slipping down her cheeks. Even though Hedda didn't know the codes, she was desperately trying to guess. After several incorrect entries, the Bear Coin sign-in page automatically locked her out. Suddenly, she leaped up and ran, but Khodorovsky raced after her and seized her by the hair.

"Where are you going? Panic room?" He took out his pistol. "Time to panic."

Now or never. Tya reached into her purse and got the Magnum. She stood tall, spread her feet, and clicked off the safety—just as she had done a hundred times at the gun range. But this wasn't the gun range, and she wasn't aiming at a can of Diet Coke. Tya's hands trembled. Her vision blurred. *Bang.* The gun went off in her hands. The kickback was so strong that it flew out of her hands. Where did it go?

Anatoli Khodorovsky fell backward like he'd been hit by a train.

He screamed. There was blood everywhere. The bullet had caught him in the shoulder, tearing through the fabric of his suit coat, shirt, and skin, and some bones were poking up like antlers.

His pistol landed on the carpet near the eagle statue, and even though he was wounded, he immediately started crawling towards it.

Where was her Magnum? Where did it land?

"Run!" Tya shouted.

Hedda had fallen, too, but she scrambled to her feet, and together, they raced for the panic room.

CHAPTER 72

Guesswork

The flashlight from the glove box was a dollar store cheapy. It was ideal for reading maps or unwrapping an Egg McMuffin at 5:00 AM, but chasing a suspect through an old gold mine at ten thousand feet? Not so much. Breck just wished he had Cash's fancy flashlight. What did he call it? The Night Blast? Something like that.

Behind him, Matthews kept stumbling over rocks and old beer cans.

Breck turned around and shined the light in his eyes.

"Dude. You need to be quiet."

"I'm trying, okay? I can't see."

The atmosphere in the mine was completely different. Outside, it was snowing, hailing, wet, and windy. Inside, everything was dry, dusty, and silent as a tomb.

The central tunnel went straight back, but several side tunnels shot off in different directions. But Breck knew where Aleks was going. That dynamite box was on the "three hundred level," three hundred feet down. And to get there, they had to climb straight down a vertical shaft using a rickety wooden ladder.

Breck started down the ladder, but Matthews grabbed his shoulder.

"How do you know they went down there?"

"That's where we found Jansen Asbjorn."

"So?"

"I think that's where he took Aspen."

"You think?" Matthews hissed. "We don't have time for guesswork."

There was no time to argue with Matthews, but it was more than guesswork. Anatoli had given them the hint—the fuse burns at forty-six seconds per foot.

That was a direct reference to the dynamite box. It could also be a red herring, luring them into a trap. Aleks could be hiding somewhere, waiting for them to pass, and then set off an explosive and cave in the mine. Or worse, Aleks may have already shoved Aspen down into the same pit they found Jansen. She could be dead already. Was this his sick way of leading them to her body?

It was a dangerous game of cat and mouse.

Breck stopped climbing and clicked off the flashlight. Matthews, a few rungs above, paused as soon as everything went black.

"What is it?"

"I heard something."

Breck held his breath, listening. Somewhere down below, he spotted the faint glow of another flashlight. It bobbed around and grew faint and then vanished completely.

"Did you see that?" Matthews' voice was a tense whisper. Then suddenly, he started yelling. "Aspen! It's me, daddy!"

His voice reverberated off the rock walls. Immediately, Aspen's voice bounced back from somewhere in the lower tunnels.

"Daddy!"

"Aspen! . . . Aspen?"

But the echoes faded into silence.

Breck clicked his flashlight on, again. Matthews' face was white as a ghost. He shined it down the shaft. The ladder rungs faded in the distance. They still had a long way to go to get down to the third level.

"Aleks! It's me, Sheriff Dyer. I have what you want. Let's make a deal."

Of course, Breck didn't have what he wanted, but he needed to buy time. He held his breath and waited, but there was no answer. He shined the light up in Matthews' face again, making him squint.

"Listen to me. Climb back up, go to the Jeep and try the CB again. See if you can get Chief Waters. Alma isn't too far away. He could be here in a half-hour if he tries."

Matthews frowned.

"But the CB didn't work. You tried to get the State Patrol on the radio when we first got here, remember? So why would it work now?" He shook his head. "Don't sideline me. Not now."

Breck shined his light down the shaft again. The good news was that Aspen was still alive. But the bad news—he was going to have to confront Aleks to save her. It was pretty unlikely the man would simply let her go, lay down in the tunnel, and allow Breck to handcuff him. A second civilian in the crossfire was an extra worry he didn't need, but Matthews was determined to come along.

"Things may get tense, so stay behind me. If you see me draw my weapon, you hit the deck. Hear me?"

"Okay."

They descended the ladder until it bottomed out on the three hundred level. Breck shined his flashlight into the tunnel. A white, glittery quartz vein ran the tunnel's length, and an ore chute was sticking out of the roof. It was a familiar sight.

"It's just up ahead," he whispered. "Watch your head. The ceiling is low here."

He placed his palm on his revolver grip. The last thing he wanted to do was fire a weapon underground, in a rocky tube. It would ricochet like crazy. The noise alone could blow out their eardrums, or worse, cause a cave-in. But he might not have a choice, depending on what Aleks chose to do.

The dynamite box was still sitting on the ground, where it had been, marking the side tunnel where Jansen had been killed. *Fuse Rate, forty-six seconds per foot,* stenciled in black paint. Breck carefully lifted the lid, but it was empty. Was it empty before? They never checked, did they?

Clicking off his light, Breck hoped to see the telltale glow of Aleks' flashlight, either in the main tunnel or the side tunnel leading to the pit, but both tunnels were completely dark. The obvious thing to do was check the pit first—so why did it feel like an ambush?

Breck turned on his light again and shined it further down the main tunnel.

"What's that?" Matthews whispered.

Something shiny was lying in the dirt next to the tram rails. Breck went to see what it was. Car keys, with a silver key chain shaped like a snaffle horse bit. When Matthews saw it, he started hyperventilating.

"Those are Aspen's car keys!"

"She dropped them on purpose."

Forget the side tunnel. That was a trap. Breck drew his revolver and moved slowly along the tram rails, further into the mountain. They were entering unfamiliar territory. Every few steps, they paused to listen, hoping to hear Aspen's voice, or footsteps, or anything. Hopefully, she was okay and was playing along with Aleks, so he didn't hurt her. That made sense since they found her keys. He was a trained killer and an expert at stealth, but Aspen was a smart girl.

They came to a fork in the road. One tunnel went left, and one went right.

"Look."

Breck knelt. He found a crumpled piece of paper on the ground, just inside the right passageway. It was a High Country Pizza receipt.

Aspen was definitely leaving a trail to follow.

The tunnel curved, and around the bend they passed some machinery, with a metal spool and circular gears—an old winch. As Breck started to walk by, the floor flexed under his weight. He took a quick step back and shined the light on the ground. The gravel was hiding several planks of thick, raw cut lumber, and the wood was covering a vertical shaft.

"Why are we stopping?" Matthews whispered.

"This is a false floor. Wait until I'm on the other side before you cross."

The wood creaked and bowed as he crossed, but it held. When he got to the far side, he waved Matthews over.

"Be careful. The wood feels rotten."

Shaking his head in disbelief, Matthews tested the boards with his foot.

"I don't know if I can do this."

CHAPTER 73

Divide and Conquer

The Presidential Suite looked staged for a magazine photoshoot. Couch cushions perfectly poised and brand new silk sheets on the bed. Carpets vacuumed, tile floors mopped, zero personal effects.

There was certainly no trace of Khodorovsky, or any sign that he, or anyone, or anyone's DNA, had ever stayed in the suite.

"Spic and span. Clean as a whistle." Jenny glared at the Russian lawyer. "Did he cut bait and run?"

"Fishing analogies are so worn out, don't you think? There is an old cowboy adage. Perhaps you have heard?" The man looked smug. "If your horse dies . . . get off."

"Where did Anatoli go? Denver?" She took out her phone. "It's a four-hour drive to the airport. Plenty of time for me to call the Denver Police Department. They'll be waiting for him on the tarmac."

Before Jenny could dial, her phone rang. The caller ID said *Quandary Ski Resort.* She hit the talk button.

"Tya? What's wrong?"

"Hey, it's Cash. I thought I dialed 9-1-1."

"I'm sure you did. When no one's at the office, 9-1-1 calls automatically get bounced to my cell phone. Is there an emergency?"

"We've got serious problems. The new panic room in Mrs. Tordenskjold's apartment has an alarm that triggers when someone goes inside and seals the door. Well, it just went off."

"What about those new fancy guards? They're right there. Send them up to check it out."

"Yeah, they bailed."

Jenny went to the window again. From the third floor of the Hyatt, she had a clear view of the ski resort. Right before her eyes, a black van squealed out of the resort parking lot and sped away into the night.

"What do you mean?" she asked.

"Not one of them even said a word. They all just up and left. Just now."

"I'll be there in sixty seconds." Jenny stuck the phone in her jacket and ran for the door, shouting at the State Patrol troopers. "Let's roll!"

She ran as fast as she could. Down the stairwell, through the lobby, and outside into the swirling snow.

It was so obvious now. The evidence bag in Aspen's car was every bit as strategic as her kidnapping. Divide and conquer. They sent Breck running to the Keystone Mine and lured her to the Hyatt—stupidly thinking she would make an arrest. And either Anatoli bought off Tya's security detail, or they were on his payroll the whole time.

Jenny wanted to slap herself for falling for it. *Damn, these guys are sly.*

While the troopers went to find their vehicles, she dashed straight across the street, splashing through fresh slush, and dodging traffic. As she ran, Jenny thought about Hedda running across the same street, in her socks, from the Hyatt to the ski resort, terrified for her life. Was her life in danger yet again?

Crossing the resort parking lot, Jenny wiggled through the automatic doors as they slowly swished apart, and as soon as she entered the lobby, Cash waved her over. His eyes were wide as saucers.

"You've gotta see this, deputy."

He showed her his computer screen.

There was a grid, with a dozen different live camera feeds—the parking lot, chair lift, alpine hut, conference room, hallways, elevators. Cash pointed to a stairwell monitor. A blurry figure was hustling down the stairs, leaning on the handrails for support. On every step, he left dark wet footprints behind.

"That dude just ran out of Mrs. Tordenskjold's apartment." Cash leaned over the desk and pointed past the elevators towards the food court. "He'll come out down there."

"I know exactly which door it is!"

She started running down the hallway, when the stairwell door by the food court banged open, and she saw Anatoli Khodorovsky stagger out, slipping on something slick. Jenny realized it was blood. He was covered in it. Judging by the way he was limping and holding his shoulder, it must be his own.

"Freeze, you Russian freak!"

But of course, he didn't. He turned and bolted for the rear of the building, hobbling past the food court and straight out to the ski slopes. Jenny hustled as fast as she could, but he jumped on the chair lift before she could catch him. It whisked him into the air.

"Where do you think you're going?" she shouted.

Anatoli laughed at her and shouted back.

"I hear the café has amazing coffee!"

But his laughter turned to a painful moan. He hunched, wincing in pain, and Jenny held her breath. Was he going to slip off the chairlift? It was a twenty-foot fall.

As she stood there, waiting for the next chair, Jenny felt a pang of fear in her gut. If Anatoli was covered in blood, what about Tya and Hedda? There could be a worse situation in the apartment. Maybe the women were wounded, too—or dead.

Jenny felt torn. What should she do? Chase this guy, or go back inside?

Stupid staties! Where were they? Stuck in traffic?

Turning around, Jenny looked back at the resort, praying the troopers would appear. She could see right through the oversized windows into the building—the food court, hallway, and all the way down to the lobby. She could see it all. As she watched, the troopers appeared, marching into the lobby, and Cash ran towards them, talking and pointing. Finally. Whatever had happened upstairs, good or bad, they could handle it.

She had a bad guy to catch.

CHAPTER 74

Think Bigger

When the next bench dipped to the ground, Jenny climbed aboard. She drew her Luger and sighted Khodorovsky, trying to see if he had a gun. But the man looked terrible. His whole back was soaked with blood.

"Hey, Anatoli!" Jenny hollered. "You need a doctor. I hope you don't bleed out before you reach the café."

Twisting around in his seat, Anatoli gave her a winning smile.

"Just a flesh wound."

Then the smile faded, and his eyes closed.

Jenny held her breath, half-expecting him to tumble off his bench. That sure would solve a big problem if he did.

The only sound was the hum of the cable overhead. As the chairlift took them higher and higher, the snowflakes became thicker and thicker. Jenny holstered her sidearm and blew hot air into her hands. Her fingers were numb.

What was going on? Was Tya safe? Hedda? Did Breck rescue Aspen from Aleks? Jenny frowned at the red flashing lightbulb on top of the cell tower, miles across town, blinking in the darkness. What was the point of having a cell phone if there was never a cell signal?

Wiping snowflakes off her face, Jenny wanted answers.

"I don't get it," she called.

Khodorovsky's head was starting to sag and jerk like he was fighting unconsciousness.

"Why do you want all that Bear Coin money?" She whistled. "Two hundred million? I wouldn't know what to do with all that money. Pay off the bills. Move to Maui. Get a tan."

As his bench passed beneath a lamppost, she could see that his face was glistening with sweat. The dude was in pain.

"Think bigger, *Krasny*."

"Aren't you freaking mega-rich already? Why do you need more?"

"Even an oligarch has a paper trail, and crypto money is invisible. No one knows what I do with it. Maybe I buy power. Or influence. Or mercenaries, to pretend they are private security team for unlucky ski resort owner."

That explained that.

"What about Hedda's island? Why do you want that? Go buy your own island."

"I like that one."

The ski lift cable bounced as her bench arm passed over a support column. They were almost at the top of the mountain. Jenny could see people inside the alpine hut, through the windows, seated at tables, and standing in line at the café counter. If Anatoli made it inside, he would have his pick of hostages, and it was going to be a stand-off until he keeled over from his injuries.

Jenny shivered. The snow was flying like crazy, and it was freezing cold. Anatoli might be lying about everything else, but he was right about one thing. The alpine hut did serve amazing coffee. It was an imported Italian brand and cost five bucks a cup, but it sounded really good at the moment.

All she could do was watch as Anatoli's bench topped the slope, and he jumped off into the snow and ran. Jenny had been counting the seconds between columns and knew that he had a thirty-second headstart. Plenty of time to order an espresso and introduce himself to a captive audience.

But instead of heading towards the café, the Russian billionaire ran the other direction, along the ridgeline. He passed beneath the outermost floodlight and then vanished in the darkness.

Jenny cupped her hands and shouted.

"Go crawl in a hole and die!"

Not her most articulate moment, but she meant every word.

Finally, the chair ride was over. Jenny slid off her bench and raced after him. The mountain ridge was dark and narrow, with drop-offs on both sides. One step in the wrong direction. . . .

The closest thing to a flashlight Jenny had was the flashlight setting on her cell phone, and it helped. When she clicked it on, Anatoli's bloody footprints in the snow were easy to follow. But the light also made her a target. Jenny had to assume that the guy had a gun. It would be so easy to wait until she was ten feet away and sink a bullet in her chest. Even in blizzard conditions, she didn't want to underestimate the man, so she shut off the light and let her eyes adjust to the darkness.

In the blowing snow, she spotted a dark figure moving slowly along the ridge.

Suddenly a helicopter came out of nowhere, and her hair whipped in the rotor wash as it flew over. It was flying dark—no red or white strobes, no landing lights, not even any gauge glow in the cabin. It touched down on the ridge long enough for Anatoli to climb on board, then it spun around and came right at her.

Jenny threw herself flat in the snow.

CHAPTER 75

One Eye Blind

"What's that?" Matthews whispered.

Something was blocking the tunnel.

Breck's dollar store flashlight was starting to flicker. Piece of junk. When it went out, he had to tap it to get it working again. You get what you pay for. Shining it ahead of them, the object turned out to be an ore cart. It was parked on the rusty rails, filled with sparkling quartz, as if the miners clocked out for lunch and never came back.

"Daddy? Is that you?"

Matthews pushed past Breck and wiggled like crazy to get around the metal cart.

"Aspen! Oh, thank God. Thank God!"

"Daddy . . . you found me. . . ."

Aspen began sobbing. Leaning over the ore cart, Breck shined the light so they could see. The girl was sitting on the tram tracks, clinging to her father. She had a black eye and some bruises and scrapes on her cheek and arms. She must have fought hard. But where was Aleks? Did he ditch her and make a run for it? Breck aimed the light further down the tunnel. The passageway made a hard curve to the left. Where did it lead? Did it hook back around? Was this tunnel a loop? If it was, then Aleks could. . . .

Breck felt an arm snake around his neck. It locked tight and began to squeeze.

Thrashing was all he could do, so that's what he did. Breck rammed his elbows into Aleks's stomach, hoping to catch him in the solar plexus and knock the wind out of him, but it was like hitting concrete. The beam of light from his flashlight waved everywhere, flickering and throwing shadows.

"Breck!" Matthews shouted.

Aleks's grip was unbreakable.

Gasping, Breck couldn't breathe. How long did he have before he blacked out? He didn't want to find out. Using his .44 Special like a club, Breck swung it over his shoulder and pounded Aleks in the face, but Aleks shook him like a rag doll until both the revolver and the flashlight went flying out of his grip.

In his ear, Breck could hear the big Russian breathing hard, and he groaned a little. Something wet had splattered Breck's cheek when he struck him with the gun, and it had to be blood. Breck must have done some damage.

Maybe he could do some more damage.

He felt around, desperately pawing for the Russian's eye sockets, but Aleks's face was slick and hard to hold onto. Then he felt mouth and teeth, and Aleks bit his finger hard and wouldn't let go, and it hurt like hell, but with his free hand, Breck managed to stick a thumb in his eye and worked it like a grape.

Aleks screamed, and Breck yanked his hand free, out of those razor teeth, but his lungs were burning, and no air was getting in—the Russian was still holding tight, and his arm was like a vice around Breck's throat.

"You're a dead man!"

That was Matthews' voice, then there was a flash of light, and a popping sound and Breck's ears rang like a bell, and it was all he could hear, but suddenly he was free, falling, and he hit the ground, inhaling deep breaths of air over and over again.

Someone picked up the flashlight and shined it around. It was Matthews.

In the beam of light, Breck saw Aleks hunched on the ground. The back of his shirt glistened and dripped with fresh blood, but he leaped up like a wounded tiger and raced away into the darkness, disappearing around the bend. A couple of seconds later, they heard wood splinter and clatter, and Aleks shouted, and they knew he had fallen through the false floor. The sound of his body tumbling, and rocks and gravel and boards, was loud in the tunnel until they heard a cavernous splash, and then it was over.

Breck rolled onto his side.

It hurt too much to get up.

Not yet.

His neck was on fire, his fingertip felt like it got bit off, and Breck couldn't get enough air into his system. He gasped and wheezed and tried to massage his throat, but that just made it worse. Was his trachea damaged? Was it crushed?

"Hey, buddy. We did it. We did it." Matthews knelt in the dirt beside him. He held his hand out, like he wanted to touch Breck's shoulder, or pat him on the head, or something. "I have to check on Aspen. Be right back."

The flashlight bobbed away.

All Breck could see in the dark was the silhouette of the ore cart and the white sparkle of quartz. Matthews was on the far side, hugging his daughter and telling her it was all over, and she was safe, and she was a Matthews, and Matthews were fighters.

When Kyle fell, it felt like Breck was the one who died. The anchor failed, and Kyle disappeared in the storm, and the silent scream of the loss was suffocating. Nickie slammed the door in his face at the memorial, keeping him from grieving, cutting him off from others' grief, and the connection of shared catharsis. The world became a strange and empty place after that. The mountains and rock and ice and snow that once drew him like a muse, once tangible, electric, had become ghosts before his eyes, or maybe he was the ghost, wandering another plane of existence, or nonexistence, and no one he spoke to could see him anymore. It took years, but at some point, he came to realize that helping others was the key to returning to the land of the living. Saving others saved him.

Gently breaking away from his daughter, Matthews squeezed past the ore cart again and cautiously explored the tunnel. Breck could see the flashlight flickering, getting dim, then bright again. Hopefully, it would keep working long enough for them to escape back to the surface. Otherwise, they were in trouble.

Breck closed his eyes. He focused on getting air in his lungs.

"How are we getting out of here?" Matthews knelt beside him again. His voice was tense. "Those planks. That guy just blew out the bridge. We're trapped."

Breck wanted to explain how the tunnel looped around if they just kept walking. It would circle right back around to the beginning. Aleks had figured it out. That was how he snuck around for a surprise attack.

As he was shining the light around, something caught Matthews' attention. He angled the light down and searched the floor. Something glistened. It looked like a wet, white, gooey gumball.

"What is that?"

"One . . . eye . . . blind."

As soon as he said it, Breck regretted the effort. He could barely get the words out. It burned like fire. Now he knew how Tya felt. And Billy James, before he died. Getting throttled by a massive Russian murderer—he could check that off his bucket list.

CHAPTER 76

Piece of the Puzzle

Winter had finally arrived. Snow coated everything. The road was slick, so Breck put the Jeep in low gear, and took his time driving back to Quandary.

The whole ride down the canyon, no one spoke. Given the condition of his throat, Breck didn't even try. Aspen was asleep in the passenger seat, completely zonked. Matthews was cramped in the backseat, with one hand resting on her shoulder. He had been sitting that way for nearly an hour. His arm must be sore, but he didn't want to let go of his daughter.

Windshield wipers on high. Swish, swish, swish.

Eventually, the dark canyon gave way to the lights of town. They passed the brewery. It was late now. Everyone had gone home, and the big Oktoberfest tent was covered in snow and sagging. Aspen's 10-speed road bike was still chained to the wrought iron patio fence.

At the stoplight on Main Street, Breck shifted gears and made a turn. The change in tempo caused Matthews to stir and look around. They passed High Country Pizza, City Hall, and the 7-Eleven. As they approached the ski resort, Matthews finally released his grip on his daughter's shoulder.

He cleared his throat. "What's going on?"

A dozen State Patrol vehicles were scattered around the parking lot, blue lights flashing. An ambulance was there, too.

"I don't know." Breck's phone suddenly buzzed a couple of times. Five new voice messages. A dozen texts from Jenny. His phone must have finally locked onto the cell signal.

One of the patrol cars was blockading the ski resort entrance, but when he saw it was Breck, he waved them through.

"Who is that guy?" Matthews asked.

He pointed at a silver-haired man in a dress blue uniform, who was talking to Hedda Asbjorn. The woman was sitting on the bumper of the ambulance, with a sling around her shoulder. Jenny was standing there, too.

"Major McMurray." Breck struggled to speak. "Homeland."

"Are you saying he's from the United States Department of Homeland Security? What's he doing in Quandary?"

"Hedda wants political asylum."

Parking near the ambulance, Breck cut the engine. Aspen was still sound asleep. With the wipers off, large wet snowflakes began to collect on the windshield. Suddenly, Matthews leaned forward and stuck his hand out for a handshake.

"Whatever else happens, I want to thank you for saving my daughter."

Breck studied him for a moment. Was he genuine? Why wouldn't he be? Breck felt guilty for being suspicious, but the man had brought it on himself. Oh, well. Might as well shake.

It was awkward, but they clasped hands.

Matthews leaned back in his seat and put his hand on Aspen's shoulder again.

"I'm just going to stay here for a little while," he said, softly.

Someone knocked on the door. It was Jenny.

He almost didn't recognize her. She was wearing a thick insulated coat with reflective yellow trim that said *State Patrol* on the front. One of the troopers must have loaned it to her. Zipping up his fleece jacket, Breck hopped out and closed the door behind him.

"Breck! What happened at the mine? How is Aspen?" Her eyes fell to his throat. "What happened to your neck?"

"Aleks is dead. Aspen is safe. I'll survive. What happened *here?*"

Jenny was bouncing on her heels. Either she was freezing, or she was buzzed on Red Bull. Probably both.

"Tya is safe. Hedda is safe. But Anatoli flew the coop . . . literally."

He wasn't quite sure what she meant, but he would find out soon enough.

Breck peered into the ambulance. A paramedic had taken Hedda inside for an examination, and was trying to shine a light on her pupils. She looked frightened and exhausted.

Tya did, too. Breck spotted her sitting on the curb beside one of the patrol cars, with a blanket over her shoulders, scrolling on her iPhone. Sven was there, too, standing off to the side, scrolling on his iPhone.

"Ask the paramedic to check on Aspen," Breck told Jenny, in a hoarse whisper. "She's in my Jeep."

"Sounds like you need a cough drop."

"I need a vacation."

"You need medical attention." She pointed at the ambulance. "Get in line."

"Maybe later."

Looking around the parking lot, Breck spotted McMurray with a group of DHS agents huddled by the lobby entrance. They were grilling Cash. As he walked towards them, Breck heard some of their questions. *Explain how an Eastern European hit squad infiltrated the Quandary Ski Resort? Who are you again? Do you have some ID?* The pitch of Cash's voice soared, and he was sweating bullets. Breck knew he wasn't to blame, and by the look of it, McMurray was figuring that out, too.

"That's not your guy," Breck told him. "He's just a local."

"You mean a local *punk*. A crew of mercenaries were right under his nose, and he had no clue. What a dumb ass." McMurray was seething. "You got a smoke?"

Jenny must have heard the magic words from a hundred feet away, because she raced over from the ambulance and crossed her arms.

"He quit."

Breck shrugged.

"I quit."

"Hey, I'm sorry it took me so long to get here." McMurray lowered his voice. "Someone in Congress wanted to slow me down, and it worked."

"Bet ya twenty million bucks I know who," Jenny said. "Dana Stayne?"

He gave her a quizzical look.

"How the hell did you know that?"

"A little birdie told me." Then she pointed at the mountain above the ski resort. "Speaking of birds, you won't believe this, Breck. A freaking black ops helicopter came out of nowhere and scooped Anatoli off the ridge. Right in front of me. If I hadn't seen it with my own eyes. . . ."

As she spoke, McMurray shook his head in disgust.

"Right here on American soil," he growled.

But after everything Breck had been through, it was easy to believe. He was just glad Aspen, Tya, and Hedda were all safe.

"Did you know Dana Stayne has twenty million dollars in a Bear Coin account?" Jenny asked McMurray. "I didn't realize senators made that kind of dough."

"They don't." The major glanced around to make sure no one else was listening to their conversation. "We're investigating Senator Stayne for pay-to-play politics. She is the chair of the Committee on Foreign Investment. Her committee reviews the national security implications whenever someone in a foreign country wants to buy a US company. For instance, the Russian airline company, Aeroflot, wanted to buy a tech company in Vermont called Oculus Aquila. That twenty million in Bear Coin was a bribe to make sure the sale went through."

"Why don't you just arrest her?" Jenny asked. "She's in Quandary right now."

But the major shook his head.

"Bear Coin is impossible to trace. We can't make a case against her. Not yet."

"Hold on." Jenny squinted. "What is Oculus What's-A-Who?"

"High tech GPS. Khodorovsky told the committee that Aeroflot only wanted Oculus Aquila because it would improve the airline's guidance equipment. Make the planes safer. But that's not what he really wanted it for. Ever since they got it, the Russian military has been using the technology to *jam* GPS satellite signals. It creates a quiet zone. Aircraft, ships, and weapons lose their guidance systems. Phone calls, messages, WiFi . . . none of it works."

Jenny held up her cell phone.

"Have they been using it in Quandary? I can't even order a pizza on this thing."

Breck smiled, but McMurray wasn't in the mood for jokes.

"The Russians have been buying islands in the Baltic Sea, from Finland to Norway, and using them as secret submarine bases. They're disrupting military surveillance, so their subs can sneak in and out, undetected. Skogsøya is a critical piece of the puzzle. It's sitting in the gateway to the Atlantic. Without it, the whole plan fails."

CHAPTER 77

Ten Gallons

There was a knock on the door.

"Trick or treat!"

"What are you supposed to be?" Jenny started handing out little bags of M&Ms. "I bet Disney makes a killing on Halloween costumes alone. Your parents must be broke. When I was a kid, I cut two holes in an old sheet and went as a ghost."

One of the kids had a giant pirate hat, black eyeliner, and a fake beard. He examined the candy and frowned.

"These are coffee flavor."

"Yeah, well, the real Captain Jack Sparrow likes coffee flavor M&Ms. Told me that himself, last time I was on a Caribbean cruise."

Jenny slammed the door and went back to the couch. Breck was sitting there, flipping through the channels. The Quandary mayoral debate was being televised on a local cable channel, and they were going to watch it together.

"Here we go. It's just about to start." He turned up the volume. "Matthews versus Tibbs. This ought to be good. Give me some of those M&Ms."

A low-budget commercial came on for Mikey's Bikeys. Jenny shook her head. Mike Jameson was wearing tight bicycling spandex, but he had pale skinny legs and a giant gut. Not a good look. He hooked a leg over an expensive mountain bike, balls to the camera, but apparently, it was hard to straddle and read cue cards at the same time.

"He's giving used car salesmen a bad name." She glanced at Breck. "I can make hot tea. You want some?"

"I'm fine."

"I'll make some anyhow. Sit tight."

His neck was one big purple stripe. It had been a week since the Keystone Mine choke fest, and even though the bruising looked horrendous, his voice was almost normal again. Still, Jenny could tell it hurt to swallow. Hot tea was the best thing for a sore throat. Didn't everyone know that?

She went into the kitchen and put a ceramic cup of water in the microwave—three minutes on high. In the cabinet, she found two colorful boxes of tea bags covered in dust. They had been in there for ages, since the last time she got sick, and when was that?

"All I've got is chamomile or peppermint."

"Surprise me."

Beep, beep. She pulled the cup out of the microwave and dropped a peppermint tea bag in it. She wished Breck would put the volume on mute. Mike Jameson's voice was getting on her nerves. Plus, wasn't it a conflict of interest for the debate moderator to be running commercials?

"What I want to know is, why hasn't Matthews resigned in shame?" The cup was almost too hot to handle. Maybe three minutes in the microwave was too long. She got out an oven mitt and carried it to the couch, and set it carefully on the coffee table. "He should be sitting in jail for tipping Stayne about our evidence locker. And she should be in jail, too, for all kinds of things."

But Breck pointed at the TV.

"It's showtime."

The debate stage at the fairgrounds appeared on the screen. Mike Jameson introduced Mayor Matthews and Johnny Tibbs and tried to joke about how the camera added ten gallons to Johnny's cowboy hat.

"Holy moly," Jenny muttered. "Couldn't they find a real moderator? This is going to be painful to watch."

Johnny and Matthews shook hands and took their places at the podiums. Mike shuffled through his question cards and adjusted his microphone.

"First question, for Mr. Tibbs. If you were elected mayor, what would you do about the poor cell service in town?"

The camera zoomed in on Johnny's confident smile. He was wearing a bright red collared shirt with white pearl snaps and a pinstriped vest. A silk scarf hung from his neck like he just stepped out of a John Wayne movie.

Breck pointed at the screen.

"Your boyfriend is a snappy dresser."

"Shut up."

The peppermint tea needed sugar, but Breck didn't complain. It was hot and hurt to swallow, but he took a few small sips anyhow. On the television screen, Tibbs leaned into the microphone and winked at the camera.

"Before I answer that, Mike, I want to let everyone know something. Moments ago, I received a phone call from Senator Dana Stayne, who represents the great state of Colorado in the halls of Congress. She is endorsing me for mayor of Quandary." He turned to Matthews. "Wasn't she supposed to endorse *you?* What did you do to make her mad?"

But Matthews didn't seem fazed and even faked a cringe.

"Haven't you heard, cowboy? There's a rumor going around—she's under investigation for taking bribes. How much money did you pay her for that endorsement?"

The smile on Johnny's face evaporated.

"I'm the one running a clean campaign. And I know you sent the neighborhood brat pack to vandalize my signs."

"Vote for Johnny Tibbs, everyone, if you're biggest concern is kids on skateboards with magic markers." Matthews looked indignant. "I've made it a hallmark of my term as mayor to root out government corruption at the highest levels. That is no easy task—for example, Quandary County Sheriff Breckenridge Dyer. Read the newspaper lately?"

"Everyone knows you hate Breck and want him gone."

"This isn't about grudges, Johnny. Three unsolved murders in one week. A horse rescue scheme. What about the billionaire, arrested for no reason? The drug cartel chaos last year? Breck may be innocent of it all, but it's the mayor's job to ask difficult questions."

While Matthews was talking, Jenny threw the remote control at the TV.

"Didn't you just save his daughter's life?"

She glared at Breck, waiting for him to chime in. But what good would it do to get upset? He knew the truth. And the truth was, Matthews had stabbed him in the back more than once over the years. Why should this be a surprise?

Breck blew steam off the hot peppermint tea and took another sip.

It was sad to see Johnny floundering. He tried to shift the debate's momentum in his favor by bringing up Quandary's high taxes and how small businesses had been choked by overregulation, but Matthews had a slick answer for everything he said.

Mike Jameson tapped his microphone.

Boom, boom, boom.

"That's the end of round one. Now it's time for a commercial break." He gave the camera a thumbs up. "And don't forget to support our local sponsors."

The television cut away to the same Mikey's Bikeys commercial, which had run earlier, in all of its spandex straddling glory.

"Seen enough?" Jenny asked.

"Way too much."

The remote control was lying on the carpet. As Jenny picked it up, the doorbell rang, but instead of answering it, she went to the candy bowl and treated herself to a package of coffee-flavored M&Ms.

"You going to get the door?" Breck asked.

"I've seen enough scary people for one day."

Once again, the doorbell rang. Once again, she ignored it.

Then somebody pounded their fist on the door impatiently.

Jenny grabbed her Luger off the kitchen table and looked through the peephole.

"It's Johnny frickin' Depp."

She hid the pistol behind her back, tucking it in her belt before she opened the door. The little boy in the pirate costume was standing there, holding out his trick or treat bag expectantly.

"I don't do repeat customers," she said. "Beat it."

But the kid gave her a fake-gold-tooth pirate smile.

"You got anything besides coffee M&Ms? I like Twizzlers and Reese's Peanut Butter Cups. But I'll take cash if that's all you got."

Jenny looked him over.

"You're just here because everyone else has turned off their porch light. But you're bold. I like that. How do you feel about Yoplait?"

CHAPTER 78

Destiny

Seneca Matthews for mayor, check.

Aspen looked over her shoulder, but inside the privacy booth, no one could see who she was voting for.

Breckenridge Dyer for sheriff, check.

After she filled in the election form, Aspen fed it into the voting machine and watched it disappear. Her father was waiting in line to use the booth, and as she walked by him, he gave her a quick peck on the forehead.

"You voted Matthews-Waters, right?" he whispered.

She smiled and winked, and her father winked back. Maybe later, she would tell him the truth, but why spoil brunch? The fact was, Breck saved her life, and there wasn't even a question in her mind who was going to get her vote. Besides, Chief Waters was a turd. And Aspen didn't vote for turds.

While she waited for her dad to vote, Aspen sat on the fender of a large firetruck. For Election Day, the Quandary County Firehouse was transformed into the town's one and only polling station. Aspen checked the time. How long was this going to take? Brunch was going to be lunch, at this rate.

Valerie came and sat down next to her. "What are you going to order?"

"French toast and a hazelnut caramel cappuccino." Aspen said it without thinking. She always ordered that whenever she went to the Blue Moose.

Her mom smiled and squeezed her hand.

Ever since the mine rescue, Valerie hovered like a hawk. She insisted on riding along on all her pizza deliveries and sat in the back of the classroom at Quandary Community College. But Aspen didn't mind. Valerie had given up mimosas, and without alcohol pumping through her veins, she was an entirely different person. Except when her dad was around, then drama oozed from every pore.

Aspen's phone buzzed. It was a text from Jamey Frederick at the Law Offices of Hoyt, Hoyt, and Frederick.

"Who's that, honey?" Valerie asked.

"My lawyer."

"Are you suing someone? The motel? The mine?"

"Nope. But I just legally registered my business name."

"Your horse rescue? What did you decide to call it?"

Aspen flushed with pride.

"The Aspen Equine Sanctuary."

Valerie put her arm around her shoulder.

"That's perfect. I'm so proud of you."

Even though she knew that running a horse rescue would be a ton of work, and there were a million unknowns, Aspen wasn't intimidated. This was her destiny. She could feel it in her soul.

"Well, if you ever need help shoveling horse manure, your father knows a lot about that department."

Valerie scowled as Matthews exited the voting booth. Instead of joining them, he started shaking hands and chatting with everyone standing in line.

"Seneca sure is taking his sweet time. Doesn't he know we're waiting on him?"

CHAPTER 79

A Chorus of Hell No's

An enormous flat-screen television balanced on top of the bar. "There's nothing quite like Mike Jameson in spandex on a life-size screen." Jenny squinted but couldn't look away. "It's like he's standing on the bar, wagging his junk at me. Do we have to watch this?"

"Ask Breck. It's his party," Danny said. Then he raised his voice so everyone in the brewery could hear him. "Does this make anyone wanna buy a bicycle?"

There was a chorus of hell no's.

Breck pulled a flyer out of his pocket. It was an advertisement for an election night viewing party at the brewery and a coupon for fifty percent off a basket of chili fries. Danny had printed them himself. There was a photo of Breck on one side and a photo of Chief Waters on the other, but Waters' face had a gun target drawn around it like he was on the wrong end of a sniper scope. When Waters got wind of it, he left a message on the Sheriff's Office answering machine, complaining about how it was mean-spirited, insensitive, and incited violence. Blah, blah, blah.

"Where are my chili fries?" Breck asked. "I ordered them a half-hour ago."

"You'll get them when I get my camera."

Breck hoped beyond hope they would find Danny's DSLR. Aleks had stolen it when he raided the Sheriff's Office, but they never found it. Would it matter if they did? Even though Tya shot Khodorovsky in the shoulder and he was bleeding profusely, he didn't forget to take the Skogsøya real estate agreement when he fled the apartment—with Hedda's signature. The island was officially his now. The key card to the Asbjorn's suite in the Hyatt, which Aleks had left in Aspen's car, had been wiped clean of fingerprints, so that was a loss, too. So if they somehow recovered Danny's camera, the crime scene photos were moot. There was no one to prosecute. Aleks was belly up in the bottom of the Keystone Mine, and Anatoli had vanished in a helicopter.

Danny disappeared into the kitchen. The place was packed, and it was obvious he was overwhelmed trying to keep up with food orders. Breck glanced around the room. It was nice to see how many people had come to support him. With all the slander, lies, and misconceptions, it was a wonder anyone showed at all.

"What is taking him so long?" Jenny asked. "I'm getting hangry."

The front door opened and Breck spotted Jamey Frederick walk inside the brewery. Beneath her winter coat, she was wearing a Nordic sweater and blue jeans. It was strange to see her dressed casually. Every time Breck met her at the attorney's office in Frisco, she had on professional attire, and her hair pulled tight.

"Hey, that's my lawyer," he said and waved her over.

When Jamey came to their table, Jenny held out her hand.

"So, we finally meet in person."

"Nice to meet you, too. Did I miss the results?"

"Not yet." Jenny shrugged. "The polls closed hours ago. I don't know why it takes so long to count the votes in this Podunk town."

Jamey took off her coat and settled into a chair. She gave Breck an optimistic smile.

"My money's on you."

"Thank you," he said. "Can I buy you something to drink?"

"I would love a Diet Pepsi."

Danny was still in the kitchen, and judging by his performance so far, he wasn't coming back anytime soon. The soda fountain was behind the bar. Breck knew right where it was.

"I'll get it for you."

He walked around the bar, grabbed a pint glass, and filled it with Diet Pepsi. Sometimes he wished he was the one who owned a brewery. Pour a drink. Cook some chili fries. Swipe a credit card. Go home at the end of the night, and not worry about Russian thugs or corrupt senators or conniving mayors. But five minutes alone with Danny always spoiled that daydream, didn't it?

"One Diet Pepsi, my treat." Breck set the soda on the tabletop. "Anything new with the DA's office?"

"Nothing," Jamey said. "It's kind of weird. They were constantly calling me with document requests and follow-up questions. But now, not a peep. They've gone radio silent."

The Mikey's Bikeys commercial was playing on the television for the second time in a row. Jenny shielded her eyes with her hands as Mike Jameson pranced around again in his spandex.

"I bet they've pulled the plug," she said. "It was just a matter of time until they realized there's nothing to investigate."

Danny popped out of the kitchen again, carrying a giant bag of pretzels this time. He went from table to table, pouring them into bowls, so people would have something to snack on while they waited for their meals. When he got to their table, the bag was nothing but crumbs and salt.

"Hey!" Jenny glared at him. "Did you forget about our chili fries?"

"We ran out of chili an hour ago."

"What? You could have told me that an hour ago."

"You want pretzels?"

"No!" But then she shrugged. "Yes."

As Danny poured pretzel powder into their bowl, the Mikey's Bikeys commercial faded to black, and a podium inside City Hall appeared on the screen. The county elections supervisor, a woman named Linda, approached the podium with a sheet of paper in her hand.

She adjusted her reading glasses.

"Polls closed at 7:00 P.M., and my team finished counting every ballot just a few moments ago. All precincts in Quandary County have reported in, but before I announce the final results, let me explain a few things first."

She went into unnecessary detail about voter turnout percentages, absentee ballots, population counts, and a litany of useless statistics that no one cared to hear. Breck took a sip of water. This whole process was nerve-racking.

Danny pulled up a chair and sat right beside him.

"I voted for Waters."

"No, you didn't." Jenny threw a wadded napkin in his face. "Besides, there is no possible way Maxwell Waters is going to be sheriff of Quandary County. There may be kids starving in Ethiopia, and alligators eating puppies, but the universe is not *that* cruel."

Breck laughed, but his heart wasn't in it.

Was this the night he lost his badge? It was possible. He realized he was holding his breath. He exhaled soft and slow and tried not to look too nervous. Jenny reached across the table and grabbed his hand.

Linda finally ran out of statistics.

"Final results. For mayor of the city of Quandary. Jonathan Tibbs received forty-nine percent of the vote, and incumbent Seneca Matthews received fifty-one percent. Matthews wins re-election."

Breck and Jenny looked at each other. That was not what they wanted to hear.

The brewery got quiet as Linda readjusted her reading glasses.

This was it.

"For sheriff of Quandary County . . . Maxwell Waters received eight percent of the vote, and incumbent Breckenridge Dyer received ninety-two percent. Dyer wins re-election."

CHAPTER 80

The Ball Is Already
In Motion

Watching Matthews preen on television proved to be too much to handle sober. For anybody. A line formed at the bar. Since Danny was busy shuttling food, Breck took command of the taps, which was kind of fun since people seemed genuinely happy that he was still the sheriff of Quandary County. Or maybe they were just pleased Waters didn't win.

Ten Mile Milk Stout, Red Mountain Amber Ale, Blue Spruce IPA. Breck's favorite was the Sawtooth Ridge Cream Ale, and as soon as everyone else got what they wanted, he poured one for himself. But before he took the first sip, he saw Tya walk inside the brewery. Making eye contact, she came right over and sat on a barstool.

"Sorry, I'm late! Hey, you just won the election. What are you doing behind the bar?"

"I'm undercover. The guy who owns this place is a crook." He picked out a new pint glass. "What can I get you? And I feel it's my duty, as the newly sworn-in bartender of the Quandary Brewery, to warn you there's no wine on tap."

She smiled.

"Whatever you're drinking. Pour me one of those."

"Coming right up."

Since the giant television was parked on the bar just inches away, the sound of Matthews' voice was obnoxiously loud. *I'm going to install a second cell phone tower in Quandary. Everyone deserves a stable cell signal. And decent WiFi. I will work with the phone company to improve the landline infrastructure with fiber optic cables so everyone in Quandary can get affordable DSL service. I love this town and I won't rest until these goals are accomplished.*

"Can you turn up the volume any higher?" Tya asked, laughing.

"I wish."

"You know, this spiel sounds mighty familiar. Didn't Matthews give the exact same speech four years ago?"

"Word for word."

She raised her glass and clinked it against Breck's.

"Congratulations, sheriff. Here's to you."

"Thanks."

They sipped their ales while Matthews wrapped up his speech.

"Hey, look at us," Tya said. "We're both able to swallow like normal human beings again. You know we have matching throat bruises?"

Breck studied her neck but hardly saw anything.

"I cover mine with makeup," she said. "That's the advantage of being a woman."

"I can't argue with that."

"You want to get dinner sometime?"

He smiled, mainly out of surprise. Tya Tordenskjold just asked him out on a date. It had been two years since the last time Breck went on a date with anyone. It had been a train wreck. Dating a married woman sounded like a train wreck, too.

"I don't think Sven would like that."

"It doesn't matter what he thinks. We're getting a good ol' fashioned divorce, remember?"

Breck's cell phone buzzed in his pocket. He pulled it out to make sure it wasn't a 9-1-1 forward. But the caller ID simply read, *Unknown Caller.*

"Do you need to take that?"

"I bet it's Waters calling to concede." He started to answer but paused. "Why don't you ask me again when the divorce is finalized? Dinner sounds nice."

"Fair enough."

Tya took her pint glass and headed over to Jenny's table. Their voices carried. Jenny wanted to plan a trip to the gun range. Shooting Coke cans in the snow would be good practice. Jamey Frederick was still sitting there, said it sounded like fun and asked if she could tag along and watch.

Breck hit the answer button.

"Hello?"

"Is there a new sheriff in town?"

It was a familiar, clunky voice. Khodorovsky.

"Anatoli? Which federal prison are you calling from?"

The oligarch let out a hearty belly laugh.

"You wish. I am sitting in my private jet, flying high over Baltic Sea. I heard the news you won and simply had to call. Yet another victory. How can you keep track of all these victories? Do you have special notebook in which you keep tally?"

It was hard to hear with the television blaring. The Mikey's Bikeys commercial was back on. Where was the mute button? Forget it. Breck dashed into Danny's office and closed the door.

"Why are you calling?"

"Another victory for your special notebook. Skogsøya was just raided by strike team commandos—Norwegian Special Operation Forces. Black ski masks, high-speed motorboats. Pity. It was such a perfect location."

"Pity."

In the background, Breck could hear the hum of jet engines on the phone. The clink of ice in a whiskey tumbler.

"How is Mrs. Asbjorn adjusting to new life in United States of America?"

"I'm going to hang up now," Breck said.

"Our entire Baltic Sea submarine program is in jeopardy because of that woman. Certain people in Moscow are very upset. I hope nothing unfortunate happens to her."

Breck knew Hedda was in witness protection. But would that stop him? The fake security detail that Tya had hired was on Khodorovsky's payroll. And where did that helicopter come from when it plucked him off the ridge in the middle of a dark snowstorm? Anything was possible with this guy.

Mental note. Call Major McMurray.

"You know your name is on Homeland's watch list, right? If you ever set foot on American soil again, you'll be adjusting to a new life in the United States, yourself. Behind bars."

Ice cubes clanked. He was pouring another whiskey. Or was it vodka?

"You are very brazen for a man with no money in his bank account. And no security system at his little mountain cabin. I must warn you that Aleks missed the plane ride home. I would not be surprised if he paid you a friendly visit."

"I would be. Aleks is floating in the bottom of the Keystone Mine. The only way he's returning for a visit is in a shimmering poltergeist fog."

Khodorovsky didn't say anything. Breck could still hear the hum of jet engines, but he double-checked his phone to make sure the line was still open. It was.

"Whatever you're thinking about doing . . . don't."

"What is that adage?" Anatoli asked. "The ball is already in motion? Enjoy your party."

That was it. The line went dead.

Breck put his phone in his pocket and headed back out into the brewery. Someone had flipped the channel. One of the Denver news stations was on the big screen, and the anchors were discussing the governor's race. Loopenhicker had won re-election, too. He was still the governor of Colorado.

"Where did I leave my ale?"

As he walked towards the bar, the front door swung open. Governor Loopenhicker marched inside—along with Mayor Matthews, Chief Maxwell Waters, District Attorney Brownton, and a dozen State Patrol troopers.

"Dyer!" the governor shouted. "We need to talk."

CHAPTER 81

The Die Was Cast

E veryone in the brewery stopped talking.

Jenny twisted around to see who had yelled at Breck.

"What's going on?" Tya whispered.

"I don't know."

Matthews, Waters, Brownton, and Loopenhicker. None of them spoke a word, which was odd since any one of those guys could suck the oxygen out of the room all by themselves. And why did they bring along so many State Patrol troopers? Jenny didn't recognize any of them. They must be from the Front Range division. One thing was for sure, they weren't there to buy Breck a congratulatory beer.

Danny muted the TV. The sudden silence was unnatural.

"Since I have everyone's attention, and the office of sheriff is an elected position, there's no reason to hide this from the public eye."

Loopenhicker gestured at Breck, beckoning him to come closer.

"Sheriff Breckenridge Dyer. I'm here to make you aware that Colorado Fifth District Attorney Charles Brownton has determined sufficient probable cause to file a complaint. His investigation has shown strong evidence that number one, you conspired with the Los Equis drug cartel, based in Monterrey, Mexico, to create an illegal, large scale cannabis operation in Quandary County last year, and planned to benefit from it financially. Two, that you conspired with local horse trader Luke Roberts to buy auction horses at low rates, and sell them, via a false horse rescue, at inflated prices. And three, that you had Roberts murdered when he exposed your role in the scheme."

Chief Waters cleared his throat with a melodramatic *a-hem*, and Loopenhicker snapped his fingers.

"Oh, yeah. Number four. Election fraud. No one in the history of elections ever received ninety-two percent of the vote. That seems a little fishy, and we're adding that to the list."

Jenny couldn't believe what she was hearing.

"None of those accusations are true." She stood up, her heart pumping like crazy. "Breck's the most upstanding, ethical lawman I've ever worked with. There are rational explanations for everything you just said, so listen up. We're the ones who busted that cartel last year, and Breck led the charge. The horse rescue situation was a set-up. And there is a simple reason Waters got eight percent of the vote. It's because he's a douche."

Loopenhicker turned his gaze upon her.

"Deputy O'Hara, I am glad you are here." Then he nodded at the District Attorney, who handed Breck a sheaf of documents. "That is a formal list of the charges I just described. Please give them to your attorney."

Jenny slowly sank into her chair. She turned to Jamey, who was still seated next to her, at the table, eyes as big as saucers. The girl was so young. Could she handle this level of pressure? It didn't look promising. Maybe if the city council hadn't decimated their budget, Breck could have afforded a high powered team of Harvard grads. A chill went through Jenny's gut. Was *she* going to need an attorney? Were they going to scoop her up in their dragnet, next?

"Good times." Breck tossed the paperwork onto the bar. He looked at Matthews for support. "You got anything to say?"

"Don't respond to the question, Seneca." Then Loopenhicker raised his voice, addressing everyone in the brewery. "Since these charges are so serious, as governor of Colorado, I am formally asking Breck Dyer to voluntarily step down as Sheriff of Quandary County, and take a leave of absence. Until this case has been resolved in a court of law."

On the television, the news anchors were mouthing words. Voting percentages scrolled across the bottom of the screen. Then it cut to video footage from earlier in the evening. The governor stood on the steps of the state capitol building, shaking hands with Dana Stayne. Jenny felt her heart drop.

The deck was stacked. The die was cast.

Mustering an unexpected gravitas, Jamey rose to her feet and cleared her throat.

"As Sheriff Dyer's attorney, I am confident that the sheriff has not violated any criminal laws in the state of Colorado. The Law Offices of Hoyt, Hoyt, and

Frederick are committed to aggressively defending him against these baseless allegations."

But Loopenhicker didn't even acknowledge her presence. He held out his palm expectantly. He wanted Breck's badge.

CHAPTER 82

American Spirit

Heated seats? There was a button on the dashboard, and as soon as Jenny pushed it, she felt the leather beneath her start to get warm.

"What will they think of next?"

She was driving a new Chevy Tahoe, just like all the deputies had over in Park County, only better. They didn't have heated leather seats. Plus, it had a black grill guard welded onto the front bumper, which meant she could ram anything she wanted. Fences, cars, deer, moose, wheelchairs, little old ladies— whatever jumped out at her. But she was really on the lookout for jaywalking mayors. Hit the gas, squish the ass. Problem solved.

Another snowstorm had rolled through, and the asphalt was buried beneath a foot of snow, but Jenny had never felt more at ease cruising up the canyon in lousy weather. The defroster worked. The gas gauge worked. Windows rolled down with the flick of a toggle switch—no zipping required, unlike Breck's old Jeep. Not that she was going to roll the windows down at the moment, but it was the principle that counted.

The back road where Breck lived was streaked with tire tracks. Hopefully, he was home. Jenny called and left a few messages that she was on her way, but he never called back. There was no way he was fishing. Not in this weather, and the lake by his cabin had to be frozen solid by now. Maybe he was eating fish sticks in front of the TV. That's what she would do if she got ousted from her job by a cadre of dirty politicians.

Yep, he was home. Gray wood smoke was churning out of the chimney, and the Jeep was parked by the deck. Completely buried in snow, but it was there.

The snow was still falling, and there was more in the forecast.

If she weren't a deputy sheriff, Jenny would love to be a meteorologist. The worst news the weather girls had to deliver was the temperature. When was the last time a Russian psycho choked out a newscaster behind the green screen? Or the DA investigated them for forecasting with Mexican thermometers?

But Jenny wasn't a deputy sheriff anymore, technically speaking. Wearing Breck's badge felt wrong, but the governor had given it to her and christened her the "acting sheriff" until the investigation was over. Was that even legal?

If the District Attorney was genuinely interested in the truth, Breck would get it back. But what if the DA was just as rotten as the rest of them? Chief Waters was in Matthews' pocket. Matthews was in Governor Loopenhicker's pocket. Loopenhicker was in Dana Stayne's pocket. The DA was probably swimming around in someone's pocket, too, covered in the lint of duplicity.

She parked next to the Jeep and shut off the engine.

Before she could knock, the front door of the cabin opened.

"Hey, Jen. What are you doing here?"

"Welfare check. You don't answer your phone. What if you broke a hip in the tub?"

The deck hadn't been shoveled, so she kicked her way across it. As soon as she got inside, Jenny took off her coat. There was a fire blazing in the fireplace, and it was putting out some serious heat.

"Did an REI explode in here?"

The living room floor was covered in mountain climbing equipment: ropes, carabiners, crampons, nylon webbing, ice axes, a tent, bright-colored boots, thick winter gloves, and goggles. A backpack was propped against the couch, big enough to hold it all, and a sleeping bag dangled from the bathroom door.

Breck didn't say anything. He slid a fresh slice of wood in the fireplace and stirred the embers with an iron poker. Flames licked up. Pine sap bubbled and hissed.

"Hear anything new from your lawyer?"

The landline telephone was sitting on the kitchen counter. Jenny could see it was unplugged.

"What about Danny?" she asked. "Has he called? He was pretty ticked when I finally told him his camera was stolen, and he said he was going to send you a bill for three grand. But he'll get over it. Right? Or what about insurance? Do we have insurance for stuff like that?"

No reply.

Breck propped the iron poker on the brick hearth, and began sorting through a pile of old, scratched Nalgene water bottles. He unscrewed the lids and sniffed them for mildew.

Jenny was getting annoyed. She hated being ignored.

"Breck? Hello? People are worried about you."

As she walked around, she noticed a worn book on the kitchen counter. It was a guidebook to Annapurna, the Himalayan mountain. She flipped through it. Each chapter described a different route to the summit, and the pages detailing the south face were dog-eared.

"Annapurna? Isn't that the mountain where your buddy Kyle died?"

"Yeah."

Finally. A spoken word. Jenny spotted Kyle's battered helmet on the fireplace mantle. She cringed when she thought about the night Nickie brought it to the brewery. Poor woman. Ten years of not knowing where your husband's dead body was must take its toll—along with ten years of bottled-up bitterness.

"Food for thought." Jenny tapped her forehead. "It might not look good if you leave the country while you're under investigation. And isn't mountain climbing in the Himalayas super expensive? I saw a documentary about Everest one time, and they said permits alone cost fifty thousand buckaroos."

"Everest is so commercialized," Breck muttered. He ran his thumb along the sharp teeth of an ice ax. "So I talked to the president at the American Alpine Club. Down in Denver. There's a small expedition team heading to Nepal, and they have an extra spot on their permit."

Jenny flipped through the book again, searching for photographs. Every angle of the mountain was steep and terrifying and caked in snow.

"Isn't it a little late in the year to try something like this? Why don't you save it for next summer?"

"Summer is monsoon season in the Himalayas, when all the fresh snow falls and avalanche danger is the greatest. But I just want to hike the glacier. See the crevasse."

"Where they found Kyle?"

"Yeah."

A pack of American Spirit cigarettes was lying near the guidebook. It was the only brand Breck ever bought. Jenny studied the Indian chief pictured on the artwork. He was bare-chested, wore a long feathery war bonnet, and held a peace pipe. It made absolutely no sense to her. What was the point of inhaling smoke deliberately? The pleasant scent of a fireplace was one thing, but tobacco and nicotine were quite another.

Taking the cigarettes over to the fireplace, she chucked the whole package into the flames.

"Doing you a fav. You'll need every bit of oxygen you can get in the Himalayas."

"I suppose."

"Cigs are expensive. Save your pennies for the trip."

She was trying to rile him up, get a reaction. But Breck didn't even blink. It was like he didn't care. Jenny studied his face. What was going on in that brain? It was strange to see Breck like this, without a badge, without a purpose. It had taken a lot of twists and turns and hi-jinks and back-stabs to get him to this point.

"You are coming back, right? Because even witch hunts have to end, eventually. Forget about Mayor Cashews and Governor Loopy Loser. Keep your chin up. Turn that frown upside down."

Breck carried the water bottles to the kitchen sink and began rinsing them out. Some of the Nalgene bottles had stickers on them. Brand names. Boreal, Black Diamond, Marmot, La Sportiva. One had that classic John Muir quote: *The mountains are calling, and I must go.*

"You *are* coming back. Right?"

Breck squirted dish soap onto a bristle brush. The water streaming from the faucet was hot, and steam rose out of the sink in wisps. One of the bottles had dark green fuzzies in the bottom, and he began scrubbing them out.

"You're going to make a good sheriff," he said.

"*Acting* sheriff. Big difference."

"Can you give me a ride to the airport tomorrow?"

"Sure. You seen my new wheels?"

He leaned over the sink so he could peer out the window. The Tahoe was all black, with a thin blue stripe down the side, and big knobby winter tires. It had the Quandary County Sheriff's Office logo painted on both doors, a low-profile light bar on the roof, and another row of emergency lights built into the front grill.

"Don't tell me Matthews boosted the budget after they kicked me to the curb."

"It's a thank you gift from Major McMurray. And you would know that if your phone was plugged in. I've been trying to call you all week."

No one had been able to reach Breck since the night at the brewery when Governor Loopenhicker asked him to step down from the Sheriff's Office. Making matters worse, the DA's investigator, Dempsey, dropped by the office looking for answers. *Running only makes him look guilty,* he said. *Breck didn't run,* she explained. *He is merely taking some personal time. Cut him some slack. He's been through a lot.* Good thing Dempsey didn't know about the ticket to Kathmandu.

"When you get to Nepal, call me so I know you made it safe. Or text. Or email. Something, okay?"

Even though Breck needed space, Jenny hated radio silence. She wanted to give him a lecture about good communication, but she didn't. She wanted to ask how he was coping, but she didn't. She wanted to tell him he had friends on his side, that the truth would prevail, and everything was going to be all right, but instead, she took a kitchen towel and began wiping Nalgene bottles until each one was dry.

About the Author

MARK MITTEN an American author whose work is primarily set in the Old West or contemporary Colorado. His novels *Sipping Whiskey in a Shallow Grave* and *Hard To Quit* were both nominated for Peacemaker Awards. *Ghosts of the Past* is the second volume in the Breckenridge Dyer series. Mitten is a member of the Western Writers of America. He resides in Winsted, Minnesota, with his wife Mary.

Made in the USA
Middletown, DE
04 December 2022

17047623R00184